a little naughty

USA TODAY BESTSELLING AUTHOR

TIA LOUISE

This book is a work of fiction. Names, characters, places, and incidents are products of the author's imagination or are used fictitiously. Any resemblance to actual events or locales or persons, living or dead, is entirely coincidental.

A Little Naughty
Copyright © TLM Productions LLC, 2024
Printed in the United States of America.

Cover design by Kari March Design

All rights reserved. No part of this publication can be reproduced, stored in a retrieval system, or transmitted in any form or by any means—electronic, photocopying, mechanical, or otherwise—without prior permission of the publisher and author.

Playlist

"Tim McGraw"—Taylor Swift

"Mean"—Taylor Swift

"I Did Something Bad"—Taylor Swift

"willow"—Taylor Swift

"Gorgeous"—Taylor Swift

"Perfect"—One Direction

"Style"—Taylor Swift

"Gypsy"—Gardens & Villa

"Hannah Hunt"—Vampire Weekend

"Angel"—Fleetwood Mac

"Blue Jeans"—Lana Del Rey

"Me and Mrs. Jones"—Billy Paul

"Don't It Make My Brown Eyes Blue"—Crystal Gayle

"The Second Line"—Stop, Inc.

"Don't Mess With My Toot Toot"—Rockin' Dopsie, et al.

Scan to Listen

"We're all born naked. The rest is drag."
—RuPaul Charles

"If you believe in yourself, with a tiny pinch of magic all your
dreams can come true!"
—SpongeBob Squarepants

For my longtime Mermaids, and for everyone who knows you
should never judge a book by its cover.*

(*except this one, of course, because it totally lives up to that
gorgeous cover—can I get an Amen up in hur?)

Prologue

Jemima

Here's what you need to know…

"**I**WANT A LITTLE BLACK DRESS AND A PICKUP TRUCK, AND I WANT A guy to tell me my blue eyes put the stars to shame." I'm sitting on the ground with my big sister Cass in front of our aunt Carol's house in Eureka, South Carolina.

The sun is bright yellow in a pale blue sky. Not a cloud is in sight, and if you hold your breath, you can hear the ocean hissing a little ways away.

We've been at Aunt Carol's a few months now, since our mom decided she wanted to be a big country-music star in Branson. She's back for a visit, but I'm not interested in what she does. I love being here, near the beach, with my sister.

"I wouldn't argue with him either."

"There's something wrong with you," Cass scolds gently, brushing my blonde hair into ringlets around her fingers. "You're too little to be thinking about boys so much."

"I'm not too little." I look up at the big sky. The heat toasts my skin and the humidity makes me sweat, but the ocean breeze is always blowing. "I want to get stuck on backroads and dance under the moon."

"Until you have to walk all the way home in the dark."

"What do you know? You've never kissed a boy."

"I've been in a broke-down car, and it's not as romantic as the song makes it sound."

"You've been in a broke-down car with *Mom*."

Cass wraps my hair in a band, lifting it off my neck, and I think nothing could be better than spending a summer riding around Eureka with the windows down and staying up all night dancing.

"I can't wait to kiss a boy."

Turning, I lay my head in her lap and wrap my arms around her waist. Cassidy is three years older, but she's sweet to me. When we sleep together at night, she sings Abba songs and scratches my back until I fall asleep.

She has a better singing voice than our momma, but she says she's too embarrassed to sing in front of people. I'm not embarrassed, but I don't sing as good as either of them.

"Get in the car, Jemima." Momma's voice is sharp, and I can tell she's been fighting with Aunt Carol again.

Every time she fights with Aunt Carol her cheeks flush, and she jerks my arm too hard.

I sit up slowly. "Why? Where are we going?"

Cass nudges my side, and I stand with her. Then I reluctantly follow her to where our mom is throwing suitcases into the backseat.

She turns and puts a hand on her cocked hip. "We're going back to Branson."

Her dark brown hair is long to her knees, and she has blue eyes like mine. It's the only thing we have in common—except the little fly-aways haloing her face in the humidity.

"I don't want to go to Branson." I put my arm around Cass's waist. "I want to stay here."

My sister stands straighter. "I'll go with you, Momma."

"You're too big. Jemma's little. She needs to be with her mother."

"No, I don't!" I shriek.

"Shut up, Jemima, and get in the car." Mom jerks my arm so hard, it feels like it might pop out of the socket.

I try to struggle against her. She's too strong, and I'm shoved into the backseat of her gold Ford Taurus like another piece of luggage, trapped by the slamming of the door.

"You need somebody to take care of you." Cassidy jogs around the car beside her, and I almost wish Momma would listen.

I don't want to leave Cass, and I want to stay in Eureka. Branson is big and cold and not like here. The people look at you with distrustful eyes, and I'm always alone.

"I'll send you some money once we get settled." Mom lifts her chin, yelling over Cassidy's head. "Because we don't take handouts from anyone."

Tears burn in my eyes, and I think about pictures I've seen of protestors going limp and lying on the ground. I wonder if I could lean out the window and fall to the ground and just lie there so maybe she'll forget me.

Momma gets in on her side and slams the door, and with the roar of the engine, we start down the gravel road, kicking up dust in our wake. The car is so old, I wonder if we'll even make it all the way to Missouri.

I'm on my knees in the backseat, crying hard as I wave at my sister. Cass stands in the driveway frowning as we fly away, as my heart breaks in two in my chest.

"I said shut up, Jemima!" Momma cranks up the radio to drown out my tears.

My arm starts to cramp, but I keep on waving, watching my sister fade away. Watching my happiness grow smaller and smaller in the distance.

Then three months ago...

Branson, Missouri, is no place to chase down a dream.

It's the place you go when you have no other options. When you've been rejected everywhere else, and you think you can at least be as good as what's happening here.

Or in my case, it's the place you wind up through no fault of your own, and you're forced to figure out how to survive or get the hell out.

That's where I am—stuck in the middle of surviving and leaving.

Crystal Gayle Dixon (a.k.a., my momma) brought me to this broke-down Nashville-wanna-be town when I was nine so she could become the next big country music star.

She dreamed of some talent scout out in the audience plucking her from obscurity and catapulting her to stardom.

Almost as soon as we got here, she ditched me in a hotel room while she went out every night searching for work and her big break. I took care of myself and did my best to live a normal life.

When we ran out of money, I ate crackers and jelly for breakfast. It's like toast and jam. Peanut butter on white bread was my lunch, and I pretended scrambled eggs and government cheese was breakfast for dinner.

Occasionally, if I managed to find a few dollars lying around, I'd get a real hamburger from McDonald's.

I went to school on the internet, and all the while, my mom went from one low-rent club to the next, doing her best Crystal Gayle impersonation, dreaming of hitting the big time while she sank deeper and deeper into drugs and debt.

Look, I'm not here to point fingers or to try and earn sympathy points. I never understood why she didn't leave me with Cass and Aunt Carol.

I did understand abandonment, and I learned quick how to make friends and who was safe.

So here I am, eighteen years later, sitting on a park bench outside Buster's food mart, watching the sun rise and waiting on a friend to finish up after working the night shift.

A little girl with olive skin and wavy brown hair sits on the concrete across from me. She's dressed in a faded, long-sleeved jersey and threadbare jeans. A pink rubber ball is in her hand, and I watch as she lets it bounce while she scoops up shiny silver jacks.

One bounce, ones. One bounce, twos. One bounce, threes.

Her hand moves quickly and with such precision, I'm hypnotized watching her. Or maybe it's because I was up all night doing my set.

I didn't even know kids played jacks anymore. I sure as heck didn't.

My eyes track her movements, and when she gets to tens, I involuntarily gasp as she swoops up all ten jacks in the space of one bounce, catching the ball in the same hand.

"You won." Our eyes meet, and hers narrow.

A faint smile curls her lips, and I can tell she's smart. She's little, but she's clever. She's a survivor like me. We're the same in this city, working class, scrapping and surviving.

"What's your name?" She looks about the same age I was when Momma brought me here.

"Nikki." Her voice is soft with a hint of an accent I don't recognize. "What's yours?"

"Jemima." My voice is tired from singing all night. "Think I can do that?"

With a shrug, she passes me the small rubber ball and the handful of warm jacks. "You can try."

"Oh, it's going to be like that, is it?" I tease her, and she lifts her chin, nodding her head like *yes, it's going to be like that*.

I toss the silver jacks carelessly across the table, then I chew my lip at my mistake. Her technique is more controlled, keeping them in a tight circle. I'll have to do better next time. At least the first round is ones. I only have to pick up one jack at a time as I let the ball bounce.

Imitating her practiced moves, I quickly repeat the process. Up next is twos. I do it all again, five bounces. Then threes, fours… The game grows more difficult as the numbers go higher.

It's like my life as the years rolled slowly past.

Mom dies, and I'm left alone. *Bounce.* The building manager takes pity on me and gets me a job answering phones at a hair salon. *Bounce.* I teach myself to sew, which leads me to repairing costumes. *Bounce.* Costumes lead to drag shows. *Bounce.* Drag shows lead to drag queens, who teach me how to work a crowd. *Bounce.* I find a new place to live and a job that pays tips. *Bounce.*

I'm getting better, I'm finding a way to live, and I'm proud of my ability to survive…

But it's always the same. My stomach is always tight, and the chance of losing everything always lurks at the door.

I've made it to sevens. I'm going to heaven when a sharp male voice interrupts us.

"Time to go," he snaps, and Nikki's amber eyes widen.

She's been so confident up to now. I don't expect her to cower, but playtime is over. I glance up at the guy standing over us, but she doesn't respond to him like he's her dad. She doesn't belong to him.

He's probably in his forties, interesting-looking in a dried-out cowboy kind of way. He's wearing dark-blue denim Wranglers with a crease down the front, and his black tee is so tight, I can see the lines of muscle in his torso. A leather jacket is on his shoulders, and a cowboy hat is pulled low over his glittering black eyes.

"What's your name?" His voice is like sandpaper.

He's a smoker, no doubt, and I think about the right thing to do. I'm still in my beaded, champagne dress, my long, curly blonde hair hanging loose down my back. I still have on my fake eyelashes and stage makeup from last night's show where I impersonate America's sweetheart.

Taylor Swift, if you've been living under a rock. I impersonate Taylor Swift at Trixie's Vixens.

You'd think here in Branson there'd be a lot of money in that, wouldn't you? I did, too.

Well, there's not.

Half the old drunks don't know who I'm supposed to be, and the other half think she's annoying or overexposed. Or both.

Still, I make three hundred bucks a night plus tips, and every now and then I'll find a fan to sing along with me. Those are the good nights.

Pressing my lips together, I rise to my full five-foot-eleven inches. "Taylor."

I say it like, *Duh.*

I know he probably wants to know my real name, but I've learned to be careful with things like real names and addresses on this side of town.

"That so?" Sliding his hands in the front of his jeans, he squares off in his alligator boots.

"Yeah." I lift my chin. "And you are?"

He swaggers closer, and the scent of tobacco and leather wraps around me, tightening my throat. He's cocky, and his crackling grin says *bad man.*

"Wolf."

Of course.

"You a working girl?" His black eyes move from my face to my neck to my small breasts.

I'm not wearing a bra with this dress, not that I need one, and he's mentally undressing me like the creep he is. "I have a job, if that's what you mean."

The muscle in his jaw moves, and he's calculating, sizing me up. Momma used to say, *Stay away from bad men. They'll beat you.* Like living with her was any better.

He should scare me, but he doesn't. I'd let him walk on, but

I'm curious about his relationship to Nikki. I've heard rumors of kids being forced to work in hotels or sew clothes or do other stuff I try to believe isn't possible.

"How old are you, *Taylor*?" He knows it's not my name.

"Twenty-seven."

I wince. I'm getting too old for this life. If I stay here any longer, I'll never leave, and I know what that looks like. *Not pretty.*

His eyes narrow. "You look seventeen."

"People say I'll be glad of that when I'm fifty." At present, looking young is more a liability than an asset.

Fine lines appear at the corner of his eyes, and he reaches up, threading his fingers in the side of my hair. He curls them, holding my head tight, then he presses his thumb against my full lips, dragging it down and smearing red-velvet lipstick on my cheek. My heart beats faster at his rough confidence.

"What are you doing?" It's a hoarse whisper.

He only holds me tighter, stepping so close, his nose brushes mine. A knot is in my throat, but I won't back down. I won't show any sign of weakness.

"You're beautiful." He catches my wrist, pressing my palm to the front of his jeans. "Feel that?"

His erection is thick in his jeans. I try to jerk my hand away, but he holds it, looking straight into my eyes like he's assessing my ability to fight.

"Let me go." My jaw is clenched, but there is no fucking way I could beat this guy in a fight.

Still, I could try.

"We could make a lot of money." Black eyes hold mine. "I'd never let anyone hurt you."

His grip finally loosens, and I jerk my hand away. I might have a taste for adventure, but I also have self-respect. Just where I learned it is anybody's guess, considering I've never had any good role models.

"I don't do that."

He lifts his chin as if my response amuses him. "Too bad."

Our eyes are still locked, and I'm not going to blink first. I'm not going to let him win.

"Hey, girl, hey. Sorry to make you wait." Monay is breathless as she hustles up to where we're standing then skids to a stop. "What's this? Are we making new friends?"

My roommate is a six-foot-two drag queen, who likes to wear two-inch platforms. Towering over us, she sizes up the situation, and her eyes narrow.

"No." My tone is flat.

Wolf takes a step back, snapping his fingers. The little girl jumps up and runs to his side, but she doesn't take his hand. He says something to her in a language that is not Spanish then smacks the back of her head.

I flinch, knowing how that feels, and I grind my teeth, watching her rub the back of her neck. I hate men who treat children like animals. I also hate men who treat animals like punching bags.

"Get in the truck."

She turns, walking slowly to the parking lot, leaving her jacks behind.

The tiny metal pieces pierce my skin, and I realize I'm making a fist. The breath in my lungs stings as anger grows hotter in my chest. It's fueled by every slap, every lonely night, every time I went to bed curled tight in a ball, cold and starving and dreaming of my sister scratching my back and singing me to sleep.

I'm going to rescue this little girl.

My mind races as I quickly form a plan, switching my demeanor from insulted to interested. I channel all the stage-performance I've learned—*find the one who's not smiling, and make him love you.*

Swaying my hips side to side, I bite my bottom lip. "You're so strong." I slide my fingers down his jacket, giving his forearm a squeeze. "I don't have to work for you to have some fun."

His dark brow arches. "Is that so?"

"Yeah, girl, is that so?" Monay crosses her arms.

He said I'm beautiful, so I tilt my head, blinking up at him with baby-blue eyes. "I could come by a little later, and we could blow off some steam."

"You just said last week—" my roommate starts, but I cut her off.

"Give me your address." I hold out my phone. "Maybe you could tell me more about your offer. Show me what I'm missing."

He's not as dumb as I need him to be, but he's horny. I felt the boner in his pants, and I only hope his dick-brain is stronger than his man-brain.

He sizes me up again then taps his phone to mine, airdropping his address. "I'll be alone at six."

"I'll be awake at seven."

Turning, I sway my hips as I walk to where Monay is waiting, tapping her platform boot, her dark brow lowered over her eyes. Before we go, I glance over my shoulder, giving him a little wink and swishing my long hair.

Monay catches my arm, muttering under her breath about how she thought only gay guys were *that* horny. It's all good. It plays into my act.

I force a silly giggle as I jump into her yellow Suzuki, slamming the door and letting out a loud, *Woo hoo!* as we take off. The more unhinged I appear, the better.

Once we're away, I fill her in on my plan, and what I hope is a situation so bad, one little girl won't even be missed.

Chapter 1

Jemima

Today, Eureka, South Carolina

"Upstairs is a bedroom and a half bath. It was Ryan's room, and I think it'll be perfect for Nikki." My boss Piper Jackson is giving me the tour of her tiny house behind the newspaper office. "It has a lot of *character*, but you know, it's a hundred years old."

Honestly, I wouldn't care if it was a million years old. It's clean, solid, and cheap. Piper's letting me have it at a big discount because she's moving in with her fiancé Adam Stone, and she's best friends with Cass.

It's possible she also took pity on me for being a poor "single mom," which has tension hanging in the air everywhere I go. I'm back with a kid who looks nothing like me, and in a small town like Eureka, everybody wants to know everybody's business.

Nikki takes off running up the stairs to check out the room, and Piper's eyes follow her curiously. She's politely waiting for me to spill the beans on what's going on, but so far I haven't formulated a good enough cover story.

Still, the pressure is rising.

"It's small, but we made a lot of good memories here." Piper pushes a pair of dark-framed glasses onto the top of her red head. "I hope you two are as happy as we always were."

She has no idea how happy I am to be home. Stepping forward, I give her a hug, doing my best not to squish her baby bump.

"I know we will be." I shove my blonde hair behind my ears. "First you gave me a job, now you give me a place to live. How will I ever pay you back?"

"Stop with all that." She waves me away. "What do they say? It takes a village?"

"If you're lucky."

She was lucky—her village consisted of her mom, and a pretty decent support network of friends. It's what I was counting on finding when I came back for my sister's Halloween wedding.

Of course, I wouldn't have missed the wedding regardless, but I needed to see if there was a place for Nikki and me to hide out.

My plan to save her just happened to coincide with an ICE raid of Wolf, first name Bill's place, and as I suspected, he was running a low-key sweatshop staffed with kids ages nine to thirteen.

I didn't stick around to find out where they all came from— maybe they were runaways, maybe they were illegal. All I know is, I'd just sneaked in the back door when the front door was blown open.

Nikki's eyes met mine, and she took my hand. As the SWAT team stormed in the front, we ran out the back, and I stashed her with Monay and the other girls while I came here.

But that wasn't the end of it. Bill decided we had a beef, and once the feds were off his back, he came looking for us.

We weren't too hard to find either, considering Monay is pretty unforgettable with her height and Dolly Parton wig. Not even Trixie could keep us off his radar.

That combined with the war on drag queens, Monay sold her car, we hopped on a bus, and got the hell out of Branson.

I'm pretty sure nobody knows where we are now, but I'm not resting on my laurels just yet.

Working with Piper at the newspaper is a big plus. I can keep an eye on the news wires and police reports. Only one job would be better—working with Cass's other best friend Britt Bailey at the courthouse, but I don't want to be that close to law enforcement until I know more about Nikki's backstory.

"Are you planning to come back to work?" She lingers at the front door, her hand on the knob.

"If you'll have me. I need money to pay you rent."

Another grin. Another dismissive shake of her head, as if she'd let me stay here for free. She probably would.

"How soon can you start?"

"Is today too soon? I hate sitting around doing nothing." Or not knowing what's happening.

"Your desk is waiting for you just like you left it."

My job with Piper was supposed to be as an office assistant, but I quickly transformed it into reporting. I'm actually pretty good at it, too. I go beyond the boring old facts and get right to the juice of the story.

Piper tries to edit me, saying the *Eureka Gazette* isn't a gossip rag, but it's hard to argue with success. Circulation went up 10 percent after I joined the staff, and I even started a paid *Personals* section to cover my salary.

With Martha her mom writing snappy headlines, we had everybody in town talking.

And they say newspapers are dying out. Not in Eureka, South Carolina.

"You left town so fast, I never got to thank you for that engagement performance." Piper squeezes my arm. "I'm pretty sure Adam would never have come up with something like that on his own."

"It was all because we love you." I boop her shoulder. "Honestly, I don't know why more people don't use 'Love Story' for proposals. It has the perfect setup, and I bet it was your favorite song when you were fifteen."

I don't mention I had my first French kiss to it at twelve. Not everyone agrees with me that kissing boys is the best, and the badder they are, the better they kiss. I suppress a little shiver.

Although, now that I'm taking care of Nikki, I'm doing my best to be more respectable and not go around kissing bad boys all the time.

"I was more of a No Doubt fan." Piper shrugs. "But who didn't like 'Love Story' at fifteen? It's *Romeo and Juliet.*"

We're standing at the front door, and even though it's January, a warm breeze blows outside. The sun is shining, and it's really lovely.

I walk to the bottom of the stairs and call up to Nikki. "What do you think?"

Her dark head appears, and she's smiling so big, it makes my chest hurt. "It has a real shower with a door, and a room just for me!"

Smiling, I hold out my hands. "What did you expect?"

"It's good that you're getting here in January," Piper continues. "Cass was able to get her enrolled at the elementary school. We guessed she's in fourth grade—?"

My brow furrows, and I think about it. Since I home-schooled myself, I have no idea what age goes with what grade. "I think so?"

"No worries. Ms. Edison is great with the boys, and Dr. Bayer will make sure she's where she needs to be."

Chewing my nail, I think about it. "I should go with her. I don't even know if she's ever been to school before. What if she's scared?"

Piper's eyes narrow, and she takes off her glasses. "That

does it, Jemima. Who is this kid? Does she belong to a friend of yours? Is there a dad in the picture?"

Pressing my lips together, I swallow the anxiety in my chest. All my life I've been trying to get back here because I know this place is safe. I know the people, and I know they take care of each other.

The moment of truth has arrived, and anyway, I'm exhausted from lying and hiding. I need help, and I have to have faith I can trust my sister and her best friends.

With a heavy exhale, I confess. "I don't know."

Piper's brow furrows more. "What do you mean?"

"I met her in a park in Branson, and she was with a man who clearly wasn't her father. He hit her and took her to work in his sweatshop."

"You followed him?"

"Sort of." I'll leave out the gross details about the prostitution offer. "He gave me his address, and when I got there, his home was being raided. So I rescued her."

I say it like it's a happy ending, but Piper doesn't seem convinced. "That sounds pretty dangerous. You can't just take a child like that."

"Why not?" My heart beats faster, and defensiveness heats my blood. "He took her. I'll at least make sure she's safe and fed and loved."

"But who is she? What about her family? Where are they?"

I scratch the side of my cheek, wincing. "I was hoping you could help me find them, and in the meantime, I'll take care of her. Don't tell on us, Piper."

"Tell who?"

"Aiden, for starters. I'm not sure he'll understand."

"I'm not sure *I* understand." Piper exhales heavily, pacing the small living room.

She's quiet, thinking, and my heart is beating too fast in my chest. I'm praying I didn't make a mistake trusting her. Piper is very careful and by-the-book, and she takes her job as editor and publisher of the Eureka *Gazette* very seriously. She's a public figure, and she's pregnant.

I'm forgetting I haven't lived here all my life, and even though these people have known Cass since she was twelve, I've only been back since Halloween.

"I guess we can keep a lid on it for now."

"Oh, thank you, Piper!" Relief drives me forward, hugging her again.

"I think Aiden probably *would* understand... But we can keep it quiet for now." Her lips tighten. "It's not like he tells us everything he should as the paper of record in this town. And I know for a fact he bends the rules when it suits his purposes."

I'm so relieved, I can barely breathe. "You won't be sorry. Nikki's a great kid, and we're going to find her mom. It's all going to work out. I promise."

"Do you have any idea where she might be?"

Now it's my turn to exhale heavily. "No."

"What does Nikki say happened?"

"She said there were explosions, and she came here with her mom to be safe and find a job. But there weren't any jobs, so her mom told her to stay with her friend at Bill's until she came back. Then she never came back... That was last summer."

Piper scrubs her forehead. "So she's a refugee?"

"I don't know." I shake my head. "I'm not smart enough for politics."

"You don't have to be smart to keep up with what's going on." She frowns, studying me. "The wire reports say refugees are coming across the border from everywhere."

"Her English is really good." I hope that earns her bonus points. "It might be better than mine, and she reads everything."

"That's a plus at least." She takes another step then lifts her hands and drops them at her sides. "Whatever. We've got to come up with a story. She's obviously not yours."

"I've been trying to think of something, but nothing adds up to me."

"Can't you say she's a friend's kid?"

"A friend I don't know how to reach? Who never calls or texts?" I count off the neglect on my fingers. "What if people start asking her questions, and her answers don't match mine?"

"Don't talk about me like I'm not here." Nikki walks down the stairs slowly, and we turn to face her.

I go to where she's standing on the bottom step and take her hand. "I'm sorry. You're right. You should be a part of this conversation. What do you want us to do?"

She shrugs, stepping off the stairs but still holding my hand. "I can say I'm staying with you until my mom comes back. It's what she told me when she left."

"Do you have any idea where she went?" Piper's voice is gentle, and I remember her son Ryan is also nine.

Nikki's eyes are round, and she shakes her head no. "We ran out of money, and then we ran out of food. She said she was going to try and find a job before things got worse."

A knot is in my throat when I think of the nights I went to bed hungry, then I remember Bill's proposition to me in the park. I hope Nikki's mom didn't get into prostitution, although if she did, wouldn't she still be in Branson?

"If you think of anything or remember anything, tell us, okay?" I put my hand on her shoulder. "In the meantime, you'll like it here. The people are nice, and I'll take you to get some clothes and stuff to decorate your room. Run upstairs and make a list of everything you need. Don't leave out anything."

Nikki blinks from me to Piper, who gives her a warm smile, and back to me. "Okay."

We wait as she climbs the stairs to her room again, then Piper moves in close, lowering her voice. "I've got a bad feeling about this. This guy Bill sounds scary, and I don't know if you could be charged with kidnapping."

"Kidnapping!" My voice is a whisper-shriek, and a noise at the front door makes us jump apart.

It slowly opens wider. "Hello?" Raif Jones smiles curiously, then his eyes land on mine.

My stomach flips. "Raif…"

The last time I saw him, Piper had asked me to interview him about a new business he was starting. Then Monay showed up saying Nikki was in jeopardy, and I left that night.

We had only just started talking, but he was really thoughtful and interesting. He's got a total James Dean vibe, and the way he glances up at me from under his dark brow does crazy things to my stomach.

"Hey, Jemima." A dimple appears beside his mouth when he smiles. "Martha said to come over and see if you needed help moving in."

He's wearing jeans and a white tee that shows off his tattoos, and when he shoves his brown hair behind his ear, the muscle in his bicep flexes. It's seriously too much for my sex-deprived imagination.

"I think we've got it covered for now." Piper's tone is flat.

His eyes haven't left mine, and I wonder if he heard us talking about Nikki. His face is impossible to read—as always.

I remember to smile. "Thanks for asking."

"We can talk more later." Piper starts for the door, catching his arm as she does. "Did you walk here from Mom's?"

He nods, glancing away and breaking the spell. "She's got me doing some work around her house."

I follow as they're walking away, and when they pause, I notice what looks like soil around his fingernails. "Have you been planting something?"

He gives me a little half-smile. "What's that?"

"Your fingers." I do a little point, and he rubs them together.

He has long, elegant fingers, which is completely unexpected and entirely thrilling when I imagine them tracing along my skin.

"Maybe." His eyes slide up to mine again, and my stomach tingles.

"That's very mysterious. You can tell me about it when we finish our interview."

"Oh, yeah?"

"Yes." I lean closer, and it's possible I'm being a little flirty. "You were going to tell me all about your million-dollar idea before I left. I've got a feeling it's going to make a really good story."

His blue eyes travel to my lips and lower before he nods. "It is."

I'm not sure if we're still talking about his idea, but I'm okay with that, too. "I've got your number. I'll text you when I'm back at my desk."

"I'll answer."

Chapter 2

Raif

ON MY WAY TO THE REFRIGERATOR, I KICK AN EMPTY PIZZA BOX across the floor.

"Fucking slobs," I mutter, bending down to pick it up before continuing through our rusted tin-can of a trailer.

I am so done with this place. Only one thing keeps me here, and it's the same thing that has me going to the refrigerator on this cold January morning—it's a memory, or a *memoriam*… or both.

Opening the door, I take out the bag of bulbs. They've had enough time to chill, and I head outside in my bare feet. It's never really cold enough in South Carolina to worry about things like shoes or sweaters or wool.

A hound dog with one blue and one brown eye hops up and follows me across the sandy grass. He wandered up here about three years ago as a puppy. I expect somebody dropped him off on the side of the road, but I fed him. He's pretty much my dog now.

"Morning, Porkchop." I pat his head, and he licks my face when I kneel down beside the flower bed I've built up inside a tractor tire.

I nudge him away and take out my hand trowel. I know, it's pretty redneck, but Mom would've appreciated these beds. A smile lifts my cheek as I imagine her expression, and I feel her with me as I dig holes in the rich soil I've established above ground.

I remember a year when I was about six or seven years old, she'd seen black and red tulips arranged in a pattern like a checkerboard in one of her women's magazines, and she'd wanted to recreate it so much.

She worked all day, measuring and planting tulip bulbs in square patterns, doing her best to get it just right. Her fingers were dark brown from the rich soil she'd bought to enhance the sandy loam we have down here by the ocean.

"The dirt here is only good for growing potatoes," she'd told me as I sat and watched her work, fascinated. "But with the right soil, you can grow anything."

I'd dug my small fingers into the ground beside her, and she'd grinned watching me. She liked to sing sad songs while she worked, or maybe they sounded sad because her voice was high and lonely. I'd never heard them before, and when I asked her if she made them up, she'd laughed.

"I learned them from your grandmother. She learned them from her grandmother and her grandmother, all the way back to Scotland."

I liked the sound of them. I liked the way her voice wavered when she sang certain words. I liked spending the day with her in the yard, digging in that black soil.

Winter came and went, and those bulbs never even tried to poke through the earth. Of course, my mom had no idea what she was doing planting tulips in the south. She didn't have the internet, so she didn't know the bulbs had to freeze to sprout. They just cooked in the ground like potatoes.

Still, she wasn't defeated. She loved flowers of all varieties, and she'd try new seeds and cuttings every year. She said it was like a surprise. We never knew what we'd get.

I learned later about planting zones and how to know what would grow and what wouldn't. Even if we had enriched our yard with the best soil this side of the Mason-Dixon line, not everything will grow here.

Glancing up at the house, I decide the same is true of people.

I learned about annuals and perennials and which flowers attract bugs and which repel them. I learned to grow the flowers she loved, camellias and jasmine, and yep, even tulips.

They just take a little more work. You have to trick them into thinking we live where it snows, which it never does here.

Hazel Dale Jones died on a cold winter morning when I was thirteen years old. My daddy went into their bedroom and laid up on the bed for a month. He only got up to use the bathroom and shower—not often enough if you asked me—and get a fresh bottle of whiskey.

My older brother Bull didn't do much better, and our trailer home in the unincorporated part of the county, went to shit.

I was the only one who kept making food, washing clothes, paying bills. I was grieving, but I knew Mom would've expected me to keep going. I could've used a good dog like Porkchop then, but I was on my own.

People in Eureka assume we're all criminals, and to be fair, my dad has never been particularly neighborly. He isn't book smart, he drinks too much, and he likes to fight. My brother Bull is a straight-up asshole, who has also done some jail time, but our mother came from decent people near Charleston.

She taught me to have manners, and she liked to tell me things because I was the youngest. I was with her more. She told me never to let anyone look down on me or say I was less than them. She taught me how to act around women, and one day I intend to have a wife and a home and maybe even a family.

I wouldn't mind if that wife had curly blonde hair and long legs. I wouldn't even mind if she liked to wear red-velvet lipstick and thick black eyelashes.

Maybe she'll sing like an angel, and maybe when I fuck her hard, she'll cry my name out like she's on her way to heaven.

A slap to the back of my head sends those thoughts spinning.

"What the fuck are you doing out here?" The low snarl is laced with a laugh.

I'm on my feet with both fists up, not even waiting before I throw a punch, but I only make contact with a couch cushion as my brother laughs louder.

Bull has dark hair and black eyes. A scar from a bar fight slices his bottom lip, and tattoos climb up the sides of his neck.

"You were thinking about a girl," he taunts. "Who was it? Donna?"

"Motherfucker," I growl, ready to punch him straight in the nuts. "Next time you hit me, I swear to God…"

"What? You're going to do something about it? You'd better get up early in the morning." He points to the box of bulbs I'm holding. "What's this bullshit?"

"Something you're too stupid to understand." I pick up the trowel moving the dirt in the center of the tractor tire.

"You planting garlic?"

Glancing at the brown bulb, I guess it does look like a clove of garlic. "It's a tulip bulb."

I don't even wince anymore when I say it. I don't give a shit if he doesn't understand me planting flowers. They're not for him.

We don't have a headstone in a fancy cemetery where I can go and put a big bouquet on our mother's grave for everyone to see. All I have are these round tires, and the assortment of flowers I keep planting for her every year.

It's how I remember her. It's how I honor her memory, and in a few weeks, she'll have red and black tulips like she always wanted.

"Whatever. I'm making coffee."

He goes back to the trailer, and the metal screen door slams behind him. I continue digging and planting.

I've just put the last bulb in the ground when a serious, female voice calls from behind me, "Raif Jones?"

I stick the trowel in the dirt and look up to see Martha Jackson standing in the yard.

She's Piper's mom, and I've talked to her a few times. People say she's crazy, but I know people say a lot of things. I don't judge until I know someone better. I know what it's like to be on the receiving end of that shit.

Either way, Martha is one of those doomsday preppers, or *survivalists* if you care to be polite. I've heard rumors she has an underground bunker with enough food and supplies to last a year—everything you need to get through a zombie apocalypse or a nuclear war or a man-eating bacteria.

Actually, if you sit and think about it, Martha Jackson might be the sanest person in town. What's wrong with being prepared for the worst, especially these days?

I stand, dusting the soil off my hands. "What do you want?"

She's dressed in denim overalls and her dark hair hangs in one long, thick braid down her back. Flecks of gray streak her temples.

"I've got some work that needs to be done around my house. Adam Stone said you're strong and honest." She crosses her arms. "What do you say? I'll pay you good money."

My shoulders drop, and I glance around the yard. "What kind of work did you have in mind?"

I'm not interested in digging a hole to China if that's what she's after. As fucked up as the world might be, I'm not looking to join a cult. I have plans of my own, and they're based in reality.

"I've got a few trees that need to come down… and I've been stockpiling food and supplies for a while. I want to sort it out and donate it. Or trash it." She hesitates. "I've also been thinking about adding a deck, so I could have people over."

My brow rises. *Okay.* "I can do that."

It's how I ended up at Piper's old house on a Monday morning, face to face with the woman who's haunted my dreams since she left town three months ago.

The last time I saw Jemima Dixon was at El Rio for one of those karaoke nights. I sat at a high-top table, and she stood on the stage in a gold dress sparkling like Miss America with full, red lips, singing like a pop star.

She's as pretty as she was when she left, but standing on her front porch just now, she seemed flustered and itchy. She promised to text me, and I check my phone to be sure it's fully charged.

"I appreciate you helping out my mom." Piper walks with me to the road leading back to Martha's house. "I haven't forgotten the way you offered to protect Rosie McClure when Ethan showed up at the paper office last year."

Right. It's a side of myself I don't like letting people see. It plays into their prejudices against my family, but I wasn't about to let that asshole find his runaway wife. "I don't like men who beat women."

It comes out as more of a growl than I intend, but something about seeing a man slap a woman sets my skin on fire. It makes me want to give him a dose of his own medicine.

"Mom always said you were misunderstood. I want to apologize if I ever made you feel, I don't know… inferior?"

Hesitating, I think about it. Piper's a few years younger than I am, so we were never in the same grade at school. She was always with the guys out surfing, although she wasn't on the waves. She had her nose stuck in a book. Now she runs the town paper.

Her red hair is orange in the sunshine, and she's got the start of a pregnant belly going under her denim jacket. She's engaged to Adam Stone, who told Martha I was honest and a hard worker. I didn't expect that from a Stone.

"You never did."

She smiles, seeming genuinely relieved. "I'm glad to hear it. Be sure to get with Jemima on that story. We like to support small businesses in Eureka at the *Gazette*."

"Thanks." I shove my dirty hands into my pockets before continuing to her mother's house.

I'll be happy to talk to Jemima Dixon.

Chapter 3

Jemima

"YOUR HAIR LOOKS AMAZING." I'M STANDING BESIDE NIKKI IN FRONT of the bathroom mirror downstairs. "I love your style. That top and those jeans are a total vibe."

It's her first day at Eureka Elementary, and after checking in at the newspaper office yesterday and setting up my desk, Piper let me have the rest of the afternoon off so I could take her shopping.

We drove to Richmond to get her clothes and school supplies at the Walmart there. She got some high-waisted jeans and a rust-colored, long-sleeved crop top sweater with a baby-blue stripe across the front.

For her new room, I got her a pale pink sheet set with a matching white duvet that has little pink flowers on it. She picked out a fuzzy purple heart-shaped pillow, and I threw in a Taylor Swift blanket.

"Do you like your room?"

We walk out to the small kitchen where I've arranged bagels

and English muffins and cream cheese on a platter along with some Jimmy Dean sausage links I bought at the store.

I'm drinking coffee.

She spears a sausage link and hands me a card. "I found this under the bed."

It's the size of a baseball card, and it has a picture of a guy on a skateboard.

"Tony Hawk," I read, placing it on the table. "Must be Ryan's. You'll meet him at school today. He's really nice. You're the same age, so he'll be in your class."

She nods, quietly taking a bagel off the plate and slathering it with cream cheese. I watch as she takes a big bite, and I'm learning she gets quieter when she's worried.

Still, she trusts me so much, it's terrifying. I don't know if it's because I do my best to project an air of confidence. She has no idea how much I'm playing "fake it til you make it" all the time.

From the start of our journey together, she's been so brave. Even when she's calm, she's not much of a talker. At first, I thought it was because she didn't speak English very well. *Wrong*—she's fluent.

Then I worried it was because she was traumatized—until I found her helping Monay style her wig, and they were talking all about Monay's career as a drag queen and how she got started.

Monay loves to tell her backstory about growing up poor in New Orleans to anyone who'll listen. Nikki was wide-eyed and curious and asking questions like she wanted to know more.

Now I think she's either the strongest kid I've ever met, or she's better than I've ever been at white-knuckling it. Either way, I try to include her in all our decisions.

She did *not* want to go back to Bill's place, and I don't blame her for that. She *did* want to come with me to meet my sister, and she seems excited about starting school, or at least willing to give it a try.

Once she finishes her bagel, she looks at me expectantly.

I down my last sip of coffee and put the mug in the sink. "Brush your teeth, and we can head to school if you're ready."

Without a word, she climbs the stairs to her small bathroom, and my stomach is in knots. I never went to a real school. All I know is what I've seen in movies, and I'm praying Eureka is *not* like the movies.

I pick up one of her shiny silver jacks from the table, turning it in my fingers. It broke my heart when I had to leave her with Monay the first time. She hugged me for a long time, and all I could think of was her mom leaving her the same way.

Then when Monay and I went back to get her, she ran to me and hugged me so hard, I almost burst into tears. I never want to leave her again.

She walks back down and puts her hand on my arm. I drop the jack and stand, picking up my purse.

"Ready?" I smile, hoping to put her at ease. "Want some lip gloss? It always makes me feel more confident to have a little lip gloss. Not that you need it."

I pull a clear tube from my bag and hand it to her. She takes it, turning it in her fingers before putting it into her backpack. "I don't think I can wear makeup."

"How old are you supposed to be?"

"Thirteen?"

"Holy shit, I'm the worst!" My nose wrinkles.

"I'm pretty sure you shouldn't cuss either."

My eyes widen, and I try to remember what I said. *Shit.* I said shit. "I'm sorry. I won't do it again. Maybe we should start a swear jar."

She exhales a little laugh. "Because you might do it again?"

"I might." I wince. "I'm pretty good at remembering things, but sometimes I forget."

We walk to the kitchen, and I hesitate at the door. "Do you need a lunch?" I try to remember what Piper said, then I think of the movies. "Is eating the school lunch gross? I should call Piper and see what Ryan does."

"Stop!" Nikki grips my hand. "You're making me nervous."

"Sorry. I'm sorry." I close my eyes and take a deep breath. "I just want you to have a great first day. I don't want to mess anything up for you. I want you to love it here as much as I do—"

"You said this was a nice town with nice people, right?"

"Yes." I nod emphatically. "And very safe."

"Okay, then." She pulls my wrist. "Let's go."

Smoothing my hands down the front of my flowered dress, I grab the tan felt hat off the table and pop it on my head.

The school is close enough to walk, being down the block from the newspaper office. I show Nikki where I'll be and make sure she has my number in the iPhone Cass helped us get.

My sister added both of us to her family plan.

"Hey, you two!" Cass pops out of the kindergarten room as soon as we enter the building. "You look adorable. I love those shoes!"

She points to Nikki's white, thick-soled tennis shoes, and I whisper in her ear as she hugs me. "Thanks for putting money in my account."

"Thank Alex. You know he's a girl dad—every little girl could be Pinky in a few years in his mind."

Cass married Adam Stone's second brother Alex, who is the total middle-child overachiever. He's the richest man in town, a sexy bourbon distiller with a tornado of a five-year-old daughter Penelope, who everyone calls Pinky.

"AJ, you're back!" Pinky runs out of the classroom, squealing and throwing her arms around my legs in a big hug. Cass taught her to call me AJ instead of *Aunt*… you know. "You missed *everything* at Christmas. Fudge made his bed in Baby Jesus's manger, and Daddy said we should just dress him up in swaddling clothes and let him be the star of the show, since he clearly wants to be."

"Who's Fudge?" I frown at my sister.

"The cat—"

"Ryan's cat—don't you remember?" Pinky interrupts,

shaking her strawberry-blonde head like she's so disappointed in my memory, until Nikki catches her attention. "Who are you?"

I look up at Nikki, who's watching us curiously.

Cass steps over to wrap her arm around Nikki's shoulders. "Penelope, this is Nikki. She's staying with AJ in Aunt Piper's old house."

"Are you going to be my cousin now, too?" Pinky frowns up at my little friend. "Ryan was just my friend, but now he's my cousin because Aunt Piper is going to marry Uncle Adam. Will Fudge be my cousin too, Mamma Cass?"

"You are very obsessed with Fudge these days!" I boop my little step-niece's nose. "I have a friend coming for a visit, and she has a pink poodle you are going to *adore*."

"A pink dog?" Her eyes widen, and I think I blew her mind.

I give my sister a wink that says *you're welcome*. I happen to know Cass does not want to get a cat, but Ryan's stray isn't helping her case by being the star of all the town's misadventures.

Pinky takes Nikki's hand. "Mama Cass says we're going to have a baby instead of a cat, but it's taking a *long* time. Come on. I'll introduce you to Ryan and Owen. They're my other cousins."

Nikki looks up at me, and I smile. "I'll be right there, okay?"

She looks down at the pink tornado holding her hand and seems slightly less anxious.

They take off down the hall, and I turn wide eyes on my sister. "I don't care how much money Alex Stone has, I don't think I could *ever*—"

"I know you're not about to say something negative about my Pinky." Cass arches an eyebrow.

"She's a little…" I fumble to find the right word.

"She's five." A wry smile crosses my sister's face. "And I happen to remember another sassy five-year-old who grew up to be a Taylor Swift impersonator."

"I only wished I had that much personality at five." I peek into my sister's classroom at the little kids milling about, waiting for the bell to ring. "They look like babies."

"Aren't they the cutest?" She steps up beside me, surveying the room with warm blue eyes. "It's their first exposure to school. For most of them, I'm their first teacher, their first chance to learn the confidence they need for twelve more years…"

"Is this the start of a Disney movie?" I shake my head. "Do woodland creatures help you get dressed in the morning?"

"Shut up." She pushes my shoulder.

"Seriously, you must be every mother's dream of a kindergarten teacher."

"I hope so." Concern lines her face. "I remember how terrified I was when we dropped Pinky off for her first day."

"You were *not* worried about Pinky going to school."

"I was. Not everyone appreciates her big personality."

"Trust me." I pat her arm. "Pinky will be fine."

"Everyone's afraid sometimes, Jem." My sister looks at me like maybe she's thinking of another time, years ago. "It's hard when they're little. They don't understand why things happen, and they don't know it gets better."

Does it? Her words hit me where it hurts, and I look up the hall. "I'd better check on Nikki."

My sister nods like I've come around to some knowledge I didn't already have. I leave her, and when I get to Ms. Edison's class, I hesitate.

I don't know this teacher, but Pinky is standing at the entrance with Nikki. Owen and Ryan are listening to her explain how Nikki is new, and she's living with me in Ryan's old house. Owen is getting impatient with his cousin—like he always does—and I figure I'd better save them.

"Hi, guys!" I smile, a little breathless. "Nikki, did you meet Ms. Edison?"

Worried amber eyes meet mine, and I can tell she's overwhelmed. A protective urge squeezes my throat, but Ryan pushes off the doorjamb.

"It's okay, I'll look out for her." He says it with all the

Adam-Stone confidence I recognize, and I realize Adam is the only dad he's ever known. "You can sit with us, and I'll make sure you know where to go."

He waves Nikki towards the class, and it takes all my will-power to wait for her to answer Ryan's very chivalrous offer.

"Thanks." She lifts her chin in a cool-girl way that makes me so proud and follows him into the classroom.

"I'll be at the paper office when you're done." I keep my voice even, doing my best not to gush or embarrass her. "Ryan can show you the way if you don't remember."

"My mom runs the paper." He shrugs like it's no big whoop. "You're living in our old house now."

Nikki blinks from him to me, and for a brief moment, I think I see a flash of separation anxiety on her face. Blinking quickly, I give her my biggest, most confident smile and a quick little thumbs-up.

She shakes her head like I'm a dork, and I swallow the knot in my throat as she continues following Ryan.

Shit, this is awful. I almost wish she were five, and I was leaving her with my sister, who I now realize has this whole school thing all figured out.

Rocking back on my heels, I want to call out to her and remind her she has my number if she needs me, but I know she knows. Owen follows them into the classroom, and I clasp my hands together, holding them in front of my mouth.

When she reaches her desk, Nikki glances once more over her shoulder at me. She does a little wave, and I unclasp my hands to wave back as I blink fast. My eyes burn, and I swear, if I don't get out of here, I *will* cry.

A small hand slides into mine, clasping it tightly. "Don't worry, AJ, Owen and Ryan will look out for her. They're really good at looking out for people, even if they are boys."

A wry smile curls my lips, and I look down at Pinky. She's looking up at me like she knows exactly how I feel, and I huff a laugh. Maybe she's not so annoying after all.

"Thanks, Pink."

We hold hands, and the bell starts to ring as we walk back to the kindergarten class. A lone tear traces down my cheek, and I don't even understand why. Nikki is at the cutest, safest little school in the world, and my awesome big sister is right here.

It's only a few steps from the fourth-grade room to the kindergarten room... and it hits me how fast these years will pass. I glance down at the little girl holding my hand with such confidence, and I think about Cass's words. *Everybody's scared sometimes.*

She's right. I was a sassy five-year-old with all the answers, but then my world got turned upside down, scattered like those jacks. I lost everything I knew, and there were times when I was so afraid.

I wonder how different I might be if I'd grown up here with Cass. There's no way to know, but I can't help thinking about what I lost, what I might have done, who I might've become.

I'm not going to let that happen to Nikki. She's going to have all the chances I never did, and she'll never go to sleep hungry or cold or scared.

"Here you are." I give my niece a hug before passing her to my sister.

Straightening my shoulders, I head out the door ready to face the world when I bump into Adam Stone, slamming the hatchback on his old Jetta.

"Jemima?" He cocks an eyebrow at me. "What the hell are you doing here?"

I've always had a soft spot for the youngest Stone brother. He's a reformed bad boy, but he's engaged to Piper now. Not to mention he's been in love with her since forever.

"Just dropped off my *daughter* at school."

"Oh, yeah." He squints one eye at me. "I heard about that."

"I'm pretty sure nobody believes that story."

"So why do you look like you've been crying?" He points a finger at my cheek, and I push the dampness away.

I shrug, and he shakes his head, exhaling a chuckle. "Why do women cry about school? I don't get it."

"Fourth grade is a big year, and she's at a new school." Sniffing, I push my hair off my shoulders. "Anyway, what are *you* doing here?"

"Dropping off some of Martha's old prepper supplies. She's cleaning out her doomsday cellar, and she thought the school could use some of these paper products."

That reminds me. "Was Raif Jones there? I'm supposed to do an article about his new business for the *Gazette*."

"No, but I think Martha was expecting him."

Chewing my lip, I consider this. "He probably can't talk to me if he's working. Maybe I could go by his house when he's done…"

Smiling to myself, I like that idea.

"You'd better let me go with you to the Jones place." Worry lines Adam's brow.

"It's okay. I can borrow Piper's truck."

"It's not a problem. Just let me know when you're going."

Narrowing my eyes, I study him. "If I didn't know better, I'd think you didn't want me going to Raif Jones's house alone."

"They're a rough bunch."

I scrunch my nose, tapping his arm with my finger. "That's very cute and chivalrous, but I'm used to dealing with rough characters."

"Doesn't mean you have to anymore." He opens the passenger's side door of his car. "Hop in. I'll give you a lift back to the office, and we can discuss it with Piper."

"You're going to tell my boss I need a chaperone to do my job?"

"I would never do that." He climbs in behind the wheel. "I'll just let her know I'm helping you out. We make a great team, remember?"

Shaking my head, I look out the window, but Adam's behavior has me even more intrigued about Raif Jones.

Chapter 4

Raif

"I MIGHT NEED A CHAINSAW TO CLEAR THIS." I'M STANDING IN THE small forest that Martha's front yard has become through years of neglect.

Her house is essentially hidden on the tail end of First Street in Eureka. It's a historic neighborhood, with some of the biggest homes in town, all owned and constructed by the town founders.

The Stones have their house right up front. It's a massive white farmhouse with a wrap-around porch and a yard filled with decades-old foliage, including a live oak with branches as big as my torso reaching down like black arms to the earth.

Closer to us is Gwen Bailey's house. Her husband Lars Bailey was an escape artist, and I remember watching his shows when I was a little boy. The day he died, he performed the biggest show on the coast.

People came from all around to watch him recreate a Houdini trick where he was strapped in a straitjacket, lowered into a waterproof tank, and then dropped in the middle of the ocean.

They put up big screens, and everyone congregated on the beach to watch. I was there with my dad and Bull, but Mom stayed at home. She didn't like big events where she didn't know what was going to happen.

Lars didn't survive that trick, and it sent shockwaves through the community. When we got home, I found my mom in her sitting room with tears in her eyes. She said she was crying for Gwen and her little girl Britt, then she voted for Gwen's mother Edna as town mayor, even though Edna was a former magician.

I think the carnival nature of the Brewer-Baileys appealed to my mom. It made us Joneses seem a little less controversial when there was such an unusual family leading things.

"I never really thought about keeping this place up." Martha almost sounds apologetic standing beside me as we survey her overgrown yard. "I didn't know how long I'd be here, and I never had company."

"My mom would've liked to have company." I bend down, inspecting the roots of the trash-trees growing all the way up to her front door. "Nobody ever came over, because people don't like my dad."

They don't like my brother too much either. I've always tried to keep my head down and fly under the radar.

Martha pushes off her knees to stand beside me. "I never knew your mother, but I'd have visited her if she'd invited me."

Pressing my lips together, I nod as I grab the axe leaning beside the house. "She probably would've invited you. She liked interesting people."

When I was a kid, I'd ride my bike down this street and look at all the big houses. Whenever I passed Martha's house, I figured it looked this way because she was hiding all the time. I guess she's not hiding anymore.

I don't know her story, but everybody in Eureka has one. This so-called "quiet little town" is a big lie. Something's always bubbling under the surface. It's why I never appreciated our family being made the scapegoats when shit happened.

I chop at the base of a skinny tree. "I won't get the roots if I use a chainsaw." Pausing, I rub the back of my neck. "Maybe if I use a backhoe…"

"You're pretty good at landscaping." Martha smiles at me, wiping a fly-away hair off her cheek. "Have you considered that for your business?"

"No." Exhaling a laugh, I shake my head. "Landscaping is hard-ass work." Then I clear my throat. "Excuse my French."

That makes her laugh. "There's worse words than *ass*."

"It's true."

People get all bent out of shape by words like *shit* or *damn* or *fuck*, but they don't think twice about calling a kid worthless or a loser or slapping a slur on someone who's different.

The thought provokes me to send another angry chop to the base of the small tree, and I'm pleased at how quickly it gives way. "These might come out easier than I expected. I'll see how it goes."

We spend the rest of the day chopping and clearing. I make a stack of logs that can be cut into firewood, and the rest we tie up and drag to the road.

When it turns four o'clock, Martha says to call it a day. I'm pretty exhausted, hot and sweaty even though it's winter in the south. We worked hard through lunch, although she provided drinks and food if I wanted anything—all from her endless, underground supply.

"Tomorrow we can see about planting rose bushes. Gwen gave me some cuttings we can use."

She shows me what she has, and I nod, turning the sticks in my hands. They're green and tender, and I feel pretty good they'll take in this yard.

"You can see your front door now." I step back, crossing my arms.

Instant gratification is the nicest thing about landscaping.

When I got here, this place looked pretty rough. Now it actually looks livable.

Martha pays me in cash and thanks me. I walk out to the motorcycle I parked at the end of the driveway this morning. Slinging my leg over it, I give it a hard push to start the engine.

It's loud and aggressive, but I keep the engine low in this old neighborhood. Once I get out on the road, I'll let it rip. Flying down the sandy dirt roads to our place is the closest I get to pure joy. That and riding on the beach with the sun going down, casting a golden glow over the wet, brown sand and the coppery waves.

I glance at the newspaper office as I zip out of town, and I think about Jemima.

She's so pretty with her bright blue eyes and sexy little smile. I think about her more than I should, considering she's part of the Stone family now.

She's smart enough to work at the newspaper, and she's been in the entertainment industry in Branson. I doubt we'd have much in common, considering I've only lived in Eureka all my life. Still, I'm thinking about her all the time.

Speeding down the dirt road, the wind pushes my hair back, and I think about men who dream big. Men who get big ideas and aren't afraid to chase them. I don't have anything to lose, so I might as well chase mine.

Pulling into the yard, I leave my motorcycle at the side of the trailer and jog up the wooden steps to the front porch. My boots scuff on the wood, making hollow thumps, and I wonder if my dad has left the bed today.

Bull works down at the docks as a welder on the barges and whatever else needs fixing. I worked with him there for a few months loading and unloading cargo, then I quit that job. Too many people looking to sell drugs or pull me into some criminal enterprise or other.

I didn't want to skim off the containers and resell the merchandise or help anybody get out of town who ought to be in jail or beat up anybody over a stupid grudge that has nothing to do with me.

It might be a quick way to make some money, but shit like that always comes back around to bite you in the ass.

"Where you been?" Bull walks out onto the porch holding a beer.

"Martha Jackson is fixing up her house." I pass him without stopping, going straight to the refrigerator and pulling out a Budweiser of my own. "I'm working with her for a few weeks."

"Then what?" He says it all pushy, like I should have some great career all lined up.

"Then I'll find something else." I bang the cap off my beer on the porch railing. "They're building that new resort over in Ridgeland. I could get something there. Hell, you probably could too."

He huffs out a disgusted noise. "Fuck that. I'm not busting my ass for chump change anymore."

"Then what are you planning to do?" I don't really care.

Glancing at the front door, he steps closer. "I've got a job coming up, and I need somebody I can trust to serve as a lookout. You in?"

Rocking back on my heels, I walk over and sit on the couch. Porkchop puts his head on my leg, and I pat him a few times. Then he goes and lies down, and I cross my ankle over my knee and look up at my brother.

Bull isn't a good person. I imagine at one point he might've had a chance at being decent, but after Mom died and Dad gave up, there wasn't anybody left he'd listen to. Now he doesn't care about things like the law or staying out of jail. I'm not sure what he cares about.

"What's in it for me?" I'm not really planning to say yes.

Anything Bull might offer me is sure to be trouble, and I've managed to keep my record clean this long. My plans include staying that way.

"Three thousand dollars for an hour of work."

I don't react, but that's a lot of money. It would be enough to put a downpayment on a good idea, but it also has me on alert.

"Three K for one hour? Doing what?" He knows my limits. We've been over this in the past.

I don't hold guys when they're getting the shit kicked out of them. I don't carry a gun when they're sifting merchandise off the barges. I'm not a fucking mule.

"A guy I know has a shipment coming through Rockport, and he needs to get it on the trucks and out of the docks without a hitch." Bull leans against the post. "There's enough guys to do the swap, but we need a lookout, someone outside the perimeter watching. Someone to signal us if anyone comes snooping around or if the cops show up."

"So this person would be offsite?"

"Yeah, strictly a lookout."

I'm thinking about three thousand dollars combined with what Martha's paying me. I won't have to look for more work right away. I could take my time, put together a real business plan, and get the ball rolling on my ideas.

I'd be one step closer to being the next Eureka millionaire. Move over, Alex Stone.

"What kind of cops are they expecting?" Whichever branch of law enforcement he's worried about will clue me in on what I need to know about the job, and whether it crosses a line for me.

If it's FBI, they're stealing goods. If it's DEA, it's drugs. ATF means guns, and ICE means they're moving people. I don't mess with guns, drugs, or people.

His dark brow lowers, and I know he knows what I'm asking. "Any kind of cops."

No help there.

I'm quiet, thinking. "How close does this person have to get to the action?"

"As close as you need to do the job." Bull takes another long drink of beer then throws the empty can in the direction of the trash. "If you can see it from the moon, you can sit on the moon. As long as you don't let us get caught. If we get caught, you're going down with us."

My throat tightens, and a cool wave passes over my chest. Outside of the rap business, I've never heard of any millionaires who've done time, and I don't have the talent for rap.

"How soon do you need an answer?"

He straightens, exhaling before he heads into the house. "It all goes down on the fifteenth, so before then."

The door slams behind him, and I tilt the bottle on my knee, studying the elaborate red and white label a moment before putting it on the table. That's a little less than a month.

I'll case the location and decide how close I can get to the dirt without getting any on me.

If I don't help him, he'll find somebody stupider to do it. Somebody who'll blow that money on alcohol or drugs or women. I'll at least do something useful with it.

My jaw clenches, and I know the bad decision I'm about to make.

My phone lights up with a text, and I turn it over to read the screen.

Jemima: Are you available to talk to me this week? If you want to stop by the office, I could stay late or I could come to you?

It takes me a second to realize it's a text from Jemima, and when I do, a flush of heat warms that chill right out of my chest. She's a beam of sunlight in this dark place, although I don't know why she's interested in me.

I think about her coming here to talk to me with my dad and brother hanging around. *Fuck that.* Then I think about being at that office with her after everyone leaves, just the two of us, and my thumbs fly quickly over the screen as I reply.

What day can you stay late?

Gray dots float, and I wait for her answer. It doesn't take too long.

That's right. She has a little girl now. I'm pretty sure it's not her daughter, like some people in town are saying. She doesn't act like a mother.

I slide my palms over the tattoos on my upper arms. The beer sits on the patio table at my knees. I've never been much of a role model, but I don't think I'm bad for kids. I'm nothing like my brother.

Scrubbing my fingers over my chin, I push off my knees and scuff into the house. She wants to talk to me. That's all.

Hesitating a moment, I text back.

Chapter 5

Jemima

MY STOMACH TWISTS AT THE THREE SMALL WORDS ON MY PHONE, and I catch my breath at the thought of being alone with Raif Jones in the newspaper office after hours…

Talking about wild hogs.

I don't know anything about pigs. I guess that's why I'm interviewing him, but still, I should do some research before tomorrow.

My hair is twisted up on my head, and I'm standing in front of the stove browning ground turkey. The box of Hamburger Helper claims to be so easy—just brown ground beef, empty the box, and simmer.

It's more than my own mother ever did for me, and I don't mind a bit. In fact, I think it's kind of fun in a what-the-hell-are-we-even-doing kind of way.

Nikki sits at the table playing jacks while she watches

SpongeBob SquarePants on my laptop. I think the jacks help her relax.

I stir the meat in the skillet, waiting for it to change colors. "I got ground turkey because it's supposed to be healthier," I say to her over my shoulder.

"All the hip young people are eating sa-lads," she replies.

I snort a laugh, walking over to where she sits. "I can't believe you're watching SpongeBob. That show was popular when *I* was your age."

"Ryan said the best time to wear a striped sweater is all the time, but I didn't know what he meant. He said it's from *SpongeBob*, so I need to watch it."

"Ah, I see." I walk back to the stove to give the meat a stir. I know all about reading the room. "Did you like hanging out with Ryan and Owen today?"

"Uh-huh." She nods. "I gave him his card back. He said he'd been looking for it."

"What did you think about your teacher?"

"She's nice. She said I'm really good at math."

My eyebrows shoot up, and a giant wave of relief sweeps through my chest. "I didn't know you were good at math!"

"I was good at all my subjects in school, but then they all closed." Her eyes go back to *SpongeBob*. "That's why we came here, but our friends didn't meet us. So my mom went to find them."

It's the most she's ever told me, and I carefully walk over to where she's sitting. "I'm so sorry." I trace my nails lightly over her back. "Do you know where they might be?"

She shakes her head no, not taking her eyes off the screen. I hesitate a moment, wondering if there's another way I could ask this. The smell of browning meat hits my nose, and I hurry back to the stove before I burn dinner.

Grabbing the box, I dump the chili mix and macaroni noodles into the pan and stir until it's blended. Then I put the lid on and set it to simmer. Nikki laughs at something on the screen, and I decide not to push our conversation. I'll let her be happy.

Chewing my lip, I walk back to where she's sitting. "I hope this dinner's good. I've never been much of a cook. The guy at Walmart said chili-mac is the best flavor."

Yes, I took some rando's advice in the food aisle. Still, he seemed somewhat reliable, and I don't want to be hard. We're not in Branson anymore. I don't have to fight, because people here are kind and helpful.

I put my hand on her forearm. "I'll be your friend as long as you need me. I promise. And Monay is coming for a little while, and—"

"Monay?" Her eyes blink up to mine, and the biggest smile splits her cheeks. "Will she bring Angie Dickinson?"

"Duh! Like she'd go anywhere without Ange."

She hops up and hugs me around the waist, her entire demeanor transformed. I'm not even jealous, because I know the comfort of a six-foot-seven drag queen telling you everything's going to be all right—even when it looks like it's not. I've leaned on Monay's broad shoulders on many occasions.

We dine on chili mac, and when it's time for bed, I lay beside her on the twin bed scratching her back and singing "Willow" from my old set back in Branson. It's the only sort-of lullaby I know.

When we were in Branson, I told Nikki about how Cass would scratch my back and sing to me until I fell asleep, and she asked if I'd do it for her.

As if I could tell her no.

At school the next morning, we say goodbye outside the building. Nikki's not in kindergarten, and I know she doesn't want to stand out more than she already does.

I'm still a little worried about her, but she's going to be

okay. We're taking it day by day, figuring out our relationship and what happens next.

I'm on my way to the newspaper office, when I spot an unusually tall, extraordinarily fabulous woman in a huge, platinum Dolly Parton wig standing on the sidewalk in front of the Star Parlor, which is the tarot-reading studio owned by Britt's mom Gwen.

She's beside a stack of leather bags holding a pink toy poodle, and I break into a run. "Monay!" I squeal. "I thought you'd never get here!"

When I get close enough, she leans down six inches to give me a brief hug. "Hey, little girl, hey." Straightening, her nose wrinkles. "Has this place gotten smaller or am I remembering it wrong?"

Hesitating, I look around at the town square. The courtyard is at the top of the street filling the entire block. In the center is a football-field-sized green park with a cute little gazebo straight out of the Warner Brothers' backlot. Down closer to the El Rio restaurant and where we're standing is the space reserved for the monthly Movies in the Park, which I love.

"It looks the same to me."

"I guess it was dark, and we were only here a few hours."

"Hello, Angie Dickinson!" I lean forward, wrinkling my nose at the tiny pink poodle in her arms. She licks me straight in the mouth, and I squeal.

"Angie!" Monay gives the little dog a bounce. "She's picked up some bad habits since we've been on the lam."

"She's just a sneaky little lady stealing kisses." I scrub her head. "Why are you standing out here on the sidewalk? I'm staying in the house behind the newspaper office. Come with me."

"I confess, I look like a hooker out here with all my belongings on the street, but I stopped by your place. It is way too small for all of this." She adjusts the side of her Dolly Parton wig, and I think she might be right.

The cottage only has one full bathroom, and even that's tiny.

"But where will you stay?"

"I was about to call an Uber and continue on to New Orleans when this friendly psychic lady who works here said she had the perfect place for me." Monay lifts her head and points to the windows above. "I'm staying in the upstairs apartment."

"That must've been Gwen." My eyes move from the neon-purple sign for the Star Parlor to the large windows of the upstairs apartment. "And that must be Britt's old apartment. I've heard it's really cute. Not sure it's much bigger than my place, but you'll have it to yourself."

"It's a temporary stop on the road of life." Monay pulls her Louis Vuitton bag higher on her shoulder. "I can't stay in a little town like this forever. I have to have the bright lights, big city vibe or I'll go stir crazy."

"Let me help you." Reaching down, I grab two of her suitcases off the ground, and she picks up the LV duffle at her feet.

I don't ask how she's able to afford luxury luggage. She'd just tell me it's not my business anyway.

We manage to climb the narrow staircase leading to a small landing above, and Monay has to duck to enter the single room apartment. I put the bags down quickly before running over to lift the windows above the headboard.

"Angie, darling, we are at an all-time low." She puts the small dog on the floor before sitting on the brown tweed sofa.

Everything is clean, and it's not threadbare. Still, it's definitely old and definitely not luxury. My eyes move to the bathroom in the corner, and I don't even want to open the door. I really want my friend to stay, because even though I never felt at home in Branson, I don't feel entirely settled here yet, either.

"I just dropped Nikki off at school. She is so excited to see you. Seriously. When I told her you were coming, she jumped out of her chair!"

"Naturally."

"Piper said I could have my old job at the paper back. I was just heading there now. I bet she'd love to do a feature on you, and that little Mexican restaurant has karaoke once a month…"

My fingers are twisted in front of me, and when Monay looks up at me, her brow relaxes with a smile. "I'm sure I can stay long enough to help you get settled. My place in New Orleans won't be ready until next month, and lord knows I am *not* going to attempt a move during Mardi Gras."

I step forward quickly to give her a hug. "We're going to have so much fun. You'll see. There's more going on around here than you think."

"I doubt it."

"Maybe we could do our own little Mardi Gras party. I'm sure the town would love it, and we're so close to the beach."

"Do I look like someone who hangs out at the beach?" Her perfectly crafted eyebrow arches, and I laugh, shaking my head.

"No, but we can explore the area. Kiawah and Hilton Head are like thirty minutes in each direction, and they have lots of shops and spas."

"Why don't you let me settle in here, and we can talk about it tonight at dinner."

"I'll cook something for the three of us! I made Hamburger Helper last night, and it was not too shabby, if I say so myself."

"Or I'll see what we can get through takeout. Maybe those places you mentioned deliver."

"El Rio is supposed to be good." She knows I can't cook to save my life. "I'll text you so you have my number, and we can discuss it when I pick up Nikki from school."

Angie Dickinson does a scratchy little yap, and I wave to both of them as I head out the door. I have a feeling Monay just might like this little town once she gets to know it better.

"Henry Anderson is the new vet. We should do a little business profile on him." Piper has her glasses on her head, and she's standing in front of the Mac at the front desk.

"Whatever happened with the personal ads I started?" I'm right beside her, taking notes on my phone.

"We've got a ton coming in for Valentine's Day. You should get started on the layout a-sap." Her green eyes lift to mine. "We've made a lot of money off that idea, by the way."

I grin, standing a little straighter. "I have an even better idea. A Mardi Gras gala to benefit the paper!"

Piper's brow furrows, and she twists her lips. "I'm intrigued. Go on…"

"Okay!" Clearing my throat, I try to think of what all I know about Eureka from my last visit. "We could have it at the distillery, in the place where the wedding reception was?" She nods, and I tap my forehead. "If I'm remembering right, doesn't it have big doors we can open to expand the space? We could decorate the trees with beads and lights, do the catering and drinks there. For tickets, we could charge… two hundred… one fifty…" I'm watching her nose wrinkle as I bring down the ticket prices. "How about one hundred for a base ticket that doesn't include drinks, and they could add drinks from there. Maybe one-fifty for well brands and two hundred for premium spirits?"

"I like it. We can talk to Alex about renting the place, and I'm sure he'd be glad to help with the alcohol. Your sister is amazing when it comes to party planning. You should've seen Aiden and Britt's wedding."

"I saw Alex and Cass's wedding, and I thought you did a great job! The MC at the reception was hilarious. We should get him again."

"Drunk Guy? Turns out he wasn't even with the band! He was some leftover from Britt's old guest list. One of Gwen's friends from the circuit."

"Like a magician?" Laughing, I press my hands to my cheeks. "That makes so much sense now. I definitely want him back, and maybe we can find a Cajun band somewhere close—or at least a band that knows the Mardi Gras standards."

"I'll text the girls, and we can meet up for a planning session tomorrow. I know Britt will want a break from the baby, and we all want to hear what happened when you went back to Branson."

"You just want to know about Nikki." I scoop my purse off the counter. "Let me see if I can change my interview with Raif Jones to tonight after work…"

"You're not—"

"I'm not going to his house, if that's what you were about to say." I take the keys to her old truck off the hook by the door. "Although with the way you and Adam keep acting, I'm very curious."

"Adam?"

"He offered to drive me to their house. Don't worry, Raif has agreed to come here after he finishes at your mom's." My phone buzzes, and my chest jumps. "Today!"

"Is he still over there?" Her lips press into a frown, but I only wave her away. "I'm going to chat with our new vet. I'll bring back a coffee."

"Decaf!"

Hopping into her old truck, I place my hat on the passenger seat across from me and switch on the radio. This thing is so old, it only has a radio, which means I only have one choice—country!

To my surprise, "Tim McGraw" by Taylor Swift is on, so naturally, I belt the lyrics along with her as I turn onto Beach Road heading to Seamist, where Dr. Anderson's office is located.

I vaguely remember Adam saying it was "conveniently located" in the direct center of the county. Something to add to my notes.

The song has ended when I turn into a beige strip mall and park in front of Sunshine Pet Care. Another note.

Two cars are in the lot, and when I push through the glass doors, the loud squawk of a parrot echoes right beside my face.

"Holy shit!" I yelp without thinking, then my eyes widen when I see a frowning lady in a large platinum wig scowling at me. "I'm so sorry! Your bird startled me."

"You're Jemima Dixon." The lady stares at me with eyes as focused as her bird's.

"Aunt Terra, don't harass Jemima!" A girl about my age walks up and holds out her hand. "Hey, there. We haven't really met properly. I'm Julia Belle. This is my aunt Terra and her Parrot, Pat. He's got the dirtiest mouth, so don't even worry about it."

"Fuck off!" the parrot rasps as if on cue, and I snort.

"Thank goodness for that. I'm starting a swear jar at home." I smile, putting on my best Eureka-friendly face. "Julia... I've heard your name. Do you have a little girl?"

"Crimson." She nods, returning my smile. "Pinky's her best friend."

"Yes! My sister has mentioned her. It's nice to meet you properly. And you as well." I lean around to where her aunt is ignoring us. "I have a friend who will appreciate your aesthetic."

The woman's eyes narrow, and I'm back in her suspicious line of sight. "How do you feel about pickles, young lady?"

For a whole half-second, I'm lost, then I remember. "Oh! I'm a big fan. Huge. Are you *the* Terra Belle of Terra Belle's Pickle Patch?"

"I am." Her shoulders straighten, and I know I'm on the right track.

"Do you have a physical store? I would love to buy some of your famous pickles, and maybe we could do a profile for the *Gazette*. I'm their newest reporter, you know."

"I do not." I'm almost worried I've offended her until she adds, "But you can come by the house, and I'll put a little something together for you."

"That sounds perfect! I'll text you..." Her eyes narrow, and I quickly redirect. "I'll give you a call when I get back to the office."

"Um, hello—I didn't hear you come in." A smooth male voice comes from behind me, and I turn to see a guy with sandy brown hair and friendly brown eyes behind the desk. "I'm sorry. I don't have a receptionist right now. Can I help you?"

He seems very nice. A little too nice, if you ask me.

"It's okay! I dropped in kamikaze-style like one of those makeover specials." Stepping forward, I shake his hand while he frowns bewildered.

"Someone sent you to give me a makeover?" He slides the hand I've just released down the front of his pale blue scrubs, inspecting his outfit.

"Oh, no!" I shake my head. "I work for the Eureka *Gazette*. Piper Jackson, the publisher, sent me over to do a little business profile on you. I should've called first."

"You need a receptionist?" Julia's eyes light, and I glance at her.

Looks like somebody has her eye on the hottie new vet in town. Arching an eyebrow, I make another note on my phone.

"If this is a bad time, I can come back." I hold my phone to my chest, moving my index finger between the two of them. "Perhaps you'd like to do an interview of your own?"

"Julia has to drive me home now." Terra steps forward, dropping a cannonball on my little matchmaking attempt. "We need to pay our bill, and she can come back later for an interview."

"Of course." Henry nods, pulling out a long spiral-bound book. "Let me just get you a receipt."

"You're doing it all on paper?" My eyes widen. "By hand?"

"Well… I have this system, but I don't know how it works." Dr. Henry frowns at a nice desktop computer sitting dark and quiet on the empty desk. "It's better if I write it all down and figure it out later."

We wait as he writes, and my eyes land on a tray of what looks like tiny biscuits. "These are so cute. Are they free?"

"Ah, yeah. They're for dogs." He returns to the receipt book. "They prevent tartar buildup, freshen breath…"

I take two and drop them into my bag, then I nudge Julia with my elbow.

She finally gets the hint. "Let me give you my phone number, and maybe I can come by tomorrow?"

He mutters something that sounds like assent as he tears off the top layer of the receipt for Terra. She hands him a paper check, and my eyes widen. It's been a long time since I've seen one of those.

At last, Henry's eyes land on Julia's, and I need to step back so I don't get hit by the sparks. "Sorry, did you need an appointment?"

"No, I'm Julia Belle." She holds out her hand with a little laugh. "Your new receptionist."

I fight a grin, giving her a little thumbs-up below the desk where Dr. Dreamy can't see. Julia is not missing her shot, and I wholeheartedly approve.

The door opens behind us, and an older man walks in with a hound dog on a leash. "I've got an appointment for Bowser."

He's loud and gruff, and I almost laugh.

"I'll be right with you." Henry holds up a finger, giving me a worried look.

"It's okay! I can come back in a few days—once you've had a chance to get your new receptionist up and running."

I give Julia a wink.

"Everybody said it would take a while to get busy." He steps around the desk and motions for the man to follow him. "Right this way, sir. And you are?"

He bends forward to greet the dog, and Julia and I exchange an approving nod. Dr. Nice Backside seems like a great catch from the few minutes I've been here. He's hot, polite, and just clueless enough.

Piper is going to hate this story, but all the old ladies in town are going to love it.

Chapter 6

Raif

MARTHA HAD ME UNDERGROUND ALL DAY SORTING THE SHIT IN HER doomsday cellar. She has an impressive collection of radios and army surplus blankets and giant cans of soup and bleach and dry oatmeal.

She gave all the paper products to Adam Stone for the community center, but I told her to hang onto her equipment. I mean, who knows, right?

She keeps me so late, I don't have time to go home and shower before meeting Jemima at the newspaper office. I rake my fingers through my hair then pull a plaid shirt out of the side panel on my bike and slip it over my shoulders. I don't look professional, but I look better than I did in just a T-shirt and jeans.

I do a sniff test, and my deodorant seems to be holding. Lucky I wasn't working in the yard all day or I'd have to cancel.

Shoving my hands in my pockets, I walk the short distance from Martha's house to the Eureka *Gazette*.

First Street curves around and comes up behind the main

drag where it reconnects to Main Street. Everything in Eureka is connected that way, in ever-expanding circles.

The lights are on when I get to the small building, and I stand outside for a few seconds, watching her working at the large computer up front. She's so pretty.

Her curly hair hangs over her shoulders, and she's wearing a green, long-sleeved sweater. Her lips are full and red, and her brows are furrowed as she studies the screen in front of her.

I don't know what to make of my feelings for her. I've always had women hanging around, but I've never thought much about any of them.

I've never tracked the flicker of emotion in a woman's eyes, the quirk of her lips, the arch of her brow, hoping to uncover how she's feeling.

As if she can feel me watching, her gaze blinks to mine, and it's like a lightning strike through the glass, fusing my feet to the ground and humming in my veins.

What the fuck do I do with this reaction? It feels dangerous, especially knowing who she's related to—specifically, Sheriff Aiden Stone.

A smile breaks across her face, and she looks away quickly, rounding the desk and coming to open the door.

I hear the turn of the lock, and she steps outside. "Hey! Have you been out here long? Come inside. It's chilly tonight."

Is it? I'm warm. It's the male moths who burn themselves to death on the lights, right?

"I just walked over." My tone is calm, controlled through years of practice. "Looked like you were doing something important."

"Oh." She shakes her head, motioning to the screen. "I'm just working on the layout for the Valentine's Day ads. People can send pictures or poems or pretty much anything. We're running all of them, but still it all has to look nice…"

Her voice breaks off, and she clears her throat, looking

down. "Sorry. Are you ready to do the interview? Can I get you a coffee or a water or something?"

"I don't guess you'd like a beer?" I'm mostly teasing, but her eyes widen.

"That's not a bad idea! Why don't we do this at El Rio? It's always better to have a relaxed atmosphere. Isn't that how they do it in the movies?"

"I don't know."

"Me either." She skips over to the desk, turning off the computer and picking up a tan coat and a small purse. "Just between us, I'm kind of making this reporter thing up as I go."

"You look pretty good to me."

"Thank you." She blinks her eyes, and I clear my throat.

We take a short turn onto Main Street, and the sidewalk leads us directly to the only restaurant in town. Herve opened El Rio about five years ago, and it's one of the few reasons I'd ever come into Eureka besides work.

And now Jemima, I guess.

She's walking beside me, and we're both quiet, listening to our shoes on the sidewalk.

"You're tall." She smiles, looking up at me.

Her teeth are really white, or her red lipstick makes them stand out more.

"I'm six-two."

"I'm five-eleven, so most guys are my height. I can never wear high-heels—" She breaks off again, this time with a little laugh like she almost said too much.

"I like women in heels."

"Good thing I like wearing them." She gives me a little wink, and my dick jumps.

Fuck, I need to get *that* under control.

When I don't speak, she exhales again, and I wonder if she's as tense as I am. She always seems so relaxed and confident.

"I saw you have a little girl now."

"Oh… Yes. Nikki." She hesitates. "She's the daughter of a friend of mine."

We're at the restaurant, and I grab the door, thinking about this new twist. Growing up with Bull, I've learned to tell when people aren't being completely honest, and it appears Jemima's hiding something.

"Where is she tonight?"

"She's at Piper's having dinner. Since I'm working."

She walks ahead of me into El Rio, and my eyes trace her long legs leading up to that short skirt. I guess whatever she's hiding isn't really my business, but it's a curious switch from her usual openness.

"I'll get us some drinks." I briefly touch her arm. "You want a beer?"

"Do you mind if I have a margarita?"

"Sure—it's two for one, so you can have two."

"Yay!" She does a little cheer, then quickly adds, "We'll see how it goes. I don't want to get drunk."

"Right." I don't want that either.

Even if I have a feeling it might be cute, I want her fully aware of everything we do when we're together.

The bartender is ready to go with margarita mix and bottle openers, moving so fast, he's like one of those jugglers. I slide over the money and take our drinks.

She's waiting when I arrive at the booth, and I place hers on the table and slide in across from her, feeling a little more relaxed. "How do we start this?"

"Tell me all about your idea…"

We speak at the same time, and she laughs. I exhale a smile, teasing the label on my bottle. Unlike the Buds we have at home, this one is gold and swirly with two lions holding up a medal.

"You go first." She leans forward to sip her drink, sliding her pink tongue along the salt rim and causing my dick to twitch again.

I clear my throat, shifting in my seat. "My mom liked to say

I'm a problem solver. When I come across something messed up, I'll think about it until I find a solution."

Her brow furrows, and she holds up a finger and her phone. "Do you mind if I record this? I'll make notes too, but this helps me remember."

My initial reaction is to say no, but I don't. "Sure."

"You were saying you're a problem solver. Your solution is hunting and trapping these wild hogs, processing them, and using them to supply the free-range and specialty pork market." She says it like she's writing my backstory. "So what do you see as the problem? The growing demand for free-range and specialty meats? Or maybe the spike in wild hog attacks here in Eureka?"

"I didn't know there was a spike in hog attacks. I just got tired of them rooting in our garbage." The skin prickles on my neck, and I don't like her thinking I live in garbage. "They've gotten pretty bold."

She doesn't miss a beat. "I was doing some research earlier today, and did you know a pig is as smart as a three-year-old child?"

"I can believe it." Those fuckers know when I'm coming now, and they hide.

"They're smarter than dogs, and a female hog can have a litter of three to four piglets every four months!"

"Shit." I take a sip of my beer. "No wonder they're everywhere."

She sips her margarita, tilting her head to the side. "You really are a problem solver, Mr. Jones."

"Yeah, but I've got to do some research first." I lean back in the booth, turning a quarter between my fingers. "If my idea was that easy, somebody would've done it already. I have a feeling there must be a hitch."

"I can help you find out. I've got time, and I like doing research." She reaches over and taps her phone face. "We can stop there for now."

"That's it?"

"No." She shakes her head like I should know better. "We'll talk more when we've got more answers and I've got better questions."

"Okay." But I'm not ready to let her go yet.

Mexican music drifts through the sound system, and I remember how she sang that night Adam Stone proposed to Piper. She has a great voice, and I wonder if she'll go somewhere like Nashville next.

I watch her trace her finger around the lip of her glass then lick the salt off her finger. Her lips are so full, I want to pull one between my teeth like a juicy berry.

Blue eyes land on mine, and I think it's only fair to interview her. "How long are you planning to stay in Eureka?"

She exhales a sigh. "Forever, I hope. When I was a little girl, I always dreamed of living here."

"Why didn't you?"

"My mom wanted me with her in Branson. At least that's what she said." She shifts in her seat, her smile darkening. "Then she left me alone all the time in a hotel room."

I don't like the sound of that, and I definitely don't like the shadow that crosses her face. I try to steer us back to the light. "Why Eureka?"

She shrugs. "My sister was here, and back then, when people would discover something great, they'd always yell, *Eureka!* I guess I thought it had magical powers or something." Her face turns pink. "I guess that's pretty stupid."

"I don't know."

She's embarrassed, maybe a little defensive, but her willingness to share a memory like that makes my stomach twist. It's like she's asking for something, and I want to give it to her.

I want to make her childish dream come true, even if it's silly.

Glancing out the window, I notice the sun dropping lower in the sky, and it gives me an idea.

I slide out of the booth and hold my hand to her. "Come with me." She frowns, hesitating, and I shake it. "Come on."

Her lips press together just before a smile lifts her cheeks. "Okay!"

She hops out of the booth, leaving her half-drunk margarita behind and taking my hand. I don't let go as we hustle up the street the way we came, but it's taking too long to get to my bike. I'm worried we're going to miss it.

"Stay right here." I hold up both palms then take off at a sprint to Martha's place, wondering why I didn't park at the paper office.

The minute I get to the carriage house, I hop on my bike, kicking the starter. I don't like disturbing the peace on this pristine lane, but tonight I've got other things on my mind besides the comfort of old people.

I wheel out of Martha's driveway in the roar of an engine and zip up to where Jemima now stands with her eyes wide and her lips parted.

"Are you serious?" It's practically a squeal, and she hops on the back of my bike before I even answer.

A low chuckle rumbles in my chest, and I grasp the handles, opening the throttle and roaring out of town, towards the old beach road in the direction of the ocean.

I don't like that she's not wearing a helmet, but we don't have much time. I'll be extra careful, and cars don't take this route anymore, choosing the better, paved Beach Road. I only have to watch out for critters crossing our path.

My eyes are on the sun getting closer and closer to the edge of the horizon, and my stomach is tight when I feel her arms around my waist holding her body flush against mine.

Her thighs are warm against the backs of my legs, and her chin is on my shoulder. We're racing down the dirt road, and it's fucking perfect.

I slow down to take the turn onto the sandy path leading out to the beach. The fat tires on my bike are designed to navigate soft sand, and it's not long before we're at the water's edge, where the ground is firmer.

"Oh my gosh! Look!" Jemima's voice is breathless in my ear, and pride rises in my chest.

It's a perfect night, and only thin, wispy clouds are in the sky, enhancing the colors.

The sun is a red-orange ball lowering to the horizon, painting the water, the sand, everything in shimmering gold, fiery orange, pink and purple.

We're far enough away that the beach is completely deserted, and I push the throttle down, opening the engine and shooting us across the edge of the surf, chasing the sunset.

A thin sheet of water laps in and out in front of us, and the bike slices right through it, creating a spray of salt water all around us. Briny wind pushes our hair back, and it's just the two of us, the sun, and the glittering waves.

Jemima's arms loosen from my waist, and I feel her throw them over her head in a *V* as she yells out a loud, "Eureka!" at the top of her lungs.

I start to laugh. Racing the sunset is one of my favorite things, and she's the first person I've ever shared it with. Not every sunset is this good, and having her here, on the back of my bike—yeah, that's right. *Eureka.*

The sun is moving fast, but so are we. We're racing to the curve, to the long stretch of rocks that reaches out into the ocean. It's where this stretch of secluded beach ends, and as much as I hate it, I have to ease off the gas.

Her arms are tight around my waist again as I pull the brakes. The bike comes to a quick stop, causing the back tire to curl a bit, throwing sand in an arc beside us.

The breakers are small here, and it's a quiet swishing mixed with the wind and the scree of bugs and frogs. We're both breathing like we ran the whole way. Our hair and faces are damp, and I rotate in the seat to look at her.

Her eyes meet mine, flashing with excitement. "That was amazing!"

My heart thumps hard in my chest. "It was pretty good."

"Did you know it was going to be like that tonight?"

Shaking my head, I exhale a laugh. "I took a chance."

"Thank you." Her voice is shy, and I reach for her cheek.

My fingers thread in her soft hair, and my thumb slides from her bottom lip to her chin. "You're welcome."

She doesn't break our gaze, and I'm thinking of how much I want to kiss her when she grasps the front of my shirt and pulls me forward to press her mouth against mine.

My fingers curl in her hair as our lips slide and seal. Her mouth is warm and soft, and heat burns in my chest down to my stomach. Her tongue touches mine, and I groan. My dick is as hard as a fucking teenager's.

I'm frustrated with our position. I'm frustrated I only have one hand free. I want to pull her to me, crush her soft body against mine, but I have to hold the bike up.

She places both palms on my cheeks, pulling my lips with hers once more before dipping her chin and leaning away with a soft laugh. "I'm sorry."

"For what?"

"Stealing a kiss." She blinks up again, and fuck me.

"You can't steal what I wanted to give you."

"You wanted to kiss me?"

"I want more than a kiss, pretty girl."

A lot more.

Chapter 7

Jemima

I THINK RAIF JONES MIGHT BE THE PERFECT MAN. HE'S DIRTY AND SEXY, and he kisses like a rockstar. He's quiet, but he sees everything. And his eyes…

Not to mention, he totally gets it. Eureka *is* magical.

Flying across the sand on the back of his bike, I've never felt so happy and free in my life, like there was nothing else on the planet but him and me and the enormous sun setting on the water, turning everything to gold.

I took a chance kissing him, but it was the only thing that could happen in that moment. There was no other choice.

Now we're racing back the way we came with the moon growing brighter overhead. It's almost completely full tonight, and it's so bright. The ocean is bathed in silver, like it did a wardrobe change just for the occasion, day to night.

My arms are tight around his waist, and his back is warm against my front. I nestle my face in his shoulders, and my insides tingle as his hand slides down to my bare calf. He gives it a gentle squeeze, and his grip is firm and possessive.

The space between my legs clenches, and I swallow the tightness in my throat. *I want more than a kiss, pretty girl…*

Me, too, sexy man.

When we get back to where we left the road, he slows to a stop, killing the engine. He steps off the bike, and I hesitate before doing the same, watching as he pulls down the kickstand.

He turns a small dial on the dash, and a radio comes to life, playing that old Fleetwood Mac song "Angel." *Can this night be any more perfect?*

I exhale a laugh, and he looks up at me in that way he does. It's impossible to read, and it's *so* James Dean. "What's making you laugh?"

I like how he says it that way. It's not pushy like a "What's so funny?"

Excitement sizzles in my veins, and I only want to close my eyes and dance.

"I've never watched a sunset that way, on the back of a motorcycle flying at a million miles an hour."

"Forty-five." His voice is quiet, sexy.

"Now we're here with the moon growing brighter and the radio playing that song. It's like you planned the perfect night for me."

He shakes his head, leaning back against his bike and crossing his arms, his muscles stretching the sleeves of his plaid shirt. He wipes a hand over his mouth as if to hide his smile, but it's too late. He can't cover that dimple in his cheek.

"I got lucky."

He's so fucking hot, this bad boy from the wrong side of town with tattoos on his arms and long hair and a sketchy past. This man, who nobody—not even him—will let me see where he lives.

"You're saying it's not like this with all the other girls?" I add a little extra tease to my tone.

"I usually do this by myself."

"Why?"

"I've never met anyone I thought would appreciate it."

Pride surges in my chest. He saved this experience for someone special… *me*.

It's another piece of the puzzle, but it's not enough. I want to know everything about him. I want to know what he was like as a little boy. I want to know what kind of trouble he got into at school. I want to know what kind of problems he solved.

I step a little closer to where he's propped against the bike, watching me. "You mentioned your mom before. Do you think I might interview her?"

His brow furrows. "She died when I was a kid."

"Oh, I'm so sorry." My chin drops. "We have that in common. I lost my mom, too."

The muscle in his jaw moves, and his expression hardens. "You'll be okay. You have your sister and her friends to take care of you. You have a good family who'll make sure you survive."

"In Eureka, but not in Branson." I give him a half-smile. "I guess that's why my dream was getting back here. It's the only place I knew I'd be safe and have food and a bed."

He watches me, not speaking as usual. The music changes to "Gypsy" by Fleetwood Mac… *a two-fer!* I start to sway, turning to face the ocean and lifting my hands over my head. I'm singing softly when I feel his warmth behind me.

Warm hands slide around my waist, and he pulls me closer. "Dance with me."

I turn, putting my hand in his, and he wraps his fingers securely around mine. I look up, and when I meet his blue eyes, my stomach tingles. Every heartbeat sends a pulse of need to my core. I lean my head against his shoulder, and it's just the two of us dancing under the moon.

The song conjures a beautiful, swirling spell, and the scent of the ocean, salty driftwood, and spice surrounds us. His body is hard muscle. He holds me, and my fingers curl in the soft flannel of his shirt.

He has all the naughty impulsiveness I can't resist, but there's more to Raif Jones. He's deeper. He sees beauty and color, magic and dreams. He's good.

As the music fades, I look up at him. He smiles softly. "Thank you for the dance."

"Thank you." My heart is a butterfly in my chest, and I can't resist. "Would you say my blue eyes put the stars to shame?"

His brow wrinkles. "No."

"Oh." I drop my face, embarrassed by my little-girl fantasy.

"But I don't say things like that." His tone is gentle, and I lift my eyes to his again. His expression relaxes. "I'd just say you've got the prettiest eyes I've ever seen. If I had the choice between them and the stars, I'd choose them."

"Oh…" I whisper.

He exhales a low chuckle I feel all the way to my toes, and I stretch up once more to press my lips to his. They're so soft and warm, opening mine with a demanding part. Our tongues meet, and he groans again in that way that makes me wet.

I hold onto him to keep from collapsing. He's perfectly luscious, and I want to kiss him for hours. I want to to make out on the beach, then I want to do more than make out. I want his hands all over me, and I think he does, too.

Our mouths part, and stormy blue eyes search mine as if he's struggling with one of those problems. "I'd better take you back."

"Right." I take a wobbly step away from him, tugging at the hem of my skirt and doing my best to break the tension. "I'm not being a very professional news woman, I guess."

"It's okay, we're not recording this part." He holds my hand to steady me in the soft sand as I climb onto his bike. He's teasing me, which is a relief.

"This part is definitely off the record."

He steadies the bike, throwing his leg over the seat and starting the engine. I wrap my arms around his waist again, and he takes it slow, crossing the short distance to the narrow path out to the road.

He continues at a slower pace on the drive back to town, and I guess it's because neither of us are wearing helmets, which I know is very bad. I didn't even think about it before. All I could think of was him and me and whatever was about to happen.

I snuggle my face between his shoulders. My arms are tight around his waist, and his hand is over mine. With my eyes closed, I feel the cool wind swirling around us, and I inhale slowly, salt air, sweet musk, and leather.

Until the bark of a siren jumps me from my dream. My eyes shoot open, and a rainbow of lights swirls around us. *What the hell?*

Raif lets off the gas, and his body tenses like he's preparing for a fight. I'm confused as a black pickup truck with police lights flashing pulls up behind us, following us slowly onto the shoulder of the road until we stop.

Raif puts his foot down to steady the bike, but we don't dismount. The truck door slams, and a tall, male shadow in a ball cap walks slowly to where we are. His body is straight and fit in jeans and a dark, long-sleeved shirt, and his boots crunch on the sandy gravel.

"Get off the bike, please," Aiden Stone orders from the darkness like a drill sergeant.

He is not smiling, and the muscle in his square jaw is tense.

Raif puts the kickstand down and helps me off the bike. We stand beside it as Aiden pauses, first to study me and then to cut his eyes to Raif.

"Where have you been?" His voice is sharp, almost like he's been searching for us.

"We were just riding on the beach—" I start.

"Without a helmet?"

"It was very spur of the moment. Raif wanted to show me something. For the story I'm doing for the paper…" I'm talking too fast, like I do when I'm nervous.

Because even though he's Adam's older brother, Aiden Stone is also a former Marine and intimidating as fuck.

"Is that why he's wearing red lipstick?" My cheeks heat, and Raif slides the back of his hand over his mouth. "Your sister was worried about you."

"Cass called the cops on me?" I'm not sure how I feel about this piece of information.

"On me." Raif's tone is a mixture of annoyance and defiance. "She called the cops on *me*."

I'm confused. "Why would she do that?"

Aiden answers. "You were supposed to be doing an interview at the *Gazette* office. Piper went by to check on you, and you weren't there."

"I didn't know I was on such a tight leash."

"Having people worry about you isn't being on a leash." Irritation enters Aiden's voice. "I'd better drive you home."

"You're not driving me anywhere." I'm ready to fight, even if he is the sheriff.

"I'm looking out for your safety, Jemima. I'd rather not give you a ticket for riding without a helmet."

"Right." Raif clears his throat, straightening. "You'd better let him take you home."

Seriously? I'm not sure whether to be pissed as hell or surprised my sister made all this fuss. She freaked out and called the cops? No one's ever done something like that to me.

"I'm fine with Raif, thanks." My tone is firm. "We were heading back to my place now anyway."

"If you think I'm letting you ride off in the dark without a helmet—"

"He's right." Raif's voice is louder. "Let him drive you home. It's safer."

My lips tighten, and I want to argue. But I guess I can't fight both of them.

"I'll catch up with you tomorrow," I say as Raif mounts his bike. "Thanks again… for all of it."

I wish I could kiss him goodnight, but that's out the window with Sheriff Dad glowering at both of us.

Raif is still as a statue, watching Aiden nudge my arm. I can't imagine what he must be thinking.

"Let's go," Aiden says, and I follow him slowly to his truck with the red and blue lights still flashing all around us.

When I get to the passenger's side, I glance back to where Raif sits on the bike. His expression is steady, but when Aiden's back is turned, he gives me a wink. My lips press together, and I fight a grin before climbing into the truck. *Bad boy.*

We're pulling onto the dirt road when I hear the sound of his motorcycle engine roar to life. It's almost like a middle finger, and my core tightens in response.

Aiden is quiet as we drive back to town, and I feel very rebellious in his giant pickup, buckled in on my side with only the lights from the dash creating a faint green glow. The radio softly plays an old George Strait song I should know.

I turn my phone over in my hands wondering why they didn't just text me, and I realize it's not on. I must've turned it off when I was trying to record my interview, which has me worried I didn't actually get anything on the record.

As soon as my phone finally powers on, sure enough, a missed call and several texts appear from Piper and Cass wanting to know where I am and why I'm not answering my phone.

We're entering town when Aiden breaks the silence. "I'm sorry if that came on a bit strong." He doesn't take his eyes off the road, and I study his profile in the dim light.

I guess I can see why Britt is so into him. He is handsome—for an officer of the law. I can only think of one guy in Eureka I want to know better, and he is definitely *not* in law enforcement.

"It felt like I was being arrested." It kind of still does, but he hasn't read me my rights. He's not in uniform.

He glances at me briefly. "It was more for his sake than yours. I know you're just doing your job, but you need to watch yourself around those Jones boys. They're rough characters."

"Raif has only ever been polite to me." I was the one kissing him, after all.

At least the first time.

"You didn't grow up here." Aiden's dark brow lowers over his blue eyes. "You don't know their family."

He's right, but it feels prejudiced to me. Also, Aiden has no clue what my life in Branson was like. I've seen much worse.

But this is what I wanted, right? Protection, safety, people looking out for me, worrying about me. Aiden is pretty much the head of what Raif would call my "good family," making sure I'm okay.

We're at Adam and Piper's house when he stops, but he doesn't move to get out. "You're not coming inside?"

"Nah, I'm headed home. Gotta work tomorrow."

Right. "Well, thanks for the lift." *That I didn't ask for or need.*

"No problem." He looks at me once more. "I'm not your enemy, Jemima. You can call me if you're ever in trouble. Okay?"

My lips tighten, and I blink down to my lap. "Okay."

As soon as I walk through the door, Piper lets out a little yelp. "You're here!"

"She just walked in the door!" Cass turns her phone to face me, and I see Britt holding a baby on her shoulder.

"Oh, thank goodness!" Britt cries, then she waves, smiling. "Hey, Jemima! Where in the world have you been, girl? Eureka is not that big."

"Just down at the beach." I gesture in the direction of the ocean.

"Well, Aiden must be headed home. Gotta run. I'll see y'all tomorrow night, and you can tell me *everything*."

She disconnects, and I'm embarrassed, confused, and honestly, a little mad. "Seriously, Cass? You called the sheriff on me?"

"I know that feeling." Adam grins from where he's sitting at the bar, taking a sip of amber liquid.

"We didn't know where you were." Cass walks over to pull me into a hug. "The lights were off at the paper and at your house, and you wouldn't answer any of your texts. I was terrified. You haven't been here that long, and you have no idea the stuff that's been happening lately."

"I accidentally turned my phone off."

"I care about you, Jemima, so I'm just going to say this." My sister looks down at our clasped hands. "It's not a good idea for you to be running around with Raif Jones."

I walk over to where Adam is sitting and pick up his tumbler, polishing off what's left in the glass. "That is so wrong. I was working on my story, and I'll have you know, there's a lot more to Raif Jones than everyone thinks. He's thoughtful and intelligent, and I think he's a bit of an artist."

"An artist?" Doubt is in her tone.

"Yes, and he was a perfect gentleman." A little too perfect if you ask me. "We were actually on our way back when Aiden stopped us on the road."

"Back from where?" She's still skeptical.

"He brought me out to see the sunset on his motorcycle. It was very beautiful."

Piper and Cass exchange a look. "Were you wearing a helmet?" Cass asks.

"You know, you can miss some really amazing things if you're always worried about safety."

It's a lame argument, I know, but I don't have a leg to stand on. I'm grasping at straws.

"Except it's not just you now." Piper's voice is quiet.

"Oh, shit, where's Nikki?" My stomach drops. "Was she worried?"

"She's fine. She's watching *SpongeBob* with Ryan and Fudge."

I jog down the short hall behind the kitchen, and peep through the door to see them sitting on the wood floor in front of the television, facing each other. Fudge is stretched out on the bed, but Nikki is teaching Ryan to play jacks.

"The trick is not to throw them too far apart when you get to the bigger numbers." They're practically head to head, and her hand is moving fast, scooping up two rounds of fives.

"Hi, guys, how's it going?" I walk over to sit beside Fudge on the bed, and Nikki hops up to walk around and join me.

"Mr. Adam made boiled shrimp for dinner, and he taught me how to peel the tails!"

"I noticed it smelled like crab boil in here." My stomach rumbles, and I give her a hug. "How was school today?"

"Great! I taught Heather and Claire to play jacks, and Owen and Ryan learned, too."

The soft noise of the pink ball bouncing punctuates the scoop of metal over the floor. "I got it!" Ryan calls, and she returns to where he's sitting.

"You did tens?"

He nods. "I didn't throw them so far apart like you said."

They high five, and all the drama of this night fades away. I'm happy to see her having fun, playing with Ryan, finding her place in the group.

"Ready to head home? You've got school tomorrow."

"Okay." She takes my hand and gives him a little wave. "See ya tomorrow, Rhine-o."

"Not if I see you first, Neek-o."

My eyebrows pop up, and I purse my lips. *Okay!*

My sister is still in the kitchen talking low to Piper when we return. When I enter the room, Piper straightens, smiling at us. "We're all set to meet with Alex tomorrow night at the distillery to discuss your Mardi Gras idea."

She seems to have forgotten all about the drama of tonight as well, and I decide to let it go. "I'll see if Monay can watch Nikki."

"Oh! I want her to come and help us plan." Piper walks around to hand me a plastic container of what looks like shrimp and grits. "Adam made this for you."

"Aww!" I look around, but only Cass is still in the kitchen. "Tell him I said thanks. I'll get Monay to come to the office one day and help us."

"I wonder if she'd be interested in reading to my kindergarten class." Cass walks with me to the door. "I have a Little Golden Book about Dolly Parton, and she could come in costume. The kids would love it."

"I'm sure she'd love it, too. I'll give you her number."

We hug Piper goodnight, and Cass, Nikki, and I head out the door.

"Need a ride?" My sister asks.

Alex's large house is on a big stretch of land farther out of town—too far to walk unlike everywhere else.

"That's okay. It's a pretty night."

"I think it's cold." She shivers, and I step forward to hug her.

"Don't call the sheriff on me again," I say in her ear.

"Don't give me a reason." She lightly pinches my arm.

I exhale a little growl. Welcome to small-town life, I guess. Cass leaves in Alex's Tesla, and Nikki squints up at me. "Why did she call the sheriff on you?"

"Owen's dad is the sheriff. They didn't know where I was, so they asked him to find me."

"Why didn't they just text you?"

"I accidentally turned my phone off."

She makes a disappointed face, and I laugh. "I know. Duh."

We walk a little ways, holding hands. "I think it's cool you're teaching the kids to play jacks. That's how we met."

"My mom taught me to play." Her voice is quiet.

An ache is in my chest, and I don't know what to say to that. "It's a great game."

When we get to the house, I send her up to brush her teeth while I put my dinner on the counter. Then when she's done, I climb into bed to scratch her back as she falls asleep. I sing our favorite bedtime song, and she blinks slowly, watching the stars projected from her lamp onto the ceiling.

I trail my fingers along her back, feeling like shit for making everybody worry tonight. "I'm sorry if I'm doing all this mom stuff wrong. Nobody raised me, so I'm kind of learning as I go."

"I think you're doing okay." Nikki turns onto her side to look up at me. "I like it here."

I lean forward to give her a little hug. "Me, too."

Chapter 8

Raif

THE TRAILER IS DARK WHEN I PULL INTO THE DRIVE, PARKING MY BIKE beside the truck under our makeshift carport. I walk slowly to the house, thinking about kissing Jemima, thinking about her soft body in my arms in the moonlight, thinking about sliding my fingers up her thighs and what she might sound like if I made her come…

Then my jaw tightens when I think about Aiden Stone pulling us over like I'd robbed a bank or stolen precious jewels.

"You made a decision on that job yet?" My brother's voice startles me.

He's sitting in the darkness on that couch, smoking a cigarette.

"I'm still thinking," I growl.

I'm about to walk past him and go inside when he stands and grabs me by the shoulder. "We don't have forever to wait." He's in my face, and his breath smells like whiskey.

"Get off me." I shrug my shoulder out of his grip, but he's too buzzed to back off.

He grabs me again, this time harder, his nails cutting through the cotton of the T-shirt under my flannel. "I'm not waiting til the last minute for you to leave me hanging. You give me an answer by next week or you're out."

I grab his forearm and spin him around. I slam his chest against the post, pulling his arm up his back. "I said get off me." My voice is a growl in his ear.

"Let me go, motherfucker." He snarls, trying to jerk away, but I pull his arm higher up his back. "I'm going to kick your ass so hard, you'll see stars."

"I'd like to see you try." I happen to know he still hasn't recovered from the ass-kicking he got down at the docks two years ago.

He and a bunch of idiots got into a brawl, and his shoulder still isn't set. In fact, if I pull it any higher, it'll pop out of joint. We both know it.

"Let me go." It's a hoarse plea, but I hold him a little longer.

Long enough for him to know I can take him. We're both breathing hard, and I shove him against the post before taking a step back.

The fire burning in my stomach is only partly eased from Aiden Stone leaving me feeling like trash on the side of the road.

Nothing like a Stone-family bucket of ice water in the face to remind me of our place in this town.

"I'll give you my answer by the weekend. For what it's worth, I'm thinking I'll do it. I just want to check the place out first."

He nods. "I knew you weren't stupid. You only act that way sometimes."

Those times I'm sure are when I do things like pick up his garbage and put it in the can or mow the fucking grass or get the mail out of our overflowing box.

I really need to get my own place, especially if I'm thinking about seeing Jemima again. Everybody's right. I don't want her coming out here.

Bull rolls his arm, rubbing his shoulder. "You been working out?"

"No. I've just been working. What's your excuse?" I'm about to open the door when it opens on its own and Willie "Bender" Cartwright walks out onto the porch.

He's an old friend of my dad's. They grew up together, and from what I hear, they used to get rip-roaring drunk together.

Until Bender cleaned up his act and started telling people who curate whiskey and smoke cigars which ones are the best. Somehow this old coot manages to make a really good living doing it, too.

Bender the influencer.

"Hey there, Raif." His low voice is thick and gravelly, and he reminds me of Jeff Bridges in that cowboy movie with his long gray hair and beard.

"What the hell are you doing here?" Now I know why my brother smells like whiskey.

Bender always brings a bottle of Alex Stone's most expensive bourbon when he visits. It's the only way our family can afford a taste of that high-priced liquor.

"Just in town for a visit. Thought I'd make sure your old man's still alive."

I expect he's headed to Gwen Bailey's house next. From what I've heard, those two are sleeping together now.

"How's it going with that business idea of yours?" He cocks an eyebrow before putting a stogie between his lips. "I'll be interested in trying some of your wild hog."

"I've been working with Martha Jackson. Haven't had much time for hunting."

"I wouldn't sit on that idea. Somebody might steal it out from under you." He reaches out to grip my shoulder, giving me a lipless smile. "You've worked hard, and I've noticed. Your momma would be real proud of you, Raif."

His words hit me hard tonight, and I clear the thickness in my throat. "Thanks."

I'm still thinking of Jemima and her sitting behind me on that bike, sliding my hand down her soft leg and kissing her full lips. Aiden Stone might be right. I might not be good enough for someone like her, but that doesn't mean I can't try and prove everybody wrong.

"I'll see about getting something together for you this weekend."

"Good." Bender's boots thump as he walks down the steps, and I notice his truck parked on the other side of the trailer where I couldn't see it when I drove up on my bike. "I'll be ready to put a good word in for you."

His words send a hot ball of urgency rising in my chest. Despite what my brother says, I'm not stupid. Everyone knows Bender's recommendation is what made Stone Cold Single Barrel as famous as Blanton's. Alex Stone can't distill it fast enough to meet the demand, and now he's the richest man in Eureka.

A word from Bender could change my life, and I glance over at my brother, who's now snoring on the couch. Grinding my teeth, I know I'm going to do the job he's offering me. I need the money now. I need to get my ass out of this shithole if I'm going to prove I'm good enough to be with Jemima.

The only way to make money is to have money.

Leaning against the post, I look up at the moon overhead. It's not quite full, but it's big and full of promise. *Would you say my eyes put the stars to shame?* She blinked those bright blue eyes up at me when she asked, the stars shining in them.

I guess I could've said yes, but I think the truth was better.

The truth is always better, and the truth is I'm going to do whatever it takes to change my situation, even if it means doing something stupid for my idiot brother.

I'm out of bed before sunrise the next morning. I don't make any breakfast. I don't even have coffee. Instead, I pull on my jeans and a clean tee. I brush my teeth and hair, then I shove my feet into my old brown work boots.

Before I go, I grab the small bag out of the refrigerator. Bull made it from the couch on the porch to the couch in the living room, and he makes a noise when I pull the door open.

"Hey," I call to him sharply, nudging his leg. "Hey!"

"Fuck you," he barks back. "What?"

"I'll do the job. Text me what I need to know."

"Fuck no, I'm not texting that shit to you. I'll tell you what to do when it's time."

Asshole. I don't have time for his cloak and dagger. "Fine. At least send me the address."

I'm out the door with one thing on my mind.

The moon is a faint shadow in the sky as the sun peeks over the horizon. I roll my bike out and walk it up the driveway out to the road. Passing the yard, I notice the tulips I planted are starting to poke through the soil, and the small, green sprouts give me a sense of hope.

Rolling down the dirt road a little ways, I'm far enough out not to be rude when I kick the bike to life and take off in the direction of town.

Martha's not awake when I cruise up to her house, and I leave my ride in the garage before snatching the brown bag and jogging up the street towards the newspaper office. I have to hurry if I'm going to beat the school kids.

When I passed the house on my way to meet Jemima last night, I noticed her flower boxes had soil in them. It only takes a few minutes to dig several small holes in each one and drop the small, garlic-clove-shaped bulbs in them. I cover them quickly with soil and give them a little press. I wish I'd brought a bottle of water, but the soil is damp enough. I have to trust they'll take.

I wad the paper bag and shove it into my pocket. I pocket the trowel as well, backing away from the house and turning towards Martha's when a sweet voice stops me.

"Raif? Is that you? Wait!" Jemima calls to me from the house, where I see she's holding a travel mug in one hand and a set of keys in the other.

A little girl with curly brown hair and curious brown eyes stands beside her watching me. She must be Nikki.

My throat is tight, and I couldn't leave this spot if I wanted to. Jemima is dressed in white cargo pants and a long-sleeved blouse with large flowers printed all over it. Her blonde hair is loose today with no hats or ponytails, and I want to slide my hands in it.

Now I know it's as soft as it looks.

"Are you on your way to Martha's?" She jogs up to where I'm standing and Nikki follows behind her, albeit at a slower pace.

"Yeah. I'm a little early."

"You've been planting again." She narrows her eyes at my fingers.

Fuck, she knows. "Just doing something…" *I'd wanted it to be a surprise.*

"Always so mysterious, Mr. Jones." She says it like one of those girl detectives. It's cute. "Listen, I want to apologize for Aiden coming and getting me like that last night, and being all…" She waves her hands in front of her. "Yeesh. Over-protective, big-brother vibes or whatever."

"It's okay." I shove my dirty hands into the pockets of my jeans and glance at my work boots. "I get that a lot."

"So I've learned." A frown lines her forehead, and she puts her fingers on my arm. "It's not right. You didn't do anything to be treated that way."

"I should've made you wear a helmet." I lift my finger and slide it along the line of her jaw. "I'd never forgive myself if I did something that hurt you."

Her skin is soft like velvet. Her lips part, and she doesn't speak. She only stares at me blinking several times like a deer when you shine a spotlight at its face.

"You okay?" the little girl at her side asks.

Jemima shakes her head, blinking faster and exhaling a little laugh. "Yes! Sorry. I was just… um… oh! Taking Nikki to school." Her cheeks flush a pretty pink, and she motions between the two of us. "Nikki, Raif. Raif, Nikki."

I nod at the little girl, but she only watches me curiously.

"I'd like to keep going with our interview. I've got some more questions for you. Do you have time to talk some more?"

My answer is yes, always, but I gesture in the direction of the old carriage house. "I'm supposed to be at Martha's."

"We could do lunch?"

"We usually work through lunch and get off early."

She chews her lip, looking back and forth from me to where Nikki is walking on without her. "I'll text you, and we'll figure something out. I had a really great time last night."

Heat spreads through my chest, causing the corner of my mouth to rise. "Me too."

"Okay." She blinks rapidly, her smile growing, and she turns, hustling after Nikki.

I take a few steps backwards, watching her cute little ass shake before turning and walking to Martha's.

Chapter 9

Jemima

"**Y**OUR FACE IS ALL RED." NIKKI SQUINTS AT ME WHEN I CATCH UP to her. "You like him."

"My face is all red because you made me run to catch up with you."

"Whatever." She shakes her head like she's so wise.

I catch her hand, swinging it in mine, happy I got to see him this morning, and he doesn't seem angry or weird about what happened with Aiden.

"He is pretty hot." I glance over at her. "What do you think?"

She turns, very obviously looking back at him, and I huff a laugh, glancing back as well and relieved to see he's gone. "Don't be subtle or anything."

I elbow her in the shoulder, and she cracks a smile. "I like his hair. He has nice blue eyes."

Most of the kids in Eureka walk to school, but there's still a car line for the newer families moving in, who live farther away.

As we get closer, I notice a big, cream-colored Cadillac SUV with shiny chrome pulling into the lot.

"Wow," Nikki whispers. "Who's that?"

"I have no idea." My voice is equally quiet.

We watch a man in a gray suit with a stern expression climb out of the SUV and go around to help a little girl out of the side door. She's wearing jeans and a fluffy white, faux-fur coat with a white fuzzy bucket hat. I'm pretty sure she's also wearing Ugg boots.

"I like her hat," Nikki says wistfully.

"I bet we can find you a hat like that." I'm chewing my lip, wondering if this girl will be in Nikki's class.

Nikki stops walking and turns to give me a quick hug. "I'll see you this afternoon."

She pulls away, walking faster, and I can tell she wants me to leave her here. I kind of hate it. I also get it.

"Have a great day!" I call after her. "You look awesome."

She gives me a little wave, and hustles on to the building. I linger a few minutes longer, watching her go and wishing being a kid didn't suck so much sometimes.

Piper is at the front desk when I get to work. "Is that profile of Dr. Andrews ready to go?" She's digging around in front of the large computer. "These Valentine's Day ads look really good, by the way. What's this one?"

She points to the screen where two blocks of text are highlighted, and I groan. "I need to ask you about these. What do you think?"

Piper reads the first one aloud. "Dear Mary, You don't need a spoonful of sugar to make me go down. Love, Bert." Her eyes meet mine, and we both start to laugh. "Oh-kay?"

"What about this one?" I point to the second one, reading

it aloud. "Dear Albus, Souls aren't the only thing I suck. Love, Voldey."

She puts her hand over her nose and snorts. "Definitely not!"

"Do you think they're real? Maybe Adam's pranking us?"

"I don't know. You'd be surprised what people will send in." She shakes her head. "We'll have to refund their money and run a disclaimer. Only G-rated Valentine's Day poems allowed."

"I didn't get to interview Dr. Andrews last week." I hang my purse on the coat rack. "He was running around like a long-tailed cat in a room full of rockers."

"What? Why?" Her nose wrinkles, and she shoves her glasses onto her head.

"His receptionist quit, but good news. Julia Belle was there, and I got the feeling she's going to take care of him in more ways than one."

"Call him and see if he can do a quick phone interview." She waves over her shoulder as she heads for her office. "I've got room for one column of copy on the front page, and I think folks will be interested in his story."

"They sure will," I call after her. "Dr. Hottie McAndrews is going to be the heartthrob of the county. Too bad he's proba-bly already off the market."

"Just the facts, Jemima." She counts off her fingers. "Where he's from, where he went to school, what brought him to the area, if he has a specialty. That sort of thing."

"Boring!"

"I've got to finish the article on the bridge repair in Freemont. It's going to snarl up the main beach road and prob-ably increase traffic in town for a few days."

"That sucks." I walk to the one empty office up front so I can call Dr. Hottie.

"The old folks will complain, but businesses like it. Brings in new customers." She hesitates before closing her door. "We're still on for the distillery tonight? Alex said to be there at five so it's not too busy."

That reminds me, I need to check in with Monay, who is probably going stir-crazy right about now. "I'll be there!"

Monay is in her thick rainbow robe with a fuzzy pink turban around her head when I arrive to drop off Nikki before heading to the distillery.

I got the interview with Dr. Andrews done. He moved here from Florida after finishing vet school because the girl he was engaged to ran off with his work partner. It was all I could do not to go down that road, but I stuck to the facts as Piper insisted.

He inherited Sunshine Pet Care from the previous vet who retired last year and was a friend of his family's. Piper said she vaguely remembered a previous vet, but Fudge is their first pet. I made a mental note that the previous vet clearly wasn't very newsworthy.

"I mentioned Julia Belle is his new receptionist, but I didn't even include the part where sparks were flying the day I was out there."

"How is that news, *cher*?" Monay goes to the kitchen, taking a bag of chicken nuggets out of the freezer.

I learned a while back that in New Orleans *cher* is slang for *sweetheart*. Monay is all about playing up her Crescent City culture.

"It's interesting." I wave my hands. "Sure, people want to know the basic stuff, but that's just it—*basic*. The spice is what keeps them coming back for more."

"You don't have to tell me about spice, honey, I'm from New Orleans. But you're writing for a newspaper, not Harlequin romance!" She holds up the bag. "Will chicken fingers work for the girl?"

"They're as good as anything I'd make."

"I'll add a little Tabasco." Monay switches on the oven. "What did you say you made last time? Hamburger Helper?"

"Chili Mac. It was actually pretty good." I take a sip of the rosé wine she poured for each of us. "Cass asked me to see if you'd be interested in reading a Dolly Parton book to her kindergarten class in drag."

Her dark eyes narrow. "Is that okay here?"

"She wouldn't ask if it weren't." I walk over to where Nikki is on the couch with Angie Dickinson in her lap. "She knows her class."

"Well, I'm always happy to help educate the children about the queen, but I don't think they're ready for this jelly." She waves a hand, and I grin.

"She said Dolly, not Beyoncé."

"Another queen."

I squat beside the couch to pet the little pink dog. A rerun of *Friends* is on the television, but Nikki's not watching it. She's been quiet since she got home from school, and I haven't had a chance to talk to her about her day. I'm a little worried after the Escalade we saw this morning.

"I shouldn't be too late." I look up at her. "You okay?"

She presses her lips together and nods. A pang of guilt hits me right in the stomach.

"I can't bail on this meeting since it was sort of my idea to have a Mardi Gras gala."

"She'll be fine." Monay walks over to sit beside her on the couch. "Won't you, sweetie? We'll eat chicken fingers and watch Romy and Michelle."

"What's that?" Nikki squints up at her.

"One of the funniest movies of the nineties—and it has Phoebe in it."

Nikki shrugs, unconvinced. "Okay."

"If we have time, I'll paint your fingernails. I've got a new color, Lavender Haze."

"That sounds fun!" I infuse my voice with optimism, but it only earns me a tiny smile.

Chewing my lip, I'm afraid I'm screwing up the mom thing

again. I bet a good mom wouldn't leave her daughter with a friend after said daughter has clearly had a bad day. I bet a *really* good mom would drop everything and take her out for hot chocolate or a slushie from the Pak-n-Save or something like that instead of working late.

"I really won't be long." I go to the door and pick up my purse. "Oh! I got this for Angie Dickinson."

Hurrying back to the couch, I pull out a packet of dog treats. Angie hops to her feet, the little pink bows on her pink ears twitching with curiosity.

"That's right!" Using my good doggie voice, I hand the treats to Nikki and continue digging. "And I have more…"

As I rake my hand through the cracker packets in my bag, Monay walks over to me, crossing her arms. "Girl, I thought you had stopped doing this."

"What? They're good for her teeth. Dr. Andrews said they prevent tartar buildup." I speak the words precisely, like I'm reading an ad.

Nikki is opening the packet, and Angie's little pink butt shakes as she tries to wag her stump of a tail.

"I get her milk bones for tartar."

"Here it is!" I pull out the other one. "Should I have gotten more than two? They look so small now."

Monay puts her large hand over mine, taking the plastic bag of treats. "You're hoarding again."

"I am not!" Straightening my shoulders, I push my bag behind me so she can't see it. "I thought it would be nice for Angie Dickinson, since she's new in town. Look how happy she is!"

She's lying in Nikki's lap with her paw on the treat, doing her best to gnaw it.

"Show me inside that bag." Monay levels her brown eyes on me. "If there's less than three cracker packages in there, I'll give you five dollars."

"Show me the money first."

Monay crosses her arms, shaking her head in a disapproving way. "You need help."

"I need to get to the distillery. Bye, Nikki! Bye, Ang!" Grabbing the handle, I hurry out the door before she asks any more questions.

We haven't even gotten to my bad-boy addiction and Raif Jones.

"Have you set the date yet? This is so exciting!" Britt sits beside me on a stool, her blonde hair pulled up in a ponytail, and she takes a big sip from her tumbler of bourbon. "I haven't been to a party since Bonnie was born. Heck, I've barely slept since she was born. There's a lot they don't tell you about babies. I've never been so exhausted in my life."

"Tell me about it." Piper sips hot tea, resting her hand on her belly. "I don't know how Adam talked me into doing this again."

"From what I understand, there wasn't much of a discussion." Alex gives her a wink.

"It's true," Piper snorts. "Your brother knocked me up. I don't know how I'm going to keep the paper going with a newborn."

They're joking around like old friends and siblings—both of which they all are—but none of them notice Cass has fallen quiet as she sips her tumbler of bourbon.

"I'll help you, of course," I say. "And we've got to get your mom back writing headlines."

I have a tumbler, too, but I'm taking it easy. It's practically the weekend, but I want to talk to Nikki when I get home, and I don't want to be buzzed or smell like alcohol when I do.

"And it's all worth it when they get here." Cass's voice is wistful, and she exchanges a glance with Alex.

He smiles at her warmly, reaching across the bar to squeeze her hand.

Then he tops off Britt's glass and changes the subject. "So about this Mardi Gras ball… What are we thinking? Eight to midnight? Eight to two?"

"I think midnight is long enough. Especially for parents." Piper leans against a barstool.

"What?" Britt's voice goes high. "If we're going through all the trouble and decoration and asking people to dress up, we should at least go until two. You're just saying that because you're pregnant and tired."

"And still working full time." Piper holds up her hands. "But okay—two it is."

"You don't have to stay that late," I tell her. "I'll be here, and I'm glad to oversee the late shift."

"I would think by that time, everything will be running smoothly," Cass adds.

"Don't get too optimistic. It's my event, after all," Piper deadpans.

"I thought we'd moved past all that 'bad luck' thinking." Britt waves a hand at her. "Everything you call bad luck actually turns out wonderfully for you."

"Including that wedding reception?" Piper hesitates, placing a hand over her lips. "Alex, do you have any saltines back there? I'm feeling ick."

"I do!" I pull my purse out and dig in it, feeling vindicated after Monay tried to shame me. "I have lots of saltines. I also have these little biscottis I got at a hotel in Branson. I got these at a McDonald's outside of Rayfield. Who knew McDonald's gave away cookie samples?"

I put several small, plastic packages on the bar in front of Piper.

"Oh, I love McDonald's cookies!" Britt picks up the small bag, inspecting the character's faces. "Look, it's Grimace!"

"Isn't a grimace a frown?" Piper tears the plastic off the saltines. "I never understood why they called him that. He's always smiling and sweet. What is he, anyway?"

"I also have these." I pull out another package of oyster crackers. "They're fun to eat. You can break them in half with your tongue."

Cass leans over to look into my bag. "Why do you have so many condiments in your purse?"

"Is that so many?" I blink up at her, smiling nervously and moving my bag to my lap again.

It's possible I got too excited about being helpful.

Cass rakes everything I've put on the bar into a pile. "Umm… yes. And there's more in there?"

Pressing my lips together, I carefully pick up the cookies, returning them to my purse. "I didn't steal them. They give them away for free at the restaurants."

"But you don't need five thousand little bags of crackers." She leans closer. "What else do you have in there?"

"Just a few things." I don't show her the pots of jelly and the tiny bottles of Tabasco sauce. I even have a few envelopes of honey, which I consider to be the jackpot. Honey is so expensive. "I have a child now. She needs snacks."

"Nine-year-olds don't snack." Cass looks from me to Piper, who's opening her second two-pack of crackers. "Do they?"

"Ryan doesn't." Piper shrugs. "But every kid is different."

"Owen eats everything." Britt dunks a cherry up and down in her drink before biting it off the stem. "I guess he doesn't snack that much, though."

"Nikki isn't even from a snacking culture!" Cass returns to me.

"How do you know?" My tone is defensive. "Anyway, you never know when you're going to be stuck somewhere and need something to eat. Or run out of food."

"Jem." Her voice turns soft, and she places a hand on my arm. "Are you hoarding food?"

Heat rises in my neck, and my throat tightens like I'm being strangled. "I just like to be prepared!"

"I have a great therapist." Piper leans between my sister and me. "Seriously, you'll love her. I wanted to hire her for Mom, but that was before I knew Mom had an actual reason for all her weird behavior. Anyway, then I started seeing her about all *my* shit, and she has helped me so much."

"I don't need therapy." My face is too hot, and I pull away from the group. "I need to get home. Nikki had a hard day at school today, and I told her I wouldn't stay out late."

"But we haven't finished planning the Mardi Gras ball," Britt complains. "I had a fun idea. Mom knows a group who can twirl fiery batons. Hell, she probably knows all kinds of circus performers. Wouldn't that be fun?"

"Yes. Very fun." I take a step back. "I'll see you at work tomorrow."

"You're not walking!" Cass hurries up beside me. "I'll drive you. It'll give us a chance to talk."

"I'm really not in the mood for a heart-to-heart." I can only handle so many problems at once.

"It's too far to walk." Britt appears at my other side. "Take my bike. The lock code is 8786."

"Are you sure?"

"Definitely. I can't drive home like this. I'll have to pump and dump as it is, and I don't want to have to come all the way back here tomorrow to get it."

People are filtering in through the glass doors, and I give my sister a hug. "We can talk about it later." Then I hug Britt. "Thanks. See you at work tomorrow!"

Piper does a little wave, eating another cracker, and I leave them at the bar, my sister watching me with a troubled expression and Britt swaying her hips to the jukebox cranking up what sounds like Del the Funky Homosapien—music I did not expect billionaire Alex Stone to have on his jukebox. Then I remember the Tony Hawk card under Ryan's bed, and realize Adam must've loaded it.

It only takes a few minutes to unlock Britt's light blue beach cruiser and pedal off down the long, narrow road leading to town. I'm a little wobbly at first. I didn't ride bikes much growing up, and I haven't been on one in probably ten years. Still, it comes back pretty quickly, and the road is straight and flat.

The sun recently set, so the sky is still a little glowey. I glance up to see the moon is fuller tonight, and my mind drifts to dancing on the beach with Raif. I wonder what he's up to right now.

I wonder if he might be with another girl, and a bitter pill lodges in my throat. Cass and them have never mentioned him with anyone, but it's not like we're exclusive… or hell, even dating for that matter.

My mind is stuck on where he might be when I notice a truck coming up behind me. "Great," I mutter to myself, slowing down and doing my best to move to the shoulder without crashing. It's getting darker on the road, and I don't want to fall into the grassy ditch.

My front wheel wobbles the slower I go, and I'm trying to stay upright and out of the way so the person can pass me.

"What the hell is taking so long?" I growl, but tightness creeps across my shoulders when I realize they're *not* passing me.

Whoever it is is following me, staying right on my tail on this deserted country road.

Fuck. I stand in the pedals to pick up speed. Sure enough the truck does the same, and the faster I go, the closer it gets. I'm completely alone, and I have no idea what to do or how far I am from help.

I don't have Mace or any kind of weapon. I have my purse and my phone. Swallowing the panic in my throat, I do the only thing I can. I veer off the road into the field, drop the bike, and start running as I dig in my bag for my phone.

The truck stops, and I hear the slam of a door followed by the crunch of shoes on gravel. Then they're running, chasing after me. I hear their body swishing through the grass, getting closer.

Little whimpers come from my throat as I dig frantically in my purse. My fingers finally make contact with hard plastic, and I rip the device out, stopping to wake it. But before I can call Cass, a large hand reaches past my arm and snatches it away.

"No!" I scream, spinning around then yelping again when I realize I'm face to face with Bill. "What are you doing here?"

He drops my phone in the grass. "You didn't really think I wouldn't find you."

"What do you want?" My heart's beating hard.

He, by contrast, is calm, sinister. "We haven't spoken since you showed up at my house."

"That's because there's nothing to say."

"There's plenty to say." He gets closer, but I take a step back. "You stole something from me."

"I don't know what you're talking about."

"The little girl. I want her back."

"Nikki doesn't belong to you, and she's staying with me until we find her mother."

"Her mother gave her to me." He reaches behind him, and I tense, fearing he'll pull out a gun. It's only his wallet, from which he slides out a narrow strip of paper. "I have a signed affidavit right here."

My brow furrows, and I step closer. It's too dark to read what he's holding, but it doesn't matter. It sounds like bullshit.

"I don't believe you. No mother would give a child to you." I'm not super confident in that statement, considering how I grew up. "Anyway, I've already started the adoption process."

"Now who's lying?" A smirk is on his lips, and I swallow hard.

He's right. I'm totally lying right now.

"No *judge* is going to give a child to you," he continues. "You're unemployed, you're not married, you don't even have a home. You're just a broke-ass, lying little cock-tease."

My front teeth clench, and my fear turns to fight. "You're a disgusting predator, and I do have those things." *Most of them.* "Not only that, I've got powerful friends who'll support me against you."

He steps closer, gripping my upper arm and jerking me to his chest. "You're a failed lounge singer who came to me for sex work."

"I went to your *sweatshop* to find Nikki and take her from you."

His hand moves to the back of my hair, fisting and pulling it hard. "You know what I do when a bitch crosses me?"

His fist goes up, and I bend my knees in a defensive crouch, screaming, "Don't you hit me! You'll start a war if you do." He hesitates, and I've got seconds to save myself. "Aiden Stone is sheriff in this town, and if he finds out what you've done, he'll bury you. He doesn't let girls get hurt."

I'm terrified, but I can say that part with conviction.

Bill's eyes narrow, and his fist is still up. His fingers tighten harder in my hair, wrenching my neck and forcing tears into my eyes. "You're not getting away with this. Give me what I want and nobody gets hurt."

My whole body shakes, but I grind my teeth. "I'll never give her to you."

His expression turns cold. He studies me with his jaw clenched and rage burning in his eyes. He really wants to hurt me, but if he's followed me all the way to Eureka, he has to know about Aiden.

"She's mine," he growls. "I'll have her, and that's a promise."

"Over my dead body." My voice is hoarse, and I gasp through my nose. "*That's* a promise."

His eyes flare, and we're face to face. "Don't tempt me with something I want."

He jerks my head again then throws me onto the ground. When I hit the earth, an *oof* huffs from my lungs. Clasping my hand over my mouth, I lie still as he storms away, allowing him to think he won this round.

Far from it. He'll never win.

I wait until he gets into the truck and slams the door. When he finally pulls away, I move to my hands and knees slowly. I'm shaking, and my upper arm aches as I reach out, circling my hand all around the grass as I search for my phone.

It takes a minute, but my fingers hit hard plastic. I'm relieved it isn't broken.

Standing carefully, I go to where I left the bike on the road. I'm shaken up, and I'm sure I'll have a bruise on my arm tomorrow. Otherwise, miraculously, I'm okay. Still, my entire body shakes as I pedal as fast as I can for Monay's apartment.

Chapter 10

Raif

IT'S LATE WHEN I LEAVE EL RIO, HEADED BACK TO WHERE I LEFT MY bike at Martha's when I got off work.

My deal with Bull has been on my mind all day, especially after bumping into Jemima this morning. I'm having second thoughts about saying yes, but I don't have any other way to make that much money that fast.

So I've been trying to rationalize it.

Whatever my brother is doing, I'm not doing it. I'm just watching. He told me the address and dock number, so I can ride over and case the area. I'll check it out and find a location far enough away that if anything goes wrong, I can dip without being noticed.

No harm, no foul.

Thinking of Jemima's pretty face makes me smile. Her blue eyes are so bright, and her teeth are straight and white behind her red lips. I was sure she'd busted me planting those bulbs, but now I don't think she did.

They should sprout pretty quickly in this temperature, and I try to picture her expression when she sees the bright pink flowers filling the boxes. Most people like tulips. They're one of the first flowers to bloom after the cold winter. Tulips and daffodils—two plants that do *not* grow naturally in our tropical zone.

Her house is dark when I pass it, and I wonder where she is tonight. Considering it's Eureka, there are only a few places she could be, and both prick at the leftover anger in my chest. She's either at her sister's, which means she's with Alex Stone, or she's with Piper, which means she's with Adam.

I don't know how close she is with Britt, which would put her at Aiden's house. My jaw clenches. The Stone family has never been our friends. Aiden is fair enough when the rubber hits the road, but he's never missed a chance to come after us for the slightest thing.

Something bad happens in Eureka, round up the usual suspects—the "no-account" Jones boys.

I keep walking past Martha's place in the direction of the bigger, nicer houses on First Street. These old mansions loom like hulking reminders there's a difference between them and me. I'm a guy who lives in a trailer outside the county lines, while they founded this fine town.

Gwen is the closest to my type of people. Her big house is the last one before Martha's, and the scent of roses meets my nose mixed with the sharper bite of cigar smoke.

Looking up, I see the orange glow of a cherry, and I know who it is. With my hands in my pockets, I walk up the driveway, pausing when I reach the edge of the yard.

"What are you doing out here?" I call up to Bender, who's leaned back in a wooden chair on the front porch.

"Who's that?" he growls, rising slowly to his feet. "Raif? Is that you?"

Exhaling a *yeah*, I walk closer, and he jogs down the steps, crossing the yard to meet me with his hand extended.

We shake, and he steps back, placing his hands on his hips. "What are you doing walking around here after dark?"

"Picking up my bike from Martha's." I nod in the direction from where I came. "I walked over to El Rio after work for a beer. What are you doing?"

"Gwen doesn't care for cigar smoke in the house." He takes another puff, letting out a stream of blue smoke. "I don't antagonize her. Her mother talks about turning people into donkeys."

"You're already a jackass," I tease, and he barks a laugh.

"No shit." He leans back, looking over his shoulder. "There's nothing like a powerful woman."

Jemima crosses my mind, and I think there's nothing like a pretty woman with full red lips and long, silky legs.

"What's on your mind?" Bender's watching me, and I'm not about to tell him that.

"Just thinking about things."

"The future?"

"Maybe." This old coot is sharp as a tack. "I was thinking about the people here, and how the way they look at me will never change."

He nods, his eyes traveling over my shoulder to the road. "Maybe you're right, but then again, I wouldn't have thought they'd ever change the way they looked at me." His gaze lands on mine. "I was wrong."

We're quiet, and I turn this over in my mind. "How'd you do it?"

"Time." He walks over to the wooden rail-tie fence and stubs out his cigar. "Consistency. Showing up and doing the right thing again and again—more times than I did the wrong thing."

"How much time?"

Bender's been around Eureka as long as I've been alive. He got himself straight a while back, but as far as I know, he's only been with Gwen the past year. I don't want to wait that long to be with Jemima.

"I think the time it takes depends on the nature of what you've done." He returns to where I'm standing. "From what I know, the only thing you've done is be born with the wrong last name. Am I missing something?"

"No." I've never broken the law. At least not bad enough to get arrested for it.

"So you're starting at zero, which is a helluva lot better than where I started." He exhales a chuckle. "I had to prove I wasn't the same man I was. You have to prove you're not who they think you are."

The weight in my chest eases a bit. What he's saying makes sense, although, "You were always a good man, Ben. You just liked to drink too much."

"I wasn't so good." He gives me a tight smile. "I'm still not, but I'm getting better. Now bring me something I can sell. I want to see you prove them wrong."

"Okay." I huff a laugh. "Thanks."

I leave him in the growing darkness, feeling a little more optimistic about my future and my plans for a certain young lady.

When I reach my bike, parked outside Martha's house, I look up the road in the direction of the *Gazette* office, in the direction of the small house behind it where she lives.

I crank the bike, but I don't rev the engine. I get up just enough speed to cover the short, wooded stretch of road separating the neighborhood from the town.

When I reach her little house, it's still dark. I cut the engine, wondering if she's on her way back here. Then I realize if she is, she probably has that little girl with her.

Taking out my phone, I open the messages app, rereading the texts she sent me earlier. She wants to talk more about the story, but I don't have any more information than I did the other night. I do have more of a sense of urgency, though, from what Bender's saying and from my need to improve my reputation.

Not to mention, I'd really like to spend time with her again. I'd like to kiss her again.

I'm getting ready to send her a text when a noise from the street interrupts my thoughts. Looking up, I see someone headed in my direction fast.

Chapter 11

Jemima

Nikki is curled up on the couch when I get to Monay's place. My friend holds a finger over her lips and motions me inside. I tiptoe over to find my little friend sound asleep with Angie Dickinson right beside her, snug as a pink toy bug.

My lips tighten, and I look up at Monay. "Should I wake her up or let her spend the night with you?"

"That's your call, little mamma. You can wake her up, but then she has to walk all the way home."

It's true, and she might have a hard time going back to sleep once we get there.

Exhaling heavily, I nod. "I'll come and get her first thing in the morning. If she wakes up and asks where I am, tell her I came, but I didn't want to disturb her."

I don't want her to think I stayed out partying all night and didn't give her a second thought. I know how that feels.

"I'll tell her. Don't worry." Monay pats my shoulder, and we go to the door.

She follows me out onto the small landing, closing it quietly behind her. "What's wrong?"

"What makes you think something's wrong?"

"Girl, please. I've known you since you were fifteen years old eating government cheese for dinner. What happened?"

"Bill's here. He chased me into a field and threatened to take her."

"What?" Monay's eyes widen, and she grabs my hand. "Did he hurt you?"

"Almost." I pull up my sleeve, and we inspect the mark he left on my arm. "He was going to do worse, but I threatened him with the sheriff. I don't know how long that will work."

"Was Cass with you?"

"I was by myself." I shiver at the memory of quiet wheels creeping up behind me on that dark country road. "It's all about saving face now. I made him look weak."

Monay frowns. "So he's coming back?"

"Most definitely." My heart beats fast, and all I can think about is protecting that little girl sleeping on the couch. "I am not letting him get his hands on her again."

"You don't have to worry about that. None of us are."

Chewing my lip, I try to decide what to do. I need to talk to my sister. Maybe her super-rich husband can make something happen. I've always heard billionaires get whatever they want, although I don't know if he can convince a judge to let someone like me adopt a little girl.

"Did she talk to you at all tonight?" I look up at my friend. "She seemed unhappy when I left."

Monay pats my arm, and we sit on the top step of the stairs leading down to the exit. "Have you ever heard of Koala Kups?" I shake my head, and she continues. "Apparently it's some trendy kid thing she wants."

Pulling up my bag, I dig out my phone, not even caring if the whole purse crackles with plastic. Nikki is more important than my issues.

"I'm going to find out." My thumbs fly over the screen, and I make a quick group chat including Cass, Piper, and Britt.

> What's a Koala Kup?

I hit send, and instantly gray dots appear on the screen.

Cass: I take it you're home safe?

> I'm at Monay's. Nikki said something about a Koala Kup tonight.

Britt: I swear, I'm going to talk to Dr. Bayer and have them banned from school.

> Why would they be banned?

I'm so confused.

Britt: Because I'm not paying $35 for an insulated cup that leaks, and I'm sick of the cup-bullies.

She adds the red-face, angry emoji, but I still don't understand.

> Do all the kids have them?

Piper: Yes, but it doesn't matter. Everywhere is sold out.

Britt: Owen doesn't have one. See above.

Piper: Adam drove over to Hilton Head, but they don't even have them there.

I quickly text a thanks, and look at Monay. Her brow arches, and she knows what I'm thinking. "Where are you going to find an overpriced, leaky cup if everywhere is sold out?"

"Amazon?" I open the app on my phone and do a quick search. "Here. They have all kinds."

"Do you know which one is the cool one?"

"No, but I bet it's this one." I turn my phone face so she can see. "It's on backorder for three weeks."

"That sounds right."

I chew the side of my fingernail. These freaking things are expensive, and my paycheck's not that big. "What should I do?"

"You should wait and talk to her about it tomorrow." Monay pushes on her knees to stand. "From the sound of it, her closest friends don't even have one, so maybe it's no big deal."

"She looked so sad, though." I stand slowly, staring at my phone. "She's been through so much. I only want her to be happy now."

"Possessions don't make a person happy. Talk to her tomorrow."

"Okay." I hug her, still worried, then start down the stairs. "Don't forget to tell her I came by tonight."

"I won't. Text me when you get home, so I know you're safe."

"I don't expect to see Bill again tonight." I stop at the glass doors, thinking about his face when I mentioned Aiden Stone. "He's gone for now."

Monay locks the door behind me, and I ride Britt's bike to my tiny place behind the paper office. The sun is completely gone. It's dark with only the tin street lamps creating circles of light with large patches of shadow between them.

When I get to the house, I hop off the bike and chain it to the fence. My purse is on my shoulder full of assorted condiments, and I remember being Nikki's age and having nothing. I remember opening the cabinets in the hotel room and them being black and empty.

The first time it happened, I'd never been so scared. I didn't know what it meant to have no food in the house. It's when I started collecting crackers and whatever else was out on the tables in restaurants or in diners or at gas stations.

Every place had something a little different. Some places had ketchup, although by itself, ketchup isn't so great. Hotels that provided breakfast would have jelly and sometimes even plastic cups of peanut butter. Then I discovered honey…

"What are you doing out here?" The male voice makes me scream.

My heart is in my throat, and I grip my purse like I'll use it as a weapon.

Raif steps out from the shadows, holding up both hands and doing his best to hide a grin. "Sorry—I didn't mean to scare you."

He's in his usual work uniform, jeans and a T-shirt, and tonight he's wearing a motorcycle helmet.

"Jeez." I huff a breath, lowering my purse and pushing my hair back. "I should ask you as much. Are you snooping around my house?"

He takes off the helmet, and his brown hair slips around his face in messy waves. I remember threading my fingers in it the other night when we danced. It's soft and thick. He steps closer to where I'm standing, and now my heart's fluttering for a different reason.

"I went to El Rio after work to have a beer. Then I came back to get my bike and bumped into Bender." He glances at my empty house. "Where's the little girl?"

"Spending the night with a friend." I cross my arms. "I had to work late, so I'm just getting home."

"Why are you working so late?" A hint of a smile still lifts the corner of his mouth, and he's so damn sexy.

"We're planning a Mardi Gras ball to raise money for the paper." I don't add *to cover my salary*. Instead, I tap his shoulder. "And you're invited."

"Oh, yeah?"

"Yes. Maybe you could even be my date." A thrill tightens my stomach. *Did I just ask him out?*

He glances up at me, and I chew my bottom lip. "Did you just ask me out?"

"I guess I did."

"Then I guess I have to say yes." That dimple is in his cheek, and in my head I jump up and down and scream *Eureka!*

Outwardly, I'm very casual. "It's a date then."

"What does a guy like me wear to a Mardi Gras ball?"

"They're traditionally white-tie affairs, and you'll need a mask. I expect most of the men will wear those little Zorro ones."

"Is that okay?" He sounds like he really cares, and I run my eyes over him, thinking how sexy he'll be all dressed up.

"I think a Zorro mask will suit you perfectly. Wasn't he an outlaw?"

"I don't know." His chin lowers, and he glances up at me. "I'm not exactly an outlaw. I just have a bad reputation."

"I can work with that." I picture him in a tux, wearing a Zorro mask, and I want to swoon. Instead I wrap an arm around my waist. "What are you doing here?"

He slides a hand into his pocket and shrugs. "Heading home. Unless… you wanted to do something?"

"I do, actually. Would you give me a ride to the store?"

This time, I wear a helmet when I sit behind him on the bike. It's one of Ryan's old skateboarding helmets we found in Piper's old garage, but Raif said it would work for a quick trip to the store.

He takes me to the Walmart outside of town, and I go straight to the girl's clothing department. If I can't get Nikki a Koala Kup, I can at least get her one of those fuzzy bucket hats.

Shuffling through the stack, I settle on a green one with a mermaid on the front. "What do you think?"

"Are kids really wearing these things?" Raif pulls a black one onto his head.

My nose wrinkles, and I do the same, pulling a rainbow one with sparkles on mine. "What do you think? Yes?"

"No." He laughs, and I pull it off quickly, my cheeks heating. I scrub my fingers in my hair, picking out my bangs with my fingertips. "I guess I have all kinds of hat hair between that helmet and this hat."

"I think your hair is pretty." He reaches out to move a piece behind my ear, and the slide of his finger over my skin is electric.

It reminds me of this morning when he touched my cheek, and I nearly burst into flames.

He takes the hat off his head, tossing it onto the pile. Then he scrubs a hand through his long, shaggy hair, and it falls perfectly messy.

"Is that all you need?" He nods at the hat.

Hesitating, I look in the direction of the camping gear. "I wonder if they have any of those Koala Kups. All the kids have them, and I don't want Nikki to feel left out."

"We'd better check." He's so ready to help me. I kind of love it.

We walk down aisle after aisle, looking at all kinds of insulated bags and coffee mugs and fire starter and radios. They have thermoses, but no Koalas.

"Piper said they were sold out everywhere," I sigh, feeling defeated. "I thought they might have gotten a new shipment or something."

"They get shipments of this stuff all the time at the docks. I could check and see if any are down there." He hesitates. "I was headed over there tomorrow anyway."

"Would you?" My eyes brighten, and I want to hug him.

A satisfied grin relaxes his face. "Of course. You just want one?"

"Oh…" My bottom lip slips into my mouth. "Do you think you can get three? I think the boys want one, too."

"I can try. Any particular color or style?"

"I'll find out tomorrow and let you know."

We pay for the hat, and we're on the road back to my place. It's much later now, and my arms are around his waist. It's not like flying across the beach in the glow of the setting sun, but it's still our bodies pressed together, the tops of my thighs against the backs of his legs.

I'm hugging him and resting my cheek against his back, and I know in my bones he is good. He even wants to help me make Nikki happy.

The one traffic signal in Eureka is red, and as we wait, he slides his hand down to cup my calf, giving it a squeeze. Heat surges straight to my core, and I want to kiss him again tonight.

My mind drifts to Nikki staying at Monay's, my empty house, and I want more than a kiss.

He pulls up behind the *Gazette* office and steps off, putting down the kickstand before taking my hand and helping me off the bike.

"Thanks for the ride. And for the cup." I'm still holding his hand as we walk to my front door, wondering the best way to invite him to spend the night.

We stop, and I turn to face him. "Why do you keep doing these things for me?"

"I like to see you smile." His eyes linger on my lips, and I slip my tongue out to wet them.

"I think you want to kiss me again." I trace my finger along his forearm.

"You do?" He steps closer, sliding his hand up my neck and into the side of my hair.

I nod, heat rising in my body. "I do."

"Would you like me to kiss you again?"

He's so close, and I remember what he said this morning. *I'd never forgive myself if I did something that hurt you…*

It's followed closely by calm satisfaction. Nothing can hurt me when I'm with Raif. People can say what they want, but he'll protect me. He's a badass.

"Yes." My nipples tighten, and I'm sure they're visible through the thin material of my dress, since I'm not wearing a bra.

His fingers curl in the side of my hair, and he lifts his other hand to my cheek. His thumb tugs at my lower lip, and hungry blue eyes hold mine. My breath hitches just before his mouth lowers, covering mine and melting my knees.

Our lips part, and when our tongues slide together, a whimper aches in my throat. He answers it with a hot growl, pulling my mouth with his before sliding down to bite my chin. He's confident, demanding, possessive, and I'm ready to submit.

"Jemima…" He trails his lips along my jaw, up to the side of my ear. "You're as pretty as the sunset on the ocean."

My fingers curl at his waist, and I can't speak. No one's ever said the things he says to me. Our eyes meet again, and his gaze roams over my face like he's memorizing it.

With a great effort, I grasp his wrist, stepping out of his arms. "Come inside."

It takes me a minute to unlock the door, and he follows as I push it open and step into the dim living room. A light is on in the kitchen, but it's otherwise dark. I place my purse on the table, and I feel his heat behind me.

A large hand slides around my waist to flatten on my stomach, and I stop in my tracks, leaning my head back against his shoulder.

His mouth is at my ear. "I like this dress."

I'm so happy I wore it.

He kisses a line down my neck, sliding the dress off my shoulder. I'm breathing fast, quickly unbuttoning the front to give him access. His hand moves around me, reaching inside my open top to cup my bare breast.

"Yes…" I hiss as he lifts and kneads it.

His hand drifts lower to the front of my skirt, gathering it higher until his fingers slide over my bare legs. I rise onto my toes as if that will make it easier for him to touch me. He can do anything he wants to me right now. I want it all.

His fingers curl around to my inner thighs. "Your skin is so soft."

My cheeks heat, and I'm a little embarrassed I haven't shaved in a few days. "I don't grow much hair on my legs, so I don't have to shave a lot."

"What about your pussy?" His hand moves higher, and my stomach twists in anticipation.

"Waxed," I gasp.

"Mmm…" His voice vibrates in my ear, and his fingers find the center of my panties, sliding back and forth before moving beneath the fabric to my bare skin. "Perfect."

"Oh, God." I can't move. One strong arm is a band of muscle around my waist, and his face is in my hair, kissing my neck as he fingers me.

He strokes and circles my clit, and my hips rotate in time. I'm a rag doll under his touch, bending as he wills. A thick digit slips inside me, and I yelp, rising onto my toes.

"Fuck, you're so wet," he groans.

I'm about to come, and I reach behind me to palm the front of his jeans. His cock is thick and long beneath the fabric and so hard. I turn, reaching for the top button, but he stops me.

In a sweep, he lifts me off my feet, placing my ass on the table. His hands grip my knees, and he lifts them, opening me as my skirt falls to my waist.

"Raif…" I gasp as he grips the sides of my underwear, jerking them down my legs.

I help him, shoving them lower and wiggling my foot out of the opening. I've only gotten one leg free when his mouth comes down, covering my pussy in a long, hungry tongue-kiss.

Another cry escapes my lips, and I arch my back. His face is between my thighs, moving back and forth, and my eyes roll shut.

His tongue slides hungrily up and down and around and around my clit, and I'm losing my mind with every sizzling swipe. My stomach quivers, and I whimper and buck, threading my fingers in the sides of his thick hair as he eats me like his favorite meal.

His mouth moves to the crease of my leg, and he kisses and licks me there. I'm so sensitive, my thighs jump, but he doesn't waste time. He's back on my clit, sucking and tasting. He's not letting up as I rise higher and higher, my orgasm tingling and twisting my stomach tighter with every pass.

Little growling noises come from him, vibrating against

my most sensitive skin. My brain burns, and I'm lost in sensation, flying higher and higher. Another warm, wet stroke of his tongue, and I feel his fingers tickling at my ass, moving closer to my pussy.

He slips two fingers inside me, curling them, and with a buck, I come so fast, I nearly fly off the table.

"Fuck!" I yell. "Fuck yes!"

He keeps licking and pumping his fingers until my legs are shaking. My hands are in his hair, and I twist to the side with a scream of ecstasy. "Raif..."

He pushes me onto my back again, and when I look down, I see his blue eyes twinkle at me from between my thighs. He rises higher, kissing the top of my hip, my lower belly. A sex-drunk laugh ripples through my body, and he bites my stomach just hard enough to make my legs shake again.

"Fuck, Raif!" I squeak, reaching for him. "You melted my brain."

He stands straight between my legs, looking down at me like I'm a feast, and he's starving. I'm pretty starving myself, and I put a hand beside me on the table, pushing up slowly to sitting.

Our eyes never part, and I reach for the hem of his shirt. "Take this off."

In a sweep, both of his shirts are gone, and he's standing in front of me bare chested, his body as perfect as a statue.

He's all tanned, lean muscle, like someone who works hard instead of working out. I trace my fingers over his broad, tattooed shoulders, down to the lines that carve out his biceps. His muscled forearms are beside me as he leans forward on the table.

The front of my dress is open, and he lifts a hand to my breast, cupping and sliding his thumb across my hard nipple. Then he leans forward and sucks and bites it.

The sensation registers straight to my throbbing pussy, and the mind-bending orgasm he gave me revives with a tingling heat. I want to rub my bare body all over his.

His chest is broad, and more lines of muscle cut along his

ribs and across his stomach. A perfect V disappears into his faded jeans, and I lick my lips.

He cups my face in one hand, forcing my eyes to his once more. "You like what you see?"

I nod, leaning forward to press my open mouth against the hollow of his throat, sliding my tongue along the hot skin covering his collarbone. Salt fills my mouth, and my hard nipples rake against his chest. He exhales a groan, his hand moving to grip my bare ass on the table.

"I want to fuck you." It's a rough order, and my hands immediately go to the button of his jeans.

"I want that, too." My voice is low, almost wild with lust.

He reaches behind him, digging in his pocket. He removes his wallet, and I'm relieved to see he has a condom. I'm only halfway through unpacking all my shit, and I don't want to break this spell.

I'm focused on getting his jeans open and down. My mouth is watering to see his cock. From the feel of it through the fabric, I expect my legs will be shaking again soon.

He steps back to finish getting them off, and when it bobs out long and thick, I drop to my knees.

Chapter 12

Raif

I TOLD JEMIMA DIXON SHE'S AS PRETTY AS THE SUN SETTING OVER THE ocean.

It's a lie. She's even more beautiful.

I can't keep my hands off her face. I can't stop kissing her mouth. I want to devour her body, and when she said her pussy was waxed, I was a goner. I couldn't keep my mouth off her.

The sounds she made when she came on my face had my dick weeping to be inside her.

Now she's on her knees, swallowing my cock, and it's all I can do to stay on my feet. My fingers are in her hair, and her lips move to my tip as her fist works my shaft.

One hand slides up my thigh, moving around to grip my ass, and she attempts to swallow me again. I groan deeply. I don't want to stop her, but I don't want to shoot my load down her throat.

Looking down, I slide my thumb across her face, moving her bangs off her forehead. It takes all my strength to cup her cheeks and move her back. Her mouth comes off me with a pop, and my dick bobs heavily, pointing straight at her.

"Get up here," I groan, lifting her to her feet.

Her lips are swollen and shiny, and her red lipstick is smeared. She's a fucking wet dream come true.

"What's wrong?" Her voice is thick.

"I don't want to come down your throat the first time."

Her nose wrinkles, and she leans closer. "I came all over your face the first time."

"That's different." I intend to make sure she comes every time she's with me, and I knew if I was inside her, I might lose control.

Her dress is pushed back on her shoulders, giving me a teasing glimpse of her small tits. Hard nipples peek at me from behind the fabric, and I cup them again, lifting and squeezing them. They're small, but they're perfect handfuls.

"Turn around." It comes out sterner than I intend, and she complies immediately.

I didn't expect to be so turned on by how obedient she is. She follows my every word like she's eager to please me, which makes my dick harder and my imagination run overtime.

I slide my hand up the back of her dress, lifting the skirt over her waist. Her sexy little ass is round, and I put my hands on her butt cheeks, spreading them apart. She exhales one of those fuck-me noises, and her thighs squeeze together.

Her bare pussy taunts me, and her arousal coats her like a peach. "Fuck, Jemima. Your pussy is so pretty."

My thumb slides up and down her wetness, and she moans again, this time louder. Her hips start to move like she'll fuck my finger, and my dick aches with need.

I quickly roll the condom over my hard-on then I coat my fingers in her wetness. Gripping my shaft, I rub it over my cock, then I step closer to her shimmering core.

When I insert the tip, my stomach muscles seize. My thighs jump, and I have to hold. She's so warm and snug.

"Fuck, you feel too good," I hiss, watching her stretching for me as I insert more. "How does that feel, pretty girl?"

Another whimper shudders through her body as I go deeper. "You're so big."

I trace her ass with my fingertips, doing my best to take it slow. "Is it too much?"

"No…" Her hand flies around to my thigh. "Keep going."

My lips pull away from my clenched teeth as I comply, slowly sinking my cock all the way into her slippery depths, watching her pink lips swallow me until I'm fully seated.

"Fuck me," I gasp, leaning forward over her.

I've got to find my control, so I don't come too fast. I move my hand around her thigh to the center of her legs. Through the ultimate bliss blanketing my mind, I find that swollen little bud and gently begin to circle it.

"Ohh…" she moans long and low, and her ass starts to bob up and down.

She's pulling my cock with her movements, and I can't hold out any longer. My hips start to rock, thrusting in and out to meet her. My hand is on the table, and we're fucking hard and fast.

My eyes are shut, and the legs of the table squeak against the floor with our violent movements. She breaks with a wail, and wetness covers my hand.

I grip her hips and thrust hard, three more times until I have to hold steady, moaning and trembling as the orgasm racks my insides. Pulse after pulse, I fill the condom until my knees bend.

She rises off the table, pressing her back to my chest, and my hands are all over her, sliding over her stomach and up to her breasts. My mouth covers her neck in kisses, and she rocks her hips against me a few more times.

I'm still inside her, and her movements make my legs tremble. I groan in pleasure mixed with pain as another pulse of orgasm electrifies my lower pelvis. Reaching down, I grasp the condom as I pull out, quickly tying it off.

"This way." She takes my arm, waiting as I jerk my jeans over my hips with one hand.

I follow her into the small kitchen where she opens the cabinet beneath the sink.

"Trash," she notes, and I quickly toss the condom.

She takes my hand again, and I follow her to the bedroom. "Take off your clothes."

I'm mesmerized watching her slide her dress off her naked body. She's standing in front of me like a painting. Her skin is ivory, and her body is curved and beautiful.

Her nipples are hard and pointed on teardrop breasts, and she licks her bottom lip as I step out of my boots then shove my jeans off my ankles.

I'm sated, but my dick isn't finished with her tonight. When I'm completely nude, she holds out a hand, and I follow her into the small bathroom.

"We can get cleaned up before bed." I wait, watching as she reaches into the shower and turns on the water.

"Are you asking me to spend the night?" I want to pull her naked body to mine and slide the full length of her down the full length of me.

"Do you have a previous engagement?" Her eyebrow arches, and I exhale a short laugh.

"No, ma'am. I'm all yours tonight."

"I like the sound of that."

She starts to step into the shower, but in this light, I see red marks on her upper arm. It looks like someone grabbed her hard enough to leave a bruise, and my brow lowers.

"What's this?" I gently touch the marks, anger burning in me at the thought of someone hurting her. "Who did this to you?"

Her lips part, and she inhales slowly, blinking fast. "I had a run-in with this guy. It's nothing."

Like hell it's nothing. "A guy here in Eureka?"

I know everybody in this town, and I'm going through the

list of names trying to figure out which high-end abuser just made my To-Do list.

"No!" She shakes her head, reaching for my hand. "He's from Branson. He kind-of showed up here, passing through, I guess. We didn't part on good terms, but I dealt with him. Or I should say I threw Aiden Stone at him, and he went away. I guess knowing Sheriff Stone has its benefits after all."

"I wouldn't know." And I'm not satisfied.

Moving closer to me, she rises on her toes to kiss my cheek. "I don't want to think about him." Her body moves against mine, soft breasts against my chest. "I want to think about you, and what we came in here to do."

She steps into the shower and turns her back to the spray. Bending her arms, she reaches up to slide her hands over her face, up to her forehead, and the water runs through her hair, tracing rivulets over her shoulders, down her breasts, to her bare pussy.

She lowers her chin, fixing darkened blue eyes on me, and I step inside, going to her. I'm still heated that someone touched her in anger, but I can put that away to deal with later.

For right now, I can't deny her effect on me. I'd say she's like a centerfold, but she's so much better.

Pulling her bare chest against mine, I cup her cheeks in both my hands. She looks up at me, blinking with complete openness. I lean forward to kiss her, sliding my mouth across hers before sealing our lips together.

She tastes like fresh water and something a little sharper. Whiskey, I think, or fine bourbon. Her body is soft and slippery, and I could so easily slide my dick into her again. I don't have a condom handy, so instead I pull back, kissing the tip of her nose.

"Turn around."

She does as I say, putting her back to my chest, and I reach for the shampoo, pouring some into my palm before massaging it into her long hair. She leans her head to the side, and her eyes close with a hum. I massage her scalp for a little bit, then she turns to rinse.

When she's finished, she rotates us so I'm standing under the water. "My turn."

I watch as she puts the floral shampoo on her hands and rubs them together before threading them into my hair. The primary scent is jasmine, rich and sweet as honey.

"I'm going to smell like you." I reach up to help her, since she's not as tall as I am.

Our eyes lock, and we're caught in a moment. Her soft body presses against me, and her arms are raised to my hair. My hands cover hers, and our fingers thread. We're breathing fast, and I lean down to kiss her again, sliding my tongue with hers, bodies flush and warm.

She lowers her arms, resting her hands on my shoulders. As I finish rinsing my hair, she drags her palms over the planes of my chest, down to my waist, and her lips press hot kisses to my sternum.

My heart beats a fast rhythm in my chest as her mouth moves over my skin. She circles my tight nipple with her tongue, and it registers straight to my dick.

"I need another condom," I rasp.

"God, I pray I have one in this bathroom." She rises onto her toes and kisses me before opening the shower door.

Grabbing a towel, she quickly dries herself and wraps it around her body before dropping to her knees at the small sink and digging through the cabinet beneath it.

While she's doing that, I grab my own towel and quickly scrub it over my hair and my body then wrap it around my waist. Why the fuck didn't I get more condoms? I can't believe I only came here with one.

To be fair, I didn't know we'd end up this way when I left the trailer this morning to work all day at Martha's house. I didn't know I'd be spending the night with Jemima's body, naked and willing to be wrapped all over mine. *Fuck.*

"A-ha!" she cries, lifting a square packet over her head and shaking it. "I found one!"

I scrub my palm over my face, doing my best not to groan. She found *one*. I almost laugh, but instead I reach for her.

"We'd better make it count." I pull her to her feet, then I lift her into my arms, carrying her to the bedroom.

Placing her on her feet again, I toss my towel to the side, watching as she scrubs her hair with her fingers. "I'm going to look like something in the morning."

"Something fuckable." Turning, I sit on the bed, holding out my hand. "Come here."

She drops the towel and skips over to where I'm waiting. She lifts her leg as if she'll straddle my erection, but I stop her, lying back on the bed instead. "Get on your knees and get up here."

Her brow furrows, but she does as I say, climbing onto the bed on her knees beside me. "What do you want to do?"

"Come here." I reach for her ass, moving her higher and lifting her leg. "Straddle my face."

"What…" she starts to argue, but I shift closer to her, lifting her leg and pulling her over me and down until her pussy brushes against my mouth.

"Oh my God…" she gasps as my tongue slides over her clit.

My hands grip her ass, and I move her up and down over my mouth and nose as I drag my tongue along every part of her soft core.

Her eyes are fixed on mine, growing darker as her lips part. I continue moving her back and forth, but it's not long before she's moving on her own, riding my face like it's a saddle.

Her eyes blink shut, and she reaches down to grip my cheeks as I trace my fingers along her ass, around the outer edges of her thighs and lower stomach. She starts to moan, and she leans forward, bucking her clit directly on my mouth.

My tongue circles and strokes, and her stomach quivers against my palms. She tastes like the ocean. She's clean and musky, and I slide one hand around her ass so I can plunge my thumb into her slippery core.

"Fuck," she gasps, and she's rocking faster.

My tongue moves in circles over her clit, and she jerks as little gasps come from her throat. Her stomach curves inward, and her gasps turn to yelps as I lick her again and again.

My cock is hard and heavy on my stomach, and I reach down to give it a tug. It makes me groan, and with a squeal, she breaks into shudders, bending at the waist and falling forward onto the bed beside me.

"Oh my God!" It's a high-pitched moan.

Her hands are between her thighs, and I quickly grab the condom off the nightstand. She's still gasping as I roll it on, and she rolls onto her back, reaching for me with both hands. I don't hesitate. We fall back together, and I slide my cock balls-deep into her spasming core.

"Yes," she wails, and I groan feeling her orgasm ripple around my dick.

She's still coming, and I wrap my arms under her, holding the tops of her shoulders as I thrust fast and hard. Her knees rise, and she holds onto me as I chase my own release. Our bodies rock together in a rhythm, and she reaches for my face, pulling my mouth to hers.

Our lips fuse, tongues curling, and the orgasm already burning in my pelvis shoots through my inner thighs. With a low groan, I come in her arms, pulsing and arching forward as her legs tighten around my waist.

"Fuck," My mouth breaks away, and I shudder with a groan, holding as I thrust slower, again, again, one more time.

My forehead is against her neck, and I exhale heavily. "Jesus."

Her arms are around me, and we're both panting. We're both holding each other like we've flown through space then fallen into the ocean and are now drifting to shore.

I lift my head to kiss her shoulder, the side of her neck, her lips. I never want to let her go. Her fingers thread in my hair, and she holds my face in her hands.

"I've never done that before." Her blue eyes sparkle like we're sharing a secret.

It makes me grin. "You're a fast learner."

"I have a great teacher." She leans up, kissing me, sliding her tongue into my mouth and making me groan.

My hands are on the sides of her face, smoothing back her hair as I look into her pretty eyes. I only ever want her to feel good.

"You liked it?"

"It was unbelievable. I thought I was going to kill you."

My brow furrows, and I start to laugh. "Kill me how?"

"I thought I was going to smother you! When I started coming, I couldn't stop."

"It was sexy as fuck." I nod, dipping my face down to kiss the side of her jaw.

"At first I thought you wanted to sixty-nine or something."

"We can do that, too." I reach down to quickly remove the condom and dispose of it.

"Come here." She crawls to the head of the queen-sized bed and pulls the blankets down. "Get in here with me. I have a feeling you're going to teach me all kinds of things."

She has no idea all the things I want to teach her, but first, I hold out my hand. "Be right back."

Returning to the small bathroom, I clean up quickly. Then I crawl beneath the blankets and pull her onto my chest. Her arm slips around my waist, and I thread my fingers in her wavy hair. It's drying, and I comb out the snarls as she traces a finger along my shoulder.

I feel her cheek rise against my chest, and she laughs softly.

I give her a little nudge. "What's so funny?"

"I made a New Year's resolution. No more bad boys." Lifting her head, she rests her chin on her hand. "I almost made it a whole month."

Her makeup is gone, and she looks so innocent in my arms. I trace my finger along the top of her cheek. "I'm not so bad."

"I know." She nods. "You're dangerous. Everyone thinks you're a bad boy, but you're really sweet."

My brow lowers. "I'm not sweet either."

Her head tilts to the side. "You help Martha."

"She pays me."

"But you were good to your mother."

I can't argue with that. It actually reminds me of a question I've had since the first day I met her. "What's your favorite flower?"

"Hmm…" Her lips press together, and she slides her blue eyes to the side like she's thinking. She's fucking adorable. "I think I like pansies. Those are the delicate ones with the little faces, right?"

I nod. "Any particular color?"

"I don't know. I like them all." She lays her cheek against my chest. We're quiet, and I slide my fingers over her shoulder. She listens to me breathe. "Remember when people used to call women's pussies flowers?"

"Yeah, that was kind of weird."

"We're not supposed to give it away." She looks up at me again, humor in her eyes. "Oops."

Now I really laugh, rolling her onto her back and sliding my hand down between her legs. "You didn't give it away. It's right here."

She arches her back with a moan, lifting her soft breasts and hard nipples, and fuck me. "We're going to need more condoms if you start doing that."

"Or you could pull out." Her fingers thread in my hair and I lean forward to kiss her breast, pulling a nipple into my mouth and giving it a firm suck.

She moans again, and I want to put my mouth all over her. I don't want to stop until she's screaming my name again, because as beautifully as she can sing, Jemima Dixon crying out my name as she comes apart in ecstasy is the best thing I've ever heard.

Chapter 13

Jemima

I'M WRAPPED IN STEEL BANDS FLOATING ON A CLOUD OF BLISS AND feeling safer and more secure than I've ever felt in my life when persistent bells start ringing in my ears.

My brow furrows, and I growl, not wanting to leave this delicious place. It smells like my soap and my shampoo and sweat and sex.

But those damn bells won't stop going, and I groan, opening my eyes. "It's too early!"

"What's happening?" Raif's deep voice rumbles at my side, and a thrill of bliss shoots through my core.

It's followed quickly by panic.

"Shit! What time is it?" I toss the blankets aside and fly out of the bed. "I've got to get Nikki!"

He sits up, rubbing one eye with the heel of his hand, and I stop moving. My shoulders drop, and I exhale an audible sigh at the sight of him. He's completely nude, all muscle and tattoos and messy hair, his erection tenting my sheets, and he's as hot this morning in the bright sunlight as he was last night in the near-darkness.

"What's wrong?" His hand drops to his lap, and I can't resist.

I walk over to where he's sitting, and I cup his cheeks in my hands and kiss him. Warm hands cover my waist, and he starts to pull me to him. His morning wood is impressive, and I want to ride it so much.

With another groan, I catch his wrists, pushing out of his grasp. "I've got to get Nikki. I told Monay I'd be there first thing to pick her up this morning."

"Okay." He nods, swinging his legs over the side of the bed.

His sexy ass flexes as he walks into the bathroom and closes the door. My eyes go to the bed, and it's a mess. Running out of condoms didn't stop us last night, and I've got to wash these sheets.

He was thoughtful enough to clean me up after every time—when he came all over my stomach, then all over my back after a hot round of doggy style, then sometime early this morning it was between my legs after I woke up with him inside me.

Chewing my lip, my cheeks are hot, and my pussy is wet and achy. I lost count of how many orgasms I had last night, and he's right here, inside my bathroom.

Then my eyes land on the clock.

"Shit," I hiss, grabbing a pair of jeans out of my drawer and jerking them over my hips.

A long-sleeved ivory sweater is over my head, and I twist my hair into a messy bun on my head. It'll have to do.

"I'll call you later!" I yell, stepping into my clogs and scooping up the bucket hat as I run out the door.

I've never been so thankful to have a bike.

"What have you been up to, Miss Thang?" Monay's dark eyes

move from my messy bun to my clean face and bare lips. "You're glowing, and you didn't text me last night."

"New skincare routine." I breeze past her to where Nikki is sitting at the small table. "Hey, how are you feeling this morning?"

She looks up from her bowl of Lucky Charms. "You look different."

"I'm not wearing lipstick." Reaching into my bag, I pull out the hat. "Look what I got you!"

Her eyes widen, and she stands out of her chair, taking it from me. Walking over to the mirror, she pulls it on her head then turns it side to side. It fits neatly over her brown curls, and she's really cute.

"You have got that look on lock." I walk over to bend down and give her a hug. "I look like a dumbo in those hats."

"It's too little for your head." Monay walks over to stand beside us looking in the mirror. "Miss Nik looks like a fashion model. You'd better work it, girl!"

"Are you saying I have a big head?" I elbow her in the side, and she arches an eyebrow.

"What happened when you left here last night?"

I shake my head, careful to avoid Nikki's notice. "Why don't you come to the office today so we can talk about the gala? Mardi Gras is only two weeks away—February 13, no less."

Her eyes widen. "We've got a lot to talk about and not much time to do it."

"Tell me about it." I tap Nikki on the shoulder. "Do you need to go by the house before school?"

"I don't think so." She motions to her backpack on the table. "I brushed my teeth, and I have my stuff here."

"Let's get going then." I give Monay a side-hug and scratch Angie Dickinson's ears. "I'll see you in a few hours?"

She sees us out, and I walk with Nikki the few blocks to school. It's on the other side of the courthouse beside the small church.

"I'm sorry I had to work late last night." I look over at her, but her eyes are hidden by the brim of her hat. "It seemed like maybe it wasn't such a great day yesterday?"

She shrugs, and we walk a few steps in silence. My insides are buzzing and happy, and with every step I can feel how many times Raif and I fucked last night. Still, thinking she's unhappy puts a damper on my otherwise sunny mood.

"I heard something about a Koala Kup?" Her lips tighten, and I wait, hoping she might say something.

More steps, and still no reply. Looking up, I see the school rising before us, and I wish this town wasn't quite so small.

"What if I have a friend who might be able to get you one? Do you have any particular color in mind?" She stops walking, and I do the same, turning to face her. "Lavender haze?"

Amber eyes meet mine, and she shrugs. "Or green to match my hat."

She's still not smiling, so I give her one of mine. "You know, even in the best places, things don't always go the way you want. But I've learned if you just keep swimming, somehow it always seems to get better. Maybe not right away, but eventually. The best thing is to be with people who lift you up and who love you, and you have that here."

Her expression doesn't change, and I can't tell if anything I'm saying makes a single bit of difference. I don't know how it could. I know from personal, first-hand experience, life can get pretty dark, and no amount of positive thinking can take the pain away.

But I can give her something I never had. A person who'll be here fighting for her.

"Have a great day, and maybe we can do something fun after school, okay? Anything you want."

"Okay." Her voice is quiet, but she steps forward and gives me a hug.

I wrap my arms around her, closing my eyes and hugging her with all the hope in my heart.

Then I let her go.

"You look different today." Piper's at the front desk when I arrive at the office again, and she shoves her glasses onto her head. "Is something wrong?"

"Everybody's commenting on my looks today." I hang my purse on the coat rack at the door. "I have an idea. Let's normalize not commenting on people's appearance."

Piper squinches her face and crosses her arms. "That's pretty rich coming from you, Gossip Girl."

I exhale a little growl, stomping over to the front desk. "Okay, something did happen, and I need your help with it."

Her arms drop, and she comes around to stand beside me. "I'm all ears."

"When I was riding back from the distillery last night, I had a very dangerous surprise visitor."

"Raif?"

"I'm going to pretend you, as an objective newswoman, didn't just say that." My eyes narrow, and she holds up both hands.

"Sorry."

"I'm talking about Bill Wolf, the man I took Nikki from. He tried to run me off the road, and then he threatened me. He said he's going to take her, and when I threatened him with Aiden, he said he's coming back."

"Shit." Piper's eyes are wide. "Cass was worried something like this might happen. She said you can't just take a child and expect no one to come looking for her."

"She never said anything like that to me." I think about the other night. "Is that why she called the sheriff on me?"

"That might have been a bit of an overreaction." Piper has her phone out, and I watch her thumbs flying over the screen as she texts. "We didn't want to make you nervous, but we've been keeping an eye out for suspicious characters."

"Well, you missed one." I can't keep the sarcasm out of my tone, especially after that Raif crack.

"Aiden's on his way. I'm sure Britt's coming with him." Piper chews her lip, looking towards the door. "Cass will be upset she's not here, but she has school."

"You called Aiden?"

"If this guy is here and threatening you, Aiden needs to know. We have to come up with a plan to keep you and Nikki safe."

Frowning, I walk to the window and look out at the small house behind the office. Drumming my fingers on my arm, I try to think about this. I have a plan of my own, but I guess I can't execute it without the help of law enforcement.

Britt is the first to appear, walking fast up the sidewalk, but Aiden is right behind her. My eyes land on the flower boxes lining the house, and I notice tiny green stems poking up through the soil.

"Looks like your flowers are coming back."

She steps up beside me at the window. "I never planted flowers in those boxes. Mom always said I should, but…"

Her voice dies out when the front door opens. Britt leads the way, worry lining her expression. Aiden steps inside tall, frowning, and dressed in a tan uniform with a big gun on his hip.

"Are you okay?" Britt's blue eyes are wide. "Tell us everything that happened. Don't leave out any details. You never know what might turn out to be important."

I feel slightly overwhelmed, then I remember she's a forensic investigator. Her job is to obsess over every detail looking for clues. It's partly why she owns a bloodhound.

"Okay…" Blinking up at the ceiling, I try to recall every little thing. "I was riding the bike, he was in a truck. I pulled off the road and started to run, but he caught me…" Aiden makes an irritated noise, and my eyes fly to his. He looks seriously pissed, but I continue. "He showed me a piece of paper he claimed was signed by Nikki's mom, but it was too dark to read it. I told him

I didn't believe it, that I was going to adopt her, and I told him Aiden wouldn't let him take Nikki. That got his attention. He let me go, but he said he'd be back."

"That's everything?" Britt presses, and I nod.

"He was insulting as usual—said I wasn't fit to be a mother."

Her face puckers into a frown, and she reaches out to squeeze my hand. Then we all three turn to Aiden.

He shifts, putting both hands on his hips. "About that piece of paper, was it notarized?"

"I don't know. It was too dark." My chest tightens. "Are you saying he might really be able to take her?"

Aiden's brow furrows, and he rubs the back of his neck. "I'm not up on family law, but it sounds like he might have a temporary guardianship. For her to be fully his, he'd have to go to court."

Swallowing the knot in my throat, I step forward. "How long would it take for me to adopt her? Can you help me with that?"

Concern flashes in his blue eyes. "Are you sure that's what you want to do? Raising a child is a lot of work and responsibility, and you're..."

Britt clears her throat, interrupting gently. "She's the same as any other person who might unexpectedly become pregnant and have to figure out what to do."

For a second, no one speaks, and embarrassment heats my face. "It's okay." I force a smile, looking down. "I know what you mean. I don't have that great of a track record."

Aiden's tone is measured. "You're just getting on your feet, and I know from personal experience it's not easy to be a single parent. You're young. You might meet someone or decide you want to do something else down the line."

"I won't abandon Nikki." Determination sharpens my tone. "I promised her I wouldn't let him take her, and I won't."

"And we're going to help you keep that promise." Piper smiles, touching my arm. "We've got your back the whole way."

Britt steps closer, putting her arm around my waist. "We love Nikki and you."

"Adoption requires a background check and a home visit. I can help with those." Even Aiden sounds like he's on my side now. "It helps to be married, but it's not impossible if you're single. You'll have to have a physical, and they'll want you to prove you earn enough to meet her needs. Then it's just a matter of time, getting it before a judge."

My mind filters through the items as he lists them. Nothing stands out as a problem except… "How hard is it to adopt if you're single?"

"I don't know. What I do know is we need to make sure you're both safe. I'll give you my number, and I want you to call me if you sense you're in danger. Any time, day or night. I can be there in seconds."

I unlock my phone and hand it to him. He taps on the face, entering his contact information, but my mind is miles away thinking about a man with the reputation of being a problem solver.

Chapter 14

Raif

ROCKBROOK PORT ISN'T LISTED AS A MAJOR SHIPPING AND RECEIVING location. It's mostly used for restaurants to get their seafood, but a few area businesses and the local big box stores receive shipments there. It's a small yard, but a surprising amount of freight moves in and out of the docks.

Two trucking lines handle all that freight, Campbell and Harris. Most of what goes on is completely above board and legal, but not all of it, as I learned the short time I was a dock worker, loading and unloading what couldn't be done by crane.

My brother told me it's where the job will go down mid-February. He wouldn't write anything down, and he wouldn't send me a text or show me any communications. The fact they're paying three thousand for a simple lookout makes me believe it's significant.

Martha likes to work half-days on Fridays, so I head out on my bike before lunch to scope out the place. It's less than an hour's drive south of Eureka, turning towards the shore before you get to Hilton Head.

Jemima is on my mind the entire drive, her bright blue eyes and pretty smile. The echo of her sighs is stronger than the noise of my bike, and I can still taste her on my lips, still feel her kisses on my neck and skin. Her shampoo scent is still in my hair, and while it's warm and enticing, unease churns in my stomach.

For starters, there's this asshole from Branson who dared to touch her. She claims he's gone, but I intend to keep an eye on her just in case. Eureka's not big enough to hide strangers. It's the one comfort I have in all of this.

I took my time getting to Martha's, taking the long way through town and looking in at the gas station, the Pak-n-Save, El Rio. Nobody had seen any strangers in town.

That asshole better hope I don't find him.

The other thing causing me unease is this fucking job hanging over my head. My reasons for saying yes haven't changed, but all my thoughts about doing it have been called into question.

Jemima believes in me. She defends me to her friends, and when I hold her face in my hands, she looks at me with so much trust.

Now I'm using her for a cover story. She texted me this morning, lavender or green for Nikki, and brown or black for the boys. I'd run this errand for her regardless of my need to case the location, but an uncomfortable knot lodges at the base of my throat. It's a pill that won't go all the way down.

Pulling up to the entrance, a guy I recognize is standing in the guard shack when I slow to a stop and raise the visor on my helmet. He's dressed in black pants and a white, uniform shirt with a walkie-talkie clipped to the front.

"Hiya, Raif." He steps out of the small booth, smiling under his heavy mustache. "Haven't seen you around in a while."

"Hey, Chip." I nod, thinking about my cover story. "What's it been, a year?"

"Something like that." He lights up a cigarette and takes a long pull. "You coming back to work?"

"Nah, I got something going in Eureka. Just checking on things."

"Anything in particular?"

Blue smoke circles around his head as he speaks. Looking around, I make quick mental notes of all the access points to this area. This is the dock, and this is the only way in.

"I've got a friend with a couple of kids."

"Don't tell me…" He starts to laugh then breaks into a wheezing cough.

It takes him a minute to catch his breath, and I nod at the smoldering cigarette in his hand. "I've heard those things will kill you."

He shakes his head, waving me away. "Yeah, yeah. So as I was saying, you're looking for one of them Koala Kups?"

"You got me." I hold up my hands. "Make me a hero, Chip."

"Do you have any idea how many people come out here asking about those things? Really nice people, too, in Range Rovers and whatnot."

"It's crazy." I shake my head, looking at the front of my bike. "What's the word?"

"Well, it just so happens, I might have something for you." He waves me over to the side. "Totally hush-hush, of course."

"Of course." I walk the bike through the gate, guiding it around behind the guard shack.

When I worked here, I wasn't thinking like a lookout. I was thinking like someone who didn't like my job and really wanted to get the fuck out of here.

Now I'm thinking like a criminal, and it makes me feel like the person everyone suspects me of being. My eyes trace every inch of the place, noting all the spots a person could hide.

Putting the kickstand down, I kill the engine and follow him down the line of cars to a silver Dodge hatchback. We're standing close, and he looks over his shoulders.

"See what you think about these." He lifts the back, and two cardboard boxes sit open on the bed.

Inside are plastic-wrapped cups in assorted colors.

"Got one in lavender or green, two in brown or black?"

He digs around, taking out what I need and slipping them to me in a black plastic bag. "Make that an even sixty."

I dig a fifty and a twenty out of my wallet and pass it over. "Keep the change."

"Thanks." He quickly pockets the money, and I put the bag inside my denim jacket.

"Hey, thanks. I knew you were the man." We walk slowly towards the guard shack again, and he stops, crossing his arms and studying me as I move the bag to the side compartment of my bike.

"Your brother's still coming around." My chest tightens, and I'm not sure where he's going with this.

While I've never done anything to get arrested, Bull's been in jail a few times. It's where my "guilt by association" comes into play.

"I heard he's doing repairs on one of the barges." I try to play it off like I'm not still living with him.

"He's not the worker you were. I bet if you wanted, you could get a raise, maybe some benefits. We never had any trouble when you were here."

"Thanks, Chip." I slide my hands down the sides of my jeans, pushing the guilt trying to rise in my chest back down. "I'm going to pass on that, but I appreciate the offer. And thanks for hooking me up. You've helped me score some serious brownie points."

"Offer stands if you change your mind."

I give him a wave and hop on the bike again. This time, when I leave, I head in the wrong direction intentionally. I follow the road creating a perimeter around the shipyard to be sure the gate is sound and nothing has changed when it comes to access.

It's still chain link and razor wire all the way around, with no apparent breaks.

When I get back to where Chip's standing, confused, I wave and shake my head as if to say I forgot where I was going. He waves me away, and I open the throttle, heading to the trailer to get cleaned up and change clothes.

"Where you been?" Bull is on the front porch when I get home. "The fella running things stopped by last night. He wanted to meet you."

Taking out my phone, I glance at the face. "You didn't message me."

"Of course, I didn't. You think I want somebody tracking my calls?" He shoves his hands in his back pockets as he stomps around in a circle on the porch. "Since when don't you come home at night?"

Since I met the most beautiful girl in the world.

"Why do I need to meet the guy? All he wants is a look-out, right?" That fucking better be all he wants, because that's all he's getting.

Bull's jaw clenches, and he growls like he's holding back a punch. He'd better keep on holding, because I won't hesitate to lay him out if he tries to start something again.

"Will you be home tonight?" he snaps.

"Probably." I've got to get those cups to Jemima, and I'd like to spend some time with her.

But I know she has a little girl.

"I'll see if he's still in town. He's one of those woo-woo types. Likes to get a feel for the team."

I don't like the sound of that bullshit. It's more like he's an asshole who wants to put on a show of force to be sure I'm not going to fuck up his job.

"I'm not living my life by this job." My voice grows stronger. "I told you I'll be there, and I will. Now get off me."

With that, I leave him on the porch while I head inside to shower and change and get ready to see my girl again.

"You did not!" Jemima's blue eyes widen, as I pull the bag from behind my back and hand it to her.

We're standing on the small porch of her house, and I hear the sounds of some kids' show coming from inside. It's early in the afternoon, and I imagine they just got home from school.

I couldn't wait to see her anymore. When I got out of the shower at the trailer, I shot her a text saying I had something for her. She asked if I'd meet her at the house, to which I immediately said yes.

Now she's standing in front of me in jeans and an ivory sweater that's falling off her shoulder. Her hair is still in a bun on top of her head, and her face is fresh and clean with no lipstick. I can't decide which look I like best, but this one is pretty damn good.

She lets out a little squeal that makes me chuckle as she takes the bag from my hands and opens it, looking inside.

Then she pushes my shoulder. "You did! How much do I owe you?"

"Nothing. It's a gift."

"Raif!" She starts to protest, but I reach out to take her wrist, pulling her closer to me.

"Just say thank you."

She blinks up at me, and a pretty shade of pink floods her cheeks. It reminds me of the pink that bloomed across her breasts when she came on my face.

She exhales a little laugh before rising quickly onto her tiptoes to press her lips to mine. It's sweet and closed-mouthed, but it fires a surge of energy from my chest to my groin.

"Thank you," she whispers, her nose brushing mine.

But I want more than that.

Catching her cheek in my hand, I hold her steady as our mouths open and our tongues curl together. The heat between us is instant. A soft whimper comes from her throat, and it doesn't take much for me to remember her on her knees swallowing my dick, or me lifting her onto that table, the top of her dress open for me to see her tits as I buried my cock into her slippery-wet heat.

She smells like that shampoo of fresh jasmine, and her mouth is cool and sweet like a slushie.

I move my lips to the side, speaking in her ear. "I couldn't stop thinking about your pretty flower all day."

She laughs, pulling away and wrinkling her nose. "I felt you inside me every time I moved."

Fuck me. I'm frustrated we're on her front porch with a little girl right inside. I'm frustrated I can't lift her over my shoulder and carry her to the bed.

Lifting my head, I look into her darkened eyes. "Don't want you to forget me."

"I couldn't if I tried." She blinks a few times, and we only breathe, all the things we want to do playing out between us in our eyes.

I release her cheek and take a step back, putting my hands in my pockets so I won't touch her again. "I had an idea about your story. I was planning to go hunting tomorrow. You could come with me."

I need to get something to Bender while he's still in town, and it's a great excuse to spend time with her.

Her brows rise, and she nods. "Yes! Let me see if I can get someone to watch Nikki for the day. When do you want to meet? Where?"

"Well, it wouldn't be until later. Hogs are nocturnal. We could meet up after dinner, and go out for a few hours. It shouldn't take too long to bag one."

"Oh, and I bet I'll get some great photos!" She glances down at her clothes. "What should I wear?"

"Something black and quiet. No perfume or any type of scent."

She nods, eyes wide as she leans closer. "Do I need a gun?"

Fuck, she's so damn cute. I take another step away before I pull her into my arms again and kiss her. "I'll take care of everything. Just be here ready to go."

"I'll be ready!"

I'm off the porch when I can't resist one more hit. Hopping onto the porch again, I catch her by the cheeks and kiss her once more. Her hands close over my wrists, and she kisses me back, moving in closer and exhaling a whimper that has my dick hard in my jeans.

I'm exhausted from fucking her all night instead of sleeping, then working all morning on Martha's addition. Still, adrenaline surges in my veins, and it takes all my strength to pull away from her.

Then it takes even more when I step away and see her breathing fast, her hair slipping out of that messy bun, her lips swollen from my kisses, and her nipples peaked beneath the loose weave of her sweater.

She might be a nice girl from a good family, but she's even more beautiful on her hands and knees getting dirty for me. I can't wait to do it again.

Chapter 15

Jemima

THE MINUTE MY EYES OPEN SATURDAY MORNING, MY PHONE IS IN MY hands, and I'm sending a text to the group.

> I've got a big surprise for the kids. Meet at the Weenie for lunch?

I Dream of Weenie is a new hot dog shop that just opened in the small strip mall outside of town on Beach Road. It's tucked in between The Human Bean coffee shop and Harold Waters's Popcorn Palace.

> **Cass**: Can't—Pinky has a birthday party at lunch for one of her classmates. What am I missing?

I open a separate text and reply to her only.

> Shit! Raif Jones got Koala Kups for the boys and Nikki. Does Pinky want one?

I add the emoji of the monkey with his hands over his eyes. How could I forget the pink tornado?

My sister's reply floods me with relief.

> **Cass**: NO! I don't need that nonsense sweeping the kindergarten class. Speaking of, Monay did a FAB job yesterday! All want to know when Miss Dolly and her pink puppy are coming back.

She includes a photo of my former roommate in full Dolly attire, massive blonde updo with a flower behind her ear, purple-rhinestone bell-bottomed pantsuit, and pink Angie Dickinson peeking out of her bag. I reply with one word…

> LOVE!

My phone buzzes with a reply from the group chat.

> **Piper**: Just us or everyone?

I tap out a reply,

> Def the boys, and whoever else is around

> **Britt**: We'll be there! Noon?

I reply with a thumbs-up emoji then check the clock. It's already eleven! Throwing back the covers, I hustle into the kitchen, where Nikki is sitting at the table coloring on her phone with her finger.

"Sorry I slept in… I guess I was more tired than I realized."

I guess having sex all night will do that to a person. A grin curls my lips as I switch on the coffee maker and drop a pod in the slot. When it's ready, I hit the brew button and walk over to where she's drawing the pink starfish guy from *SpongeBob*.

"What's his name again?"

"Patrick," she answers without looking up. "You fell asleep on the couch last night."

"I was pretty busy when you were with Monay." I take

my coffee and sit beside her at the table. "There's something I need to talk to you about."

She puts the phone down and looks up at me. When I took her for slushies yesterday, she told me the new girl Annabelle made fun of her accent. She called her Ninny instead of Nikki and she even whispered something about her clothes being from Walmart.

I told Nikki she must shop at Walmart if she knows the clothes they carry there. It only helped a little. Then Raif showed up like a hero on a chrome-metal horse bearing Koala Kups.

I can't wait to give them to her and the boys at lunch, but now that I've slept on it, I think it's time to discuss my plan and see what she thinks.

"You said your mom left you with Bill. Do you remember if she said anything about guardianship, or did she ever use that word?"

Nikki's brow furrows, and she shakes her head. "She just said she'd be back, not to worry."

"Do you remember if Bill made her sign something?"

Again, she shakes her head, and I guess she didn't have to be in the room for it to happen.

Chewing my lip, I sit straighter. "I was thinking... To keep you with me and away from him... How would you feel if I talked to a judge about adopting you?"

Her eyes widen, but she doesn't look excited. "Isn't that what orphans do? I'm not an orphan. My mom's coming back for me. She said she would."

"Hey, hey, it's okay..." Reaching out, I slide my fingers along the sides of her hair. "I know she will if she can. I just don't know when that might be, and I don't want Bill to take you away from me. I think, for now, it might be safer if I adopt you. Then if your mom does come back—"

"She will!" Nikki's eyes shine with growing tears, and I scoot my chair closer to hers, pulling her into a hug.

"Of course, she will." My tone is soothing, and I rub my hand up and down her arm, doing my best to ease her tension. "I didn't mean to say she wouldn't. Just until she does, would you like to stay here with me?"

She sits back in the chair, and her eyes are on the front of my robe. She blinks several times without answering, and my chest is tight. I don't know what to think. I took her from Bill, and brought her here. The whole time, she never fought me or cried or asked to go back to Branson.

Up to this point, I've interpreted that to mean she wants to do this. Now a knot is in my throat, and I'm afraid I might cry. Maybe I did kidnap her like Piper said… Am I the monster?

Finally, she looks up at me. "If I say yes, does that mean I gave up on her?"

"Oh my goodness, no!" The word comes out in a rush of breath, and my eyes prick with tears. "I would never ask you to give up on your mom."

I hug her to me again, and this time, her arms slide around my waist. For a moment, I hold her, wondering what all this little girl has survived in her short life. I can't take away her hope as well. We rock side to side, and I wait as the tension slowly leaves her body.

When she's ready, she sits back in her chair. Her lips tighten, and my heart twists as I watch her choose her words. "You're really nice to me. I like being here with you and Monay and Angie and Ryan and Owen."

I slide my thumb over the tear on her cheek, wiping it away. "You do?"

She nods, and our eyes meet. "Yeah, you guys are okay."

She's teasing, and a smile curls my lips. I lean forward, hugging her again. "You know I'm not very good at being a mom. We'll just be a special family that gets each other through the hard times. Okay?"

"Okay."

"I heard this place started out of a VW van in Nashville." Piper walks out to a picnic table with two trays of hot dogs in her hands.

"Sounds like our next story," I call to her.

Nikki has her phone out and her green bucket hat on, and she's showing her SpongeBob drawings to Ryan and Owen while I sit beside Britt. Bonnie is awake and waving her tiny fists, and I cup her little white-blonde head in my hand.

"She's so cute," I coo, leaning closer to kiss her, taking a big sniff of baby scent. "She smells so good."

"Johnson's baby wash and Baby Magic baby lotion." Britt says it like she's reading a recipe. "Ooo, what have you got?"

"Mac-n-weenie for you…" Piper sets a bun full of what looks like macaroni and cheese in front of Nikki, then a plain hotdog with mustard, ketchup and relish in front of me. "One Frank-n-weenie, hold the onions. Chili weenie for you guys…" She sets two chili-covered hot dogs in front of the boys. "Pimento and cheese weenie for Britt, and a weenie without a cause for me."

"What's that?" I frown at her dog.

"Veggie weenie."

"There truly is no cause for that." Britt laughs, taking a sip of her lemon water. "We can get caramel corn after."

"We're speaking to Harold again?" I arch a brow, looking up at her.

The last time I was here, Harold ran his dog Bo against Britt's grandmother in the mayoral race, then he yelled at Piper for calling his dog a delicious snack in the paper, which was really Martha's fault.

Basically, we were not speaking to him when I left to get Nikki.

"He did a really great job apologizing to Gran." Britt nods, stuffing a french fry into her mouth. "If she forgives him, I will. He does make the best popcorn on the coast."

I'm all set to make a witty comeback when a little girl prances out of the Popcorn Palace in the direction of Heaven Scent, the aromatherapy and candle store I did one of my first business profiles on for Piper.

It's Annabelle, and she's dressed in jeans and cowboy boots with a lavender plaid shirt and a flat-brimmed hat. She looks like a little fashion model, but from the glint in her eye, I can tell she's a mean girl.

My eyes fly to Nikki's, and she's looking at me as well. Cheese is smeared on both her cheeks, and I quickly tap my face to let her know.

She grabs napkins and starts to wipe just as Owen leans forward. "Oh, look, it's Dumbbell."

Ryan snorts a laugh, but Nikki looks down at her lap. Britt's brow furrows, and she looks up to where Annabell jerks her chin as she quickly steps into Frangelica's store.

"Owen!" Britt's voice is kind but stern. "You know better than to make fun of people. Why would you say that?"

"She's a little brat." He sits back, crossing his arms hard. "She sits in the front of the lunchroom and puts out her Koala Kup at lunch like she's the queen of the class and Debbie and Vanna are her dumb minions."

"I don't know any of these little girls." Britt blinks several times, and I can tell she's stumped. "That's weird, isn't it? We used to know everyone in Eureka."

"Cass probably knows them." Piper takes a bite of her veggie dog. "This is not bad! It's spicy—that must be the rebel part."

Britt tilts her head in the direction of the boys, making wide eyes at her friend.

"Oh, yeah." Piper clears her throat. "Don't be mean to little girls at school, Ryan. Even if they act like little twits."

"That's just great, Piper." Britt rolls her eyes, and I decide it's time.

"Who's ready for the big surprise?" I hold up both hands and wiggle my fingers.

Nikki looks up from her lap, and the boys shift in their seats. "Is it somebody's birthday?" Ryan asks.

"It's a special, *welcome to Eureka* present!" I pull out the black bag and take out the cups one at a time. "Koala Kups for all!"

Nikki's is an iridescent green and purple and the boys' are black and tan camo-style.

"What?" Ryan hops onto his knees, lifting the cup, and Piper's jaw drops.

Britt's brow furrows. "I didn't know you were doing this."

My chest squeezes, and I'm afraid I fucked up again. "I'm sorry! I didn't want to get one for Nikki and leave out the boys." My voice is quiet. "Should I have asked first?"

"Of course not." She puts her hand on my forearm. "It was very sweet, but how… Did Alex pay for them?"

"Where did you get them?" Piper asks at the same time.

"Nope." I smile proudly, ready to prove them all wrong. "Raif Jones got them for me. He said it was a gift for the kids."

Owen's eyes widen, and he whispers, "You got this from the no-account Jones boys?"

"Owen!" I look from him to Britt, who shakes her head quickly. "That's not very nice. I told him about the situation, and he said he might know a place to get some."

"Are they stolen?" Piper jokes, picking up Ryan's cup and inspecting it.

"Not funny!" My voice rises. "I told you he's not like that. He had a friend who was able to get some, and I texted him the colors and everything."

Nikki has her cup open and is already pouring her fountain drink into it. Owen quickly does the same.

"We should probably wash them first…" Piper starts, but it's too late. Ryan is already following suit.

I can't decide if I'm happy or frustrated until Britt inhales slowly and forces her frown into a smile. "Thank you, Jemima, and please tell Raif I said thank you as well. I know what it's like to be pre-judged because of your family, and I think we owe it to him not to do that."

A surge of joy shoots through my stomach, and I hug her side so hard, she squeals. "Don't make me drop the baby!"

"You're going to see. Raif Jones is a little rough around the edges, but he has goals. He's going to prove you all wrong."

Piper is nodding, but I can tell she's worried. "I hope you're right."

I don't even waste time telling her I am.

Chapter 16

Raif

THE SUN IS SETTING WHEN I PULL MY BIKE UP TO JEMIMA'S SMALL house. For a moment, I sit on the bike and watch the sun-streaked sky change from pink and blue to blood-orange and black.

I remember the night I took her down to the ocean, how tense my muscles were, how tight my hands were on the handlebars as I rode through a surge of adrenaline strong as a cocaine hit.

I wanted her to see it the way I did, to understand what it meant, and she did. I huff a soft laugh remembering her on the back of the bike, throwing her arms into the air and cheering us on.

She changed everything.

Before I had goals, but no real reason to pursue them. I wanted to accomplish things, but in the back of my mind was always the question *why?* Now I have a reason, and I wonder why I wasted so much time.

These thoughts root in my mind as the door opens, and she steps out before quickly locking it. She's dressed in all black, like I said, and her blonde hair is hidden under a black beanie. She's not even wearing her red lipstick, but her lips are glossy as they part in a smile that hits me right in the chest.

"Hey!" She scoops the old skateboarding helmet off the porch before jogging to the bike. "Is this okay? I figured if my clothes needed to be black, my head probably did, too, and I didn't wear any perfume or anything."

"You're perfect." My lips part, and I swear, I don't think I've smiled this much in my whole damn life. "Ready to do this?"

She removes the sock hat and nods as she fastens the helmet under her chin. "I have my camera. I'll put it on silent mode so it won't make any sounds. Remember how I did all that research before? I forgot to mention pigs can detect a human whisper up to one hundred yards!"

Her eyes are huge, and with that helmet on and no lipstick, I can't resist. I catch her chin and pull her closer for a kiss. It's just a quick, closed-mouth, temptation of a kiss, but it does the trick. Her cheeks flush, and she puts her hands on my chest.

"What was that for?"

"Nothing. Now get on the bike."

She hops on quickly, and I take us out that same dirt road we used the first night we were together. I'm working on instinct here, but there's an old homesite where a mansion burned to the ground years ago. Only the brick chimneys remain, but it's possible they're rooting under the old satsuma trees.

I love the feeling of her arms around me, her body tucked tightly against mine, and I almost wish it were farther away. I almost wish we could blow this off and do something a little more fun with her free evening.

Then I remember my reasons.

When we reach the turnoff, I cut the engine and stop the bike. "We'll leave it here at the road and walk the rest of the way."

She cups her hand over her mouth and speaks right at my neck. "So we don't scare them away?"

My lips tighten on another damn smile, and I nod, taking the bag of supplies out of my side compartment and tucking a handgun into the back of my pants.

She waves quickly, and I glance up to see she's holding up one finger as if to say stop. I pause, and she takes out her phone, snapping a few pictures. I'm not sure how interesting they'll be. I'm only wearing jeans and a black tee with a black jacket over it.

Holding two fingers over my lips, I motion for her to follow me, and we start out for the house. The walk is farther than a football field, so I don't think we've alerted any animals to our presence yet.

When we get within sight of the house, I start looking for a place we can hide. The area around the house was cleared ages ago, but as we get closer, I notice an old oak tree past the second standing chimney.

It's a risk, since we'll have to get all the way into the yard, which is where I hope they'll be coming to feed. Lifting my hand, I motion for her to follow me, and we make a large circle around the perimeter before cutting up close.

She's a good hunting partner. She's quiet, and she stays close. When we reach the tree, I point up and clasp my hands to give her a boost. She only hesitates a moment, shoving her phone into the pocket of her black leggings before holding my shoulders and letting me boost her into the oak.

I follow next, catching the thick limbs and pulling myself up behind her. We're not too far off the ground, but one thing I do know about hogs—they don't look up when they're rooting.

The sun is essentially gone, but it's a cloudless night. The sky is full of stars, and the half-moon is slowly making an appearance. We're sitting on the wide branch of the tree like two kids riding a hobby horse, and I have no idea how long this might take.

Her back is to me when my phone buzzes in my pocket. I frown, sliding it out.

Jemima: You're very sexy as a macho hunter man.

She includes one of those red-faced sweating emojis, and my shoulders lift with a silent laugh. But her next one makes my dick hard.

Jemima: I wonder if pigs can hear a blow job from 100 yards away?

This one's followed by a sly-faced emoji, and my thumbs start to move.

Lean back, and we'll see if they hear you come on my hand.

Her head ducks forward, and she cuts a look at me over her shoulder before turning back to text more.

Jemima: If you lean back against the tree, I could straddle your lap and see who comes first.

This has to be a first—sexting in a live oak tree while waiting for wild hogs to appear below. I'm seriously considering it when the crack of a twig interrupts our flow.

Her head snaps around again, eyebrows raised in question. I nod, reaching back and sliding the gun from the waist of my jeans. I'm a pretty good shot at close range, and it isn't the first time I've done this.

Lifting my leg, I turn so I'm no longer straddling the branch. I have a straight shot, directly down to the ground below, where a pig the size of a large dog is rooting around the base of the tree. He's too close, and I'm afraid he's going to catch our scent if I don't act fast.

The gun is in my hand, and I pull back the hammer as slowly as possible, doing my best not to make a noise. I'm all set to shoot when a camera flash lights up the ground, and the animal startles.

Exhaling slowly, I don't let it rattle me as I pull the trigger, aiming for the back of its head as it starts to bolt. The gun blasts, and it drops right on the spot a few feet away.

I hop off the limb, landing on my feet on the ground when Jemima's voice rings out in a wail.

"Raif!" I look up fast. Is she freaked out by the actual kill? "I'm so sorry! I thought I'd turned the flash off!"

I reach up to help her out of the tree. She lands on her feet in front of me, her hands on my wrists, and my hands on her waist. She looks up at me with her cute face all scrunched, and I can't help kissing her nose.

"You don't have to apologize since I got him."

"Still, I nearly ruined everything!"

"But you didn't." I walk over to where the animal's stone dead and grab the rope out of the bag, quickly tying its back hooves together.

"You're really good at this." She has the camera out, taking more photos. "You're like one of those people who could survive an apocalypse."

That makes me laugh, since I've been working the last several weeks with Martha. "I'm not sure how long I'd make it, but at least we'd have something to eat."

"Which is very important," she notes quietly.

Tossing the rope over the low branch where we were just sitting, I lift the animal off the ground. It's heavy as fuck, and it takes all my strength to get it high enough to drain. I hear her phone clicking, taking photos as I tie off the rope. Returning to my pack, I take out a pair of black latex gloves then pull my buck knife out of my back pocket.

With one quick swipe, his neck is open, and the blood starts to flow out.

"Ugh, that's gross." She's frowning again, and I step back to where she's standing with a hand over her mouth.

"All part of the process." I wipe the knife in the grass, doing my best to get it clean before wrapping it and the gloves in a towel. "You have to drain the blood so it doesn't settle in the muscles. Otherwise, you can't eat it."

I touch her arm, and we walk back around the tree to get away from the sound and the smell of the dead animal.

She has her phone out, and she's back in professional mode. "How long have you been hunting? All your life?"

"No, I just started when the hogs started getting bad. My daddy was always too drunk, and Bull would rather get in a fight than sit in a deer stand."

A proud smile curls her lips, and she tilts her head to the side. "But you weren't like that. You wanted to be something better?"

My stomach tightens, and I inhale, wiping my hand across my mouth. "*Better* feels like a loaded term. I'd rather say, I didn't want to live like that."

"Okay." She makes a note on her phone.

I bend my knees, sitting on the cool grass. She walks over and sits beside me with her legs crossed.

"For someone who just started hunting, you look like a pro. You've got all your gear, the rope, that knife… I didn't know you could hunt with a Glock."

"You can hunt with any kind of gun, Jemima."

"You're a great shot, too. You dropped that pig just like that." She snaps, her eyes shining.

"It was pretty close range."

"And you knew exactly where he'd be."

"I got lucky." Crossing my legs, I move closer so our hands are almost touching. "I'd been scouting around for signs of them. Since I shot one on our property, they've moved away. Like you said, pigs are smart."

"So it was a little more than luck. You had a hunch. A feeling like before—with the sunset."

That makes me smile. "I'm batting a thousand."

"What does that mean?"

"It means all my attempts to impress you have been successful."

Her head cocks, and she smiles up at me. "Extremely successful, Mr. Jones. In fact, I'd say you were batting three million."

I reach for her waist and pull her onto my lap. Her knees go down on each side of me, and I kiss the side of her neck. "You're a pretty good hunting partner."

She pulls the hat off her head and drags her fingers through her hair. "Is it a mess?"

I reach up to slide a stray curl off her cheek and behind her ear. "It's beautiful."

Her arms are on top of my shoulders, and she leans down to press her lips to mine. Our mouths open, and for a minute we make out like a couple of kids on a first date. She holds my cheeks, and I hold her waist. Our tongues curl together, and she exhales a sigh.

My eyes are closed, and my sole focus is her sweet mouth, the softness of her body pressed to mine. My hands move under her shirt, tracing the warm skin of her back, and she shivers, exhaling a laugh against my cheek.

"Are you ticklish?" I grin, meeting her eyes.

She shakes her head. "I never was before. I think I'm sensitive to your touch."

I unfasten her bra and move my hands around to cup her breasts. "How's this?"

"Mmm…" She leans forward, nibbling my top lip. "Very nice."

Lifting my chin, I claim her mouth, tracing my tongue along hers and shifting her body so she can feel the erection growing in my pants. I pinch her hard nipples, and she exhales a moan, rocking her hips against me, making me want more.

My hands move to her ass, and I squeeze her soft cheeks, sliding her faster up and down my dick. Her eyes are closed, and she grips the tops of my shoulders, moving with me, grinding on my lap.

"Do you think anyone would see us if we…?" She looks around, and I'm already unbuttoning my jeans.

"Nobody's out here."

She stands at once, shoving her black leggings down and off, along with her underwear. She steps to me, and I catch her legs, holding her in place so I can drag my tongue between them, circling her clit and tasting her.

"Oh," she yelps, catching the back of my head. "I'm so close."

I keep going, only breaking away a moment to roll on the condom. "Sit."

She holds my hand, reaching down to fist my shaft and guiding it into her. The tip goes in, and we both groan when she hesitates.

"So big." She's on her knees, and she lowers slowly, pulling up again to tease me.

"Jemima," I groan, lifting my hands to squeeze her bare ass. "What are you doing to me?"

"Making you crazy, I hope." Her hands are on my cheeks, and she covers my mouth with hers before dropping all the way and starting to ride.

"Fuck," I exhale against her lips.

My fingers tighten on her ass, and I move her faster to match the burning need in my pelvis. I'm on fire. Sensations radiate from the arches of my feet up my thighs, and shaky whimpers slip from her throat as I move her on my cock.

At some point, she takes the reins, wrapping her arms around my neck and pushing her chest to mine, grinding faster and harder. I lean back on my hands in the grass, watching my own private lap dance. Her eyes are closed. Her forehead is furrowed, and her lips part as she rotates her hips, bucking again and again until she comes apart on my cock.

Reaching behind her neck, I roll us so she's on the ground beneath me. I prop on my forearms and thrust. Her thighs start to shake, and she wails, digging her heels into the ground as if she'll try to squirm away.

It flips something primal in my brain, and my orgasm roars through my pelvis. With a shout, I come violently hard, my cock pulsing and jerking. Her body spasms around me once more, and I moan, holding onto her as I almost black out from the sensation.

"Fuck me." My forehead drops to her shoulder, and I try to steady my breathing. "That was intense."

Her arms are around my shoulders, and she's panting as well. When she speaks it's a whisper. "I've never come so hard."

Lifting my head, I look into her eyes. "So you like hunting?"

She starts to laugh, and I start to slip out. "Fuck." I reach between us and catch the condom, quickly putting it away so I can trash it later.

I'm on my knees, holding her hand, and she stands, going to where she left her clothes. I jerk up my jeans, grinning like an idiot as I watch her cute little ass disappear in her underwear then into her leggings.

A thought crosses my mind that ought to scare the shit out of me, but it doesn't. I want to be like this with her always. I never want to let her go.

When she turns to face me again, her brow is furrowed like she's just discovered a serious problem. My stomach drops, and I catch her chin.

"Hey, you okay? Was I too rough just then?" I remember the part where it seemed like she might squirm away.

"No, you were amazing." She blinks up at me, and her blue eyes are so bright. "I need to ask you something, and it's going to sound crazy. But just hear me out."

"Okay." I slide my thumb along the line of her jaw, thinking I'm ready to do just about anything for her.

Clearing her throat, she reaches up and takes my hand, holding it in both of hers. She presses her lips together, sliding her thumbs along the top, hesitating as if she's suddenly afraid. I'm so confused, but she inhales slowly.

Then, lifting her chin, she holds my gaze, and with all the sincerity in the world, she says, "Raif Jones, will you marry me?"

Chapter 17

Jemima

THE WORLD GOES COMPLETELY SILENT.

The wind isn't blowing. There are no frogs croaking. Even the bugs seem to go still.

I'm standing in the middle of an empty field after another mind-blowing round of hot sex, waiting for Raif Jones to answer me.

Baby, just say yes…

His brow lowers, and his lips part as if he'll say something. Then they close again, and he blinks a few times. His eyes hold mine, which I appreciate, but I can see he's completely confused.

"Are you serious?" It's a gentle question, which I also appreciate. "You want to get married?"

"Just for a little while." My heart beats fast as I try to explain. "I'm trying to adopt Nikki, you see, and it would be so much easier if I were married. Like it's nearly impossible if you're single, but if you're single like me, it's even worse. We don't have to do a big wedding, and I'll be happy to sign a prenup—"

"Prenups are for rich people." He's still frowning, but I'm encouraged he's not coming back with an emphatic *no*.

"I'll be a good wife, I promise. I won't nag you or ask you to do things you don't want to do."

His brow relaxes, and it almost seems like he'll laugh. The fist of panic in my throat starts to unfurl, and I figure I should lay it all out on the table.

"Nikki's nine, so she's pretty self-sufficient. I'll take care of everything when it comes to her, so you don't have to worry about a thing—"

"I don't mind helping."

Warmth fills my chest, and I kind of love him for that.

"I can't cook, but I'd be willing to take lessons. Adam's a great cook, so maybe he could teach me?"

That seems to piss him off. "I'll teach you how to cook if you want to learn."

"Are you a good cook?"

"No."

"But…"

"I don't need Adam Stone teaching my wife to do anything."

I press my lips together, fighting a little squeal. "Okay."

He called me his wife.

Sort of.

"Speaking of the Stones, what will they think about this?"

"They probably won't like it."

He nods, but I'm moving fast. "Is that a yes? I know it's crazy, but it's only for a little while—three months tops—and I promise not to make your life miserable…"

"I can't imagine you'd ever make my life miserable." He reaches for my waist, pulling my body flush with his. "But what about me? You don't know anything about me."

Resting my hands on his chest, I look up at him. "I know a lot about you. I've been interviewing you for almost two weeks."

"What do you know?" His eyebrow arches, and I internally sigh.

He's so sexy.

"For starters, you have an entrepreneurial spirit."

"Big word."

"You're a good son, a problem solver… a dependable worker, and you know how to treat a lady." I count them off on my fingers.

"It's true, but that's not enough to marry a man."

He's right. I think about what else I know about him.

"You're a bad boy." I study my hands resting on his chest. "My momma used to say never fall in love with a bad man, because he'll beat you. Will you beat me?"

I look up, and when our eyes meet, anger mixes with confusion in his gaze. "Is this about that asshole from Branson?"

My ears are hot, and I look down again. "No! He was never my boyfriend."

"Look at me." He gives me a little shake, and when I look up, his eyes are deadly serious. "I would never hurt you, Jemima Dixon, and I'd kill anyone who did, including him. In fact, I like this arrangement. If that guy does show up at your place again, I'll be there to teach him a lesson."

A surge of energy tingles in my stomach, and I exhale softly. "That sounds good to me." His jaw is tight, and I really like this side of him. Sliding my hair behind my shoulder, I throw a little sass. "You sound like my kind of bad boy."

"Don't get it twisted." He leans forward, speaking in my ear. "I'll still spank your ass if it gets you off."

The tingle in my stomach shoots lower, making my pussy wet. "I think it might."

"I figured as much." He releases me, catching my hand in his. "You're a bad girl."

"You're a tease." I skip closer, holding his arm in my hand.

"I wasn't teasing."

Our fingers thread, and he leads me to the road, where we left the bike. I'm a little timid to ask my last question, but I guess if I'm ever going to do it, I'd better do it now.

"I know it's not a real marriage, but… will you cheat on me?"

He stops walking and gives my hand a tug so I'm back in his arms, flush against his chest. Then he kisses my lips softly. "Never."

Our eyes are locked, and I believe him. Every word. "That's all I need to know, I guess."

"Well, I'd better get you back. You've got a little girl to put to bed, and I've got a pig to process."

The whole ride back, my cheek is pressed against his shoulder, and I'm smiling, staring dreamily at the sky full of stars. Even if it's not a real marriage, even if he's only doing it to help me adopt Nikki and there's a deadline on our arrangement, I'm so happy.

It's like I've found something I didn't know I lost. My arms are clasped tightly around his waist, and when his hand covers mine, I feel so safe and protected.

He waits for me to walk up the steps to my little house where Monay is staying with Nikki, but I hesitate on the top step, not really wanting him to go.

"Thanks for the hunting lesson."

His blue eyes shine from beneath the helmet with the visor pushed up. He rolls back, but I can tell he's smiling.

I don't miss his parting words, "See you soon, Mrs. Jones."

"You've got that look again." Monay is sitting on the couch when I walk through the door. "I thought you said this was a work trip."

"It was, look!" I hop onto the couch beside her.

Her eyes narrow, but I pull out my phone, scrolling through pictures of Raif looking super hot in his hunting gear, him walking out to the site, the tree where we waited, and the final kill.

"Look at that. Raif and Jemima, sitting in a tree." She's still suspicious in her sky-high Dolly wig and flowery blouse. "And you expect me to believe there was no K-I-S-S-I-N-G?"

"We had to be very quiet so we didn't scare away the hogs."

"So I guess this glow means you really like hunting?"

I squeeze my lips so I don't laugh and glance around the room. "Where's Nikki?"

"She's upstairs. It's not a school night, so I figured she could stay up a little later."

"Hang on. Wait right here." I scrub Angie Dickinson's pink head then jog up the stairs.

Nikki is in her bed with her eyes on her phone, and she's wearing headphones. I wave before sitting on the bedside, and she pulls the headphones off, studying me curiously.

"Hey, can you talk a minute?" My voice is quiet, but she nods. "So, remember Raif? The guy you met before school that day?"

"The one with the dirty hands?"

I frown, then I remember. "Oh, yeah." I kind of forgot about that. "What do you think about him?"

"I don't know." She shrugs, sitting up straighter in her sea-green pajamas. "He has nice eyes."

"How would you feel if he came here to live with us?"

She looks around the small space. "Where would he sleep?"

Hesitating, I think about her question. I don't know if anyone would ask her about this in court, but I decide it's better to be safe. "We're getting married, so he'd sleep in my bed."

Her eyes widen. "Are you pregnant?"

"No, no…" I exhale a laugh, shaking my head. "No. I am *not* pregnant."

She blinks down to her lap, and I can't tell what she's thinking. I want her to be happy, but maybe she's worried I'll abandon her for him? But how can I let her know this is all for her without saying it straight out? Chewing the side of my finger, I try to think of something.

Her light-brown eyes lift to mine. "Does he like children?"

"Yes!" I catch her hands in both of mine. "He knows all about you, and he's totally fine with children. I have an idea. Why don't I text him, and we can meet up for slushies at the Pak-n-Save. Then you can really talk, not like on the street on the way to school."

"I like slushies."

I slide a dark brown curl behind her ear. "Trust me, you'll like him a lot. Nothing's going to change."

"It'll change some. We'll have a boy in the house."

"But it's only our special family getting bigger."

"The one that gets us through the hard times?"

"Right." I boop her nose, then I point to her screen. "*SpongeBob?*"

She nods, and I give her a side hug. "Just one more episode then get some sleep, okay?"

I'm not sure I've convinced her, but I'm feeling optimistic about our arrangement. Having Raif here will be a good thing, not only in my adoption efforts, but also to keep away any unwanted visitors.

When I get to the bottom of the stairs, I check the lock on the back door. It's securely in place, and when I turn, I let out a little yip.

Monay towers over me in the kitchen, arms crossed and frowning. "I heard all of that. Are you pregnant for real?"

"No!" I exhale a laugh, shaking my head as I catch her arm, pulling her into the living room where Nikki is less likely to overhear us. I know her headphones are on, but I'm not taking any chances.

Monay lifts her arm out of my grip when we reach the sofa. "Then why are you marrying a man you've known, what? Three months?"

"I'm doing it for the adoption. I did some research after I talked to Aiden, just to find out how long it could take and how to speed things up. It said single people can adopt, but it sounded very hard. A lot more hoops to jump through. Raif is willing to help us, and he knows it's only for the adoption."

"Will it help if everyone knows it's only for the adoption?"

"You're right." I pace the living room, thinking. "I was going to tell Cass and Piper and Britt, but if Britt knows, she'll have to tell Aiden. I don't know if that will have to go into his report."

"He's writing a report?"

"He offered to do my background check and my home visit. As sheriff he can do that for me to speed up the process."

"Girl…" She shakes her head and picks up Angie Dickinson. "Just as long as he doesn't have to look into my background for anything."

"I think you're safe." I follow her to the door. "Although, I might ask him to find out how you can afford all that expensive luggage."

She holds up a finger. "That is not your business."

"I like to imagine you had an affair with a senator. It checks all my boxes—forbidden love, billionaire, enemies to lovers…"

"Why do we have to be enemies?"

"Because he's in Branson."

Her red lips pucker, and she nods. "I see your point. It's a fun story. You just keep on believing it." I think she's distracted from my new situation, but she's not. "While we're on the subject of money, does James Dean have any?"

"I don't think so, but that's not the point. The point is to help me."

"Hmm…" She evaluates me. "I take it he's good at consummation?"

"He's very good, and we get along." I think about what he said about not letting anyone hurt me and never cheating. "He's a good man, and he wants to help us."

"I'd like to be part of this slushie sit-down. I have a few questions of my own."

"In that case, I think we should meet for drinks."

"It won't be anything he can't handle."

"I'm more worried about the kids."

"I know how to act around children, and I know how to look out for them, too." She leans down and air-kisses both my cheeks. "Lock this door behind me."

"I will."

We say goodnight, and I lock the door, turning to lean against it. Then I take out my phone and send Raif a text.

Chapter 18

Raif

"Y EP." BENDER SITS ON THE PORCH, NODDING AS I WATCH HIM stuff his face with barbecue pork. "This is good. Now tell me about it."

"It's leaner than beef, it has more vitamins, it's more humane…" I scratch the back of my neck, running through all the facts I jotted down in my research. "No GMOs, no hormones. It's better for the environment."

He squints an eye, pointing at me. "You've done your homework. How soon can you get me enough to sell?"

I have done my homework, and this is the part I've been dreading.

"They're smart, so I'd have to figure out a way to capture more than one. Maybe build a pen. Then I'll have to find a butcher who'll cut me a deal. It could take a while."

"Is it sustainable?" He wipes the sauce off his beard.

"Maybe." I remember what Jemima told me she'd learned. "The sows have about ten to twelve piglets a year."

"I'm ready when you are. I think we can make this work. Free-range pork sells for sixteen to twenty dollars a pound."

"I heard." At the same time, I'm calculating how long it took to get one sandwich.

"It's dirty work, but it's good money." He pushes off his knees. "It's a growth industry. Before long you can hire some guys, and you'll be the boss. You can sit back and rake in the profits."

Three thousand dollars would go a long way towards getting me there. I watch as he picks up the bottle of Stone Cold single barrel, and I think about the deals I've made with my brother, with Jemima.

I step over to shake his hand. "I appreciate it. You've always been more of a dad to me than my own."

"Just repaying my debts." His brow softens. "Your momma took care of me more times than anyone should've. She had a good heart, and I've always seen a lot of her in you."

My jaw tenses, and I release his hand. "I'll let you know when I'm ready."

All the way to town, I do my best to make it okay. I do my best not to think about jeopardizing what I've built up with Bender, Jemima, the memory of my mom.

I think about the old timers and the kind of things they had to do to achieve their goals. Hell, even Alex Stone couldn't be where he is without his family's bootlegger past. Everyone has to color outside the lines a little.

It takes money to make money, and at this point, I only have one option. Sometimes you agree to do things you wouldn't want exposed to the light of day. Then later, you have to be a man of your word and stick to it.

Everything's going to work out.

But nothing can go wrong.

Jemima's waiting for me on the sidewalk when I pull my dad's old truck up to the Pak-n-Save. She's wearing a long-sleeved gray T-shirt tucked into jeans with a bow on the front. Her hair hangs in curls around her shoulders, and she's holding two large cups.

She looks like someone worth risking everything for, and heat tightens my stomach.

I step out, and she steps closer, shaking her head. "I have to warn you, everyone is waiting for us at the gazebo."

"Who's everyone?" I glance across the street at the white structure in the middle of town square.

When she texted me about meeting her and Nikki here for slushies, I thought it would be just the three of us. Now I see Nikki running around the grassy field with Piper's son Ryan and Owen Stone.

Britt's bloodhound sits on the gazebo steps watching them, and inside it are Piper and Britt and the drag queen who came here and got Jemima before Christmas.

"I'm not worried about them." I walk to the back of the truck and open the tailgate.

"Who is this?" Her voice rises, and she reaches out to run her hand over Porkchop's head.

I snap a leash to his collar. "Jemima, meet Porkchop." He immediately tries to bolt to where the kids are playing when I help him out of the back, but I'm ready for him. "He's not used to being on a leash. Or being in town. Or pretty much behaving ever."

"You named him *Porkchop*?" She passes one of the large cups to me.

"He stole a pork chop off my daddy's plate one night, and Bull named him that. I'd have named him Lucky, because if my dad had caught him…"

She doesn't need to know the rest of that story.

"Well, it's definitely unique." She slides her hand into the crook of my arm, hugging her body to my side and speaking low. "They know we're engaged, but only Monay knows why. They all think I'm pregnant, and I'm just letting it ride."

A tiny explosion goes off in my brain at the thought of Jemima pregnant with my child. In its aftermath is an unexpected sense of pride. I picture her walking around here, her belly growing round with our baby. I think about lying in bed with her coming up with baby names.

It's something I didn't even know I wanted, but I like the idea. A lot.

"We might have to work on that." I glance at her, and she bites back a grin.

"I like practicing with you."

Heat surges below my belt, and I lean closer to her ear. "You'd better stop teasing, or I'll have to take you around back and spank that ass."

"Oh my gosh." She fans her flushed face, and I hear Piper in the gazebo.

"That's what I thought. Pregnant." She stands, walking to us. "You were supposed to do a business profile, not do *the business.*"

"Stop saying that." Jemima gestures between me and the other two. "Raif, I think you know everybody except Monay."

Monay stands, and from the top of the gazebo in a full platinum wig and platform heels, she's a pretty intimidating height. "It's nice to finally meet you, Mr. Jones. I've heard *a lot.*"

I can believe it.

Jemima puts her hand on my arm. "All good things."

The boys run past us, but Nikki peels off, going straight to my dog.

"Who's he?" She looks up at me, scratching his neck. "Is he yours?"

"Yeah, but you can play with him. He's a little wild, but he's friendly."

As if on cue, he starts licking her face like it's an ice cream cone.

"Oh, okay! Down, boy!" She falls back on her butt, and I take a knee, pulling him off of her.

"Slow down, Porkchop." Then I notice her blue cheeks. "He probably tastes the slushie on your face."

"Oh, yeah." She blushes, pulling a long sleeve down and scrubbing her cheeks. Then she's back in front of him, holding his neck. "His eyes are different colors!"

I lean on my forearm, still holding his collar. When I pat his head, he licks me in the face, and I catch his muzzle, gently moving it away. "It's called heterochromia. He was either born that way or it happened because of trauma."

"Trauma?" Nikki's eyes flash, and she moves closer, pulling the dog into a hug and rubbing her hands down his back.

Porkchop stands, wagging his tail so hard his whole butt moves.

"He's perfect." Her voice is quiet, and she meets my eyes again. "Will you bring him with you when you come to live at our house?"

"Is that okay with you?"

She has the most serious brown eyes I've ever seen, and she hesitates as if she's considering my question. "We don't have a lot of room inside, but we have a fence around the yard. He could stay out there."

I slide my palm over his black and white head. "Maybe you could train him. I haven't had much time, but I think he's still young enough to learn."

She reaches out to pet him again, and he lowers his ears, tongue out and panting. "Maybe I could teach him to shake hands."

"I don't know if he's smart enough for that, but you can try."

The two boys have noticed us talking, and they run up to where we're standing.

"That's the dog who was in the race at the fair!" Owen shouts. "Your girlfriend gave him hot dogs to make him run."

Jemima's eyebrow arches. "Your girlfriend?"

I exhale a laugh. "She was just some girl I knew."

"She cheated." Owen frowns.

I slide my hands into my pockets. "They didn't say we couldn't use food, and Porkchop's not very smart."

"That girl wasn't very smart. Every dog on the field ran after her except Edward." He goes to where Britt's bloodhound is sitting. "Edward's the smartest dog in the world."

Dropping my chin, I wonder how I can get out of this. "He's pretty good. Who knew a bloodhound could run so fast?"

"That girl was lucky she could run fast. She almost lost her tube top."

"So you two are getting married." Britt interrupts, shifting her baby to her shoulder. "That doesn't seem a bit sudden to you?"

I can't tell if she's trying to distract her son or if she's really grilling me. My eyes go to Jemima's, and she's blinking fast. I've learned that means she's nervous.

I shift the ball cap on my head. "We don't want to wait."

"Marriage is a big step." Piper's tone is more measured. "Are you sure you're ready for it?"

"I'm sure about Jemima." Her eyes meet mine, and I give her a wink.

"Can we be sure about you?" Monay watches me closely, and I don't know which of us would win in a fight.

My money's on her.

"Yes." I meet her gaze without hesitation. "Jemima wants this, and I want it. I guess we have as good a chance as anybody else, and I intend to take care of her. You don't have to worry about her with me. Ever."

"Oh!" Britt puts a hand over her mouth, and she looks like she's going to cry.

I don't know if that's good or bad, but Piper nods. "Cass might not agree, but you sound all right to me."

Jemima walks to where I'm standing and slips her hand into my arm again. This time she couples it with a kiss on my cheek, and I feel good. I feel happy.

And I push back on those other feelings building like gray clouds on the horizon.

Chapter 19

Jemima

CASS STANDS IN FRONT OF A MINT-GREEN CUISINART MIXER IN THE middle of her pristine, white kitchen in Alex's big house outside of town.

My sister is an excellent baker—she used to have her own business making cakes until she said it took over her life. I did not inherit that skill, or at least I never learned it.

Today she's mixing icing to go on her signature snickerdoodle cake, and I feel like I'm under the interrogation lamp. "You barely even know him, Jemima! He could be a drug dealer for all you know."

"He's not a drug dealer." I slide my finger across the screen of her iPad, where we've been looking at Mardi Gras decorations for the gala. "I've interviewed him for the paper, I've asked him all kinds of questions, he got cups for the kids—"

"Drug dealers don't tell you they're drug dealers. They simply do what they do, then you both get gunned down in a dark alley one night because somebody didn't get paid or something went wrong or somebody's trying to move up in the hierarchy."

"I think you've been watching too much *Ozark*." I lean forward to dip my finger in the icing bowl. "Where's Pinky?"

"Alex took her to Julia's. She has a playdate with Crimson, and that's not what *Ozark* is about. It's about money laundering."

"I thought it was about drugs." I shrug. "Anyway, I've known him long enough. I know what drug dealers are like, and he's not one. He's a hard worker, he's very goal-oriented. Piper's mom loves him."

"I guess. Who am I to judge?" She sighs, turning off the mixer. "Aiden said he's never been in trouble, and I guess how well do you ever know anyone these days?"

"See!" I hold out my hands. "It's all good."

"It's not all good. I still think it's too fast." She puts both hands on the countertop beside the mixer. "Are you pregnant?"

"No!" I laugh. "Everybody keeps asking that. I'm not pregnant. We're just in love."

The words fly out before I have a chance to catch them, and my throat tightens. *Are we?* That *would* be too fast… Wouldn't it?

"Really?" Her voice takes on a hopeful pitch, and my insides squirm.

Up to this point, I haven't really been lying to anyone.

"Yeah." I smile, blinking down and doing my best not to appear guilty.

She walks over and takes both my hands in hers. "Okay, then." She pulls me into a tight hug. "Starting now, there'll be no more negative talk. I'm so happy for you, especially after all you've been through. I want you to have all the good things in the world, and that includes marrying the man you love."

I swallow the lump in my throat and manage to squeak out a thanks.

She steps back, her gray-blue eyes so full of warmth. "Piper said he was very convincing at the park yesterday, and she said he brought a dog for Nikki to play with?"

"Yeah… Can I have a glass of water?"

"Of course." She takes a glass out of the cabinet and brings it to me. "I remember the day Mom took you away so clearly. There were nights I could still hear you crying in my sleep. I was furious at her for leaving us behind, but when she came back and took you away, it was almost worse. I struggled for a long time wondering why."

"I wondered that too." I drink the water, not really wanting to take this trip down memory lane. "I would go to sleep at night and imagine you were there, singing to me."

"I'm sorry." She slides her hand down the side of my hair. "Maybe she thought she was doing good? Maybe she didn't want to be alone, or maybe she thought you were too little to understand being left behind?"

"Maybe she was just selfish." That old anger is in my chest again. "She'd stay out all night, then she'd get up the next evening and do it all again. Like she was so determined to hit the big time, she forgot everything else. She said it was for us, but she left me behind as sure as if she'd left me here with you."

My sister is quiet, and she holds my hands gently. "Aunt Carol said she died alone in a hotel room."

A frown pulls my brow, and I draw back my chin. "Mom died at the hospital." Cass looks up at me confused, and I explain. "She tried for a while to get clean, but it was too late. Her heart gave out."

"I don't understand. Why would Aunt Carol tell me that?"

"Because she's mean?"

She doesn't answer right away, but after a few moments she nods slowly. "She is… or she always was."

I glance around this beautiful kitchen all stainless steel and white tile and reclaimed wood. My eyes drift into the living room, where massive couches are arranged in front of a theater-sized flatscreen television. These are the things my momma always wanted. She never got them.

"I wasn't with her when she died."

"What?"

"She fell, and I called 9-1-1…" It's a memory I'd be glad never to relive. The flashing sirens, workers yelling, me being pushed aside as they rushed in and took her away. "I waited, but no one ever came back for me, so I crawled into her bed. I never saw her again."

"Oh…" Cass slides her hand over mine, and I look up to see tears building in her gray-blue eyes. "I didn't know."

"They wanted to send me to live with some relative, but I wanted to be with you. Then they said Aunt Carol didn't want another child."

My throat tightens, and I don't know why I'm telling her this. I don't like these memories. I've accepted they're a part of who I am, but they're the past. I'm in Eureka now, and I want this to be the part where I get the magic, the love, the life I always dreamed about.

"It doesn't matter now."

She closes the space between us, pulling me into a hug. "It does matter."

I feel her hiccup a breath, and I hug her back. "But we can't change it. I learned who I could trust, and I learned to be strong." I take her hands in mine, something I always wanted. "Now I'm building my own family, and we'll always be there for each other."

Wiping the tears off her cheeks, she squeezes my hands. "I hope you'll let me be a part of it."

"You already are."

The justice of the peace's office in Ridgeland is a small room in an even smaller building in a strip mall off the highway north of Eureka.

Monay parks in the empty space next to Raif's shiny motorcycle. "I guess I see how you're getting home." She glances at me across the console. "Miss Nik and I will be at the Pak-n-Save getting red vines and slushies for Movies in the Park tonight."

"You're going to have so much fun. *The Princess and the Frog* is one of my favorites." I look over my shoulder at Nikki in the backseat.

She's wearing a pretty, hot pink dress with eyelet embroidery, and her hair is brushed smooth with a little flower headband.

Monay is wearing a full face of makeup, her best Dolly wig, and a pale pink sheath dress and matching coat. It matches Angie Dickinson's dye job, and of course, Ange is with us, wearing her best puppy tiara for the occasion.

"I expect you'll be having your own fun tonight." Monay gives me a wink, and anticipation shimmers in my stomach.

I step out of the car, straightening my skirt. I chose a simple white tunic dress with eyelet embroidery and tan cowboy boots. I pulled my hair back in a bow, and I only put on mascara and lip gloss.

"You look pretty." Nikki takes my hand, looking up at me. "Even low-key."

"Thanks." I put my arm around her shoulder, giving her a squeeze.

We agreed this would be a low-key event. No fanfare, no bachelorette, no reception—much to my sister's and her friends' dismay.

The last thing I need to do is build this up to more than it is or get too attached. It's why I didn't want Cass or any of them here.

I said it was because Raif wasn't inviting family, and I didn't want him to feel outnumbered, but the truth is, I don't want anyone broken-hearted when the adoption papers go through and we shake hands and go our separate ways—including me.

"Let's do this." Monay adjusts Angie under her arm, and she leads us through the glass door with the bell on it.

A woman is at the front desk, and when she looks up, her eyes widen. "You must be here for the wedding." She hops up, clasping her hands together. "We get so few of these, the girls and I've been so excited."

I have no right to be nervous, considering this marriage is only a means to an end, a thought that puts a lump in my throat, which I know is ridiculous.

"You'd better turn that frown upside down," Monay murmurs in my ear. "What will people say?"

The woman leads us to a smaller door with *Justice of the Peace* engraved on a plaque out front. "Your groom is waiting for you inside."

I take a deep breath, putting a smile on my face, but when the door opens, I falter. The room is larger than I expected, and Raif is speaking to a man up front. He's dressed in a dark gray suit and slim, black tie. His hair is brushed back into a small ponytail, and he looks like something out of a magazine.

He's gorgeous, and when his eyes meet mine, his lips stop moving. His expression takes on an intensity that flushes my entire body with heat. I can't move. Everything else fades away…

Until Monay nudges me in the back. "That's more like it."

A smile curls his lips, and he dips his chin before walking to where I stand.

"You're beautiful." His voice is low like we're sharing a secret.

"Thank you," I manage to answer.

"I got this for you." He's holding a small bouquet of flowers.

They're light blue with dark blue little faces, and they're tied with a baby blue bow.

"Pansies?" I take them from him, holding them to my nose.

"Your favorite."

They don't have a scent, but I don't care. "They're perfect."

"They're the color of your eyes." He grins, and that dimple pierces his cheek.

"You look really good." I reach out to slide my hand down the lapel of his jacket. "I've never seen you dressed up before."

"It's a special occasion." He takes my hand and pulls it into the crook of his arm, and all my stoic intentions fly straight out the window.

All I want is to give my heart to this moment and to him and to the beautiful story unfolding in this sterile government office. I want my gorgeous husband, who gives me my favorite flowers and doesn't hesitate to make my dreams come true…

Or help me solve my problems.

"If you're ready, we can begin now." The older man at the front of the room draws our attention.

Raif escorts me to stand before him. It's a straightforward procedure. Monay and Nikki and the ladies from out front are our witnesses. We recite the standard promises to take care of each other, to be true to each other, in sickness and in health.

Nikki's eyes are bright as she watches the whole thing, and the hint of a smile is on her small face. Monay has an elaborate handkerchief in her large hand, and she keeps hugging Angie Dickinson to her side and dabbing her eyes.

Then the old man says the words, "Til death do you part," and my breath catches.

Raif repeats the words without missing a beat, and with a steadying inhale, I do the same. Monay huffs a little noise that sounds like a sob.

"Do you have the rings?" the man asks.

Monay steps forward to hand me the simple gold band Cass helped me buy online from James Allen. A half smile curls Raif's lips as he watches me hold his hand and put it on his finger.

"Never thought of myself as a ring guy." Warmth is in his tone, and he slides it around with his thumb. "I like it."

I feel bad we didn't really talk about this part. "It's okay if you didn't—"

"I hope you don't mind." He holds my hand in his and slides a delicate, gold-filigree ring on my finger. "It was my mother's."

Emotions flood my chest, drowning my already aching heart. My lips part, but I can't speak. The ring is beautiful with tiny diamonds wrapped in filigree swirls. I lift my finger, holding it close to my chest like a precious treasure.

"You may now kiss the bride." The man holds his hands up, and Raif touches my chin.

My eyes are on his tie, and my bottom lip goes between my teeth.

"Look at me, Jemima." It's a low order, but I shake my head. "I can't."

"Why not?" I hear the grin in his voice, and I force my eyes to blink up to his.

The intensity is stronger than ever, and I can't hold his gaze. "I thought I could do this, but now I don't know. I'm afraid."

"What are you afraid of?"

"You… this. You're so gorgeous, and it's all so beautiful." *And I want it to be real so much.* I don't say that part out loud.

"Just hold on to me, pretty girl. I told you, I'd never let you get hurt." He cups my cheek in his hand, placing his thumb on my chin. "I'm going to kiss my wife now."

My eyes slide close, and his lips cover mine, warm and possessive. Our mouths don't open. We're not French kissing in front of all these people and Nikki, but I lift my hand to hold his face.

The sound of a phone clicking photos brings me back to reality, and I look into his blue eyes one more time. It's a shot straight to my heart, and I hear the man say it.

"I now present Mr. and Mrs. Raif Jones."

We take Raif's motorcycle back to the house. While we were signing off on the license, Monay sneaked out and attached a "Just Married" sign to the back along with a few streamers.

My arms are tight around his waist, and my head rests against his shoulder blade as we fly down the highway. The one wedding gift I would allow is Nikki spending the weekend with friends so we can have a "honeymoon sexcation," as Monay put it.

When we finally arrive home, balloons are tied to the front door along with a curtain of white and silver streamers, and I'm struggling with not getting too emotional about the whole thing.

This isn't real is on repeat in my brain like a mantra, and I don't want Raif to think I'm trying to trap him into something permanent after I told him it was only temporary.

"I asked them not to do this." Apology is in my tone, and he steps off the bike, removing his helmet.

"I think it's nice." Pieces of his hair have escaped the ponytail, and it hangs attractively around his face. He reaches out to hold my hand as I dismount. "Don't apologize."

He smiles, and I do my best not to swoon over his dimple. I leave him to secure the bike, while I jog up the porch steps and unlock the door. I'm about to step inside when strong arms catch me around the waist.

"What do you think you're doing?" In a swoop, he lifts me off my feet, holding me like a real bride. "I'm supposed to carry you over the threshold."

"Raif…" My ability to resist him goes up in smoke, and I rest my cheek against his chest. "I'm trying to stick to the script."

"What script is that?" He walks over and sits my butt on the back of the sofa.

My legs are straddled, and he steps between them. The brush of his slacks against my bare thighs has me very aware of my short skirt and thong underwear.

"The one where we're only doing this so I can adopt Nikki."

Leaning down, he traces his thumb along the side of my jaw. "I thought you promised to be a good wife."

A twinkle is in his eye, and I pull my bottom lip between my teeth. "I did."

He puts his thumb on my lip, tugging it free, and I pull that thick digit into my mouth, giving it a suck.

A hiss slips through his teeth, and his eyes darken as he watches me. "Then pull up that dress and show me your pretty pussy."

Chapter 20

I NEVER THOUGHT MUCH ABOUT GETTING MARRIED. I'M NOT OPPOSED to it or anything. It's more that I've never had time for it, at least not the way I would want to do it, and for that matter, I've never met a girl who really interested me enough.

Not to be judgmental, I've met some nice girls. I just never met anyone who made me want to settle down and build a home or have a family. Until a sassy little blonde with full red lips batted her lashes at me in the newspaper office.

Still, Jemima caught me completely off-guard with this marriage. If it had been up to me, I'd have spent a little more time getting to know her.

But when she walked into that justice of the peace's office in her pretty lace dress with her bright blue eyes and soft pink lips, something clicked inside me. It felt right, and while I don't want to hijack her show or make her stay in a marriage she doesn't want, she's mine now. I'm planning to enjoy her being my wife.

Particularly when she's bent over the back of the couch with her white lace dress riding up her thighs, and I'm holding my hard cock, slowly dipping the tip into her slippery core.

"Fuck me, that feels so good." I'm going to have to work to keep my promise of never leaving her behind.

"You like that?" She lifts her juicy little ass, looking back at me over her shoulder.

"Yes..." I reach around to slide my fingers between her legs, under that scrap of a thong, to massage her clit. "How about you?"

"Oh, God, yes." Her knees bend, and her face collapses into the pillows with a moan.

She's so wet, and pleasure snakes up my legs with every tantalizing inch I drive into her. "Look at that greedy little pussy taking my cock."

She moans again, moving her ass higher, closer, pulling me deeper into her warm body. Gripping her hips, I jerk her hard against my dick. Her wails are muffled in the cushions, and my body is on fire.

The sensation of her, watching her creaming my cock hypnotizes me. Moving my hand around front again, I slide my fingers rough and fast over her clit. I need her to come with me, and I can't stop.

"Come on, baby."

She pushes up on the couch, gasping. "Spank me."

A surge of orgasm hits, and I groan, doing my best not to finish. She collapses forward again, and I do what she asks. Reaching back, I slap her butt, and a bright pink flush colors the skin.

She moans, turning her head to the side. "Harder..."

"Fuck, princess." I pull back and slap her ass again with a little more force.

She shrieks, and her hand goes between her thighs massaging her clit. I do it again on the other side, and her pussy jerks around my cock. Her knees bend, and her thighs quiver, and I lose it.

Gripping her hips, I hold, shuddering through an orgasm so intense, I'm lucky my own knees don't give out. We're leaning forward on the couch, and I feel her fingers fumble between us, holding the base of my shaft as I pulse harder, grinding out a swear of intense pleasure.

Leaning down, I wrap my arm across her chest, lifting her to me. "Kiss me."

She complies at once, turning so her head rests against the front of my shoulder. My fingers hold the sides of her face, and I pull her mouth to mine.

When the man at the courthouse told me to kiss the bride, I had to hold back out of respect for her friends and the witnesses helping us.

Now I want to kiss my wife properly.

I curl my tongue with hers, and she exhales a little noise that makes my dick pulse once more inside her. I flatten my palm against her stomach, pressing her ass against my pelvis.

"That's what you do to me," I speak in her hair, against her ear. "You make me so hard."

She whimpers, and again I take her lips with mine, sliding my hand from her stomach up to her breasts, lifting and kneading them in my hands.

Our mouths break apart as she moans, and she bites the side of my jaw as I twist her tight nipples with my fingers. We came hard, but this afterglow is blowing my mind.

I reach down again, dragging my fingers under that tiny scrap of fabric covering her bare pussy, and she exhales soft grunts in my ear.

"Are you still coming on my cock?" My mouth is at her shoulder, and I watch her hips rotate in time with my finger circling her clit.

"Yes…" She nods as she moves her hand to grip my ass, pulling me to her.

I exhale a low groan, and she curls her fingers to trace her nails along my thighs. I'm pretty fucking sensitive right now, but when I look down and see her beautiful body in my arms, her head back as her body rotates in time with my hand on her pussy, I can't stop.

Her nipples are taut little spikes, and she's so fucking gorgeous. Her hair falls around her shoulders, and I drag my fingers up and down her center until her stomach quivers again, and her lips part with a soft cry.

Her body shakes, and she grips my forearm as she shudders through another orgasm, her pussy spasming around my cock. Her fingers thread in mine as I lift my hand to her stomach, and she turns to face me.

I swallow air at the sight of her. Her blue eyes are darkened, her cheeks are pink from my beard scratching her skin, and her bare breasts rise and fall quickly with her pants.

"You are so fucking beautiful."

"You were right." She traces her finger along my jaw, pressing her forehead to my lips. "I like when you spank my ass."

"Oh my gosh, this is so delicious." We're sitting on the floor in the living room with a white cake between us and two glasses of champagne.

She's adorable in only my shirt, holding a fork and shaking her head as she takes another big bite of cake. We didn't even bother with plates. We're eating it right off the platter.

"I told Cass not to do anything. Can you believe they didn't listen to me?"

"They love you." I grin, watching my cute little wife stuff her face.

"They're welcoming you, too." Her eyes meet mine, but I'm skeptical. "Seriously, Cass said they would drop their suspicions. Britt in particular said she knows what it's like to be judged by your family and not your own merits."

"Yeah." I've pulled on my boxer briefs, and I'm sitting beside her, our legs touching and the fingers of our free hands entwined, stabbing my fork into the white cake and doing my best not to feel guilty.

I am committed to Jemima's happiness. They're right to trust me in that aspect.

My eyes land on my mother's ring on her finger. She's the kind of girl who should wear it. She's the kind of girl my mom would have loved. She's optimistic and kind, and she encourages the best parts of me the way my mom did.

The justice said something about two becoming one during the ceremony, and as I watched her pretty face so nervous and earnest, I could sense it happening. When I'm inside her, and she's coming in my arms. When I'm holding her, kissing her soft lips, we're one.

She's mine.

"I think it's almond." Her brow furrows as she continues chattering, taking a sip of champagne and looking up at me. "Isn't that the traditional wedding cake flavor?"

"Hell if I know." I exhale a laugh.

Sometimes I think she forgets I wasn't raised as privileged as she was. Although the crazy questions she asked me when she proposed got me wondering. *Would I beat her?* That one had me seeing red.

It made me wonder if her childhood wasn't as privileged as I thought, if she's been in a situation where some asshole tried to hurt her. I haven't seen any signs of it, but I'd better not find out it happened. I'd hate to go to prison for murder when we're starting off so well as newlyweds.

"Ha, now they're confessing." She holds up her phone so I can see the text notifications.

"What does it say?"

"Since you wouldn't let us have a reception or even a bachelorette," she reads aloud, "we hope you enjoy your gifts." Her brow furrows, and she looks up and around the room. "Gifts?"

She hops onto her feet, and I watch as she scampers to the bedroom door then lets out a shriek. "Look what they did!"

Dropping my fork, I hustle over to where she stands. Inside the small bedroom, someone made a heart out of rose petals on the bed, and two thick white robes are folded on the end. They're monogrammed in gold, and one says *Husband*. The other says *Wife*.

"Oh…" She exhales a whimper, and I frown, following her to where she traces her finger over the words. "Why did they do this?"

"Hey." I catch her chin, making her look at me. "What's wrong?"

"This is putting a lot of pressure on you, and I don't want you to be sorry you agreed to help me or feel uncomfortable in any way."

That almost makes me laugh, and I take the robe off the bed, quickly pulling it around my body. "Damn, this thing is soft!" I slide my hands up and down the velvety material. "Do I look uncomfortable to you?"

"No." She blinks those pretty blue eyes up at me.

"Good, because so far, you're shaping up to be a pretty good wife, and as your husband, I plan to enjoy this arrangement."

Her lips tighten as if she'll fight a smile. "Is that so? And how do you intend to do that?"

Stepping closer, I put my hands on her waist, dragging her to my chest. "I can think of several ways." My hand lowers between us, and I slide my thumb up and down her clit. "I could put my tongue right here." I drag my hand around, tracing my finger lightly along her ass. "Or here. I could spank your pussy next time…"

A sharp inhale parts her lips, and she grabs the front of my robe. "I want it now."

I quickly shrug off the garment, letting it fall to the floor. She palms my growing erection through my thin boxer briefs, tracing her nails over my dick.

"Damn, girl." I shove my underwear off, kicking them to the side before quickly lifting her off her feet.

Her legs wrap around my waist, and she covers my mouth with hers. I step to the wall, pressing her back against it and reaching between us to guide my cock into her.

"Fuck," I groan.

She's so damn wet it almost sends me over the edge.

"Oh, God," she gasps, tightening her thighs over my hips and lifting her body up and down my pelvis, pulling and massaging me.

"Jesus, I'm going to come." My hands grip her soft ass, and I can't believe I'm so close so fast.

"Me, too," she gasps, kissing me more.

It's too late to slow down at this point, and I step forward, nailing her against the wall. Her head falls back, and her soft breasts bounce between us with every hard thrust.

She's driving me crazy. I lean down to pull a taut nipple into my mouth, and she rasps a loud, moaning cry. My lips pop off her so I can close my eyes. It's all too much. I wrap both arms around her waist, lowering to sit on my heels as my orgasm surges hot and fast.

She straddles me, bracing her knees on the floor to ride my body, dragging her pussy back and forth over my cock until I'm going blind. The moment she breaks, my hands grip her ass, and with a shout, I fly off the cliff.

My lips part, and another guttural groan rises from my chest. I'm holding her tight as I ride out this sensation, this mind-altering pleasure.

Her body trembles and pulls, and I groan again, filling her, claiming her, speaking her name as mine.

Chapter 21

Jemima

MY HEAD IS AGAINST RAIF'S BARE CHEST, AND WE'RE SWEATY AND breathing hard from another round of orgasms. After doing it against the wall and then on the floor, we crawled into bed for a nap. Then I woke up a few hours later with his head between my thighs.

He made me come all over his face, then he fucked me so hard from behind, I'm pretty sure my legs won't work anymore.

So far, married life is pretty damn hot.

"I was just thinking, this house is small." His fingers are in my hair, and he wraps a curl around one. "What will we do when Nikki's here?"

Lifting my head, I rest my chin on my hand. "We'll have to invest in soundproofing for our bedroom walls and door."

A smile curls his lips, and he leans down to kiss me. "That's my good little wife."

His praise twists buzzy satisfaction low in my stomach. It's funny, I've never cared two cents what men thought about me—in fact I used to be kind of bratty about not caring. It was like the tough-girl survival act I needed to protect myself when I was in Branson. It meant I was strong.

Now I seem to live for Raif's proud smiles and sweet compliments. I especially lose it when he tells me how sexy I look riding his cock or how pretty my pussy is. Just thinking about it makes my cheeks flush. It makes me want to please him even more.

"What are you thinking about?" His eyes are on me, and I should know by now he doesn't miss a thing.

"I was just thinking about how sweet you are to me. No one's ever treated me so good."

His brow furrows, and he shifts to the side, leaning his head on his hand. "What happened in Branson?"

The position makes his bicep bulge. The muscle in his jaw moves, making it nice and square and strong. He's a sculpted god with ink covering his shoulders and messy hair falling around bad-boy blue eyes. I exhale a sigh.

It's very distracting.

"Hey." He reaches out to touch my chin.

"I'm sorry, what?" I laugh, kissing his finger.

"Branson? What happened there?" An undercurrent of protective anger is in his tone, and I slide my hand into his.

"Nothing I couldn't survive."

"What does that mean?" He's not letting up, and I figure he might as well know the truth.

Inhaling slowly, I roll onto my stomach beside him. "When I was about Nikki's age, my mom took me away with her. I don't know why she didn't leave me in Eureka with Cass, but she didn't."

He traces his finger along the line of my hair. "And?"

"And she left me alone every night while she tried to become a country music star. Then she got hooked on drugs. Then she lost all our money, and things got pretty dark." I clear my throat and just say it. "Then she died."

"Shit, I'm sorry." His hand is warm on my shoulder. "Fuck, Jemima."

"It's okay now." My shoulder rises beneath his touch, and I blink up at him. "I'm actually lucky, I guess. I didn't meet anybody like Bill until I was living with Monay and old enough to handle it."

"Is Bill the fucking asshole who hurt you?" Ice enters his tone.

"Yeah…" Tucking my chin, I wince. "I took Nikki from him. I guess you could say I kidnapped her, but he's a bad man. He wants her back, but Aiden is protecting me from him."

Catching my chin, he guides my eyes back to his. "You're *my* wife now. *I* protect you from him. Where is he?"

"I haven't heard from him since that night." I shrug. "I'm pretty sure he's back in Branson."

"He'd better fucking stay there."

"I'm not afraid of him." Shifting onto my side again, I scoot closer, hugging my body against Raif's. "I'm living in this cute little house with a sexy husband who makes me so happy. I'm going to adopt Nikki, and it's all going to work out."

His blue eyes soften, and he moves closer, wrapping his arm around my lower back and pressing his lips to the top of my shoulder. "I like making you happy."

"Good, because I like it, too." I can't keep the smile off my lips, and he exhales a laugh against my skin.

He lifts his chin. "I want you to be proud to say I'm your husband."

I stretch taller to kiss his full lips. "I already am."

The sun breaks warm through the window of our bedroom, and I rise onto my elbow to study Raif lying on his back. His skin is golden, and a lock of hair is across his forehead.

My husband. It's too late for me to resist falling for him.

He's so handsome, and when he says he wants to protect me and make me happy and make me proud of him, I fall more and more.

This weekend has been so perfect. I move the blankets aside and quietly slip out of the bed and pull my fluffy *Wife* robe over my naked body.

Every single one of my muscles is sore from all the sex we've been having, and my core aches with every step. It's delicious and amazing. I've never felt so satisfied in my life.

I start the coffee in the kitchen, and as I stand gazing out the window at the growing sunrise, my eyes land on a sea of hot pink blooms in the flower boxes attached to the fence.

Going to the door, I cross the small yard in my bare feet to find dozens of tulips bursting happily through the soil in the white wooden boxes.

Reaching out, I touch them carefully as I try to understand. Piper said she never planted anything here, and I don't think I've ever seen tulips like this anywhere except in pictures.

"Do you like them?" Raif's voice behind me makes me jump and turn around.

He's standing there in jeans and no shirt, and the memory rushes back. I remember that morning when Nikki and I caught him here as we were hurrying to school. Dirt was on his hands, and he shoved them in his pockets like he'd been caught.

"You did this?" My eyes are wide.

He exhales a laugh, rubbing his hand over the back of his neck. "I thought you might like them."

I rush into his arms. "You planted these for me all those weeks ago?"

"I had extra bulbs."

"Extra bulbs?" My brow furrows. "Where were you planting them before?"

"My mom always wanted tulips, but she didn't know how to grow them this far south." He turns me so my back is to his chest and wraps strong arms around me. "I did a little research, figured out how to make them grow, and I planted some in our yard for her."

Resting my head against his jaw, a sad mix of emotions fills my chest. "But she's gone."

He turns to kiss my temple. "I still like to think it makes her happy to see them… if she ever passes this way again."

I reach up to place my hand on his cheek. "You're so good."

A low hum vibrates from his throat, and he kisses my ear. "I had some left over, so I planted them for you."

"I love them." I pull my phone out of the pocket on my robe and snap a photo of the brilliant, waxy blossoms.

Look what my husband gave me.

I attach the photo and hit send to the group.

Britt: Raif!

She adds a crying emoji.

Cass: He grew tulips? Send him to my house.

She adds a laughing emoji.

Piper: Damn, how long has he been in love with you?

Joy pinches my stomach, and my cheeks warm. I wonder how long I've been falling in love with him.

Chapter 22

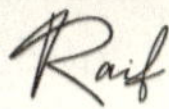

"WHAT'S THIS I HEAR ABOUT YOU GETTING MARRIED?" BULL bursts through the screen door as I'm zipping up my suitcase. "Chip said it was in the paper, but I said he was shitting me. You can't believe nothing in that paper. It's run by the Stones."

I adjust the ball cap on my head and haul the large piece of luggage off the bed. I'm surprised our wedding announcement was in the paper. I guess Piper must've slipped it in there. She loaned me her truck to make this trip, after all, since I can't haul shit on a bike. I'm still getting used to having people wanting to help me everywhere I turn.

"I'm married." My voice is flat, and I walk over to where my dad is standing in his robe.

His hair sticks out around his head, and he rubs his hand over the yellowed T-shirt covering his stomach. "Your momma would be real proud of you, son."

I pull him in for a hug, wondering for a brief moment

who'll look out for him when I'm gone. "I want you to eat something today, and I'll swing by and check on you after I'm settled."

I know my brother won't do anything, and I don't know when Bender's planning to be back in town.

"Who's going to keep the place looking nice?" His old voice is scratchy, and I glance at Bull hulking in the doorway.

Yeah, not him.

"Were you even planning to tell me you're moving out?" Bull straightens when I approach like he'll block my way.

All my shit fits in one suitcase, but I have an extra bag of supplies for Porkchop. "I'm moving out."

"The fuck?" He grabs my arm. "Who the fuck did you marry?"

I jerk my arm out of his grip and carry the bags through the door. "Nobody you need to worry about."

The last thing I need is his dumb ass thinking he'll get anywhere near Jemima or Nikki.

"I didn't even know you were serious about anybody." He follows me into the yard.

"There's a lot you don't know."

I turn back, and he pokes a finger against my shoulder. "I don't like your attitude. You can't just make a life change like this without telling me. You think you're better than me or something?"

"No." My jaw is tight. I'm not planning to fight my brother before I leave today, but I will. "I just think I make better choices than you do, but that doesn't make me better than you. It makes me smarter."

"Is that so?" He puts a hand on his hip.

"Yep." I give a sharp whistle through my teeth, and Porkchop comes running around from the back of the shed.

He hops all around me, and I lean down to attach the leash to his collar. His tongue is out, and he looks for all it's worth like he's smiling.

"You're not taking that dog." Bull steps between me and the truck, and I stop.

"Get out of my way."

His scarred lip tightens, and instead of stepping back, he crosses his arms. "You'd better show up for the job. I already said you'd be there, and it's too late to find a replacement."

"I'll be there." It's a heavy weight in my chest, but I'm keeping my word.

Reaching for the passenger door of the truck, I move him out of the way.

His arms uncross, but he's not backing down. "Good, because these guys don't respond well to people breaking their word. I'd hate to be part of a team coming to find you."

"Would you?"

I know first-hand my brother really enjoys beating the shit out of people when they're being held on the ground. Street justice, he calls it.

"Don't fuck around and find out."

My jaw tightens, and a new layer is added to this fucked up mess I've gotten myself into. I still need the money, but if that's all it was, I could still walk away. Now everything I do impacts Jemima and Nikki, and I can't let them get hurt.

Fuck. And I just said I was smarter than this asshole.

"I said I'll be there." My tone is flat.

"Good luck, son." I look up to see my dad standing in the doorway, and my stomach twists.

The old man. He has no idea the devil's lurking around his door.

"Thanks, Dad."

One day I'll be back to get him, but today isn't the day. Today I'm getting out of hell.

I'm doing what I should've done years ago. I just never had a good enough reason.

"Porkchop!" Nikki is waiting when I pull into the parking lot in front of the newspaper office.

She opens the latch on the wooden gate surrounding the small yard and runs to the side of the truck. I lean over to un-lock the door for her.

Porkchop sat on the seat the whole drive, and when we got into town, he bobbed his head, looking all around like he was on some kind of doggy adventure.

Now Nikki is sitting in the truck hugging him, and his tongue is hanging out.

"I'm pretty sure he has no idea what's going on." I hand her the leash. "It's only the third time he's been out of our yard."

"He's going to like it here. You'll see." She leads him out of the truck, and he jumps forward so hard, it jerks her whole body.

"You got him?" I lean forward, watching as she guides him to the small house.

"I've got him!" She opens the gate and pushes him inside with her butt as she pulls it closed again. "He's the coolest dog ever, and I'm going to teach him how to mind."

Exhaling a laugh, I close and lock the truck before grabbing my suitcase and setting it inside the fence. "Good luck with that."

Leaving home wasn't as bad as I'd anticipated. I knew Bull was going to be a pain in the ass, and I fully expect the place to turn into a dump now that I'm not there to pick up the trash he drops on the ground beside the garbage cans.

I do worry about my dad, though. He's getting worse, and his disability check only goes so far. Getting him off the hooch is at the top of my to-do list once I get my shit straight.

"That's a very serious look, Mr. Jones." The sweet voice melts all the worries pressing against my chest, and I turn to see Jemima stepping across the small alley that separates her office from our house.

Our house. It's a strange thought to hold in my mind. This

little place where we're getting started. Or something. I guess it's all temporary, even if it keeps feeling like it's real more and more.

I put an arm around her shoulders as she hugs me. "Just thinking about my dad."

"Was he sad to see you go?"

"I don't know." I exhale a breath. "I expect he'll miss me after a while, but I don't know how much he's drinking these days."

Her telling me what she did about her own childhood formed an unexpected bond between us. I never would've thought Cass's little sister would've grown up almost the same way I did. The primary difference between us is having somebody somewhere waiting at the end to throw you a lifeline.

I guess I have something like that now, too.

"I'm sorry." She looks up, and knowing the empathy in her eyes is real makes me hold her closer.

It makes me want to track down that Bill character and kick his ass.

"We don't have to worry about it tonight. I'll check on him, and my brother's there."

"I've never met your brother." She tilts her head to the side. "Is he like you?"

"No."

That makes her laugh, but she has no idea.

And I have no intention of her finding out how different we are.

"If he comes snooping around here, you text me. He's not a nice person."

Her eyes widen. "Do you think he'd try to hurt me?"

A low fire ignites in my chest at the suggestion. I don't think he'd be that stupid, but I can't guarantee it.

Even if he behaves, I don't want him insulting her, and I really don't want him telling her things she doesn't need to know about me. I'm stuck doing this last job, but when it's done, so is my affiliation with him and his outlaw friends.

"Just text me."

"Okay." She kisses my cheek. "I've got to finish up a lay-out, then I'll head home. Want me to give Piper her keys back?"

"Yeah, thanks." I catch her cheeks in my hands wanting a better kiss. I slip my tongue in for a sweet taste of sugar, and she blinks a few times like she's in a daze. It makes me chuckle. "Don't worry about dinner. I'll take care of it."

Exhaling a hum, she does a little twirl towards the alley. "Good, because I told you I'm a lousy cook."

By the time she shows up for dinner, I've got meatloaf with mashed potatoes and gravy ready and waiting. It's not super complicated. The potatoes are from a box, and the meatloaf is about the only thing that took any effort, although it's a pretty simple recipe—one egg, breadcrumbs, and Worcester sauce.

All through dinner, Nikki wears her headphones and watches *SpongeBob SquarePants* on her phone. Jemima has her phone beside her plate as well, and her foot is in her chair with her knee bent.

"Oh! Look at this one." She swipes through pictures of Mardi Gras decorations. "What do you think?"

My brow is furrowed, and I'm not sure if I should say what I think so soon. I watch as she taps and sends the pictures to her group of friends.

She and Nikki do the dishes, and then Nikki runs outside to tell Porkchop goodnight and make sure he likes his new home. When we're finally alone together in bed, I pin Jemima beneath me, holding her shoulders and kissing her soft neck.

"I know you and Nikki have a system going here, and I'm just along for the ride—"

"What?" Her brow furrows, and she puts her palms against my chest, holding me back. "You're not just along for the ride. You're part of the family. We're a team."

"In that case, I think we ought to talk to each other at dinner."

Her eyes widen, and she appears genuinely confused. "What do you mean? I was talking to you! I showed you all the costumes and garlands and…"

"Nikki had her headphones in and she was watching cartoons the whole time."

"She loves doing that." Jemima smiles like it's nothing. "All the kids are into *SpongeBob* now. Isn't that funny?"

"She needs to talk to us. How else will we know what's going on with her?"

Jemima's brow furrows, and she looks to the side. "I always talk to her on the way to school or at night when I'm scratching her back at bedtime. Although, I guess I haven't done that in a few days."

"After my mom died, nobody gave a shit what I thought. I don't want her to feel that way."

"You are so sweet." Jemima slides her finger up and over my ear.

"I told you about that."

She exhales a soft laugh. "Right. You're *not* sweet, but you are making our little family better."

A strange sense of pride swells in my chest, and I study this woman in my arms. My wife, who sees me as trying to make things better. Nobody has ever suggested the Jones boys made anything better until her. Hell if I know what I'm talking about, but I fucking want to prove her right.

Leaning forward, I cover her mouth with mine. A sigh of pleasure slips from her throat, and a surge of heat moves through my pelvis. Covering her body with my lips, it's too late to call this temporary. She's too precious to me, and I want to make her feel how much has changed. I want her to know I don't plan to walk away when this is over, and I want her to feel the same.

"Porkchop knows his name!" I'm standing at the stove when Nikki runs in from the yard.

Her face is flushed, and she's breathing fast. "He only poops behind the shed, and I think he's getting better at not jerking on the leash!"

"My dad didn't like dog crap in the yard." God forbid he'd clean it up. "The dogs learned to hide to do their business."

She doesn't need to know why.

My brow lowers, as I think. Jemima said I'm improving the family, but maybe they're improving me as well. I can't remember the last time I said *crap* and *business* instead of plain ole *shit*. I sound like some kind of fucking librarian.

"That means he's smart!" She's so determined to make Porkchop a hero, I don't want to burst her bubble.

"Wash your hands. I can't vouch for how clean he is."

Jemima breezes in the door. "Not too late, I hope?" She skips over to kiss my cheek, and I catch her face, pulling her to me for a quick tongue kiss.

I like the way it makes her sort of melt every time I do it. I guess I'll know we're in trouble if that ever changes.

When I turn to the stove again, she stands behind me, digging her thumbs into the tight muscles of my shoulders. "This smells good."

Lowering my arms, I exhale a groan. "That feels good."

She exhales a soft laugh, looking over my shoulder. "Is it a Jones family recipe?"

"No." I lean back to kiss her cheek before she skips off to our bedroom, and I catch Nikki watching us with a frown.

When our eyes meet, she looks down at her phone. "Why are some animals black and white?"

"Don't know." I take the pot of spaghetti off the stove and dump it into the colander in the sink, then I go back to the stove where the meat sauce is bubbling.

"Britt's mother Gwen would say it's remnants of a time when the world was only light and shadow." Jemima spreads her hands and wiggles her fingers as she returns to the kitchen in black leggings and a pale blue sweater that falls off one shoulder. "She's a mystic, you know."

"I thought she was a psychic." I take the spaghetti sauce off the fire and pour it into a bowl for the table.

"Psychic, mystic. Same diff." Jemima shrugs, sitting down and putting her foot in her chair.

Her phone is out by her plate as well, and I watch as she pulls up her group chat. Nikki is still frowning at me, but I'm frowning now, too as I put the spaghetti in a bowl and carry it to the table.

"What's wrong?" I sit at my place, meeting Nikki's disapproving gaze.

"That's not how Jemima does it." Her lips poke out. "She puts the sauce on top of the noodles and stirs it all together."

Jemima blinks up to join the conversation. "Oh, Nikki, that was when I made Hamburger Helper. What Raif made is a lot better—"

"He's not better than you!" Her voice rises. "That's not how we do it."

Jemima exhales a nervous laugh, glancing from her to me. "We don't have a way of doing it…"

"Yes, we do!" Nikki stands out of her seat, frowning harder.

"What's our way, honey?" Jemima tilts her head, and the worry in her eyes makes my chest tighten uncomfortably.

"You make the meat in the pot, then you dump the box in!"

"But, sweetie—"

"And you sing to me at night, and you scratch my back!" Nikki runs up the stairs, and Jemima's foot slips off her chair.

She watches her go, then looks at me. "What just happened?"

Passing a hand over my mouth, I stand slowly. "Let me talk to her."

When I reach the top of the narrow staircase, I hear muffled crying from her room. A pang of guilt is in my stomach, and I try to think what I would've done at her age if I'd been living with my mom and somebody like me suddenly joined the party.

I was only a little older than she is now when I lost my mom, and the only thing I wanted was everything to go back to the way it was before.

Reaching out I tap lightly on the door. "Nikki?"

She sits up fast, wiping her face on her sleeve. "Yeah?"

"Hang on." I step across the hall into the small bathroom to grab a washcloth, holding it under the cold water and giving it a squeeze.

I walk over to sit beside her on the bed and hand it to her. "I'm sorry if I made you cry."

"She said nothing was going to change." A pout is in her voice, and I press my lips together. "Now everything is changing, and she loves you more than she loves me."

Those words hit me right in the gut. I imagine Jemima loving me, and I confess, it makes me feel a little winded and a lot good.

Clearing my throat, I know Nikki is important to her. I know if I have a snowball's chance in hell, this is one problem I've got to handle correctly.

"I don't think Jemima loves anyone more than you." I put my hand on her little shoulder. "I wouldn't be here if she didn't love you."

Her nose wrinkles, and she looks up at me. "What does that mean?"

Then I realize she's clueless about why we really got married, so I redirect. "She knows how much you love Porkchop, and I guess she thought I'd be useful to have around to cook for you all and keep you safe."

"And sleep in her bed."

Nodding, I can't argue with that. "She was wrong to say nothing would change, but we're trying to make them *good* changes."

Her small mouth presses into a line, and she holds the wash-cloth against her cheek. "Porkchop's a good change."

"He's your friend." I clear my throat. "I'd like to be your friend, too, if you'll let me."

Her brown eyes slide to mine, and I can't remember a time when I was vulnerable, when I wasn't fighting everybody. Now I'm in this house with this kid and this woman who's turning my world around.

"You want to be my dad?" The skepticism in her voice breaks the tension building in my chest.

I exhale a laugh, shaking my head. "No, I can be more like an uncle or maybe a cousin you like hanging out with. Is that better?"

"Hey…" Jemima's soft voice warms the room, and I look up at her thinking about words like *love* and *family*.

Maybe it's too soon, like a fine suit of clothes I can't afford to buy yet, but I sure like the way it feels when I try it on.

She walks over and sits on the other side of Nikki. "I'm sorry. I'm messing everything up again. I'll scratch your back and sing to you tonight and every night—that's not changing—and Raif really likes you, and we can have Hamburger Helper some nights if you want it."

Nikki falls into Jemima's chest, pressing her face against her sweater and hugging her arms around her waist.

"I'm sorry." The little girl's voice is muffled in the layers, and tears flood Jemima's eyes as she hugs her back.

I scoot closer, putting my arms around both of them. I guess this is what it's like to have a house full of women, but I'll take it any day over the burping and shit-talking at my old place.

It's exactly what I want.

"You didn't mess up anything." I kiss the top of Jemima's head. "It's just a little growing pains."

She lifts her chin, blinking through her misty eyes. "We'd better have that good dinner you made before it gets cold." She nudges Nikki. "Okay?"

Later, after dinner is eaten and the plates cleaned, after Nikki has gone outside to take selfies with Porkchop again, we're back in this room. Nikki is in her bed, and Jemima is lying beside her. I sit on the floor with my back to the wall and my knees bent watching as my pretty wife scratches Nikki's back and sings a haunting song about ships and ghosts.

Her voice is so pretty, it's like I'm watching something magical happen, like a dream or a vision. She sings the words over and over, and I think about where we are and what lies ahead. How much I want to be her man and I don't want to wreck any plans.

Chapter 23

Jemima

"I CAN'T BELIEVE HOW FAST IT GOT HERE!" CASS IS DECKED OUT IN black leggings and a light purple sweatshirt with sequined king cakes all over it. "It seems like just yesterday we were missing out on your wedding."

"It was only a week ago, and you didn't miss out. We wanted it small." I pull my hair up in a green, purple, and gold sequined scrunchie.

She's standing at the door of our bedroom while I pull a gold sequined jacket over my white tank top and jeans.

"It's Tuesday, so it was eleven days." My sister's arms are crossed as she watches me, and she tilts her dark head to the side. "How is married life?"

I can feel the flush creeping up my cheeks, and she starts to laugh. "That good? In this little house with a nine-year-old?"

"I've been working late on the Valentine's Day spread all week."

"I see." She gives me a sly smile, and Monay walks through the kitchen to where we're standing.

"Is she using work as a cover story again?" My towering friend waves her purple green and gold manicured nails. "I wouldn't be surprised if the big day came and not a single Valentine's Day ad is in that paper."

"That is not true!" I follow her out into the kitchen. "I *have* been working. I've also been taking breaks every so often to recharge."

Monay shakes her elaborately up-done platinum wig, and starts to laugh. She's in a sequined purple bell-bottomed pantsuit, and her drag friends Shauntay and Zenighta are each wearing gold and green pant suits to match. The three of them are walking dogs in the Mardi Gras Dog Parade today, leading up to the big gala tonight.

"Happy Mardi Gras! Everywhere else it's only Tuesday!" Britt sing-songs, walking through the door carrying a platter of cupcakes decorated in Mardi Gras colors. "You should see the doggy floats lined up outside the newspaper office. All the trees are covered in beads, and I've never seen so many dogs in tutus and jester hats. Why haven't we been doing this every year?"

"Mamma Cass! Mamma Cass!" Pinky bursts into the kitchen right behind Britt holding Angie Dickinson under her arm and wearing a pink sweatshirt with sequined king cakes all over it that reads *Let Her Eat Cake*. Her strawberry-blonde hair is tied up in two ponytails with purple, green, and gold tinsel, and she's wearing white marching boots.

"Porkchop won't stay on his float!" Her eyes are round, and she's talking loudly. "Uncle Raif said he might have to stay home, and Nikki started to cry!"

"Uh-oh." I start for the door with my sister right behind me.

"Here we go," Cass laughs, giving her daughter's shoulder a squeeze. "Don't worry. We'll get Porkchop in the parade."

"Try hot dogs!" Britt yells after them, and I hear Monay speaking to Pinky.

"I think Angie Dickinson has found her soulmate in you, little princess."

"We're bonded." Pinky's voice is very wise.

Out on the lawn, Raif stands beside a wagon built up with wooden sides painted purple, green, and gold with matching lights and garlands. His arms are crossed, and he appears to be in problem-solving mode.

He's definitely in sexy-husband mode in his dark jeans and purple tee that reads *Throw Me Something, Mister,* with his long hair pulled back in a tiny ponytail and little pieces falling out.

Porkchop's head is lowered under the weight of a small, Mardi-Gras-themed jester hat with tiny gold bells on the points, and he actually seems embarrassed. A matching sequined bow tie is around his neck, and Nikki kneels beside him in her jeans and a white sweatshirt with a king cake on the front and *Lover* spelled out in sequins underneath it.

She's hugging him and looking distraught. "He has to be in the parade! We worked so hard."

I place my hand on Raif's crossed arms. "I don't think Porkchop likes his costume."

Raif uncrosses his arms, wrapping one around my waist and kissing the side of my head. A thrill moves through my stomach at his affectionate gesture, like it's the most natural thing in the world.

"He doesn't like it when the wagon moves." He's speaking low, like he doesn't want to agitate the situation.

"Edward can ride in the wagon!" Owen jumps up, loud as ever. "He's smart. He knows it's a special parade, and he won't mess it up!"

Beside him Edward stands placidly in a tiny purple, green, and gold glitter bowler hat, and a collar with tiny pom-poms in Mardi Gras colors and with masks around his neck. He looks ready for a nap.

"Porkchop is smart!" Nikki shouts back. "He just doesn't like being confined."

"You'll never get Fudge to ride in a wagon." Ryan seems to be trying to be the diplomat.

Fudge sits above the fray on the fence beside the flower boxes. I'm impressed he has a sparkly Mardi Gras collar around his neck. The boys are both wearing jeans and colorful T-shirts and beads. All the kids have beads and plastic top hats covered in Mardi-Gras-colored glitter.

"What if Porkchop walked in the parade like the other dogs?" I nod to where Shauntay and Zenighta stand chatting on the sidewalk.

Shauntay wears a long, straight Beyoncé wig, and she's holding a tan Pomeranian who's dressed in a sparkly Mardi Gras tutu. Zenighta is in full-Zendaya mode and holds the leash on a friendly looking lab wearing the same jester hat and bow tie as Porkchop.

"But we decorated the wagon for him!" Nikki walks to where I'm holding onto Raif. "It even says *Free-Range Pork Floats My Boat!*"

I hold back a snort, sliding a long curl behind her ear. "I know, but the main thing is that he's in the parade, right? You can walk him with Monay and the girls and the other dogs. It'll be just as fun."

"He still jerks on the leash." Her face scrunches, and she looks to where Owen is trying to get Edward into the wagon. "And we didn't decorate the wagon for *Edward*."

My eyes widen, and I look at Raif. He takes a knee beside Nikki, putting his hand on her waist. "Porkchop has a lot of energy. He'd probably prefer his old buddy Edward take his place. You know, Edward's not as young as he used to be. He might get tired walking all the way around the square."

Her eyes light, and the tables seem to turn. "Yeah, Edward's so *old*, he probably wouldn't even make it to the end of the parade route if he had to walk the whole way."

Covering my mouth with my hand, I look carefully from Nikki to Owen and back at Raif still kneeling beside her.

He gives her a little squeeze. "Now don't say that too loud. It's not nice to be ageist."

She frowns. "What's *ageist?*"

"It's when you make fun of somebody because they're old. Like you wouldn't tease Mrs. Edna because she's older, would you?"

"No!" Her eyes widen. "That's wrong."

"Good." He nods. "It's our secret."

I jump in to reinforce his brilliance. "And won't it be fun to walk with the Mardi Gras queens? You might need to borrow a wig from Monay."

"Girl, don't be loaning out my wigs without my permission." Monay walks up beside us. "What's happening?"

Pinky prances up beside her in her boots, holding Angie Dickinson like she's a prized possession.

"Are they still trying to get that dog in the wagon?" Pinky puts her hand on her hip like she's so exhausted with this scene. "Just let him walk with the queens and the princesses!"

"That's right, little cher!" Monay pats her shoulder. "You are indeed the queen of the princesses."

"Whatever that means," I laugh.

We're attaching the leash when Annabelle strolls past holding Bo's leash. "Hi, Nikki. I like your dog float."

She's less elementary-school it-girl today in simple jeans and a Mardi Gras sweatshirt, and I hold my breath, waiting to see what will happen.

"Hi, Annabelle." Nikki is very casual, giving Porkchop another hug before standing. "Edward's going use it. We're walking with the queens."

Annabelle glances to where Monay towers over Pinky, who is completely preoccupied with Angie Dickinson.

"Cool," she says, continuing on her way.

My eyes slide to Nikki. "That was… good?"

"She's okay, I guess. We decided to be friends."

Pressing my lips together, I nod slowly as Piper joins us.

She's dressed in Mardi Gras regalia like everyone else, and her face is flushed from running around.

"Doug's ready with the music, and Harold has the mic. Let's get this doggy parade rolling!"

I kiss Raif's cheek. "Looks like you've got everything under control. I have to lead us off with Piper."

"We'll be right behind you."

I wave to the queens, who are practicing their arm movements. I pass Holly with Myrtle and all her piglets out in tutus and tiaras. They're assorted colors, and some are bigger than others. Some have a bit of a wild look about them, and Holly has been making cracks about Raif's float being offensive.

I lean into Piper's ear and whisper, "I thought this was a *dog* parade."

"Myrtle is as smart as a dog, haven't you heard?" Piper winks. "Plus, she's a celebrity."

"Who got knocked up by a hog from the wrong side of the tracks." I start to laugh.

"As long as she paid the walking fee, we're not judging."

A trumpet blasts, and the second-line song begins. A cheer rises from the crowd, and it send a thrill through my chest.

Harold launches into his welcome speech, thanking everyone for coming out to the inaugural Mardi Gras dog parade, and the wagons start to roll.

Piper and I each have baskets of beads we hand to the children and shiny Mardi-Gras doubloons. The parade only goes around town square, but it's impressive to see the number of people crowding the grassy field and lining the sidewalks in front of the local businesses.

Adam joins us as we pass El Rio. "Herve said he's sold a record number of hurricanes and margaritas just since noon." He hands decorated cups to Piper and me. "Virgin margarita for you, and a fully leaded hurricane for you."

I take a sip of the bright red drink adorned with cherries

and slices of orange. "This is a dangerous drink. I can't taste any alcohol at all!"

"Take it easy. I watched him make it."

Adam takes the basket of doubloons and helps me hand them to the kids as we round the first corner. We're walking slowly to be sure none of the dogs—or pigs—get spooked. It's not a long route, so everyone should make it to the end.

I walk closer to the sidewalk, handing beads to children on parents' shoulders, when I notice a guy with dark hair watching me. He has a scar on his lip and tattoos on his neck, and he's not smiling.

Turning away quickly, I scoot back to where Adam is helping Piper pick up a fallen dog's hat.

"It's not that bending over is hard," she laughs, holding her growing baby bump, "It's just awkward in all this regalia."

"Let me help." I toss the rest of my drink into a trash can as we pass, feeling uneasy about the strange man watching me.

I take her beads and hand them to the spectators. Glancing over my shoulder, I've lost sight of him, but my eye catches Raif's from where he's several yards behind us with Owen and Nikki.

The queens are behind him waving and blowing kisses as they lead their dogs, and Pinky prances with Angie Dickinson under her arm doing the same. Nikki is behind them holding Porkchop's leash, and at a glance, it looks like he *is* getting better at staying with her. It's gratifying with how consistently she's been working with him.

I watch her fall back beside Raif, who's pulling the wagon holding Edward while Owen walks beside it handing out beads, and my heart warms when I see her hold his hand.

I almost exhale a little sob of relief remembering our difficult night. He was so good with her, then he crept into the bedroom and sat quietly listening to me sing. It was the most perfect, family moment. It's so hard to think of this as temporary.

He smiles when his eye catches mine, but as if he senses

my unease, it melts a bit. His brow furrows as if asking me a silent question. Shaking my head, I return to waving and handing out beads.

The music changes to the "Mardi Gras Mambo" as we close in on the finish line. The rest of the parade is still going behind us, and we walk to the staging area where Harold is calling out the names of all the doggy participants and their owners as they roll past in decorated wagons or baby carriages or on foot.

Piper takes a seat on the raised platform beside him, and I walk through the crowd in the grassy center of the loop handing out the rest of my beads.

I haven't gotten far when a male voice pulls me up short. "I heard you're the new Mrs. Jones."

Straightening my shoulders, I look up at the man with the scar and the neck tattoos. "I am."

"The fucking Stones." He shakes his head as if he's disgusted, and I look around quickly as if I can somehow shield the children present. "That little shit always wanted to be something we're not."

I push my hair off my shoulders. "I'm sorry, I didn't catch your name."

"I didn't pitch it." He scowls down at me like I'm a bug to be squashed.

"Are these for us?" A little girl pulls on my sequined sleeve, and I realize she's pointing to the beads in my hand.

"Yes!" I take three and loop them over her head.

More children appear, and I hand her the small bag. "Take them all, and y'all run give them to everybody, okay? Make sure all the kids have them!"

They take off running, and when I turn back, the man is still watching me.

"What's your name?" he growls.

"None of your business." Raif appears at my side, putting his arm around my waist and moving me behind him.

It hasn't been very long since I was on my own against men

like this one, but I have to confess, it sure is nice to have someone looking out for me.

"I'm not allowed to know my sister-in-law's name?"

My eyes widen, and I peek out from behind Raif's shoulder. "You're Bull?"

"Everything okay over here?" Aiden walks up, and Bull swears under his breath, shaking his head.

"Fucking Stones." Bull sneers at Raif. "I guess you think hooking up with them is going to make you legit. You think you're going to be someone?"

"I don't think anything except you'll treat my wife with respect." Raif's expression is dark, and I put my hand on his arm.

"It's okay. I'm glad to meet your brother."

"You've met him. Now we've got to get back." Raif takes my arm, pulling me behind him again.

"Unless you've got something to say, you'd better head on, Bull." Aiden straightens the top of his belt. "This is a family event."

"Family event with a bunch of drag queens." He nods in the direction of Monay and the girls, and now I'm getting mad.

"They're part of our family." I stand straighter, stepping out from behind Raif.

Bull's eyebrows rise, and he exhales loudly. "Okay, I'm starting to see what my brother likes about you."

Raif lunges, but Aiden cuts him off, moving between the three of us. "If that's all you wanted." Warning is in his tone.

"I need to speak to my brother." Bull growls at Aiden. "If that's still allowed."

"Okay." Aiden puts his hand on my shoulder, moving me away.

Raif's jaw is tight, but when he sees Aiden has me, he steps closer. The two of them turn away, but I hear Bull say something about tonight.

Raif looks up at him confused, and a lump is in my throat. I don't know what they're saying, and I don't like it. Bull isn't a good person, and I'm starting to see why Raif didn't want me around him.

His brother nods and takes a step back. "Nice to meet you, Princess." His dark eyes slide down me in a way that leaves me feeling naked. "My little brother might drag you down to his level, but I bet you're pretty on your knees."

Raif moves so fast, I almost don't see him. He holds the front of Bull's shirt, but Aiden is just as fast, catching his arm before he slams his fist into his brother's ugly face.

"Not here, man." Aiden grunts, pulling Raif away. "Time to go, Bull."

"Yeah, I'm done." Bull turns and swaggers, backing away.

Raif's nostrils flare, and I can see the flames in his eyes when he returns to me. He loops his arm around my waist, pulling me tight to his side, and all his muscles are tense with anger. I don't know why I'm shaking.

"I'm sorry about that," he says quietly, kissing the top of my forehead.

Hugging closer to him, I tuck my head under his chin. "He's not the first creep I've ever encountered."

"You're my wife now, and I'm not letting another creep near you."

Warmth squeezes my heart, and I exhale a breath of relief. I've always been afraid. I learned early to always be aware of my surroundings, but lately it's becoming less of a fact of life.

Rising onto my tiptoes, I kiss his cheek. "I love knowing you have my back."

His eyes meet mine, and his expression relaxes. "I've got your front, too."

My brow furrows, and I study the direction his brother went. "What was he talking about *tonight*?"

The muscle in Raif's jaw moves, and he hugs an arm around my shoulders, pulling me into his side. "It's nothing."

"Nothing?" I tilt my head back to meet his eyes.

"Just something he wanted me to help him with."

A trickle of worry tightens my chest. "But we have the gala tonight…"

"And I wouldn't miss it for anything."

We're approaching the mob of children and dogs and drag queens, and the music has changed to a happy zydeco classic, "Don't Mess With My Toot-Toot." The kids laugh every time the words toot-toot are spoken.

Pinky marches in her white boots, and Angie Dickinson dances all around her feet in her pink tutu. Nikki throws a frisbee, and Porkchop takes off after it while Owen watches with his arms crossed, and Ryan walks around with Fudge draped over his shoulder like a cat-fur stole.

It's all joyful and celebratory, and Piper is thrilled with how much we've raised for the paper, but when I look at Raif, I can't relax.

Whatever his brother said has him on edge, and I can't shake my sense of dread. He puts his hands on my waist and starts to dance, and I hug my arms around him hoping I'm just being paranoid.

Chapter 24

Raif

'M STANDING IN THE SMALL LIVING ROOM IN MY WHITE TIE AND white vest waiting for Jemima. My black tailcoat is lying on the back of the chair, and I'm thinking about what's coming tonight.

My brother showing up and showing his ass this afternoon has had me on edge. Jemima tried to smooth it over, but it's going to take a mighty effort not to punch him in the dick if I see him tonight.

Hell, I shouldn't see him at all. I don't plan to get that close.

The kids are all at Aiden's mother Patricia's house for the night. Piper reassured us the old lady loves keeping all the kids, and she has a trampoline, movies, and all the games and snacks to keep them entertained.

Nikki was worried about leaving Porkchop, but I assured her he'd be fine. He's like me—we're not so far removed from our old life that we don't remember it.

As for me, not much has changed other than I walk to work these days, and I go to bed and wake up with the most beautiful girl in the world in my arms. I want to give her everything. I don't want her to worry about anything, but Bull's appearance today put me on guard.

My old life is never too far away.

Going to where I stashed my bag on the very top shelf in the laundry room, I pull it down and remove the leather case holding my Glock. I haven't used it since the day Jemima and I went hunting, and I don't like having it out now.

Still, I check it to be sure it's loaded then lock it up in its case again before returning it to the top shelf. I'm just entering the living room when she steps out of our bedroom, and I stop in my tracks.

The black lace of her dress wraps around her body in a design that just covers her private parts. It stops at the top of her thighs, and the sheer overlay hangs to the floor. A sheer lace mask is over her eyes, and her red lips are full and pouty.

She takes my breath away.

"Do you like it?" She does a little turn, and I slide my hand down the front of my pants to calm my dick.

Closing the space between us, I tilt her face up to meet my eyes. "You are so beautiful. I really like this mask." I slide my finger along the sheer black lace.

"Thank you, Mr. Jones." A naughty glint is in her eyes. "We have the house to ourselves tonight."

I exhale a breath, shaking my head. "How long do we have to stay at this thing?"

She laughs, going to the kitchen counter and lifting what looks like a black silk scarf. "This is for you."

Walking to where she stands, I turn my back. "Help me with it."

Her sweet jasmine scent surrounds me when she lifts her arms and ties the mask over my eyes. It reminds me of our first night together, showering together. It feels so long ago, but it was only a few weeks.

When I turn around to face her, her eyes widen, and her cheeks flush a pretty pink. "You look really good."

A grin lifts my lips. "I guess we're learning something new."

"Masks are sexy? Is that new?"

Reaching out, I pull her to me, leaning down to trace my nose along the top of her forehead, along the line of her hair and down to her ear. "My new wife is sexy."

Her shoulder shivers, and I'm ready to ditch this gala.

"We'd better go," she sighs. "I'm afraid if we stay here much longer, we won't make it, and I told Piper I'd cover the late shift for her."

"Damn." I thread her fingers in mine, lifting my jacket off the back of the chair. "Maybe we can find a coat closet at the distillery."

"A vacant office." Her heels click on the wood as she follows me out the door.

It's the first time I've driven my bike in a week. Jemima has a better helmet now, and I wait for her to tie her long hair in a scrunchie before securing it on her head.

"Good thing I didn't plan an elaborate updo." She grins at me from behind the visor, and she's too cute. "Monay would not do well on a bike."

"She'd have to rethink that wig." I tease, giving the starter a kick.

"It would be a real test of her commitment to the relationship." Her arms are around my waist, and I lean back to kiss her cheek.

"I'd let you win."

Her face presses to my shoulder, and we cruise out of the parking lot, following the road out to the narrow highway leading to the distillery.

The parking lot is packed when we arrive. Twinkle lights and beads fill the small trees, and music echoes across the fields from the live band.

I park close to the front in the one space for a motorcycle, and Jemima takes a minute to arrange her hair, pick out her bangs and straighten her mask.

"All set?" She blinks up at me, and I kiss the tip of her nose.

"Good as new."

Twining our fingers, we walk hand in hand to the entrance. The girl manning the ticket table waves us inside, and Cass is the first person we see. She's wearing a similar black dress as her sister, although it has more fabric. She's also wearing a dark lace mask.

"You look amazing!" Cass cries, throwing out her arm. "We're twinning!"

I stand back watching them, and except for the hair color, they are very similar. They're both tall and really pretty, and I've heard Cass sing.

"Raif?" Alex Stone walks up. "How's it going, man? Is this your first time at Stone Cold?"

I look around the massive wooden structure. Huge oak barrels line the walls, and it's all polished wood and brass. It smells like leather, and it has the feel of an old lodge built from old money.

"I usually go to El Rio."

"Welcome." He shakes my hand, which is new. "I hear you've been working with Martha?"

"Yeah." I slide my hand down the front of my coat. "She wanted an addition."

"My grandfather was a contractor." Alex hands me a tumbler of scotch. "He worked hard all his life. If it weren't for him, this place wouldn't exist."

I taste the expensive bourbon and nod. I don't really know

bourbon, but I know Bender's always raving about this being the best. "Good stuff."

"That's his recipe. Pop used to say the only place you find *success* coming before *work* is in the dictionary."

"Sounds like a smart guy." I look down at the tumbler, trying to imagine any of the Stones starting from scratch.

I guess one of them had to do it.

"He loved to fish. Do you fish?"

"Never tried it."

"Tell you what, I'll get your number from Cass, and we can give it a try one afternoon."

"Okay."

"Have a good time." He points at me before stepping behind the bar.

I glance down at the crystal tumbler in my hand wondering what just happened. The richest man in town just shook my hand and welcomed me into his world, and it's kind of messing with my head. I'm trying to shake my brother's pronouncement that I'll never be one of them, but it's hard to turn on a dime.

I'm surrounded by all the people who've never liked or trusted me or my family, and they're all wearing masks. I need to find Jemima.

She's talking to Piper, who's dressed in a high-waisted shimmery beige dress. Wide gold cuffs are on her wrists, and her mask is pushed up into her red hair, which is piled high on her head.

I start to go to them when a familiar female voice stops me. "You clean up nice."

Martha Jackson is one of the last people I expected to see here. She's wearing fatigue-green cargo pants and a gold shirt with purple and yellow feathers in the pockets. It's pretty much what I'd expect to see on her.

"Thanks." I nod to her outfit. "You're festive."

"Pfft, I'm not wearing all that filmy see-through and

sequins." She waves her hand at the room full of ball gowns. "I'm not Gwen."

"Gwen's here?" I'm actually encouraged to hear this.

If Gwen is here, that means Bender might be here, and I'll feel less like the fly in the buttermilk.

"She's around here somewhere. Covered in stars." Martha surveys the room. "I don't like all these masks." She leans closer to my chest. "With those back doors open to the woods like that, anybody could walk in here."

Shit. That puts me on guard, and I stand a little straighter. I've lost sight of Jemima again. "They don't have security out there?"

"My daughter says they do, but you can't stop a determined intruder."

I'm used to Martha's paranoia, but she makes a point. All the men are in the same white tie and tails as me, and now the masks make them all suspicious.

My eyes finally land on Jemima. She's across the dance floor now, talking to Britt and Aiden. Britt is wearing a dark purple strapless dress with a bright green ribbon running across her chest and down the sides and bottom.

Aiden looks… the same as me. Gwen is not too far behind her in a black floor-length dress covered in silver stars, and I hope that means Bender is over there.

"I think I'll just stay close to Jemima. You good?"

"Of course—go." She catches my sleeve. "These people are no different than you, Raif. You just haven't been around them as much as I have. You're not who they think you are. I know what that's like."

She pats my arm, and I nod slowly. I can't tell if she's trying to warn me or make me feel better, so I go with, "Thanks."

She waves her hand. "You're welcome."

Jemima meets me halfway around the dance floor. "Sorry!" She kisses my cheek. "I got all tied up with Piper making sure she has everything she needs. She can't stay on her feet as long these days, so she'll be taking off in about an hour. Then she needed me to give something to Britt…"

"No problem." I slide her hair off her cheek, and she smiles up at me.

"Are you having a good time?"

"It's interesting." I survey the crowd filling the elaborate space.

Some people are on the dance floor doing the two-step. Some are doing their own style of dancing. All the women are dressed up in elaborate colorful dresses like fancy birds. The men are identical penguins for the most part, laughing and drinking, slapping each other on the back.

"Interesting?" Jemima's brow furrows. "That's not the same as fun."

"It's really nice." I kiss the side of her head. "Martha was just saying… something. It's okay."

"Martha's so creative." She slides her hand into the crook of my arm. "I've been trying to get Piper to hire her at the paper. She writes the wildest headlines."

"I bet." We walk through the crowd in the direction of the courtyard area, passing Cass on the way.

"Hey, I've been looking for you." She puts her hand on my arm, giving it a squeeze. "I want to apologize."

Jemima's eyes widen, but I'm curious. "For what?"

"I listened to the gossip instead of getting to know you myself. I was worried, and I misjudged you." She pats my arm. "I'm sorry."

I'm not sure what to say, since the gossip isn't all wrong, but I recognize an olive branch when I see one. Taking her hand, I give it a gentle shake.

"You don't have to apologize. I'm used to it."

"But I do." She studies my face, and I feel like she's reading my mind or something. "I can tell my sister is right about you. You're a good man, forgiving and generous."

I almost laugh at that. "I don't have anything to be generous with."

"You do, though." A warm smile curls her lips. "And you will. I can sense it."

She hugs her sister and continues on her way, and I think she's been spending too much time with Gwen.

Jemima snuggles into my side, leading us to the open back doors and out into the courtyard. "Now *that* was interesting."

The moon is a fingernail, and the surroundings are more mysterious outside. It's darker with only the twinkle lights in the trees providing illumination. Jazzy music plays in the background, and small clumps of people sit at metal café tables.

A performer in a black top hat and a vest blows fire in the open grassy area, and we pass a woman in a black mask and sequined bodysuit balancing on a cylinder juggling hoops.

"Wow," Jemima clutches my arm. "Britt's mom lined up a few of her friends to perform. I was expecting carnival stuff, but they're more like Cirque du Soleil."

"They're pretty badass."

"It's all so beautiful." Jemima sighs, taking a sip of champagne. She points to my tumbler of bourbon. "Did Alex give you that?"

"Yeah." I tilt it to the side.

"Then it's his special reserve, very expensive."

"It tastes like whiskey." I reach for her waist and pull her close. She's the one person in this whole damn place who I can relax around. "Dance with me."

Her hands slide up my shoulders, and in her heels, our faces are almost cheek to cheek. I don't recognize the slow song, but it has a steady beat.

"It's the first time we've danced since that night on the beach." She looks up at me.

Lowering my face, I kiss the top of her shoulder. "We can always dance in the kitchen."

"I'd like that." Her sweet voice is soft in my ear, and I want to be lost in this moment.

This is what I crave—her in my arms. I'd like to put her on the back of my bike and ride out of here at top speed, away from the heavy task hanging over my head to a place where it's just us and peace, safety.

The music fades, and we step apart, threading our fingers and walking to where we left her drink on the table. As we get closer, I notice a fellow sitting in one of the spindly metal chairs. His face is covered in white paint with black lines that make it look like a skull. His suit is not the standard white-tie and tails. He's dressed in black with pinstripes and purple, like the shadow man.

"That's fun." A smile is in her voice, but her fingers tighten on my arm as we get closer. "Oh…"

Her voice dies away as the man stands, placing a black top hat on his head. "Good evening, Jemima. This is quite the event you're hosting."

"Bill." Her voice is a hush. "What are you doing here?"

"I bought a ticket, of course." He whips out the paper stub like it's a rabbit from a hat. "I want to be sure you know that I know where you are. Always."

Protection surges in my chest, and my voice is a growl. "You're Bill?"

"I don't think we've met." His eyes are black. "Bill Wolf, and you are?"

He smiles, extending a confident hand as if he'll intimidate me. Only I'm not scared.

"Raif Jones." I grip his hand firmly, jerking him closer to me, so he can feel my strength. "I heard last time you were here you put your hands on my *wife*."

"Wife?" His eyebrow arches, and he attempts to look past my shoulder at Jemima.

I step to the side, blocking him. "That's right. So you'd better back up, because I'm ready to give you a taste of your own medicine."

"I'm not looking for a fight." He releases my grip, holding up his hands. "Just checking on my girls."

"Which girls are those?" My tone is ice, and it's my turn to give a menacing smile.

"Jemima and Nikki, of course. I don't want them to think I've forgotten about them." His eyes are on mine, but his voice rises to meet Jemima's ears.

Bill Wolf is slim and not quite as tall as I am, but I can tell he's the type who'd shank you in a dark alley without thinking twice. Jemima's fingers are on my arm, and the way she's clinging to me has me ready to grab him by the neck and beat him to a bloody pulp.

"They're not your girls." My voice is a low growl. "And you'd better forget them, or I'll have to erase your memory."

A smile curls his lips. "I consider myself warned."

"You're not warned. You're guaranteed."

He laughs lightly, falling back. "I'll be going then. Goodnight, *Taylor*."

We watch as he slinks away into the crowd, and I'm ready to go after him when Jemima grips my arm. "Let him go."

I turn to her, frowning. "Let him go?"

She nods, but I can tell she's shaken. "We need to tell Aiden he's here, but I don't want to jeopardize Nikki's adoption. If we do anything to him, he can use it against me in court, and trust me, I know he would."

My lips tighten, and now I really don't want to leave her alone tonight for any amount of time. I don't even like Nikki being at Aiden's mother's house without a guard.

"You're right. We need to talk to Aiden. We need to make sure the kids are covered."

She steps closer into my chest. "Thank you for being here for me."

I surround her in my arms, hoping my presence eases the

tension in her body. "I won't let anybody hurt you. I made you that promise, and I'll keep it."

With a soft exhale, she nods, resting her forehead briefly against my chin before taking my hand. The rest of the night, I'm on high alert, staying close to her.

We tell Aiden what happened, and he immediately leaves, claiming he's not much of a gala person. Ten minutes later, he texts me he's spending the night at his mom's.

> **Aiden**: All good here. Stay with Jemima. I know she's covering for Piper.

It's another twist, me joining forces with Sheriff Stone. My brother's words thump in my head with every heartbeat. *They won't make you legit*, and a fist of defiance rises in my chest.

> I don't need them to make me who I am. I'll protect my family, and I don't have time for a brother who won't even get out of his own shit.

> **Aiden**: Keep me in the loop.

I'm studying Aiden's final text when Bender strolls up to join me. "Heard we had some trouble here tonight."

He extends a hand, and I shake it. "Just an old ghost from Jemima's past."

"We get so distracted by the men, we forget the ladies have lives, too."

"The only thing Jemima's guilty of is taking the law into her own hands."

"Last I checked, the court doesn't treat vigilantes any better than regular criminals." It's almost like he's speaking from personal experience.

Glancing over at him, I notice he's dressed in the same formalwear as I am, and a crystal tumbler of bourbon and a cigar are in his hand. His silver hair is swept back, and even his beard looks trimmed.

"If I didn't know better, I'd say you were downright elegant."

A rough laugh coughs from his chest, and he slides a hand

into his pocket. "Don't get used to it. Gwen's really into this gala. Seems Mardi Gras has a lot of mystique."

"Mystique." I nod, and he narrows his eyes.

"You're a far cry from bare feet and blue jeans yourself."

"Not far enough." I turn, leading him away from the crowd of people we know. "I need your advice on something."

We stop at a tall wooden table, and he rests his elbow on the rough-hewn surface. "Shoot."

"I said I'd do something back when nothing I did seemed to matter." Scrubbing the back of my neck, I think about how that wasn't so long ago. "Now if I don't see it through, people I care about could get hurt. But if I do, people I care about could be really disappointed."

His dark brow lowers, and he studies the amber liquid in his glass. "You want to know what I'd do?"

"Yeah." I look up at him.

"I don't know." He reaches out to squeeze the top of my shoulder. "But you've shown me over and over that you're a smart man, Raif. I think when the time comes, you'll know what to do. Either way, I'll be here on the other side."

It's not the answer I wanted. It's not cut and dried, do this, don't do that. I guess it's about what I expected he'd say.

Glancing over at Jemima, I see her with Britt and Adam, and I know whatever happens, she'll be okay. They'll take care of her and Nikki.

"If anything happens, look out for my dad for me."

"I'll look out for your dad, but I'll look out for his son as well." Leaving his empty tumbler on the table, he slides his hand in his pocket as he starts to go. "My money's on you, Raif Jones, and I'm rarely wrong."

Chapter 25

Jemima

For the rest of the evening, I'm haunted by Bill's Shadow Man, looking for him around every corner or seeing his face in every mask. Raif stays close by me the entire time, and we finally decide he must've left. Still, I'm exhausted from watching by the time two o'clock rolls around.

"Congrats, baby sister. I think we have officially launched a new tradition." Cass hugs me as we walk out the glass doors to the emptying parking lot. "It's my new favorite. Right up there with Movies in the Park."

"I agree, darling." Monay is right behind us with her arm looped through Zenighta's. "We passed a good time tonight. Mamma Ru would be proud."

"I could not get enough of that snickerdoodle king cake!" Zenighta's voice is scratchy, and I expect it's from singing Creole classics all night with the band. "You have got to give me the recipe."

"That's Cass's recipe." I fall back to loop my arm around her waist.

The two of them are in sparkling purple, green, and gold bodysuits with their hair flowing all around. Zenighta's is sleek, straight-as-a-board black while Monay's is platinum, her signature color.

"I was so nervous giving out that recipe." Cass cups a hand over her eyes. "It's Britt's favorite, and I didn't want her to think I'd told a family secret."

"I think the family secret is safe." I unhook my arm from the queens' when we reach Alex's car. They blow kisses and continue in their platforms to their waiting Uber. "It wasn't as good as yours."

The guys are right behind us, and while Alex seems easy, making plans about getting together this weekend, Raif's eyes are on mine. His posture is tense, and I hate that something I did is causing him so much worry.

"See you tomorrow." I hug my sister then go to where the bike is waiting.

She grins, giving me a wink. "Have a good night, you two."

They take off, and I hesitate beside the motorcycle. He's not smiling as he lifts the helmet, carefully placing it on my head.

"Are you mad at me?" My voice is small, and his blue eyes fix on mine.

"What the hell? Why would I be mad at you?"

"If it weren't for me, we wouldn't have been on guard all night. We could've enjoyed ourselves, maybe slipped into an empty office like you said…"

He fastens the clip under his chin, exhaling a smile. It's not a full smile, though, and the weight in my stomach grows heavier.

"Let's get back to the house."

I climb on behind him, and the entire drive back, I do my best to hold onto him and not my anxiety. Aiden is watching over Nikki, and Britt said to enjoy the night, not to worry.

> **Britt**: I know what it's like to be a newlywed with a kid in the house. Enjoy.

I'd like to follow her instructions, but I can feel the tension in Raif's muscles, and it has me on edge as well.

When we reach the cottage, he parks outside the fence. Porkchop greets us at the gate, and Raif holds him back to let me enter the yard. The tulips have faded, and in their place, he planted flowering Carolina jessamine. They spill over the boxes in dozens of happy yellow trumpet-like blooms.

They're bright and full of hope, but tonight, under the waning moon, I can't relax. We carry our helmets to the porch, and I wait as he unlocks the door. Our mood is so shifted from when we left earlier. I mentally search for a way to bring us to that place again.

In the living room, he slides out of the tuxedo jacket and leaves it on the back of a chair. Next, he removes the white vest, shirt, and tie. He's so handsome in the dim light with his muscles on display.

"Are your shoulders tense? Come sit, and I'll give you a massage. Frangelica gave me some essential oil when I did her profile…"

But he doesn't come to me.

He continues through the kitchen, going straight to the laundry room where I hear him open a cabinet. A minute later he returns wearing a long-sleeved black tee. He's also carrying a leather bag that looks like a gun case.

It's the same case he brought with him when we went hunting, and my stomach twists.

"Do you know how to use this?" He puts it on the table, turning the combination lock on the zipper. "I'm going to leave it with you in case Bill shows up here."

He removes the sleek black weapon and checks the clip.

"Where are you going?" I watch as he turns it to the side.

"The safety is always on, but it disengages when you pull

the trigger." He passes the weapon to me, and when he puts it in my hand, it's lighter than I expected.

My eyes are wide, and I carefully put it on the table. "I've never shot a gun."

"Don't be afraid to use it." He walks to where I stand and puts his hands on my shoulders. "I have to run an errand, but I'll be back before sunrise. I want you to stay here with the door locked, and if Bill comes here while I'm gone, text Aiden."

"Why can't I text you?" A dry ache is in my throat, and I don't want to let him go. "Is this the thing your brother was talking about?"

His chin drops, and the muscle in his jaw moves. "It's the last thing I have to do, but it's going to be okay. I promise."

"Can I go with you?"

"No."

I step forward, wrapping my arms around his neck and pressing my body tightly to his. "Raif… I'm afraid."

His shoulders drop, and he wraps his arms around me. "I never want you to be afraid." His voice cracks. "Do you want to go to Monay's?"

"I want you to stay here with me." My body trembles, and he holds me tighter.

He presses his forehead against my neck, and for a moment, we're locked in an embrace so warm and so desperate. His breath is labored, and I'm fighting tears. Darkness seems to grow around us, but here, where we're holding each other, it's light and safety. If only I could convince him to keep holding onto me.

With a groan his arms loosen, and he takes a step back. "I have to go."

"No…" It's the faintest, broken whisper.

He catches my chin in his fingers. "Look at me, Princess."

"I'm not a princess."

"I'll be back in two hours. Don't be afraid. Go to sleep, and tomorrow, everything will be different. It'll be the start of something brand new for us. Okay?"

Blinking up at him, I want to believe him. He leans down to press his warm lips to mine. He opens my mouth with his and slides his tongue inside. With a whimper, I try to hold his shirt. I curl my fingers and try to be stronger than his need to leave me.

But he pulls away, and I know I'm not.

"Lock this door behind me."

It's the last thing he says before disappearing into the night.

Chapter 26

Raif

L EAVING JEMIMA IS THE HARDEST THING I'VE EVER DONE. THE ONLY thing keeping me going is the belief it's all going to work out. I have the power to walk away if things go bad. I've scouted my location, and I located a position where I can beat it at the first sign of trouble.

I'm not a part of this.

I'm only a lookout.

It's going to be okay.

The job is scheduled to happen at 4 a.m. The shipment will arrive, and just as fast, the trucks will be loaded and will roll out with whatever illegal cargo has been added. I'll be back in Jemima's arms before the first rays of dawn.

Bull never told me which branch of law enforcement they're worried about, and I'm afraid it's drugs. I'm afraid it's fucking fentanyl, and I don't like being a part of it getting into the supply chain.

The entire drive, my mind works overtime on a way to alert

the authorities without getting caught. If I see something, sound the alarm, and everything stops, that's a win. Stopping it is my main concern—so if I alert the DEA, then tell my brother it's a raid, I'm clean.

It's an enticing idea, but I need to know what I'm working with first.

When I reach the road leading to the dock, I cruise on by the entrance, hitting the throttle loudly so they'll know I'm here. It's my signal to Bull. The sound of my bike means the watch is in place.

I circle the perimeter like I did the last time, and I see no signs of anyone or anything. It appears everything's going according to plan. When I arrive back at the entrance, I turn off, taking a narrow road leading away from the gate and up a wooded hill.

At the top, a picnic area stands dark and empty. I pull off into a copse of trees and park the bike behind an old green dumpster. I have my phone and a small pair of binoculars that fits in my pocket. Normally, I'd also have my gun.

Thinking of it at the house with Jemima twists the pain in my chest. It's pain and anxiety and worry and heartbreak. If she knew what I was doing right now, would she understand? I said I wanted her to be proud of me. How could she be proud of this?

My hands are in my pockets as I walk down the hill. Palmettos, wax myrtles, and juniper bushes form a scratchy barrier on both sides of the road. I wish I had my denim jacket, but I can't risk being spotted in the darkness.

As it is, I'll have to push through the brambles. My phone buzzes in my pocket, and I look down to see it's a call from an unknown number. It's my brother letting me know he heard me. Now all I have to do is get in place and watch for an hour or so, until he lets me know they're done.

This is where I deviate from the plan.

I have to know what I'm allowing to happen here, and if there's something I can do to stop it. It's a big risk, and I'm taking it. It's the only way I can try and redeem myself for this bad decision.

Walking down the hill carries another risk. If their fears are justified, and law enforcement knows something is going down here, if it's a sting operation or a SWAT team shows up, I'll be arrested right along with them. It won't matter what my intentions are now. I won't be able to run away, and I'll go to prison.

Swallowing the knot in my throat, it's a chance I have to take.

I creep down to the side of the fence, to the opening behind the guard shack and through the narrow space beside the post. Staying low, I creep along the edge of the parking lot, doing my best to duck behind the line of dumpsters, the discarded wooden palettes, and the occasional parked car.

Lights blaze up ahead, and I hear the sound of voices, the metallic sliding of a cargo door. They've opened the semi truck, which means I don't have much time now. The truck is loaded, and once they're done, neither the driver nor the logistics company will know what's been added to their shipment—unless someone tips them off.

Leaning out carefully, I look down the long side of the warehouse. The truck is parked beside the loading dock, ready to take off at sunrise. I see shapes, but I'm too far to make out if one is my brother.

I count four guys, which doesn't seem like enough to move stereos or televisions. I try to rationalize—four could be enough if it's virtual-reality goggles or iPhones or some other type of small, digital equipment. It doesn't have to be drugs… or worse.

Fuck, I want this to be an old-school robbery so bad, and the dark sensation creeping up the back of my neck tells me it's not.

Swiping my hand over my forehead, I keep low as I jog up the side of the long truck to the midpoint. I'm not getting any closer. I can use my binoculars to try and make out what's happening. I just need to find the best hiding place to spy.

One step to the right, and my eyes land on a girl about

Nikki's age. Her straight, dark hair is parted down the middle, and she's wearing jeans and a gray shirt. Her eyes are downcast, and she looks behind her as she crosses the space between the dock and the truck.

Sickness tightens my throat. I'm pretty sure I know what's happening. I need to bolt, but I'm still not certain. Taking a step closer, I peek around the side of the truck. Sure enough, I see another one. This time it's a short man passing money and papers to another, leaner man in a black suit coat. His back is to me, so I can't see his face.

The leaner man waves him away. A little boy in a *SpongeBob SquarePants* T-shirt holds onto the smaller man's jeans pocket, and anger burns in my stomach. He could be Ryan or Owen. He could be Nikki.

I've seen enough—it's time to go. It's time to put an end to this.

Taking careful steps, I do my best to quietly get away. I know who to call now, but I also know the clock is ticking before these trucks pull out and are gone. They'll disappear into the night, and it'll be too late to do anything.

And I won't be here next time.

I'm at the edge of the truck when the lean man in the black coat turns to the side, and recognition like ice shoots through my veins. His face is painted white with black lines to create a skull. *Shadow Man*. It's Bill.

My throat closes, and the binoculars fall from my hand, hitting the pavement with a loud clatter. Black eyes lock on mine, and it's too late. He sees me.

Chapter 27

Jemima

IT'S TOO QUIET AFTER RAIF LEAVES. THE GUN SITS ON THE TABLE LIKE a warning, and I want to be as far away from it as possible.

If he really thought Bill was coming here, would he just leave me like that? It's not like him, and it makes me nervous, like something has happened and everything is different. I've stepped through the mirror, and I'm in a world where danger is all around and everyone is slightly mad.

"Stop it, Jemima," I scold myself. "You're imagining things."

It's after 3 a.m. It was a crazy busy night of people in masks and dancing and mystery all around. I go to the small bathroom and turn on the water in the tub. Then I pour a scoop of lavender bath salts into the flow.

It doesn't have to be madness and evil. It can be mystery and intrigue.

Standing in the dim room, a tingle on my shoulder makes me look behind me. Nothing is there, but it gives me a chill.

I didn't imagine the worry in Raif's eye, the guilt in his

expression. He tried to act like it was nothing. He said he'd be back before dawn, but I could sense something was wrong. Why would he feel guilty? Is it because he is?

No. I shake those doubts away. I know my husband better than that.

Going into my bedroom, I place my white lace panties and a thin, white nightgown on the bed. The gown is thigh high and essentially see-through, and I imagine wearing it for Raif when he gets back.

My dark areolas are visible through the thin fabric, and I can rub his shoulders with the essential oil Frangelica gave me. It's essence of sandalwood…

Massage always leads to sex, and I have to focus on what we'll do when he comes home.

Frangelica also gave me two candles when I interviewed her. One is sage and the other is tuberose. Together they make the most interesting, clean, relaxing fragrance.

Sage drives out evil spirits, she told me. I light it at once, waving my hand over it to spread the good juju around our home.

"Go away, evil spirits," I whisper as I walk into the bathroom.

Switching off the water, I place it and the rose one on the counter. They're the only light in the room, and I take off my clothes, stepping into the steamy, fragrant bath.

My hair is up, and I try to calm my anxious mind.

It keeps trying to go to the night my mother died, the chaos and confusion, the swirling lights of the sirens and the pushing of the EMS workers. The only thing that helped me be calm was singing.

I climbed into my mother's bed, and I sang a song… What was it?

The only song in my head tonight is "Blue Jeans" by Lana del Rey. It's a flash of realization in my chest, and it's been growing and growing for so long, since that first night on the beach. *I will love him til the end of time…*

After so long being strong, surviving, taking care of myself and staying out of trouble, he created a place where I can breathe.

He'll fight for me so I can stop fighting. He's a bad boy, but he's mine. I don't have to be afraid anymore, because the look in his eye, the way he stepped to Bill tonight at the gala, says *touch her and die.*

Closing my eyes, I focus on the first day I saw him in October—blue jeans, white shirt, brown hair falling over one blue eye, a naughty grin. He looked at me the way I looked at him, like we knew it was all over for us. He smiled, and I did my very best flirt, thankful I'd worn a short skirt to show off my long legs.

Long legs… A man reaches up to grab my ankle on the stage, and I kick him in the head. Shouting breaks out. He smashes a drink and tries to climb onstage. The bouncer pulls him back, but I see Trixie's scowl. Counting out my money… You antagonize the customers. They're not supposed to touch me. This isn't a strip club. I'm a singer—Taylor Swift. You're no Taylor Swift, but you could be Lana del Rey. Slimy grin, lecherous eyes getting closer…

With a sharp inhale, my eyes jerk open. I fell asleep in the tub, and I don't know what time it is.

The water has turned cold. Stepping out, I grab the towel and pull the drain. The candles have burned down, and I blow them out as I dry my body.

Going into the bedroom, I try to shake the bad feelings, the tendrils of the dream. All of that is packed away. Far, far away. I'm not there anymore. I'm not her.

"Come home, Raif," I whisper, my throat aching with fear.

I step into the lace panties, drop the nightgown over my head. It's chilly, so I pull on the plush robe with *Wife* monogrammed on the pocket. Everything is quiet and dark now. The darkest hour is before dawn.

Picking up my phone, I stare at the black face. It's after four, too late to text anyone. Or is it too early? How much longer? Has it been two hours? I didn't note the exact time he left me.

Looking at my hand, I slide the delicate gold ring around my finger. I lift it to my lips then hug it to my chest. Are promises real if they're said as a means to an end?

Only, I meant it when I said those words in front of that old man. For better or worse, richer or poorer, sickness and health. *Til the end of time...*

A noise outside makes me jump. Something is moving out there. My heart beats like a rabbit in my chest, and I go into the living room to turn on a light. Before I do, I peek through the curtain. I don't see Porkchop. I don't see anything. The moon isn't on my side tonight.

Still, someone is there. Looking to the kitchen, the gun is on the table. The door is locked, but I hear footsteps on the walk. A quake moves through my torso, shaking my shoulders, and my phone lights up in my hand as the door starts to move.

Chapter 28

BILL WOLF HAS SEEN ME, AND I CAN TELL BY THE GLITTER IN HIS black eyes he knows it's me. He knows I'm not letting him get away with this. The countdown has officially begun.

I jump to hide, but my boot hits pea gravel and slides out from under me, twisting my knee. It hurts like a motherfucker, and I bite back a swear. But I don't have time to recover. Footsteps are approaching fast, and I've got to run.

Digging in my heels, I push through the pain, doing my best to stay in the darkness, to retrace my path to the gate. They're right behind me, and they're not injured. I hear a whistle and another sound like a signal, and I'm afraid I'm not going to make it. I'm afraid they're going to circle around and cut me off.

I only saw four guys, but that doesn't mean there aren't more. I don't know where the fuck Bull is hiding, and he won't hesitate to take me down.

The guard shack is in sight, and I lower my chin, pumping my arms and grasping with my fists. It's ten yards away. The heat of another runner is at my flank. Pain shoots through my knee, but the adrenaline pumping in my veins turns it into fuel, helping me block out everything and focus on that break in the fence.

Someone grips my sleeve, but I snatch it away, tearing the fabric as I dive through the gate. Lights appear on the road, coming up fast, but I don't stop. I run hard across the street, just clearing the second lane when the semi-truck barrels past, horns blasting.

It gives me enough time to hide, and I dive into the scrub on the side of the narrow road. Curling into a ball, I clasp a hand over my mouth to quiet my gasps for breath, my scream from the pain in my knee, the branches cutting my skin.

Holding steady, I listen as the two men run around, up and down, shining lights and whispering to each other. My hand tightens over my mouth, and I grind my teeth as minute after minute passes. I don't dare use my phone—the light would draw their attention straight to me.

So I stay, vibrating in place, waiting for them to give up the search.

Bill saw me. He recognized me. He knows I'm in with the Stones, and for all I know, he's calling off the job right now—or better yet, that snake is passing the reins to another guy while he slithers out the back door.

My brother would be dumb enough to think it's a promotion. He's in charge now, and he'll be the asshole holding the bag when the cavalry rides into town. *Don't do it, Bull…* I think, but I can't warn him. I can't do anything.

The guys are slowing down, and my chest is tight. I imagine Bill in his truck right now, making a fast exit, leaving these dumbasses to take the fall.

What will he do next? Go back to Branson? I can't imagine him walking away that easily. A guy like that would want revenge. It's when the answer hits me like a sledgehammer.

A guy like that would go to my place.

He'd go after me—or he'd go after the one thing that would hurt me more than death. *Jemima…*

I can't wait any longer for these assholes to go away. Pulling out my phone, I'm about to light it up when I hear them talking. They're finally giving up, and I hold, waiting, rocking softly in place until finally they're far enough away.

My hands shake as I unlock my phone and rapidly pull up the texting app. A text is already waiting for me from the same number.

Unknown: What happened?

I ignore it, instead sending a message to the one person I know will get here fast.

Human smugglers—Dock 3, Rockbrook Port, Harris truck line. Bring backup—NOW!

I don't know if any of that will make sense to him or if I'm even using the right words. I only know I can't stick around to find out.

A cramp pierces my side as I run uphill to my bike hidden in the trees. Throwing my injured leg over the seat, I kick the ignition and hit full-throttle. Roaring down the hill, I don't stop when I see the men at the bottom, waiting to block me.

They can't touch me at this speed, but it's not over. Bill knows where we live, and when Aiden shows up with the cavalry, he'll know I tipped them off. It's just after four, and I'm pushing with all my might to get to her before he does.

The highway shines with dew, and I lean forward into the handlebars. My knee throbs, but I feel him right behind me. Glancing over my shoulder, I don't see headlights. I feel the buzz in my pocket, and I know it's either Aiden or Bull. I don't see flashing lights.

I only see Jemima's sweet face waiting at home alone with a gun she doesn't know how to shoot.

I'm afraid it all makes sense now. I'm afraid I know the truth, and Nikki's mom is long gone… We'll cross that bridge when we get to it. If we get to it. If I make it to my destination in time.

If I make it home before him.

Cutting the engine as I approach Eureka, I cruise around the back way, following First Street and coming up from behind in case he's waiting for me out front. Leaving my bike beside the small shed at the edge of the trees, I wince when I put weight on my leg, but I don't have time for that pain.

My throat is tight as I slip from shadow to shadow, getting closer to the cottage. I take out my phone and quickly tap out a text.

I'm here. I'm coming in the back door. Don't be afraid. Don't shoot.

Aiden: Omw, troopers alerted. Sending Ben to check on Jemima.

Bill was there. I'm back in Eureka, but I don't know where he is now.

Jemima: Is that you?

Everything changes when I see her question. It's not me.

Running up the path to the house, I vaguely notice Porkchop isn't chasing me, but I don't have time to look for him. My boots hit the wooden steps at the same time the sound of gunshots blast through the night.

"Fuck," I shout, turning the key in the lock and falling inside like someone shoved me.

"Raif?" Jemima shrieks as she runs to where I'm lying on my side in the doorway.

Pain radiates through my torso, and I push with my boot against the floor to get all the way inside the house.

"Get down!" My voice is ragged.

Another shot rings out, but I manage to clear my legs and push the door closed with my foot. Jemima is on her knees beside me, her hands flying from my face to my shoulders to my side where blood pulses out with every heartbeat.

Fuck, I'm going to bleed out if we don't do something.

"What do I do?" Her voice shakes, and my gun is in her hand.

"Call 9-1-1, get me towels… Put pressure on it." I'm fading fast, and I hear the sound of footsteps on the porch outside.

The door's not locked, and Jemima has run to the kitchen to do what I said. I'm lying on the floor, panic racing through my veins as the wooden door starts to open.

"Gun, Jemima…" My voice is a gasp, and I brace my foot against the wooden barrier. I'm getting weaker by the second, and I force a shout that comes out as more of a groan. "Give me the gun!"

It's too late. Bill is standing over me, eyes flashing with rage behind a mask of death. "That's the last time you fuck with me, boy."

He doesn't hesitate, raising the gun to my face.

The noise of a shot rings out, but I don't feel anything. I close my eyes, and cool white light washes over me.

Chapter 29

Jemima

THE JESSAMINE SEEMS TO HAVE GOTTEN FULLER OVERNIGHT, ALMOST like it knows today is Valentine's Day.

Soft yellow blossoms greet me with wide open faces, filling every possible space from the flower boxes down the fence post. I can't see the green leaves or even the stems for the abundance of flowers.

When I stood out here, watching as Raif planted them for me, he said they were native flowers. He said they could withstand the elements, the heat, the wind, and the rain—anything nature might throw at them wouldn't matter. They would grow happy and strong because they know how to survive in this environment, he said.

He also said the yellow flowers reminded him of my hair and my smile, bright sunshine, full of hope, never giving up no matter what life throws at me. He slid his dirt-covered finger across my cheek, and of course, it made me smile.

"I love to see you smile," he'd said, and I'd said something about him getting me dirty.

Sitting on my butt with my back pressed to the fence, I close my eyes and try to picture the dimple in his cheek, the twinkle in his eye when he looks at me in his bad-boy way, like he knows he owns me.

I try to reach out and thread my fingers through his soft hair. I think of our first meeting when he'd said *he* was the breaking news. I remember his fierce protection when Ethan McClure threatened us.

He defied the negative stereotypes and the prejudices. He was strong, a fighter, yet he handled me gently, like one of his flowers. He loved me like a fiery volcano, like I've never been loved…

I only want to hold onto the good, but the flashing lights blast through my memory. The fear freezing in my veins as he struggles on the floor, inky blood spreading around him in a circle, fighting for life. *Towels… the gun. Give me the gun!*

The door opens slowly and terror squeezes my throat at Bill's glittering eyes. He's no longer the shadow man. Now he's the angel of death.

But I won't let that happen. I won't let him win. It's over, and I said if he ever came back, I'd kill him. Lifting the cold metal in my hands, my eyes squeeze shut as my finger squeezes the trigger…

Exploding gunshots, the stench of weapons and blood, shouting voices and blaring sirens roar in my ears. I'm pushed aside and told to get back, get out of the way, let them do their work. Plastic gloves and white masks and EMS officers running back and forth, in and out, and I shrink smaller and smaller into the background, pushed out the door.

The colors are midnight blue and deep red; purple fading to orange in the growing light of dawn. Then came the silence.

Pounding silence after they left, taking him away, and leaving me here.

Alone.

A shudder moves through my chest. My skin is cold in the rising sun, but my nose is hot from crying. Streams of tears warm my cheeks. Beside me the yellow flowers hang their heads, wet with dew, mourning with me.

Wrapping my arms around my bent knees, I try to remember the gold of that sunset covering the beach. Our sunset, when I rode the bike behind him, my arms outstretched in a *V*.

It was our beginning. We were stars burning in the sky, hot as fire and so, so beautiful.

My fingertips are cold when I touch them to my cheeks. When I close my eyes, more warmth falls.

For a little while, I was the happiest girl in the world, the luckiest. He was my bad boy, and I was his bad girl.

Only, we weren't bad. We were just a little naughty.

He was my husband, and I never told him how much I love him.

"Let me search here, and I'll call you back." The familiar voice is loud in the quiet, and I look up to see the wooden gate wobble back and forth. "Open, dammit!"

Blinking through tears, it's Dolly Parton. Blinking again, I realize it's Monay trying to work the latch on the gate with her ultra-long acrylic nails. The wooden door opens, and she pushes through, stumbling a bit in her heels before pushing it shut with her butt.

"Thank goodness that dog isn't here." She looks around and down, and as soon as her eyes land on me, she yelps. "Jemima! Good lord, girl, we've been looking for you everywhere. We're all waking up, finding out all hell broke loose after we just left… What are you doing hiding out here?"

"I'm not hiding." I try to speak, but my voice is gone.

It comes out more like a frog is in my throat.

"Come on, we've got to get you dressed." She reaches down, gently grasping my arm and pulling me to my feet.

I'm surprised I can walk, but Monay has always been strong

enough for the both of us. "There's no need to disturb evidence." Her voice is all business, and I glance at my front door to see yellow police tape blocking it.

It's another painful reminder. It's why when EMS left, I sat down where I was, under the boughs of flowers my husband planted for me.

Looking down, I'm still in my nightgown and my plush white robe with the word *Wife* monogrammed on the pocket. I lean heavily on her arm, and she practically carries me through the gate to the newspaper office.

"My clothes…"

"Cass has Nikki at her house, but Piper said she didn't see you when she picked up Porkchop. He's going to be fine, don't worry. Dr. Henry said it was some kind of tranquilizer." Monay continues talking as she opens the glass front door. "They thought you'd gone to the hospital."

"I don't have a car." My voice slowly returns with each swallow.

My friend stops in place and puts a large hand on her hip. "Well, hell, I don't either." She shakes her head. "I'll message Cass and see if she can find us a ride. We've got to get you to Ridgeland. I can't believe the closest hospital is almost an hour away. What kind of backwater…"

"Why am I going to the hospital?" Hollow pain echoes in my chest where my heart used to be. It hurts so much, I rub my hand over the spot, forcing my lungs to breathe.

Monay's platinum head tilts to the side. "Don't you want to be there?"

"Not really." My voice is quiet. "Although, I guess as his wife, they need me to do things…"

I'm honestly not sure what wives do in situations like this. Our marriage was for a very specific purpose. It wasn't until later that things started to get blurry, that they started to feel like forever.

Or was it right from the start?

Til death us do part...

Panic seizes my lungs, as if they sense the tsunami of grief on the horizon surging towards me, faster than the eye can see or even understand, forging a path of destruction powerful enough to take me under.

I won't survive this.

"As a wife, you need to be at his bedside holding his hand." She shakes her head like she doesn't understand me. "I know you didn't have any kind of role models when you were a child, but honestly, girl. He's coming out of surgery any minute, and we've got to get you dressed and to the hospital."

The jolt in my chest is so abrupt, I almost vomit. I swallow and hold the counter as the blood rushes from my face.

"Surgery?" I can barely say the word.

"Yes, surgery! It's a miracle what these surgeons can do nowadays. Hell, I heard they could've probably saved JFK if he'd been shot today, but he's still looking at a significant recovery—"

I grip her arm fast. "He's alive?"

Monay blinks at me, her glossy lips part, and realization breaks over her face. "Baby girl..." Her voice softens, and she puts her hands on my arms. "Yes, he's alive. He's going to be okay."

A violent sob bursts from my chest. It's a massive heave mixed with a scream. My knees go out, and Monay catches me, moving us quickly to the bench.

I can't breathe.

I'm a fish on the beach, out of water, and another gut-wrenching sob rakes through my throat. I can't see through the tears, leaning forward as Monay holds me.

"Shh, baby, it's okay..." She hugs me to her, rubbing my back and rocking us both. "I got you. It's all going to be okay."

All the tears I never cried from all the years of not giving up, of holding on and surviving, of losing my mother, of being abandoned, of being brave when I was terrified.

Every time I fought to be strong and not hard, to love and

believe in love—it all comes bursting through like a mighty dam has ruptured.

My eyes are closed, and I hold onto Monay. I hold onto the lifeline she gives me. The safety net she's always thrown in the flood. I hold onto her until the water recedes and my toes brush against solid ground. Rocking back and forth, we make our way to the shore.

I'm shaken and weak, but I haven't lost everything.

I still have hope.

He's alive.

Chapter 30

Raif

"NORTH AMERICA IS COMPOSED OF FIVE GEOGRAPHICAL REGIONS."
The girl's voice is a steady drone as I slowly open my
eyes. My brow furrows as I try to focus, to piece together
where I am and what happened. "There's the Canadian Shield,
the Great Plains, the mountainous west, the eastern region, and
the Caribbean."

Nikki's dark head is bowed over a colorful textbook, and
she's in a reclining chair surrounded by pillows reading her homework out loud.

My brain is cloudy and thick, like I'm slowly coming out of
a dense fog. My arms and legs are too heavy to move, and I'm
so tired. Looking around, it's clear I'm in a hospital. I'm surrounded by soft beeping noises, tubes, wires, and several large
bouquets of flowers.

I recognize some of them. That one is stargazers, roses,
carnations, and two large gerbera daisies. A glass vase on my

bedside table holds a bunch of Carolina jessamine. They look like the ones I planted for Jemima in the flower boxes back home.

She was so pretty that day with her hair up in a ponytail and little pieces flying around in the breeze. She leaned in beside me, pressing her fingers into the soil, learning how to plant them. I told her the yellow would be like her hair and her smile, then I got dirt on her cheek…

Closing my eyes, the warmth moving across my chest is an ache, and I realize a tight bandage is wrapped around my torso.

With a flash, Bill's face appears in my memory. I see him standing over me with a gun pointed straight at my forehead. He's smiling like the angel of death—or the shadow man, which is essentially the same thing, right? I was pretty sure that was the end of me, but clearly it wasn't.

The gunshot didn't hit me in the head. I don't have brain damage, but I am in a hospital room. A really fucking nice hospital room with a couch and a television and a reclining chair holding Nikki, who continues reading about North American geography.

I can't tell if she's trying to wake me up or put me to sleep.

Only, where is Jemima? My head turns to the side as I search the large room for her.

Was she hurt? Is she in another room in this hospital? The gun was pointed at me, but I passed out from blood loss, I'm sure. Still, I heard the noise. She was right there in the kitchen, steps away…

The beeping noises grow faster, and Nikki sits up in her chair. "You're awake!" She puts the book on the table and rushes to my bedside, eyes wide. "Are you in pain?"

"Where's Jemima?" My mouth is so dry, I can barely speak.

She grabs a plastic cup with a straw and holds it to my lips. Taking a swift pull, I turn my head and ask again. "Where is she?"

Nikki looks over her shoulder, and it's taking her too long to answer my simple question. With a groan and a strain, I try to sit up and get out of this fucking bed.

The monitors go crazy, but I have to know she's okay. I have to know he didn't get her, he didn't shoot her, she's not lying in a bed somewhere because of my stupid, fucking mistake.

"Wait…" Nikki tries to hold my arm, and the pain shooting through my side almost knocks me out.

"Mr. Jones, stop!" A woman in dusty pink scrubs rushes to my bedside, putting her hand on my chest. "You'll tear your stitches."

"Where's my wife?" It comes out as a ragged growl.

The drugs or the injury has taken all my strength, and I can't push past a petite nurse and a little girl. I'm so fucking weak. The pain in my heart is crippling me, and the beeping grows more urgent.

"Mr. Jones, please, you have to lie down." The nurse holds my shoulders.

"Raif?" Her sweet voice hits me so hard, I almost cry. "You're awake! Oh, thank God, we've been waiting."

Nikki moves back so Jemima can access my bedside. Gazing up at her, I swallow the thickness in my throat. I'm so tired, but I need to touch her. I need to feel her warm skin against my fingertips to know she's okay.

"Jemima…" I lift my hand, and she clasps it in both of hers, hugging it to her chest.

Tears shine in her eyes, and she leans forward, wrapping her arms around my shoulders and pressing her body to mine. Her sweet body.

"It's so good to hear your voice." Her voice breaks.

"I thought something happened to you," I whisper.

I want to hold her in my arms. I never want to feel that terror again, but I'm so damn exhausted.

"Are you in pain?" Her pretty brow wrinkles, and she touches the wetness away from the corners of my eyes. *Am I crying?*

"No, beautiful." I manage a smile. "Not anymore."

Her face relaxes and tears shine on her cheeks. She kisses

my lips, my cheek, my temple. Her warmth, her smell of jasmine. She's here, and the relief is so intense, I feel myself fading.

Not yet.

Lifting my hand, I thread my fingers in the length of her hair. "You're okay?"

Her lips press into a smile, and she leans closer, hugging me again as she whispers, "I am now."

"Your brother and the rest of the men are being held on charges of human smuggling." Aiden is in my room, and I'm sitting up in bed a million times stronger than I was when I woke up two days ago.

I'm ready to get out of here.

Jemima hasn't left my room since I woke—hell, according to the nurses, she hasn't left my room since I got out of surgery.

Every night, she sleeps on that sofa, and every day, she sits at my bedside holding my hand and talking to me about everything I missed.

Bender got to the house at the same time as Bill. He found Porkchop out cold and couldn't tell if he was dead or injured. Luckily, he was only sedated, which I know means Bill had been watching our house.

He knew we had a dog, and he was ready to sedate him, which means even if I hadn't been at that dock, he was planning to show up at our place that morning.

I don't know if that makes me feel better or worse.

As for what happened to me, I was shot in the abdomen, just missing my stomach but nicking my right kidney. They were able to repair the damage, but I've got several weeks of recovery ahead of me. In the meantime, I can't lift anything heavy, and I don't know how that's going to affect my work.

"He tried to say you were involved in the job, but I told them you were working with me." Aiden is in his uniform standing at the foot of my bed. "I said you had an inside connection, and you tipped me off as soon as you knew for sure the exchange was happening. Still, the Feds might want to question you."

He clears his throat, and I wince, unsure how I feel about this not-quite-accurate cover story.

"Technically, it's the truth." Jemima's voice is quiet, as if she can read my thoughts. "As soon as you knew what was happening, you called Aiden and told him. Then you raced back to protect us."

"I shouldn't have been there at all." My tone is flat, guilty.

"If you hadn't been there, we wouldn't have stopped them, and who knows where those people would be?" Aiden shakes his head. "Now they're at least going through the proper channels and not being victimized."

"It's true." Jemima moves closer, putting her hand over mine on the bed. "You stopped a crime from happening."

It's not the greatest excuse, but I have to concede it's something. "What about Bill? Is he still threatening to take Nikki?"

I pull Jemima closer to me, putting my arm around her waist, wanting to protect her from any fallout from my actions. I was supposed to be helping her adopt Nikki, not making it a million times harder.

"Bill is dead." Her voice is quiet. "I thought you knew."

"What?" My eyes fly to Aiden.

"It was a clear case of home invasion." I can see he's more confident in this part of the story. "Bill shot you. Hell, he was about to kill you, and he was taken out in self-defense."

"By who?" I look at Jemima and back at Aiden.

He shifts on his feet. "It wasn't clear at first who fired the kill shot until ballistics came back. Bender was using a different pistol from the Glock Jemima fired."

My brow lowers. "Bender?"

Aiden looks at Jemima, and her face flushes pink. "I closed my eyes and screamed when I pulled the trigger." Then her tone turns hard. "But I'm glad it was me. He threatened all of us."

I slide my arm down, taking her hand, unsure what to say to this news. My strong girl protecting her family.

"No charges are being filed," Aiden continues. "He was standing over you with the intent to kill. There was no other choice."

Jemima lifts her head, hope in her tone. "Does that mean it's over?"

"Pretty much," Aiden nods. "Nikki can stay with the two of you for now, while your petition for adoption makes its way through the system."

She squeezes my hand. "We don't have to be afraid of him lurking around, trying to take her."

"I wasn't afraid." My voice is level, and I'm still trying to get over her saving my damn life.

"It would be helpful if we knew more about what happened to her mother." Aiden walks to the window. "Either way, after six months, she'll legally be considered abandoned."

Jemima exhales a sad sound, and I hug her closer. We're quiet a moment as the facts settle over us, as the noise of construction rises from outside.

Aiden's arms are crossed, and he watches the activity below. "Looks like Redford Park is continuing as planned. At least it's not in Eureka."

Jemima walks over to where he stands, looking over the massive development underway. "Still, it's a lot of new jobs."

"And crime and congestion and crowded streets." His tone is dismissive. "It'll completely change the community."

Back when that battle was going on, I never really took a position on whether a big golf resort would've been good or bad for Eureka. Sitting here now, the only change in the community I'm glad about is the one where I'm no longer a usual suspect.

"Stinkgazers." Aiden pulls a petal on one of the giant pink and white lilies. "We used to hate them growing up. Funeral flowers."

"Funeral flowers?" Jemima walks over and plucks them out

of the vase, tossing them in the trash. "We won't be needing that any time soon."

I exhale a smile at her defiance, my badass little wife.

"That's right." Aiden pats her on the back before going to the door. "I've got to head on back. Just wanted to give you the update."

"Thanks, Aiden," she calls after him.

Our eyes meet, and I'm about to reach for her when the nurse enters, speaking to Aiden as she passes him in the doorway. "I've got good news for you!"

She carries a clipboard to the bed. "The doctor has cleared you to go home. I've got your prescriptions here, and your care instructions. If you're ready, we can have you out of here in an hour."

She smiles, and I'm already on my feet. "I'm ready."

"Not so fast. I have to change your dressing and order a wheelchair. But you can start gathering your things." She pauses at the door. "It's not often we get to treat a hero."

My brow furrows, but she's gone before I can stop her. Jemima is picking up my few belongings. She folds the jeans I was wearing when they brought me here, and slides them along with my boots and my socks into a canvas bag. Monay brought fresh clothes when she picked up Nikki for school.

Standing carefully, I walk over to where she's packing. "I don't know what she's talking about. I'm nobody's hero."

Jemima places her palm against my cheek. "You're mine."

Reaching up, I close my hand over hers. "How could I possibly be…"

"You saved Nikki and me."

"You saved Nikki." Holding her hand, I look down into her bright blue eyes. "You saved me, too."

Her hand moves to my chest as she rises onto her toes. "Let's say we saved each other and leave it at that."

She presses her lips to mine, and I catch her face, giving her a better kiss. "And Bender saved Porkchop."

Chapter 31

Jemima

"**B**RING THE WATER TO A BOIL, THEN ADD THE DRY PASTA." Raif stands in front of the stove, showing us the correct way to make pasta. "Some people salt the water. Others don't."

"What do you do?" Nikki looks up at him from where she's standing beside me.

We're both wearing aprons, and I'm holding a wooden spoon ready to stir when told.

He gives her a wink as he picks up the jar of sea salt. "I always salt the water." With that he grabs some with his fingers and circles it into the steaming pot.

"Wait!" My eyes widen. "How much salt was that?"

He shrugs. "A pinch."

"But how do I know if your pinch is the same size as my pinch?" I wave the wooden spoon. "What if I get it too salty, and you can't eat it because I pinched too much?"

"Don't pinch too much." He says it like it's so obvious.

I exhale a frustrated noise, looking at Nikki. "Like I know how much to pinch."

"How could anyone possibly know that?" Nikki agrees.

Raif exhales a chuckle, sliding his hand around my waist and kissing the side of my cheek. "You'll get the hang of it with practice."

"First you said brown the peppers and onions until they're done, and now you're saying my pinch is the same size as your pinch."

"I think you're taking this too seriously."

"Of course, I'm taking it seriously. I don't want to ruin your dinner!"

Raif scratches the side of his jaw, and Nikki puts her hand on my arm. "Why don't you stick to Hamburger Helper? I really like that chili mac."

My lips tighten, and I lower the spoon, walking away from the stove.

"Hey!" Raif jogs up behind me, wrapping his arms around my waist. "You do a lot of things around here for us. You don't have to cook, too."

"What do I do?" My voice is pouty, and I feel like a failure.

"You sing to us!" Nikki calls from where she's watching the pot for any sign of bubbles.

"You work at the paper." Raif kisses the side of my neck, sending a cascade of tingles down my arms. "You do the laundry…"

"Oh, yes. Don't forget how I turned all the whites pink."

"Martha says I look good in pink." He stands straight, turning me to face him. "She said it flatters my skin tone."

Pressing my lips together, I do my best not to laugh and spoil my pity party.

"I can think of several other things you do *very* well." He's giving me that bad-boy grin, and I lose my fight.

Leaning down, he kisses my lips slowly, pulling the top one

with his teeth and the bottom one before slipping me a little tongue. I'm not pouting anymore.

"When is it going to boil?" Nikki's still at the stove waiting with the box of penne in her hand.

With one final peck, he starts back for the kitchen. "There's an old saying, Nik." He steps up beside her again. "A watched pot never boils."

"Then how do I know when it's boiling?"

"You'll notice when it starts. In the meantime, we'll peel the shrimp."

I walk over to the living room while he shows her the correct way to hold a knife. Cass took care of having the house cleaned while we were at the hospital. She paid a service to scrub everything so there's not a speck of blood. They even repaired the damage to the fence and the door.

A copy of the Eureka *Gazette* from that day, Valentine's Day, is on the coffee table, and I realize I've never even looked through all the personal ads I spent so much time arranging.

Piper finished up the last few, and I smile at the pictures of babies, high school sweethearts, elderly couples holding hands, Howard and his dog Bo…

Poor Howard needs a significant other. The thought passes through my mind as my eyes land on an ad I've never seen before. It's a picture of me, and I'm smiling up at Raif.

He's wearing a suit, and I'm in a white lace dress, and I realize it's one of the pictures Monay took at our wedding at the justice of the peace. It looks like it's right after we kissed.

Even in black and white newsprint, the emotion on my face is so pure, it aches in my chest to see it. It hurts even more to think we're reaching the end.

Neither of us has said anything about it, but with Bill dead, there's no reason to speed the adoption process. Technically, I don't need his help anymore, but I can't bear the thought of him not being here, teaching us to cook, planting flowers, saying how much he loves pink laundry.

Maybe we don't need him for the adoption, but we need him to complete our family. Then I read the words below the photograph.

Jemima,

I knew the day I saw you, you'd change my life.

You never judged me. You simply put your hand in mine and said you'd follow where I led.

You said I was more than they thought, and I wanted to prove you right.

I wanted to make you proud, because I'm so proud to be by your side.

You're beautiful, strong, sweet, and brave.

Every day, I want to be the man you see when you look at me this way.

I love you.

Your husband,
Raif

Swallowing the air in my throat, I look over my shoulder at him standing back as Nikki pours the penne into the boiling water. How long has he been waiting for me to see this? It's been weeks since Valentine's Day.

I love you…

My chest burns with so much emotion, I can't wait anymore. Carrying the paper to the kitchen, I stop at the table and wait for him to look at me.

"Now you wait for it to return to a boil, then cut the heat all the way down and cover it." He's still talking when he glances at me.

Then he looks again.

He sees the newspaper in my hand, and he touches Nikki's shoulder. "Keep everything going. I'll be right back."

Desire is in his eyes as he closes the space between us,

covering my hand with his and leading me straight out the front door. As fast as it closes behind us, he turns, pulling me into his arms and meeting my mouth halfway.

The paper falls to the porch, and my arms go around his neck. Our mouths open, and as our tongues slide together, heat ignites between my thighs. A whimper slips from my throat, and I want him to lift me against the door and fuck me hard.

Of course he can't do that. First, we're on the front porch of our house facing Main Street, but more importantly, the doctor said no heavy lifting for at least six months.

"What would you have done if I'd never seen it?" My fingers thread in his hair.

He grins, kissing the side of my neck. "I'd have had to show you every day… like I plan to do."

Rising onto my toes, I wrap my arms around his neck as emotion surges in my chest. Our mouths seal together, and his hands slide down my back to my ass, squeezing.

"I want you inside me," I gasp, as his hands move to the back of my legs, under my skirt.

"Fuck, I love you, Jemima." His voice is a low groan at my ear. "I've loved you since the night Aiden pulled us off the road, and you fought for me."

Pulling back, I hold his face in my hands. Our eyes meet, and we're both breathing fast.

"I love you, Raif Jones." My nose heats, and I didn't know I could cry and be horny at the same time. "I fell in love with you the day you agreed to marry me. Then I fell in love with you more when you tried to fight your brother for me. Every time you said you loved to make me smile, I fell a little more. When I thought I'd lost you, I knew I'd never love again."

His brow lowers over his pretty blue eyes. "When did you think you'd lost me?"

Exhaling a sob-laugh, I lean forward, closing my eyes and pressing my forehead to his chin. "After you were shot… I thought you had died. I was so afraid, I sat on the ground under the jessamine and cried until Monay found me and told me you were alive."

His arms tighten around me, and he pulls me firmly against his chest. "I'm not going anywhere without my girl." He leans down to kiss me again. "If anything happens to me, I'll be your ghost. There's no such thing as heaven without you in it."

"I can't imagine anywhere good without you."

I go to kiss him again when a heavy paw pushes on my back, and I jump, falling against Raif's chest and looking over my shoulder.

Porkchop is on his hind legs with one paw on the door and the other on me.

"Sit, Porkchop," Raif orders, and we both look at each other with wide eyes when he actually does it. "I'll be damned."

His black ears quirk, and he whimpers a little bark when Nikki calls frantically from inside. "Raif! Help—it's happening!"

"Gotta go." He gives me a quick kiss and charges through the door. "What's happening?"

Rolling my back to the wall, I hold my hand over my warm lips. Porkchop nudges me with his nose, and I drop down to one knee to pet his head and hug him.

Then I stand and exhale a laugh. My heart flutters like a butterfly in my chest, and I smile so big. I want to laugh and skip and run and sing. Instead, I pick up the paper and carry it inside.

I'm going to cut out this message and frame it. Then I need to get the rest of those pictures from Monay.

Chapter 32

"**T**HIS IS THE BEST PENNE PASTA I'VE EVER HAD!" JEMIMA SPEAKS WITH her mouth full from behind a giant bowl of pasta, shrimp, and red sauce with bell peppers, onions, and garlic.

"Not too salty?" I tease.

"Nope—you have the perfect pinch."

"You bet I do."

Her hand flies to her mouth as if to stop a spit-take, and it's silly and sexy, and the smolder below my belt that started with our kisses on the porch grows hotter.

"All the kids at school think Porkchop is a magic dog." Nikki spears a shrimp before popping it into her mouth. "They said he's magic because his eyes are two different colors."

"Magic?" I chuckle, ready to debunk that notion when some-one nudges me under the table. Jemima's big eyes meet mine, and I change course midstream. "What kind of magic?"

"Ryan said he can probably see ghosts like Fudge." She stabs another shrimp and eats it. "Did you know cats can see ghosts?"

"I've heard that." Jemima picks up a piece of garlic bread. "I think Gwen told me that once."

"She would know," I add.

"Pinky said she has a dog now, too. She said Angie Dickinson is her best friend, but I said Ang belongs to Monay." Nikki takes a bite of garlic bread. "Then Pinky got mad and told Mrs. Mamma Cass I was being mean to her."

"Wait…" Jemima holds up a hand. "You call my sister *Mrs. Mamma Cass?*"

"Pinky started it," Nikki explains. "She was calling her Mamma Cass, and Aunt Cass said she had to call her by her teacher-name at school. So she added the Mrs."

"I see…" Jemima looks at me, and I shrug. "Well, I know Cass wouldn't think you're being mean. She also knows her daughter, and Pinky can be a bit… ahh… what's the word?"

Her eyes drift to mine again, and I got nothing. In the short time I've known her, I've learned Pinky is a handful, but nobody better dare say so in front of Jemima's sister.

"Ryan calls her the pink tornado," Nikki says, and Jemima swallows a snort. "Anyway, Mrs. Mamma Cass told us not to compare our pets anymore. She said we had to love them all equally."

"I agree." Jemima nods, taking her last bite of pasta.

"I do, too, because Owen is *always* going on about how smart Edward is." Nikki rolls her eyes like she's so over it. "So he can find stuff. So what?"

I polish off my last bite of pasta, not really wanting to burst her bubble about the intelligence of Edward versus poor ole Porkchop.

"I was going to say Porkchop is my best friend," she continues, darting worried eyes at me. "But I guess he's not really mine."

"Sure, he is." I reach over to squeeze her forearm. "He belongs to all of us, and he can be your best friend. Do you know what he did just now?"

"Ate grass? I saw him do that the other day."

"No…" I don't like the sound of that. "He sat when I told him to sit."

"He did?" She jumps out of her chair and runs to the door. "I've been trying to get him to do that for weeks!"

"Let me know if you see him eating grass again," I call after her, then turn to Jemima feeling pretty good about what's happening here. "It's nice, don't you think?"

"I do!" Her face shines, and she steps out of her chair to kiss my lips. "I like when we talk to each other at dinner, especially now that our schedules have changed."

"He did it!" She comes running back, then she does a little dance around her chair. "Just wait til I tell Owen!"

"Okay, sit down and finish your dinner." Jemima nods to her chair as she picks up her plate and carries it to the sink.

I stand as well, collecting my dishes as Nikki grabs a piece of garlic bread. She takes a big bite and wiggles her butt back and forth in her chair. It makes me chuckle.

"What are you doing?" Jemima meets me halfway to the sink.

"Helping clean up."

"Y'all cooked." She shoos me with her hand. "Go for your walk, and I'll clean up the kitchen."

I shake my head, but I hand her my plate, gesturing to Nikki. She grabs Porkchop's leash off the rack, and when we head outside, she snaps it to his collar.

Strolling up Main Street, we nod and wave to the few folks on their way to El Rio or running errands or going home. Eureka gets pretty dead during the week after quitting time.

Nikki walks beside me, and I haven't noticed PorkChop jerk her arm yet.

"You're doing a really good job with him. I never had enough time to train him to do anything."

"He's not dumb." Her voice is quiet, and it seems like something more is on her mind.

She was telling us so much at dinner, maybe we should've kept it going. I could've dug out a few of those millions of packs of cookies Jemima carries around in her purse and called it dessert.

We're rounding the square, and it won't be long before we're back at the house. She's still walking with her brow furrowed, watching Porkchop walking at the very end of his leash. He's not jerking, but he's not walking with us.

Clearing my throat, I do my best to sound casual. "Is there something else you want to talk about?"

She pinches her lips before looking up at me, almost like she's afraid to ask.

"It's okay." I smile. "What's on your mind?"

"Is the man who shot you going to come back?"

Whoa—not what I expected. I stop, putting my hand on her shoulder gently. "No, he's gone. You don't ever have to worry about him again."

"Gone like… dead gone?"

"Yeah," I answer quietly. "Dead gone."

"Why did he shoot you?"

We decided not to tell her it was Bill, because we didn't want to scare her. Now I'm starting to wonder if that was a good idea. Still, I don't want to change it without talking to Jemima.

"I made a bad decision. Then I tried to make it right. It was almost too late, but I got lucky. I had people who care about me throw me a safety net."

She reaches up and holds my hand. "Like Jemima?"

"Yep." I nod. "And Aiden and other people. I think you were there, reading to me in the hospital."

"They said we were supposed to talk to you, but I didn't know what to talk about." She shrugs. "Monay said reading out loud would work."

I give her a little side-hug. "How'd you do on that geography test?"

"A-plus." She smiles, and I hold up my hand for a high-five.

"That's my girl."

Later that night, I'm sitting on the floor again, watching as Jemima traces her fingernails over Nikki's back and sings their bedtime song. I wait at the door as she hugs her goodnight, and we walk together downstairs.

The moon is on the rise, and she stops in the kitchen, turning and wrapping her arms around my neck as she hums the song she was just singing. For a few minutes, we dance in the kitchen with the moonlight on the floor.

My arms are around her waist, and my face is at her ear. "I hope she's never too big for that. It's my favorite part of the day."

Her head leans back, and a dreamy light is in her eyes. "You're my favorite part of every day."

My stomach tightens, and I lean down to slide my lips over hers. She exhales a hum, and we're still swaying as our mouths part and our kiss turns deeper. Heat blooms through my stomach, and I'm frustrated I can't lift her off her feet right now.

"The first thing I'm going to do when I'm well is fuck you against that wall." She shivers in my arms, turning her back to my chest.

"That wall?" She points in front of us, and I lean down to kiss the side of her neck.

"That wall, and then that table."

My hands slide over the front of her dress, covering her hardened nipples, and she exhales a little moan. "We'll need to arrange a sitter."

Hesitating, I glance at the stairs, then I catch her hand, leading her to the bedroom and closing the door. My back is to the wooden barrier, and she wraps her arms around my neck, smiling up at me.

"I'm so happy you're here, I don't even mind having to wait." Rising onto her toes, she kisses my lips. "It heightens the anticipation."

Our fingers twine, and I follow her to the bathroom. "We don't have to wait for everything."

"Shower, and I'll change your bandage."

I cup her cheeks, kissing her again before removing my clothes. Her tongue slides over her bottom lip as I remove my shirt followed by my pants. Her eyes flicker to mine, and she fans her face, going into the bedroom.

"I'll wait out here so I'm not tempted to re-injure you."

It doesn't take me long to clean up, and I'm sitting on the bed with a towel around my waist as she carefully removes the bandage covering my wound. The stitches are out, and it's healing really well, but her eyes still mist as she does it.

I touch her cheek, thinking how fast it all went wrong. How quickly I could've lost everything because of one stupid decision.

She clears her throat as if to banish the bad memories. "What does Martha have you doing now anyway?"

"I'd already finished most of the construction, so we're painting, doing trim work. That kind of thing." She finishes taping me up and sits in front of me on the bed, sliding her hands in mine. "I think I'll visit my dad tomorrow… and my brother."

Pretty blue eyes lift to mine. "Do you want me to go with you?"

"No."

I don't leave any room for discussion, and she fights a smile. "Okay." Squeezing my hand, she looks up at me. "Just know I'm there for you if you want me to."

"I know."

"I really liked my Valentine's Day wish." She scoots forward, straddling my lap.

I trace my finger along the side of her cheek, moving her hair behind her ear. "I wanted everyone to know how I feel about you. I wanted it published in the paper for the historical record."

A smile curls her lips. "Does this mean you want to stay married a little while longer?"

My hands slide up her thighs, to her ass beneath her skirt.

Her hips start to rock, and she leans down, holding my face in her hands. Her eyes are hooded, and she rubs her pussy over my growing erection.

"Yes." I squeeze her hips.

She rises onto her knees, opening the towel and stroking my dick. "Yes, what?"

Pleasure surges through my legs, and I catch the back of her shoulders. "We can keep this going." I groan, pulling the skin with my teeth. "You still have to adopt Nikki, and I'm a man of my word."

Lying back on the bed, I roll us so I'm above her.

Her eyes light, and she lets out a little yelp. "Careful!"

"Don't tell me to be careful." Bending down, I capture her lips with mine, pulling the top one with my teeth before swiping my tongue inside to taste her. "I want to fuck my wife."

She reaches down to guide me inside her, and when she wraps her legs around my waist, pulling me into her balls-deep, we both exhale a sigh. Then we start to move.

We rock together, and I slide my hand between us, massaging her clit as we move up and down. Her back arches, lifting her breasts to my mouth.

I bite and suck her taut nipples, dragging my tongue across her body as she twists and moans beneath me. It's slow and sensual. She's so beautiful, I have to close my eyes, but I can't escape the intense pleasure surging through my veins.

I'm hypnotized by her, and before long, I'm picking up speed, unable to hold back. My knee rises, and I go deeper, ignoring the pinch in my stomach as my muscles flex, as primitive need overrides everything else.

Her moans turn ragged, and her stomach begins to quiver. She grinds harder, and it's not long before I feel her coming around my dick. With a low groan, I release, holding her body as I pulse again and again.

My cheek is against her throat, and her soft breasts are

against my chest. The scent of flowers surrounds us, and when I trace my fingers down her back, she shivers and exhales a laugh.

"I love you." She says it so simply.

It's the second time she's told me today, and I lift my head, moving higher, so I can slide my hands down the sides of her face. I wrap her in my strong arms and hold her close enough to become a part of me. Because it's what she is now. It's what she's always been.

Leaning down, I kiss her lips. I kiss her cheek, and I hold her beautiful eyes with mine.

"I love you," I say, making a solemn promise. "I love you, and I always will."

The county jail is a beige stucco building with a pointed entrance and a black sign that reads *Honor and Integrity*. I'm not sure if that's meant to inspire the police officers or remind the inmates, but I don't get the feeling it's working either way.

I leave my phone, wallet, keys, everything in a tray with the guard, who doesn't smile or even make eye contact. He hits a button and tells me I've got fifteen minutes.

When I requested this visit, I'm not sure what I expected to happen. I don't feel entirely responsible for my brother being here, but I am in with the Stones now. If I can help him get a reduced sentence, I'd like to try.

The guard directs me to sit at a small table, and when Bull enters the room and sees me, his upper lip curls in disgust. Exhaling deeply, I know at once it was a wasted trip. Still, I've got to try.

"What are you doing here?" he spits out, sitting across from me. "Come to gloat?"

"I wanted to talk to you." I lean forward, placing my hands on the table.

"I don't have nothing to say to you. You're a double-crossing asshole."

"They treating you okay in here?"

"It's fucking jail, Raif. They're treating me like a criminal." He takes out a cigarette, and I watch him light it.

There's never been any love lost between us. We've had moments of near-friendship, but usually it's built on him wanting something from me or needing my help.

Maybe this time I can help him in a real way—at least I can try.

"I've been talking to Aiden—"

"Oh, you've been talking to Aiden?" His head wobbles side to side as he mocks me. "Your best friend, the sheriff?"

Ignoring that. "He said it's possible we could try and get you a reduced sentence if you say you didn't know what was going down that night."

"Why would I do that?"

My jaw tightens, and I meet his eyes. "Because I don't believe you'd be involved in something like that."

I already had no respect for people who take advantage of desperate people. The more time I spend with Nikki, the more I want to help Aiden find them all and put them in prison.

He pulls on the cigarette, blowing smoke in my face. "Those people know what they're doing when they come here. If they didn't want us to help them, they could've stayed home."

"You're not helping them. You're making money off them."

"Fuck that. Everybody's got problems."

"You knew the whole time what was going to happen that night and you never told me?"

"I don't ever say yes to a job without knowing what it is. I'm not stupid like you."

Bitterness is in my throat, and I'm done here. "Well, guess who just got wise?" Standing, I push the chair back, leveling my eyes on his. "I'm done here."

"Good."

I leave him sitting there like the dumb fuck he is. I started with this visit, because I'd hoped to bring some good news to my dad when I see him next.

As it is, my chest is heavy when I pull into the yard of our old trailer. It looks older than when I left, although somebody has at least picked up the trash and tried to straighten the yard.

The beds I made are all empty, but they're not full of weeds. The porch light is fixed, and the floor appears to be swept.

"Dad?" I bang on the door before walking in. "You around?"

I stick my head inside, and it smells a bit musty. Reaching up, I prop the screen door open and walk into the kitchen to open the window behind the sink.

"Hey, Dad?" I shout a little louder, walking down the short hall to his bedroom.

Pushing open the door, I'm surprised to see it's cleaned up and neat. It's also empty. I guess I should've called before I came instead of assuming he'd be here.

Returning to the kitchen, I open the cabinet under the sink to check the trash. I'm relieved to see it's empty, and no bottles are on top of the refrigerator. Inside the fridge is a plastic container of what looks like leftovers on the top shelf. A loaf of bread is beside it, along with eggs, milk, and a six-pack of RC Cola.

Dragging my palm across my mouth, I try to understand what this means when the screen door opens. I watch as my dad hesitates on the landing, actually scuffing the bottoms of his boots on the entrance mat.

He's dressed in clean jeans and a long-sleeved shirt that might have been ironed, and he does a little jump when he sees me.

"Raif." His face relaxes with a smile, and he walks over, pulling me into a hug. "What are you doing here, son?"

"What are you doing?" He smells clean, and I step back, noticing his hair has been combed.

"Just getting back from my meeting. Sheila gave me a ride."

I look out the door and notice a white Camry leaving the driveway. "Who's Sheila?"

"One of Bender's friends." He walks into the kitchen, stopping in the center of the room. "Why are you here?"

"I said I'd check on you. I'm just in Eureka, not Australia."

He looks around like he's unsure what to do. "Can I get you something? I only have water and RC cola to drink."

"I'm good. I don't need anything." I'm not sure how to ask this, so I just ask it. "Did you stop drinking?"

"Well…" He scratches the side of his jaw. "Maybe. Ben got me hooked up with this program. I'm not supposed to say I'm ever done drinking, but it's been a few weeks now."

A flicker of hope ignites in my chest. "The place looks good. It cleans up all right."

He nods, stepping to the door. "I got all that crap out of the carport, and I hauled a bunch of junk to the landfill. I'm not so good like you are with the beds, but I'm keeping the weeds out."

"You should've called me. I could've helped you." Actually, now that I'm saying it, I probably couldn't in my condition.

"Nah, it gave me something to do." He looks up at me. "Ben said you were recovering anyway, and you got that new wife and all."

We're quiet, and a shaggy black-and-white mutt walks across the yard and lies down in front of one of the lawn chairs facing the chiminea. Even the dog doesn't seem afraid, which always bothered me in the past.

The meanness is gone, and I never knew how much I wanted this until now, looking at the cleaner yard, the swept porch, the half-full refrigerator. It's like a fist I've been holding in my chest relaxes.

Exhaling deeply, I grip his shoulder. "Mom would be real proud of you, Dad."

He looks up with the same blue eyes as me, and his face wrinkles with a grin. "She'd be real proud of you, son."

Man, I hope she would. It was pretty much the only thing keeping me going until I met Jemima.

"Maybe you could come to town and have dinner with us some night."

"I'd like that." Hope lights his eyes, and I'm not letting this progress go.

"Thursday night work for you?"

"I'll be there."

Chapter 33

Jemima

"What do you think of Harold Waters?" Monay's long nails flick against the arcana cards as she shuffles them. Nikki sits across the table from her, watching curiously. "I think he's easily influenced."

I'm finishing up a layout on the big computer at the front of the *Gazette* office. It's getting close to Easter, and we've got pictures of babies and preschoolers coming in like crazy, all in gingham and white holding baskets and bunnies. It's another of my *fun*-draisers, emphasis on the fun, I tell Piper.

Glancing over at the two of them and Angie Dickinson in her little bed, I think about how our special family has grown in the last several weeks. Raif's dad has started joining us for dinner, and he's so deferential and kind. He reminds me so much of his son.

The first time Thad showed up at our door, Raif hugged him so long I had to dry my eyes. It was such a gift. I imagine it's how I would've felt if I'd ever been able to help my mom, and now he checks on him all the time. It's such a win.

I drag another photo onto the page and arrange it with the caption beneath. "Was there a baby boom in town I didn't know about?"

"How in the world would I know something like that?" Monay rolls her eyes, then puts the stack of cards on the table. "What do you mean by *easily influenced?*"

"He ran his dog for mayor last year against Mrs. Edna because Drake Redford was trying to bully her into approving a golf resort."

She speaks to Nikki. "Cut them." Nikki does as she's told, and Monay waves a hand at me. "We talked about that. He thought Drake was being pro-business, then he realized he was just being pro-Drake."

"Cass could've told him that."

"Anyway, since his little niece went back to Greenville, he's got more time—"

"Wait…" I look at Nikki. "Annabelle left? You didn't tell me."

She shrugs. "She wanted to be with her dad."

"And you're not sad or anything?" I watch her closely for any sign of regret over losing her new friend… *ish?*

"I mean, I miss her. But we text and stuff, and it's her dad. Of course, she wants to be with him."

"Okay…" My voice is quiet, until I open the next photo and squeal. "Oh no!"

"What?" Nikki cries excitedly, and the two of them jump up and rush to where I'm working.

I cup my hands over my mouth, but I can't stop laughing. "The poor babies!"

It's a photo of two little boys sitting on the lap of someone dressed in the ugliest, scariest Easter bunny costume I've ever seen. The rabbit's mouth is stretched in a hideous, pink smile, and the eyes are wild.

One little boy's eyes are huge, and the other is screaming so hard, his entire face looks like a tomato.

"Those boys are going to need some serious therapy." Monay dismisses it with a wave, but I have to tap the tears out of my eyes.

"Promise you won't ever do that to me!" Nikki whispers, and I can tell she's empathizing a little too much with these poor kids.

"I promise." I give her a hug, sniffing as I arrange the photo into the layout. "I might have to put that one on the front page with a warning."

"The things parents do to their kids." Monay carefully arranges the cards on the table, telling Nikki, "Hold your intention in your mind."

"What's my intention?" Nikki frowns at her.

"It's something you want to happen."

Nikki presses her lips together, and she seems to be thinking very hard. "Okay," she finally says.

Monay and I exchange a look, and she turns them over slowly, explaining each one as she does. "The tower means a visitor is coming… Pentacles means you'll find something you lost—maybe money!" She raises her eyebrows at Nikki. "And finally… the empress—"

"I'm going to find a bunch of money and become a queen?" Nikki jumps out of her chair and does a little dance.

Angie Dickinson stands in her bed and shakes her tiny butt along with her, and Nikki grabs her under her arm. "Did you hear that Ang? I'm going to be fancy like you!"

She swans around in front of the desk, holding up her arm and waving her cupped hand like Queen Elizabeth II. I shake my head, returning to the layout.

Monay pokes out her lips and shrugs. "The empress usually has something to do with mothers or motherhood, but sure, let's go with that."

"Why are you asking about Harold Waters?" I lean on my

elbow, finishing up, and Monay arches her eyebrow. Her eyes slide to the side, and my lips part. "Seriously? You and Harold?"

"Maybe." She sweeps her hand from the top of her perfect updo down her lime-green tweed minidress to her matching heels. "If he's ready for all this."

I grin, nodding in satisfaction. "I've been wanting to fix him up with someone ever since I got here. Who knew he had such good taste?"

"He is from Chicago."

Piper walks out of her office, resting a hand on her stomach. "How's it looking for the Tuesday edition?"

"I think we're all set, boss. Check it out." I motion to the screen, and she snorts a laugh.

"Oh, no!" She cups both hands over her face. "Those poor babies!"

"That's what I said!"

"Why would they do that to them?"

"I don't know!" I hit save on the pages. "Maybe they'll laugh at it one day?"

The bell above the door rings, and Ryan marches in carrying Fudge over his shoulder. Pinky is right behind him, and Adam enters last.

"Bestieeee!" Pinky cries, and Nikki hands over Angie Dickinson. The little dog's whole body shakes as she happily licks Pinky all over her face. "I love you too, stinky breath."

"Miss Ang hasn't had her Milkbone today," Monay makes a disappointed face, and I wave from behind the desk.

"I have some! Pinky, look in my bag." Monay's eyes narrow, and it's my turn to roll my eyes. "They're leftovers from before. I've stopped hoarding. These days I'm only distributing."

"Let's hope so."

"Hey, Jem?" Adam joins Piper and me, wrapping his arm around his wife and kissing her cheek.

"What's up?" I compress the file and save it to our server.

"A lady stopped by the community center just now." He

glances at the kids and steps closer, lowering his voice. "She was asking about you and Nikki."

"Was she from the adoption agency?" My heart jumps to my throat, and I grab his arm. "It's a little earlier than I expected, but…"

"I don't think so." His tone is cautious, and I meet his eyes. "What's wrong?"

"I brought her to your place. She and Raif are in the yard talking while I came to get you."

Piper steps to my side, putting her arm around my waist. "Stop being so cryptic, Adam. Who is she?"

Adam's face drops, and he rubs the back of his neck. "I don't know how to answer that. Just… Get Nikki, and let's see."

Piper looks at me, and I glance at where Nikki and Ryan are playing with Fudge. "Okay."

"We'll all go together," Piper says.

I try not to borrow trouble. I'm sure it's nothing. "Hey, Nikki? Let's run to the house for a second, okay?"

She hops up at once, hurrying over to take my hand. "What's up?"

"Uncle Adam said someone's here to see us."

"Okay!" She swings my hand a few times, then takes off, skipping ahead of us.

Following her out the glass doors, we round the corner to the narrow alley separating the office building from our house.

Raif stands in the yard with a pretty woman who has long, dark hair. She's wearing a dark, V-neck shirt with lots of necklaces, and a long, black skirt with flowers all over it. She looks about ten years older than me, and the way she smiles and moves her hands is so familiar.

Nikki freezes in place at the same time the woman looks up to where we're standing. The flash between them is unmistakable. The woman's face crumples and tears spring into her eyes.

Nikki breaks into a run, screaming at the top of her lungs, "Mama!"

My heart is in my throat, and I grip Piper's arm.

A soft, "Oh…" slips from her lips.

I can't seem to move. I'm frozen in place watching Nikki crying and hugging her mother, who's on her knees holding her and touching her hair, her body, her cheeks as if to be sure she's real.

"I never gave up on you, Mama," I hear Nikki whimper, and hot tears flood my eyes.

Adam clears his throat, putting his hand on my shoulder. "She said she'd seen the news about Bill's death. She recognized him and thought maybe her daughter was here. I knew as soon as she walked through the door…"

"It's unmistakable." I haven't taken my eyes off the two of them, laughing and crying and hugging each other like they've survived another war.

It's like a swirling, out-of-body experience, where I don't know which way is up or if happy is supposed to be this sad.

Not until I see Raif's face.

His eyes lock on mine, and he strides to where I stand, surrounded by my friends. Without a word, I rush into his arms. Strong arms surround me, and he holds me tight, as if he's pulling me back together and giving me the strength I need to face this.

"Hold onto me," he says quietly, and I do.

I feel the tension in his body, and I know like me, he's struggling with this new thing, this thing that will change everything for our little family.

Releasing me, he turns, holding my hand as we approach them. Nikki's mother rises slowly, tears coating her face. Nikki's arms are around her waist, and her head is buried against her side.

"I'm Vivienne." Nikki's mom holds out her hand. "Are you the one who saved my daughter?"

Pain aches in my chest, but I take her hand, forcing myself to smile. "I've always wanted to call it that."

She only holds my hand a moment before pulling me into a hug. Her body is so tense, and she holds me so firmly.

"Thank you," she whispers. "I haven't spent a single day without fear, trying to get back to her."

My hand is on Nikki's back. She's clinging to her mother like a baby monkey, and it twists the pain in my chest.

"Why did you leave her with Bill?" I try to keep my voice neutral, not accusatory.

"I had no choice." She cringes as if the memory hurts. "We had no food; we had no options. I couldn't work. A woman told me about a place in Canada that would help us. She said I could leave Nikki with Bill, and she would be there to watch over her."

"You trusted her?" It's hard for me to believe.

"I trusted my friend." She hugs her daughter again. "I promised I'd be back, but when I came back they were all gone."

I'm not sure if I should feel guilty. "Bill's place was raided, and they took everyone away. I got Nikki before they got her."

A shiver moves through her shoulders, and her eyes squeeze shut. "It's a miracle I found you."

I don't know about miracles, and I'm still frustrated she would leave her daughter with that man, even if she had someone watching her. Raif puts his arm around me again, and Piper steps up beside us.

"Hi, Vivienne, is it?" She smiles. "I'm Piper Jackson. This is my fiancé Adam, who you met… Anyway, are you planning to spend the night? Do you need a place to sleep?"

I hadn't even thought of that.

Vivienne looks from Piper to me to Nikki, and her face warms again. "I'd like to stay with my daughter if I can?"

Piper looks at me. "There's not much room at your place. Maybe Cass could…?"

"I could bring over an air mattress." Adam volunteers. "If you don't mind sleeping on the floor."

"I don't mind," Vivienne answers quickly. "I've slept on much worse."

"I'll go get it, then." Adam gestures to me. "That's okay?"

"Of course." I nod, doing my best to overcome the feelings fighting in my chest.

"I can make dinner!" Nikki's voice is so loud. She holds her mother's hand, bouncing up and down as she leads her to the house. "I'll show you my room, and you can see the pictures I've made. And look! This is Porkchop! He's my best friend."

Porkchop stands beside her wagging his tail and butt, and not jumping on them like the good dog Nikki trained him to be. My fingers tighten on Raif's arm, and I inhale a shaky breath.

Happy. I'm supposed to be happy as I watch the two of them going into our small house, our little home where so much has happened. Where we've grown so close.

"You okay, girl?" Monay is beside me, studying my face with worried eyes. "Want me to kidnap her and put her on the next bus back to Canada?"

"No…" I try to smile, but tears are in my eyes. "It's good. It's what she's always wanted."

Piper rubs my back. "Do you want me to tell Cass to come? I'm running Pinky home, and I know she'll drop everything."

"No. She needs to take care of her family." My voice breaks on the word, and Raif puts his arm around my waist, pulling me into his chest.

"We'll text you," he answers, and Piper pats me once more.

"I can be here in minutes." Monay gives my arm a squeeze. "One word. *Canada*, and I'm here."

Sniffing, I nod, lifting my head off Raif's chest. "It's okay. We need to do this."

He holds my hand as I force my feet to move.

Nikki insists on making the shrimp and penne dish Raif taught her for dinner. She has her mother right at her side as she explains every step.

"Did you know a watched pot never boils?" she asks, moving them away from the pot.

"I've heard that," her mother says adoringly.

"It's true! I tried to watch the pot last time, and I waited and waited, and it never boiled until I walked away."

Her mother closes her eyes and laughs.

Throughout dinner, Nikki talks nonstop about her friends and school and the Mardi Gras dog parade. Occasionally, she even lapses into a language I don't understand, and her mother responds, hanging on every word, reaching out to touch her arm, her hand.

Sometimes Nikki gets out of her chair and hugs her, and through my heartache, I see my time with her was only six months out of their life together.

It doesn't make me feel better, though.

It makes me feel small.

Raif places his hand over mine on the table, and I glance at him. Dinner smells delicious, but I can't seem to eat any of it. He opened a bottle of red wine, and I've had half a glass.

When they finish eating, we go outside so Nikki can show her mom all the tricks she's taught Porkchop.

"I didn't know he could sit until Raif told me, and I wasn't even there!" she gushes.

She tells him to shake, and instead of lifting his paw, he shakes his whole body. Vivienne puts both hands over her mouth and laughs like it's the funniest thing in the world.

I walk inside slowly and help Raif dry the dishes.

"You okay?" He looks up at me, and I nod.

"She's so happy."

Adam drops off the air mattress, and they set it up on the floor in Nikki's bedroom. It's late when we say goodnight, and they climb the stairs together.

When I've finished washing my face and putting on my night clothes, I step into the dark living room once more, looking up at the light coming from under the door.

Soft noises drift down, and it sounds like *SpongeBob*. I imagine Nikki's showing her mom her favorite clips from her favorite show.

Raif is sitting up in bed when I return, but I go to my side and climb in, lying with my knees bent and my arms around my waist. He scoots in behind me, wrapping his arms over mine and holding me tightly to his chest.

Tears run down my nose onto the pillow, and as much as I want to be happy, it's hard to let her go.

Warm lips press to the top of my shoulder, and his voice is kind. "Want to tell me about it?"

I thread my fingers with his, trying to find the words for how I feel. "I guess even when it's good, nothing lasts. We can't hold onto anything."

He doesn't answer, and I tuck my chin. For several minutes, we stay that way, quiet in the dark. His lips press to my shoulder again, and he finally speaks.

"It's true," he says. I'm not comforted, and after a little longer, he continues. "When my mom died, I got real mad about it, and I stayed mad for a long time." He pauses, and I wait. "Then I started planting the flowers she liked. Mostly because I didn't have anything else to do… And those flowers would die. They were beautiful for a week or two, and then they were gone, just like her."

He pauses, and when I close my eyes, more tears fall.

"So I planted new ones," he continues. "And when they would bloom, I'd remember my mom's smile. I remembered how we shared those moments together, how she'd hold them to her nose and then to mine, and I'd savor that time. Like your time with Nikki. Our time as a family." He kisses my shoulder again. "When I close my eyes, it's there in my bones. It's not lost, because I can time-travel back to it and have it again. But if nothing ever ends, nothing new can begin."

I understand what he's saying, but I'm pouty. "I don't want something new."

"I know it's hard to think about now." He threads his fingers in my hair. "I'm here. Keep holding onto me."

I do until I fall asleep, and when I wake the next morning, I'm alone in the bed.

The sun is shining bright, and I hear voices in the kitchen. Hopping up, I pull on leggings and a sweatshirt and thick socks over my feet.

When I step into the kitchen, I see them sitting at the table. Vivienne has a cup of coffee, and Raif is standing by the stove making eggs.

"You're up!" Nikki runs and hugs my waist, and the hole in my chest is a little less painful.

I manage to smile at Vivienne. "Did you sleep okay?"

"Yes." She nods, her eyes warm as she watches her daughter. "I slept so much better than I have in so long."

I get myself a cup of coffee, and Raif spoons scrambled eggs onto all our plates. Toast is on the table along with bacon. We share another meal, and when we're done, Nikki wants to show her mom her school.

She grabs the leash for Porkchop, and Raif follows them to the door as my phone lights up with a text.

Britt: What the hell? She can't just waltz in here and take Nikki back just like that!

She includes a red-faced, angry emoji.

Britt: Aiden says depending on the timeline, we could establish abandonment.

I did take her from Bill, though. She said she's been searching everywhere

Britt: How could she leave her daughter with him in the first place?

She claims a friend was watching over her.

Cass: I've had it with these mothers just showing up out of the blue and wrecking everything. What can we do? Alex has a lawyer.

"You coming?" Raif calls to me from the door.

"I'll catch up. Give me just a minute here."

Piper: Theoretically, I agree. She showed poor judgment, and she's got a lot of nerve. But I saw them together. Nikki is so happy her mom's back.

She includes a crying emoji.

It's all she ever wanted.

My eyes heat with new tears.

Cass: I don't like it. What will they do now?

I don't know. We're going for a walk. I'll update asap.

Chapter 34

Jemima

WE WALK ALL OVER EUREKA. NIKKI SHOWS HER MOM THE SCHOOL, then we walk over to the softball field where Adam had just started teaching them to throw softballs.

"Pinky claims she can hit a home run, but she says a lot of things." Nikki rolls her eyes, holding her mom's hand.

"I wouldn't put it past her," Raif says, and we circle back around to the square.

Owen and Ryan are in the grass throwing a frisbee with Edward, and when they see us, they run to where we are. Nikki introduces the boys to her mom, and they study her with curious eyes.

"Your mom lives in Canada?" Owen asks, scrubbing the side of his head and frowning at Nikki. "Does that mean you're moving to Canada now?"

It's the elephant in the room nobody's mentioned, and Nikki's expression freezes. I realize in all the reunion hugs and kisses, all the breathless stories they've shared, what happens next never occurred to her.

Her amber eyes fly to mine, and for the first time since her mother reappeared, she seems worried.

"I don't know." Her voice is quiet.

"We'll talk about it at the house," I say quickly.

But as we walk home, I can tell the vibe has shifted. Nikki still holds her mother's hand and Porkchop's leash, but she's not talking nonstop. Even her mother seems a bit worried.

"You know," Raif starts, unhooking Porkchop's leash once we're inside the gates. "There's lots of jobs around Eureka. That new resort is coming soon, and I'm sure they'll need workers. There's the distillery and all kinds of hotels and resorts in Hilton Head and Kiawah."

"But where would we live?" Nikki's voice is quiet. "You always say there's nowhere for people to stay in town."

"Alex has a garage apartment..." I start.

I was so upset with them last night, but now, standing here with the possibility they might be separated again, I realize how cruel it would be.

"You are all so kind." Vivienne's voice is gentle. "I have a job and a home in Toronto. I'm so happy I've finally found my Nika. I thank you so much for rescuing her. She must come back with me tomorrow. I have to return to work."

My stomach pitches, and Nikki's eyes widen as they meet mine. I swallow the lump in my throat, holding back the tears and forcing a smile. "Of course... We should have known you couldn't stay. I did sort of... kidnap her, I guess."

Vivienne takes my hand in both of hers. "I thank you so much for rescuing her. I will never forgive my friend for her lie." She pulls me closer into a firm hug, and I bend my arms to pat her back. "You took care of her so well. You will always be part of our family."

"Thank you," I whisper, looking down as she lets me go.

The rest of the evening is less animated than the night

before. We sit outside and eat hamburgers while Nikki plays with Porkchop, hugging him and patting his head. I can't help thinking she's not as happy as she seemed, but maybe it's my own selfish thinking.

At bedtime, she comes to our room, tapping on the door before peeking her head inside.

"Hey, babe." I walk over to her, and we hold hands as we sit on the bed.

"I'm sorry." A tear is on her cheek, and I reach out to wipe it away.

"What are you sorry for?"

"When Monay told me to think of something I wanted, I thought of my mom. I didn't know it would work. I didn't believe the cards were magic, but they were. Now it's all confused."

She puts her head in my lap, and I lean forward, wrapping my arms over her shoulders. Raif steps out of the bathroom in his jeans and walks over to sit beside us. Our eyes meet, and his brow furrows.

"Shh, don't cry…" I rub her back. "You never gave up on her. We talked about it, remember? You said you would never give up on her, and I said you didn't have to. It's a good thing."

She sits up slowly, but her eyes stay on our clasped hands. "If it's a good thing, why does it feel bad?"

I can't answer that question. Reaching out, I hug her to me, and we hold each other. Raif wraps his arms around us both, and we're a family of three for a little while longer.

The next morning, we take our time packing. Nikki's clothes and things have grown from the small bag we had when we arrived in Eureka. She's come out so much. Monay gives her one of her smallest designer bags to use.

"That way you'll have to come back and return it," she says, using a long nail to trace Nikki's hair behind her ear.

"You're definitely coming back for a visit." I squeeze her to me. "And we'll visit you."

Piper and Adam stand back while Ryan and Owen say good-bye. Britt is beside me frowning as she bounces Bonnie on her shoulder. Cass even drove over with Pinky, but the pink tornado is more interested in Angie Dickinson.

The only problem is Porkchop. He jumps all around, wagging his butt and sitting for all of us to see. Nikki takes a knee and hugs him, and Owen joins her at his side.

"He might not be able to find stuff like Edward can, but he's a good dog," Owen says. "He's pretty smart, even if he doesn't understand how to shake."

"He does shake," Nikki argues, and on cue, Porkchop shakes his whole body for her. "He won't understand why I'm not here," she whispers, and my heart breaks a little more.

Raif looks at Vivienne, whose face is troubled as she watches the children. Gesturing to her, they step away from the group, and I squat beside Nikki, petting Porkchop's head as well.

"I'm sure he'll always remember you. Dogs are good that way."

She nods quietly, and he licks the tear off her cheek.

"We'll all play with him," Ryan adds. "And we can send you videos all the time."

When I look up, Raif and Vivienne are returning, and her face shines with relief.

"Hey, Nikki?" Raif puts his hand on her shoulder, and she looks up at him. "Would you like to take Porkchop with you to Toronto? It's a long drive, but your mom thinks he can make it."

Nikki's eyes widen, and she looks from Raif to her mother. "You do?"

Vivienne nods, and Nikki jumps up, running to hug her first then Raif then Porkchop, then me. When she gets to me, she stays longer, and I hold onto her as long as she needs.

"We got you through the hard time." I slide my hand down the back of her hair, doing my best to hold back the tears.

"Does that mean we're not a special family anymore?" She lifts her head, and when I see the tears in her eyes, I can't stop mine.

"No way!" I manage to make my voice sound upbeat, but it breaks. "We'll always be there to help each other through the hard times. It means this is your happy ending… for now. Until you meet a boy… or a girl!"

She rolls her watery eyes, hugging me again. "I love you, Jemima. You're a good mom."

"I love you, too. You're the best daughter."

As they drive away, she's in the backseat waving through the glass. It's different from how I left here when I was a little girl.

Her wish has come true, and in our hearts, we'll never say goodbye.

As the sun is setting, when the dishes are washed and it's only the two of us, Raif holds out his hand to me. I take it, and he leads me out through the yard. I follow him to where his bike is parked, and he picks up the helmet, putting it on my head and strapping it under my chin.

He does the same with his then helps me onto the back before kicking it started. I don't have to ask as we head out the old dirt road, the same one as that very first night when I was supposed to be interviewing him—when I told him why I wanted to live in Eureka, and about magic and family and why this place is special.

My cheek is against his shoulder, and it's not long before we arrive at the narrow path leading from the road out to the isolated stretch of beach. He guns it across the soft sand, and when we reach the shoreline, the sun is just touching the horizon.

It's another perfect sunset, and he pauses long enough to remove our helmets and set them on the sand. The sea breeze is strong, blowing my hair and whipping my skirt around my legs.

Turning back, he captures my lips in a burning kiss, and just like that, we're off, racing across the surf as the sun makes its slow dive into the ocean turning the whole world to gold.

I lift my arms in a *V* and lean back, releasing the heaviness with a loud cheer.

When I lean forward again, I understand what he wants me to know—without endings there can be no beginnings, and some endings aren't endings at all.

We race all the way to where the rocks stretch into the ocean cutting us off, and we're both breathing fast as we watch the sun continue to disappear.

When it's gone, we drive back the way we came, restoring our helmets before continuing home.

The bike stays in the yard, and we crash through the front door, slamming it closed and coming together in a fierce kiss. We're still taking it easy, still inside his window of recovery, but it's good. It's healing, and when we finally collapse, sated and sweaty in the bed, his head is across my waist, strong arms holding me securely.

I trace my fingers along his back singing our song, of him being my man. His fingers slide along my arm, and he listens like he always would, sitting on the floor when Nikki was here.

Now it's just the two of us.

"You don't need me to help you adopt Nikki anymore." His voice is quiet.

A breeze blows outside the window, and the chimes on the side of the house ring like soft bells. For a minute we're all alone in the universe, just him and me, contemplating our destiny.

"I always had the things I needed in my life," he continues. "I had clothes and food and a bed, but I never had anything like you. I never needed anything like you." He lifts my hand, sliding his mother's gold ring around my finger. "I'd like to keep on being your husband if you'd like to keep on being my wife."

A surge of love radiates from my heart up to my cheeks, and

I can't stop a smile. "I'd like to be your wife to the end. Then I'd like to turn around and do it all over again."

He reaches up to slide my hair off my cheek. "We've got experience with endings. I think we should start our beginnings now."

"Our beginnings?"

"Yeah." He moves higher, caging me in his strong arms.

"And what would those beginnings look like?"

A naughty grin curls his lips, and he leans down to kiss the space on my neck below my ear. "Maybe one of them would have long blonde hair, a sassy little attitude, and a voice like an angel."

A tickle is in my stomach, and I stretch with a happy sigh. "One?"

"And another one might have a little James Dean outlaw in him."

Pushing his shoulder, I rise up on my elbow. "Are you saying we might have a little bad boy just like you?"

"I'm not so bad."

"No, you're sweet, and I would love him so much." I cup his cheeks, kissing the growl off his lips at being called sweet. Resting my hand on his cheek, I trace my thumb along his lips. "I didn't want to say anything until I was sure, but it's possible we have a new beginning on the way right now."

His expression changes, and his eyes light. "Jemima... Are you—"

"It's very early. I haven't even seen a doctor yet, but I think maybe... yes."

I'm still speaking as he's moving down my body, sliding his hand over my flat stomach that doesn't look any different than it ever did. Still, I never miss a period, and it's been three weeks.

Soft lips touch my skin, and he wraps his arms around my lower back, resting his cheek above my navel. Reaching down, I thread my fingers in his hair loving this man so much.

"Jemima..." He says my name with such reverence. "The

idea that you might be my wife was a dream too big for me to have. Now this? I'll do everything to be sure you and this baby and our family are always safe and proud and have everything you need."

I pull on his arms, and he slides up in the bed, pulling my back to his chest and sheltering my body with his the same way he did a little while ago, when I couldn't think about anything new.

"I have everything I ever need right here. My hero, my husband, my strength. You fill my broken pieces with golden sunsets and love." His lips trace the line of my jaw, and the heat rises between us. "I love you so much."

As we move together, our bodies becoming one, I realize the pain is gone. The things we've lost have become a part of our story, and I can't wait to see all the new things we make together.

Epilogue

Raif

MARTHA'S NEW DECK IS LIT WITH TWINKLE LIGHTS WRAPPED around the posts and in the trees, and citronella lanterns are placed along the eaves.

She stands beside me in her usual, long-sleeved fatigue-green shirt and brown cargo pants looking over her daughter and all her extended family.

"You did good here." She nods. "It's exactly what I pictured. The whole family together, and more on the way."

I look over at Jemima with Cass, the two of them just starting to show, comparing the size of their stomachs and trying to figure out if they're each having a boy or a girl. I can't stop a proud grin—something I've been doing a lot these days.

"We need more girls," Jemima says. "Pinky needs more members on her team."

"I don't care as long as it's healthy." Cass toes the party line, but Alex is more decisive.

"I'd like a girl." They look at him, and he shrugs. "I grew up in a house full of boys. Girls keep things interesting."

"You can say that again." I wrap my arms around my wife, sliding my hand over her round belly.

She kisses my cheek, and Deputy Doug fires up the karaoke machine. "Here we go," he says, waggling his eyebrows and looking over the crowd. "I know we want a duet from the Dixon gals, and of course, I'll be doing my usual."

As if on cue, Terra Belle walks in wearing her platinum blonde wig and red lipstick. Her niece Julia, Dr. Henry, and Julia's daughter Crimson are right behind her, and while Pinky runs with that little pink poodle under her arm straight to her friend, Terra walks straight up to me.

"Raif Jones!" Her voice is stern, and I straighten, wondering what the hell she's about to say. "I wanted to say this in front of God and everybody."

"Okay?" I square my shoulders, preparing for the worst.

"I'd like to apologize for accusing you of destroying my pickle patch. You didn't do it, and I shouldn't have assumed you did. I was wrong."

My shoulders relax, and I put a hand in my pocket. "You don't have to apologize, Ms. Belle, everybody thought we did it."

"That doesn't make it right." Terra rolls her shoulders back, lifting her chin. "The way you stepped up and helped this single mother and that little girl shows what a good man you truly are. Here's a jar of pickles from my best batch."

She holds out a big jar of her award-winning pickles, and I take it as Monay sashays up with Harold. "Terra Belle, I had no idea we went to the same hairdresser. Come sit by me, and let's get to know each other."

Terra inspects Monay, and she's clearly impressed. "Lead the way. Have I got some stories to tell you…"

Aiden looks up from where he's turning hamburgers on the grill and gives me a chin lift. I look down at the enormous jar of pickles I'm holding, and Julia hurries over to give me a hand.

"I'll put them in the kitchen for you."

"I can't believe we're all pregnant at the same time." Piper waddles up looking like she's about to give birth right here. "We're going to be outnumbered."

"Speak for yourself. I'm done." Britt has her cotton-topped little girl on her hip, and I can't help projecting into the future.

This time next year, that'll be Jemima and our baby. It makes me hug her close again.

"Raif, you are some kind of talented," Piper continues. "This place looks amazing. Is there anything you can't do?"

"I'm sure there's something." I laugh, feeling very much on the spot in front of all these nice folks.

Thankfully, Ryan runs up holding an iPad. "Look, everybody—Look! Look!"

Jemima clasps her hands when we see it's Nikki on the screen. "Nikki!" she coos.

It's not unusual—we FaceTime with her at least once a week, and we've already planned for her to come for a visit.

"Hey, everybody!" She waves hard, and I see Porkchop sitting beside her. "Watch what I taught Porkchop to do!"

She jumps up, grabbing a frisbee, and we watch as she throws it far down a long park. Porkchop runs like a greyhound and jumps in the air with more grace than I ever knew he had, catching it easily in his mouth.

All of us break into cheers and applause. I tell her how impressed I am.

Even Owen reluctantly says, "He looks more natural doing it than Edward does."

Britt passes the baby to her mom, and I wave at Bender, who's down in the yard standing beside my dad. Dad looks really good. He's healthy, smiling, and talking to Ben like the old friends they are. We've been having him over for dinners every Thursday, and it's really good.

I'm about to jog down to them when Alex catches my arm, pulling me away from the group. "Can we talk for just a minute?"

"Sure." I stop, and he motions for me to follow him inside. "What's up?"

"I want to run something past you. See what you think."

I look around Martha's well-stocked kitchen. I've never been inside her house, and she's got every kind of herb and spice you could imagine. Some I've never even heard of. *Grains of paradise…*

"What's on your mind?" I look over at Alex.

"You know Ben stops by the distillery for a drink every now and then, and we shoot the shit." He slides a bottle of his most expensive bourbon onto Martha's shelf like it's a surprise gift. "We were talking the other night, and he said you have an idea for turning these damn hogs that are taking over down here into free-range pork and selling it to specialty meat stores."

Leaning against the counter, I cross my arms. "That's the idea. I've had a little setback with the accident and then my startup money sort of fell through."

He doesn't need to know my startup money was going to come from that job with my brother.

"I have capital to invest. What if I gave it to you to help you get on your feet? Of course, it would be an investment, so you'd pay me back from your first profits. Or, alternatively, I can continue as a silent partner and earn dividends as you become more successful."

His eyes hold mine expectantly, and it's one of those strange moments when I want to look over my shoulder to make sure he's talking to me.

"You want to give me money?"

"For your business." He takes a brown folder off the counter and hands it to me. "I had my lawyer draw up a contract. Take it home and read it, and let me know what you think. I'm prepared to advance you twenty thousand to get things up and running."

He says the words, and I almost drop the folder. "Twenty thousand *dollars*?"

"Would that be enough?"

"Yeah." I nod, looking at the folder in my hand. "That would definitely be enough."

"Brilliant. You can use it to buy equipment or hire some help—whatever you need." He steps forward, extending his hand. "Just look that over, maybe run it past your own lawyer, and get back to me when you're ready."

I shake his hand, and for a minute, I have a picture in my mind of Alex Stone pulling me up to his level. It's an image I've had before, but for the first time, I see the path to making it happen.

I can't wait to find Jemima. I can't wait to read over this contract, even though I know I'm going to sign it. It's another beginning, arriving at the perfect time.

"Thanks, Alex." I nod, feeling a little overwhelmed. "I won't let you down."

He squeezes my shoulder. "I know you won't, partner."

Just then, a slow piano melody ripples across the patio, and a smooth female voice begins singing the first words to an old Crystal Gayle song my mom used to like.

"Mmm…" Alex smiles. "That's my wife's voice. See you outside."

He leaves me standing in the kitchen, and I slide the contract behind the giant jar of pickles before following him out.

I'm one step out the door when I hear Jemima singing the next verse, and I can't lie. I love that sound.

Standing on the deck that I helped to build, I look up at my beautiful wife, glowing and pregnant and singing like an angel with her sister. They hold hands, and she looks at Cass like she's on top of the world.

When her mom took her away, she said she would dream at night of her sister's voice. I guess for her this is a full-circle moment.

She looks again at the group, and her eyes find mine. When

I dream at night, it's her voice I hear, and when she smiles at me, my entire body comes alive.

They finish the song, and she gives Cass a hug before coming straight to me.

She does a little pivot to accommodate our new addition, and I exhale a chuckle. Then she puts her arms around my neck and gives me a big kiss.

I slide my hand along her soft hair. "What was that for?"

"This." She looks around Martha's place, at this big group talking and laughing, eating and drinking and just having a good family time. "You made this possible for all of us."

"I have to give Martha credit for the idea."

"But you made it a reality. You made us a family."

Doug puts on a slow, jazzy song "Me and Mrs. Jones," and when I look over, he gives me a little nod. I return it, and we start to sway.

Again, I have to give her the credit. I'd never be here right now if this girl hadn't seen me for more than a shady, no-account criminal, a usual suspect.

I was a discarded book everyone had taken one look at and decided wasn't worth reading, but she took the time to see inside the cover.

Tracing my nose along the side of her ear, I inhale sweet jasmine. My beautiful wife, who made all my dreams possible. Even the ones I didn't know I was allowed to have.

My dad walks over to shake hands with Aiden Stone, and the truth is she's the real magic in Eureka.

It was just a town, but she believed in what it could be. She brought us all together.

"Remember when you told me not to worry, it was all going to work out?"

"Yes." I nod, lightly kissing her soft lips.

"You were right."

"The prettiest girl in the world was holding my hand. How could it not?"

Her nose wrinkles, and I kiss her again. We're at an end making way for another beginning, and it's the start of something amazing.

The End.

Thank you for reading *A Little Naughty*! Don't miss your FREE Bonus scene! Scan the QR code to download now.

New in town?
Binge the complete "Be Still" series in Kindle Unlimited and on Audio.
Scan to Read

Learn about all of my books on TiaLouise.com/Books, including a downloadable Reading Guide.

Keep turning for a sneak peek at *The Way We Touch*, Book 1 of my brand new small-town, brother's best friend, sports series with four football-star brothers and one feisty little sister who find love and adventures in their small, coastal hometown. Get ready for quirky characters, cute kids, intrigue, angst, and *spice of all varieties…*

The Way We TOUCH

*My **brother's best friend** might be a **cocky wide receiver** with an ego the size of Texas, but I did not mean to almost kill him with a ghost pepper. He did that all by himself.*

Logan Murphy should come with a warning.
He's as hot as a Carolina Reaper on black
asphalt in the middle of July.
With perfectly messy dark hair and smoldering blue eyes—
and don't even get me started on the way that black tee
stretches across his toned chest...

He's my brother's best friend.
He's also **a football star** on track to win the first
wide-receiver MVP in league history.
Good thing I only date golfers… or I did.
Good thing he's only visiting for a month, because the more
I see he's not a player, the harder it is to block him from
running away with my heart.

I've always loved football, but after eight years pro,
everything about it leaves me cold.
So when I agree to head south with *my best friend*, the
last thing I expect is to have my face melted off by *his
pepper-loving little sister*.
Dylan Bradford was supposed to be a kid, not a feisty pinup
who looks at me like she's never seen a man before.

She's all curves and cutoffs, bare feet dancing
in the warm summer night,
But I'm only in town a month, and she
doesn't date football players.
Then late-night talks turn to sharing past hurts and future
dreams, and shy looks turn to confident kisses.
The heat between us can't be denied.
It's spicy and sweet, and it melts us together.
Until *the way we touch* becomes more than friendly—
it's forever.

(THE WAY WE TOUCH is a small-town, brother's best
friend, sports romance with close proximity, hilarious
"accidents," and a dirty-talking hero. No cheating. No
cliffhanger. No third-act breakup.)

Chapter 1

Logan

AN HOUR LATER, I'M IN THE PLUSH LEATHER FRONT SEAT OF HIS maxed-out, gunmetal F-150 racing south on Interstate 95 with the radio quietly playing country music.

We're facing a day-long drive, and I'm booking a room for us to crash in North Carolina. It's the first time I've made a road trip like this since I moved to the city, if ever.

"I saw you slip Wendy that extra tip." He glances at me, returning his eyes to the road.

I stretch in my chair, doing my best to get comfortable. We're going to be here a while. "You made me worry about her."

That makes him chuckle. "You're a good man, LL. I knew it the day I met you, even if you do approach the world with your guard up."

"Likewise."

"This is just what you need." Garrett glances at the lights of New York City in the rearview mirror. "Newhope will clear your head, get you back to square one, the basics."

"Does the chamber of commerce have you on the payroll?" I tease because I love.

Garrett is the poster boy for his hometown. It's all he talks about, but the truth is, at this point, I'm up for anything to kick me out of this funk.

I think about what he's told me in the few times we've spent together, shooting the shit. He lost his mom young, like I did. He's one of four brothers—all football stars—and a little sister. Although besides Garrett, only his brother Hendrix is still in the game.

I don't know Hendrix well, but we've met. He plays for a team in Los Angeles, and he's a bit of a rockstar tight end.

His second oldest brother Zane was a career kicker forced to retire last year after getting nailed pretty bad during a fake field goal. It was a dramatic injury, his foot dangling at the end of his leg like a freak show while he roared in pain.

It's the kind of injury you like to pretend could never happen when you're headed onto the field each week, and they played it on reruns every five minutes. Fuck, I still get chills remembering it.

"Jack said he'll be picking his fall lineup while we're in town." Garrett's large hand is propped on the top of his steering wheel, and he has a toothpick in the corner of his mouth. "I told him we could help him out, maybe give the boys a pep talk."

His oldest brother is a retired star quarterback from Texas. I remember watching Jack Bradford on the field and wondering how anyone with that much talent could ever retire. He did, though, at the top of his game. A legend.

Now he coaches high school ball. Friday night lights.

"Sure. Whatever he needs." I glance out the dark window wondering what my nineteen-year-old self would think of meeting Jack Bradford in the flesh.

Then I travel back a bit more, wondering what I would say to my fifteen-year-old self today. What would he even be able to hear? Certainly not that life at the top isn't as great as it looks from the bottom. Or that no matter where you go, there you are.

Hell, maybe I'm just depressed. I haven't slept with a woman in a long time, and the last time I did, it was with someone who was more interested in her social media following. I'm not being a hater. There was a time it was all I cared about, too.

"Dylan said Zane is laying low, but he's healing fine." My friend's jaw tightens, and he shakes his head. "It's going to be the first time I'll have seen him since that accident, and it was a fucking nightmare."

"Tell me about it." My lips tighten, and my stomach cramps.

It's a big switch to go from the nonstop schedule of a big game every week, seven months out of the year, traveling all over the country, being a celebrity to a certain segment of the population, to nothing.

Full stop.

From the roar of a stadium, to dead silence. Forgotten.

I've heard guys talk about the shock of retirement, and I'm not going to lie, I'm not looking forward to it. Even if I have been floating the possibility of this being my last year. It all depends on that trophy, even if that trophy means more to my dad than it does to me.

"That just leaves Dylan, but she'll be working at the restaurant most days." Nodding, I picture a kid living on the coast in south Alabama.

My mind travels a thousand miles down the dark road ahead of us, far from the lights of Manhattan. I think about the life I left behind when I graduated from UT.

Taking out my phone, I pull up my contacts and select my father's name. In the glow of the dashboard light, I text him what I've been thinking for weeks.

I'm not going back there.

Get THE WAY WE TOUCH and fall in love with this small-town, brother's best friend, football romance today!

It's FREE in Kindle Unlimited and available as an Audiobook.

Books by
TIA LOUISE

ROMANCE IN KINDLE UNLIMITED

THE BRADFORD BOYS
*The Way We Touch, 2024**
*The Way We Play, 2024**
*The Way We Score, 2025**
*The Way We Run, 2025**
*The Way We Win, 2025**
(*Available on Audiobook.)

THE BE STILL SERIES
*A Little Taste, 2023**
*A Little Twist, 2023**
*A Little Luck, 2023**
*A Little Naughty, 2024**
(*Available on Audiobook.)

THE HAMILTOWN HEAT SERIES
*Fearless, 2022**
*Filthy, 2022**
For Your Eyes Only, 2022
*Forbidden, 2023**
(*Available on Audiobook.)

THE TAKING CHANCES SERIES
*This Much is True**
*Twist of Fate**
*Trouble**
(*Available on Audiobook.)

FIGHT FOR LOVE SERIES
*Wait for Me**
*Boss of Me**
*Here with Me**
*Reckless Kiss**
(*Available on Audiobook.)
BELIEVE IN LOVE SERIES
Make You Mine
*Make Me Yours**
*Stay**
(*Available on Audiobook.)

SOUTHERN HEAT SERIES
When We Touch
When We Kiss

THE ONE TO HOLD SERIES
*One to Hold (#1—Derek & Melissa)**
*One to Keep (#2—Patrick & Elaine)**
*One to Protect (#3—Derek & Melissa)**
One to Love (#4—Kenny & Slayde)
One to Leave (#5—Stuart & Mariska)
*One to Save (#6—Derek & Melissa)**
*One to Chase (#7—Marcus & Amy)**
One to Take (#8—Stuart & Mariska)
(*Available on Audiobook.)

THE DIRTY PLAYERS SERIES
*PRINCE (#1)**
*PLAYER (#2)**
DEALER (#3)
THIEF (#4)
(*Available on Audiobook.)